Prince
of the
Doomed City
Book Five: Enthralled

Sylvia Mercedes

FIRE WYRM BOOKS

© 2023 by Sylvia Mercedes

Published by FireWyrm Books

www.SylviaMercedesBooks.com

All rights reserved. No part of this publication may be reproduced, stored in a retrieval system, or transmitted in any form or by any means—for example, electronic, photocopy, recording—without the prior written permission of the publisher. The only exception is brief quotations in printed reviews.

This volume contains a work of fiction. Names, characters, incidents, and dialogues are products of the author's imagination and are not to be con-strued as real. Any resemblance to actual events or persons, living or dead, is entirely coincidental.

Cover design by MoorBooks Cover Design

*This book is dedicated to those who love
and to those who, still loving,
are finally willing to let go.*

1

"I WILL COME TO YOU."

A sharp scent of lavender fills my nostrils, shocking my senses. I moan and turn my head slightly, fighting the pull of consciousness. I don't want to be dragged up through layers of dreaming mist back to the waking world. Not yet.

Because that voice is speaking in my head. Warm, low. Intense.

"From anywhere in all the worlds, I will come."

Another moan rumbles in my throat. I feel warm breath against my skin, panting, ragged. Ravenous. I feel the brush of soft lips, the sharp edge of teeth. Sensation travels through my veins, flooding my body with prickling warmth. I gasp, my back arching, my body eager for that touch, my soul hungry for that connection.

"Just say my name."

My lips stir, eager to form the syllables. But nothing comes. Nothing but a frustrated groan in my throat. Who is this who speaks to me in such melting tones, who caresses my body, who calls to life such fire in my core? His name is just there, resting on the tip of my tongue, but I can't . . . I can't . . .

My eyes flare open.

I stare up at the coffered ceiling overhead even as the scent of lavender overwhelms me. It's so strong, I stuff my hand under my pillow and wrench free a small lace sachet. My eyes, blurry with sleep, struggle to focus on it, struggle to make sense of anything. I hiss through my teeth and toss the sachet to the foot of the bed. Grimacing, I press both palms to my eyes, digging fingers into my head. My body is strangely alive with prickling heat, remnants of some fevered dream. There's a knot of burning tension in my loins, and I squirm with a desire for relief I don't understand.

Say my name.

That voice in my head. I try to catch it, to hold on.

Say my name . . .

. . . my name . . .

. . . my name . . .

Then it's gone. Even the last echo is lost. Was it ever there at all? The heat in my body fades, and I'm left hollow, cold. And that stink of lavender is still in my nostrils. Lavender. Of course. Lavender buds, plucked from the bush standing by the door of the gray stone townhouse on Elmythe Lane. Danny Gale's house. And this room, with its coffered ceiling and lacey curtains—this is the Gale's little guest room, the former Mrs. Gale's pride and joy, an untouched sanctuary which her children and their friends were forbidden to enter. How many times did Kitty Gale and I crouch in the doorway, peering in at all the pretty baubles and delicate furnishings? I recognize that washbasin with the painted cherubs and roses, and that hideous clock on the mantel, suspended in the arms of dancing, semi-nude nymphs. The stink of lavender in my nose carries it all back to me on a wave of memory and confusion.

What am I doing here?

The quilt feels suddenly so heavy on my body. I throw it back and sit upright, swinging my legs over the edge of the bed. Immediately a wave of nausea rises like a cloud, filling my head. My stomach pitches. I clap a hand to my mouth, gag. Then, desperately, I stagger out of bed, dragging the quilt to the floor behind me as I half-fall over the washbasin set against the far wall. For an instant that picture of cherubs and roses swims before my eyes. My body heaves, and I empty the contents of my stomach into the basin, foulness marring the dainty images. I close my eyes, unable to bear the sight, and heave again and again, even after my stomach is empty.

Hands shaking, I fumble for the little hand towel and wipe my mouth. Slowly, blearily, I lift my head and stare at my face in the little gold-framed mirror above the washstand. My eyes are ringed in dark hollows, my complexion pale, my cheeks drawn. I look like I died and reanimated. I heave a shuddering sigh and blink.

In that moment of darkness behind my eyes, an after-image appears: my own face but with long dark hair straggling in snarls across my shoulders, and my eyes, sewn shut with thick black threads.

My eyelids fly open again. I could almost swear I feel the hideous sensation of threads bursting. But that's ridiculous. It's just a dream, a nightmare. Maybe I'm delirious. Obviously I've got a touch of something. That would explain the heat in my body when I first woke, wouldn't it? Fever. I must have a fever.

A light tapping at the door startles me, and I turn my head too fast. The room spins, and I close my eyes again, willing it to stop. "Clara?" It's Kitty's voice, followed by another tentative knock. "Clara, dearest, are you awake?"

I glance down at the mess I've just made in the basin. "I . . . yes, Kitty. But I think I'm . . . unwell."

"Unwell?" The doorknob turns, the door opens. Kitty sweeps inside, already dressed for the day in a neat lawn gown, her hair swept back from a brow puckered with concern. She takes in the sight of me in my nightgown and my wild hair, bowed over the basin, and grimaces. Without hesitation she presses the back of her hand to my forehead. "You're not feverish," she says.

"I'm not?"

Tutting, Kitty steps back, takes one of my hands and pries it away from the basin. She smiles gently. "It's just nerves, dearest. That's all. Nothing a cup of tea and toast won't settle."

The prospect of either tea or toast makes my stomach knot. But I say only, "Nerves? About what? Why should I be nervous?"

At this Kitty tosses her head back and laughs outright. "Wedding jitters, of course! It's perfectly natural." She pats my cheek fondly. "After all tomorrow is your big day."

"My . . . my what?" Coherent thought refuses to form, much less a complete sentence. I watch, stupefied, as Kitty fetches a dressing gown from the wardrobe and shakes it out. When she turns to me again, holding out the garment, I can only blurt, "I'm getting married?"

Kitty chuckles. "Turn around, you goose." I obey silently, allowing her to help me into the dressing gown. She faces me forward again and hastily does up the delicate row of buttons for me so that my nightgown is entirely covered up in layers of lace and frills. When she finishes the topmost button, I catch her eye.

"To whom?" I ask.

Kitty's fingers freeze. Her brow puckers again, this time in a frown. "You are joking, aren't you?" Then she smiles again. "Yes, of course you are. Fix your hair, dearest, and come down to breakfast. If you hurry, you can give Danny a kiss before he leaves for Westbend. I tried to convince him to take the day off as he still hasn't finished packing. But you know Danny—he has to make certain all his patients are seen to one last time before he sets off on the wedding trip." She steps back, looking into my eyes once more. There's something shadowed in her gaze, a hint of worry. But she gives my hand a squeeze and says only, "Don't be long. And don't worry about the mess; I'll send a maid to clean it up."

With that she whirls in a flurry of petticoats and vanishes from the room. I hear her calling out to the housemaid, "Stephens! Miss Darlington is unwell. Clean the basin and bring fresh water, will you please?"

My knees are suddenly weak. I just make it to the bed in time to keep from sinking to the floor. Clutching the headboard, I wait for the room to stop pitching and rolling, half-afraid I'll need to duck to the basin again before the maid even gets here. The sour smell of my own sickness only adds to my nausea. To counteract it I scramble for the sachet at the foot of the bed and press it under my nose. Whereas before the sharp lavender scent had made me ill, now it steadies me, brings my thoughts into some sort of order.

Wedding.

My wedding is tomorrow.

My wedding to Danny.

But of course. It makes sense, doesn't it? I've always known I would marry Danny. We've planned it since we were children. It's only been a matter of time, of waiting for him to finish school and the initial residency at Westbend Charity Hospital. And I had to . . . I had to finish . . . I had to . . .

But there's nothing in my mind. Just a wall of mist. Whatever the end of that thought was supposed to be, I cannot find it.

Shuddering, I wrap my arms around my stomach. My body is so cold, all memory of that warm, prickling heat gone. There's nothing but the faint echoes of a voice—low, sensual. The kind of voice that could make a girl feel undressed with a few words. A voice that could slip into my secret places and make me come alive. I grind my teeth. What kind of thoughts are these for a bride-to-be? Surely this is inappropriate. Because that certainly isn't Danny's voice in my head.

When did we become engaged? I cannot remember a proposal—not unless the one Danny made when he was fourteen and I was twelve counts. And why am I already living in the Gales's household? Surely I should be home with Oscar, shouldn't I?

"Oscar," I whisper.

The door opens. Stephens, the housemaid with the sleepy eyes and the disapproving nose, appears. She bobs a swift curtsy before silently attending to my mess. Guilt pricks my conscience, but an apology feels feeble under the circumstances. Instead I do as Kitty suggested and find a comb. I don't bother glancing in the mirror as I straighten my hair; I already know I don't look like a blushing bride this morning. But Danny has seen me at my worst. Besides, there's always a chance he will have already left for the hospital by now.

No such luck.

When I finally step into the breakfast room doorway, Danny is seated at the table, a cup of tea in one hand, the daily paper in the other. A beam of sunlight pours through the lace-trimmed windows, highlighting the gold streaks in his brown hair. It creates an otherworldly glow about him, transforming him momentarily into another man entirely, a being of story, of myth, belonging to a faraway world of dawnlight . . .

He looks up. His blue eyes catch mine, and the spell is broken. He's just Danny once more. My Danny, my friend. My husband-to-be. He smiles hugely at the sight of me. It's such a spontaneous expression of pleasure, my heart hitches. My lips tilt in return, and a flush steals up my cheeks as his gaze takes me in, standing before him in my lacy dressing gown with my hair all unbound. His gaze lingers but is more concerned than admiring. He sets his teacup down in its saucer and rises, draping the newspaper over the back of the nearest chair. "Good gods, Clara, but you look pale. Kitty tells me you're not feeling well?" He comes around the table and takes my hand even as he peers earnestly into my eyes, searching for . . . something. I'm not sure what. "Did you rest last night?"

For a wild moment I consider telling him about the fevered dream, the voice. About what it did to my body. But no. What would be the good in that? "Yes, of course, Danny. I'm fine."

"Do come sit then." He draws me into the room and pulls out the chair beside his. I sit slowly. When I look up to thank him, he bends down, his lips hovering just over mine. Hastily I turn away, and his kiss lands on my cheek instead. He lingers there a moment, but when he draws back, he says softly, "Clara?"

"I'm sorry," I murmur, trembling fingers rising to my mouth. "I . . . I was sick, so . . ."

He is silent for a breath. Then, "I understand." Backing away, he steps to the buffet by the wall and rings a silver bell. "Tea and a little breakfast will work wonders for you. Just what the doctor ordered, eh?"

I attempt to smile at the joke, but my eyes stray, drawn to the paper he's draped over the back of the chair opposite me. The headline is only partially visible, calling attention to the hot topic of the day—some strike among the city ironworkers—but my gaze drifts to a small advertisement, right there on the front page. I can only catch part of it: "*—ational new story—thrills and horror—Oscar Darlin—*"

"Ah! There, you did make it downstairs after all."

Startled, I rip my gaze away from the printed words just as Kitty bustles into the room with a platter of toast and tea. "Kitty, let the maid fetch and carry, why don't you?" Danny says.

Kitty laughs. "I told Stephens to give it to me. I *am* the maid of honor, after all! It's my duty to serve the bride."

Their bickering is a dull clamor in my ears. I don't try to follow it but instead turn back to the newspaper, trying to discern those words. Danny, seemingly unaware of my attention, picks up the paper, rolls it tight, and tucks it under his arm. "I'd best get to the hospital," he says. "They're splitting my patients among Hubert, Jordice, and Phaedan, confirmed idiots to the man. I want to make certain no one ends up poisoned or maimed before I return. Kitty"—he points a finger at his sister—"don't overtax Miss Darlington with all your pre-wedding enthusiasm. It's her day, not yours."

"Oh, of course, brother mine!" Kitty rolls her eyes. "We have only to finish hemming mother's gown, arranging the flowers as soon as they arrive, and there's the last few doilies for her trousseau to be finished, not to mention the—"

Danny chuckles and pinches the bridge of his nose. "Just don't run her ragged. That's all I ask."

Kitty pops up on her toes and plants a kiss on her brother's cheek. "Not to worry. I'll see that your bride is fresh and perfect for her wedding day."

At those words Danny shifts his gaze back to me again. I look down quickly at my hands. Even so I'm aware how he opens his mouth to speak but stops himself. Instead he turns, vanishing from the doorway. I listen to his footsteps progress down the hall.

"Pssst!"

I jerk my chin up and catch Kitty's frown. She tosses her head, indicating the door. "Go on, silly. It'll be your last chance for a private word before the wedding."

I hesitate. But then, fisting my hands, I rise and, ignoring the way my stomach pitches and the room around me dips, hasten from the breakfast table and down the hall. Danny is just stepping out the front door into the bright morning light. "Danny!" I call.

He pauses, looks back at me. His face breaks from tense lines into a smile that is so warm, so melting, it steadies my thudding heart. He sets down his medical bag as I approach and takes both my hands in his. "So you did come to see me off."

"Danny," I begin then bite my lips. But I've come this far, I might as well continue. "Danny, when . . . when did we become engaged?" It's such a stupid question. I know it, even as I say it. But that wall of mist in my brain is so impenetrable, and I need to know.

Danny's fingers tighten ever so slightly around mine. Otherwise nothing about him changes. Am I imagining the sudden wave of ice that seems to ripple out from his soul? "We've always been engaged, Clara," he says at last. "Since we were children."

"Yes, but . . ."

"But when did we make it official?" He ducks his head, trying to meet my eyes. "Don't you recall? It was earlier this summer. When you returned home from Somsbury. Lord Dashwing's daughters no longer require a governess, and you let me talk you out of applying for another position. We've waited long enough, and my place at Westbend is secure for the next three years at least. It's high time we stopped waiting for the rest of our lives to begin."

His words flow over me in a steady stream of calm and confidence. It all sounds so reasonable, so real. And yet . . .

"Who is Lord Dashwing?" I ask.

Rather than answer, Danny plunges his hand into his pocket. "Here, Clara," he says. "I should have done this a long time ago." He holds out a ring, a dainty little amethyst set with tiny diamonds. His mother's ring; I remember seeing it on Mrs. Gale's hand.

Danny takes my hand now and slips the band onto my finger. He asks no question, makes no proposal. But when the ring is over my knuckle, he lifts my hand to his lips and kisses it. "There," he says with satisfaction. "You're mine now." Then he leans forward and kisses my forehead. The brush of his lips sends a chill sweeping through my body. "You're mine now," he says again, murmuring the words against my brow. When he draws back, his summer-blue eyes hold my gaze, not warm and gentle like I know them. They're cold. Cold enough to freeze me in place. "Enjoy your last day as Clara Darlington. Tomorrow morning you become Clara Gale. And all will be right with the worlds."

Worlds? The plurality of the word strikes my brain like the toll of a bell. My very blood vibrates in response. "Danny . . ." I begin.

But he bends abruptly and retrieves his bag. "I must go now. I'll see if I can finish up with Hubert, Jordice, and Phaedan and return for luncheon. After all, as Kitty keeps reminding me, I do have a wedding trip to pack for!" With that and a last beaming smile, Danny turns and strides down the front steps, through the little iron gate, and out into the street. The rising sun casts his shadow long before him as he turns west and hastens toward the hospital.

I watch him go, far too many questions filling my head. Sickness churns my gut again, and I sag against the doorframe. My gaze remains fixed on the street long after Danny disappears. He's bound for the charity hospital in lower westside, a poor part of town just clinging to the ragged edges of respectability. The same part of town where my family lived for years in a dark little house on Clamor Street.

Is Oscar still there? Did I leave him alone in that house, surrounded by all those old, haunting memories? Surely I wouldn't. Not willingly.

Is he aware of the wedding preparations? Will he come?

"Clara?" Kitty approaches behind me, takes hold of my elbow, and draws me gently back inside. "Shut the door, dear. It's chilly this morning, and I won't have you catching your death on the eve of your wedding." She tugs me along after her toward the parlor. "If you're quite done with breakfast, we do have rather a lot to finish today. Mother's old wedding gown fits your little frame nicely, but she was rather tall, and that hem—"

"Kitty," I say and pull my hand sharply free, backing up several paces. "Kitty, I've got to see Oscar. I've got to . . ." I can't even finish the sentence. Turning to the door, I take several steps.

"You can't go charging down to Clamor Street like that!" Kitty calls after me. "If you must see your brother, at least put some clothes on."

I look down at the lace and frills adorning my person. A faint blush creeps up my cheeks. "Yes. Yes, of course. How foolish of me." I turn to the stairs. "I won't be long, Kitty, I promise. And I'll come back in plenty of time for that hem."

"See that you do," Kitty says, watching me from the bottom of the stairs, her expression wreathed with concern. I cannot bear to look at her. I hasten up, eager to escape her gaze, eager to get out of this house.

2

KITTY OFFERS TO ACCOMPANY ME TO CLAMOR STREET, BUT I firmly decline. For a moment I fear she will protest or even forbid me to go entirely. I brace myself, prepared for a fight. To my relief, however, she deflates a little, shakes her head, and says only, "I know it's hard, Clara. But at some point, you are going to have to . . . to . . ."

"What, Kitty?" I demand. It's like my whole world is suspended on the tip of her tongue.

Her blue eyes flick to meet mine. "You're going to have to let him go."

"Let him go!" The words explode in my head, a dark rumble of a voice that stirs my blood and sends my pulse racing. I cannot see Kitty anymore, standing in the foyer, peering at me with

such earnest entreaty. It's a different face which swims before my vision—a beautiful face, set with intense violet eyes which spark with dark fire.

"*Free him and free yourself.*" The words, the image, they are all there in my head for a painfully brilliant instant. In the next breath they're gone. Like a world illuminated in a flash of lightning only to be lost in darkness. Nothing remains but a distant echo of thunder. Kitty stands before me again, her expression sharp. "Clara?" she says, reaching for me. "Clara, you look as though you've seen a ghost."

Without a word I turn away, pulling a veil down from my bonnet brim to shield my face. I hasten down the front steps of the Gales' tidy little townhouse and into the street, all but running as my footsteps carry me down to lower westside.

Something is wrong. Something is very wrong with . . . with all of this. This wedding tomorrow. My residence in Danny's house. It all makes a sort of sense on the surface, and yet nothing about it feels right, feels true. I love Danny, of course I do, and I've always meant to marry him one day. But I would never leave Oscar. Only it seems I already have.

I shake my head, trying and failing to clear it. Why can't I recall anything of yesterday, or the day before? Or even the last few weeks? Why is there such a huge, unyielding blank inside my mind?

I walk faster. The cool air seems to do me good, clearing my head and easing the incessant nausea. My heart beats unsettlingly fast, and I'm obliged to stop and catch my breath, leaning against lampposts for support every so often. But I could make the walk from the Gales' home to mine with my eyes closed, and the city streets are not overly busy this early in the morning. Soon enough I turn down the narrow, unkempt street where, years ago, my father moved our family when addiction and excess saw him expelled from good society.

I stop in my tracks. Morning light plays gently across the rough cobblestones and ramshackle dwellings that line both sides of this narrow street. And yet, for the briefest possible moment, moonlight fills my vision. Moonlight gleaming off the edge of a brilliant sword of otherworldly metal, held in the arms of a glorious, golden-haired being.

There's blood on the paving stones.

A body crumpled.

A head rolling. Rolling.

Stopping.

I draw a sharp breath. Nausea rushes through me so viciously, I turn and vomit right there in the street. A few passersby cast me dirty looks and take care to put distance between themselves and me. No one stops to offer assistance; that simply isn't how things are done on Clamor Street. For once I am grateful. I fish a handkerchief from my reticule and dab it to my mouth before turning to face the street again. The image is gone, both the moonlight and the gore. But it lingers in the back of my brain as I pick up my skirts and hurry on my way.

My footsteps slow against my will as I draw near the door of our house. It feels as though I've not been here for many years. Which can't possibly be the truth. I live here with Oscar. Or do I? Danny said something about me working as a governess for some lord. Is that where I've been all this time? Trying to recall only makes my head swim, and the last thing I want is to vomit on my own doorstep. So I push those thoughts back, lift my chin, and knock sharply. No answer. I wait for a count of twenty, then knock again, this time calling out, "Oscar? Oscar, are you in?"

Perhaps he's out for the day. At work? No, not Oscar. He's never been able to hold down a job. If he's out, it just means he never bothered to come home last night and is sleeping off an evening of debauchery in a ditch somewhere. I pinch my lips in a thin line. Without any real hope I try the doorknob. To my surprise, it gives. Oscar didn't bother to lock up behind him. I suppose I can't blame him—Dad sold off anything of value in the house long ago. Still I wish the boy would take more care.

I shiver as I step over the threshold. It's a strange sensation, like tiny knives are cutting away the top layer of my skin. Like I'm stepping out of one reality and into another: the reality of my childhood, of a life lived in shadow and constant anxiety. Yes, there were moments of joy, companionship, laughter. But these were underscored by tension, by the knowledge that the embodied volcano living in our midst might erupt at any moment, for any reason.

Something in my soul rebels at the notion of reentering that space.

But I force the feeling down and stride purposefully from the foyer into the conjoined kitchen and living room. It's colder here than on the street. My gaze flicks to the empty hearth. When was the last time Oscar lit a fire? He's so heedless of personal care. Which is why he needs me, why I should be here with him, why . . . why I would never leave him. Not willingly.

I cast my eyes about the shadowy room. A single beam of sunlight penetrates the window grime and gleams on the chipped skirts of Mama's porcelain shepherdess on the mantel. Even faceless and battered, she is a familiar sight, and I find courage enough to raise my voice and call out, "Oscar? Oscar, are you here?"

A scraping sound overhead, followed by a crash of shattered glass. My heart jumps to my throat. Every instinct tells me to turn, to run, to get out of this place. A cloud passes by, and the sunbeam vanishes, filling the room with deeper shadows that writhe on the edges of my vision. Footsteps pound through the ceiling. I whip my head to one side, to the narrow stairwell. It's dark—not even a shred of light illuminates beyond the first two steps. I stare at it like it's a portal from the deepest hell, listening as those footsteps thud on the treads. Darkness seems to ripple around the doorway like smoke. I brace myself for whoever will emerge.

No one does. I blink several times, but the footsteps—which had seemed so near, so threatening and imminent—are simply gone. The cloud rolls on, and filtered sunlight fills the room again. The darkness in the stairwell eases. I can see the treads leading up to the next floor. Slowly I make my way to the bottom of the stairs.

"Oscar?" I call. "Please, answer me."

Nothing. But he's here. I know it. So I climb the stairs, one hand lifting the hem of my skirt, the other pressed against the too-close wall for support. Emerging on the upper floor, I look around at the small landing and the trio of doors. My room. Dad's. And Oscar's, the smallest chamber with the steeply slanted ceiling and tiny windows with their leaded glass panes. He should have moved out of it by now, should have claimed one of the larger bedrooms instead. But he hasn't. He remains as he always has been.

The stench of strong liquor stings my nostrils. His door is partially open, and I push it wider. Glass crunches beneath my boot. I look down to see the dirty tumbler shattered underfoot, as though it had just been thrown at the door. I lift my head, fix my gaze on the hunchbacked figure crouched at the little desk beneath the window. Papers, ink, pen-trimmings, and broken quills litter the space all around him, along with empty bottles, upturned glasses, a pipe, and the stumpy ends of cigarettes.

"Oscar?" I say quietly.

He doesn't react. He sits in a pool of morning light, writing furiously, as though all the words of a lifetime are even now flooding his system and must be purged before he explodes. I've seen him like this before, recognize the manic frenzy that every so often comes over my otherwise indolent brother. Despite the glow surrounding him, the shadows beneath his desk are deep and seem to writhe with the energy of his creative force.

Licking my lips, I step closer. Something on the bed catches my eye, however, freezing me in place. It's a stack of magazines, twenty at least. I recognize the title, the familiar ornate script of *The Starlin,* the premier literary magazine in the city. Dad's old publisher. And there, just under the main title is another, set in Gothic script:

THE HOLLOW MAN
Written by Oscar Darlington

I suck in a breath. For a moment my mind tries to reshape those words, to transform them into another name: *Edgar. Edgar Darlington.* That's the name that should be emblazoned across the front page of *The Starlin.* That's the name I grew up seeing on every month's issue for years. But though I squeeze my eyes shut, shake my head, and look again, the letters will not morph into their correct shape. *Oscar,* they read irrevocably. *Oscar Darlington.*

With a wordless cry, I snatch the topmost magazine from the stack, flip to page twelve, and begin to read, heedless of my surroundings, heedless even of my brother at his desk. My pulse quickens as the words capture and absorb me, as the story drags me into its depths. It's a dark tale. A tale of obsession, violence, and possession. A tale of horror without end, passed on from one generation to the next. I come to the last page, the last sentence, the last word, knowing full well this story is but a brief glimpse of one much older, much longer. A story which has been playing out since before I first drew breath and will continue long after I've gone to my grave. The curse of the Hollow Man, a dark inheritance. Inescapable as death.

Slowly, my fingers still white-knuckled as they grip the pages, I lower the magazine from my face. Oscar has stopped writing. He's turned in his chair and leans back, one elbow propped on the desk as he watches me read his work. His expression is closed, an enigmatic mask.

"So, Clara," he says, breaking the silence at long last. "I did it. I wrote a hit."

I feel faint. Wordless, I sit down on the edge of his bed. The rest of the stack tips. The magazines make a soft shushing noise as they slide across his rumpled quilt.

Oscar reaches behind him and plucks a stack of glossy pages from the paper spike nearly lost amid the rest of the debris on his desk. He hands them to me. I accept them numbly, my eyes glazing slightly as I read the words printed on each one: reviews from every major critic in the city and across the country. All raving, all effusive in their praise of Oscar's prose, of his grasp of the genre, his themes, his symbolism, his creative courage. But most notable is the one phrase that every reviewer repeats in one form or another:

"Oscar Darlington has done the impossible, surpassing the scope of his late father's hitherto unmatched talent."

"Edgar Darlington has finally found a worthy successor in the pure, unfettered genius of his own son, Oscar."

"The son has eclipsed the father."

Over and over again with unrestrained floridity, the same idea: Edgar's sun has set; Oscar's star is on the rise. And all due to the success of a single story, if one were to believe the word of these fawning critics. The most unbelievable part? I agree with them. I have read every one of our father's works multiple times over. *The Hollow Man* beats them all. Written from the very depths of a wracked and battered heart. Unashamed and unpretentious. A true work of art.

"Oscar," I breathe, "this is . . . incredible." Tears spill through my lashes and trail down my cheeks. This is his dream come true, his darkest, most desperate dream. I laugh, shaking my head. "I can't believe it."

"Can't you?"

I look up from the sheaf of papers in my hand. For an instant— an instant so brief, I must have imagined it—Oscar's eyes are empty sockets filled with whirling darkness. Shadows like tendrils lick from the edges, fanning his cheeks. I suck in a breath. The image is gone. My brother looks at me with those large, soulful brown eyes of his. Only this time they aren't brimming with that mingled trust, hope, and fear I know so well. There's fury in his gaze. Fury and disgust.

"Oscar?" I say softly, my hands beginning to shake. "Oscar, I am so proud of you. You know I've always been—"

Oscar lunges from his chair. I utter a single cry just before his hands grip my throat and force me down upon the bed. He hovers over me like a sleep demon, smothering me with his weight. "How dare you?" he snarls through teeth which gnash like fangs. *"How dare you? You act like you love me, act like you care. You pretend to support me when all along—all along, Clara—you were trying to hold me back."*

I shake my head, struggling to force words through the pressure of his fingers. "Os—Osca—" Fear bursts in my limbs. I flail against him. He's not strong, but I am nonetheless helpless in his grasp. I stare up into the rage-ravaged eyes of a stranger, and darkness closes in around us.

A sob breaks in Oscar's chest. He releases me abruptly and backs away, staring at me. His hip hits his desk and knocks over a pot of ink, which spills to the floor in a stream of black, like monster blood. I sit up amid the scattered review notices, my hands at my throat as I struggle to draw breath back into my lungs. Instinct tells me to leap from the bed and run from the room. But I can't. Something holds me here. An anchor, a chain. I only know I cannot leave Oscar's side. Not now. Not like this.

"I knew it," he whispers, his shuddering voice both desperate and brutal. "I knew it was you all along. I knew you'd cursed me. Didn't want me to become like Dad, right? That's always been your great fear, that I'd turn into the old man. So you got that Prince of yours to put a spell on me, to bind me in chains. To hold me back."

His words ring in my ears, meaningless ranting. I've heard the like before, though never spoken with such savagery. "You're not cursed," I whisper. "Even if it were possible, I would never curse you. This is foolishness—"

"Foolishness was thinking I could trust you." My brother grasps the edge of his desk as though it's his only support in a crumbling world. The closeness of this little chamber seems to vanish. Instead I see him, a lone figure in the vastness of a huge, terrifying world full of shadows. He looks so small, so frightened. I want to reach out to him, to let him know he's not alone. "Oscar," I begin.

His eyes flash. All the sweet, boyish lines of his face transform before my eyes into sharp, dangerous edges. "Foolishness was thinking you and I would always have each other's backs. I should have known all along. You're just like *them*."

He doesn't need to speak their names. With that one word the image of our parents looms large between us, haunting phantoms of torment and accusation that live forever in our minds. Tears trickle down my cheeks. "I've always been on your side, Oscar. And I always will be. There is no curse. Curses are the stuff of fairy tales. This is real life. There are no curses, no spells, only the demon drink—"

Oscar throws back his head and utters a loud bark of laughter. It's such a bitter sound, it brings bile rising in my throat. He turns away from me, fumbling with the items scattered across his desk. His fingers close around a penknife, and he toys with it, turning it round and round. The little blade glints in the morning light. "I thought you loved me, Clara," he says, his low voice just audible with his back to me. "Now, however, I know there's only one person in all the worlds who does. And I will do everything in my power to bring him back from the hell and horror you cast him into."

He's not making any sense. Every word he speaks is more manic than the last. Has he finally lost his grip on reality entirely? "Oscar," I say softly, "who are you talking about? Do you mean . . . do you mean Dad?"

He doesn't answer. His breathing labored, he bows over his desk, one hand planted against the pages of scrawled writing, the other still gripping that knife.

"He's dead." The words fall from my lips with clear certainty even as fog roils in my brain. It's the truth. I know it's the truth, I simply cannot remember how I know. "He's dead, Oscar," I repeat more firmly and step closer to my brother, extending a hand to his shoulder. "He's not coming back. You're safe now, you're—"

With a ragged cry, Oscar whirls. The penknife flashes; pain slices across my palm. I cry out, stagger back, more shocked than hurt. Blood oozes from the cut, runs down my wrist, staining my sleeve. I clutch my hand to my heart even as I back to the open door. My gaze never leaves Oscar's face. He is white as death, his mouth open, his chest heaving.

"We're never safe from him, Clara," he breathes. "Not really. But we can get stronger. And we can do what must be done." The penknife falls from his trembling fingers. He clutches his head with both hands, his mouth a leer of pain. "Get out of here. Get out now. And don't come back."

The light in the room fades. Darkness closes in, creeps up the walls, swirls beneath the writing desk, and envelops his feet. I look into his eyes, see again the emptiness of void in his gaze, shadows licking from the corners, spilling onto his cheeks. He isn't Oscar, not anymore. In that moment he is a monster. A monster with a beloved, terrifying face.

I turn and flee that room, flee that house, slamming the door shut behind me.

3

I STOP AND VOMIT RIGHT THERE ON THE DOORSTEP. I don't want to. I'd sprint down Clamor Street if I could. The last thing I want is to remain anywhere near those shadows, those phantoms, those memories. But my body simply folds up and empties my stomach onto the broken stones.

Finally empty, dizzy, I stagger on. Only once do I look back and peer up at Oscar's window, half-hoping, half-fearing I'll see him there, watching me. Uncertain what that sight will do to me. But he isn't there. No doubt he's already bowed back over his work again, lost in the flow of words. Forgetting his sister, forgetting our bond. Forgetting everything that once mattered to us.

A little whimper escapes my lips. I didn't invite him to the wedding! How could I have forgotten? My fist closes tightly, trying to stop the throbbing pain of that cut in my palm. What should I do? Will I go through with it tomorrow? Will I walk to the chapel, make vows of eternal devotion to Danny, and . . . what then? That will be the end of it. My heart thuds, a dull weight in my chest. I will be forever drawn away from Oscar, my loyalties necessarily shifted, our paths irredeemably diverged. And the prospect feels like death.

"Stop deluding yourself."

I hiss through my teeth, closing my eyes as that unfamiliar voice appears in my head again.

"You cannot save him. How can you not see the truth?"

"Who's there?" I demand in a whisper. Opening my eyes, I turn in place. The people of Clamor Street come and go, bundled up against the frosty air, pursuing their daily business. A washerwoman with a basket of laundry on one hip pauses to shoot me an uneasy gaze before hurrying on her way. But the speaker, whose voice is so clear in my head, is nowhere to be found.

"Some people cannot be saved because they do not want to be saved."

I press my fists to my temples. "Who are you? Who are you, who are you? Why do you keep saying these things?" Am I going mad? Perhaps. Madness runs in the family, doesn't it? First Dad, then Oscar. Now me. It's the only reasonable explanation. I look back at the house, certainty swelling in my breast. I'm going mad, and those shadows that seem to pour out of the windows and beneath the door are all part of my delusion. They aren't real, they aren't real, they aren't—

Whirling on heel, panic flooding my veins, I take two strides in flight. Before I can take a third, I hit a broad chest clad in a striped waistcoat. Strong arms close around me, and a voice speaks in my ear. "Clara! Clara, what's wrong?"

"Danny!" I gasp. Relief floods my veins, so overwhelming I could faint. My knees buckle, and if his arms weren't currently wrapped around me, I would sink to my knees right there on the street. Danny slips a hand around my waist, pressing me close even as his other hand finds my cold cheek and tilts my face back so he can peer into my eyes.

"We talked about this," he says with gentle sternness. "We agreed that you wouldn't come back here anymore."

My head whirls while my stomach knots. When did we agree on anything? When did we even have this conversation? I can't remember. So I lean forward, press my forehead against his shoulder, and simply let him hold me close. Ignoring the curious stares of onlookers, he turns me gently, guides me out of Clamor Street and back to more reputable parts of town. There he finds a stone bench and guides me to sit, his manner all solicitation and concern. Just like the Danny I remember . . . from when I remember anything at all.

"I thought you had work," I say when at last I'm able to speak again.

"And you plotted to sneak away while my back was turned?" he supplies with only a trace of bitterness. He's removed his gloves and now holds my hands between his, transferring his body heat directly into my numb skin. Frowning suddenly, he turns my hand over to reveal the slice along my palm. "How did you get this?"

I don't answer. I can't. The words simply won't come. In silence I watch as Danny, ever the doctor, draws a clean handkerchief from his breast pocket and fashions a bandage. When he is done, he presses my hands between his again and looks into my eyes. "I finished what I needed to and thought I'd come home and steal you away from Kitty's fussings for a bite of lunch on Trisling Row. Only Kitty told me you'd come here." Deep wells of love and worry brim in his gaze. "Please, Clara, we talked about this. Don't you remember? We agreed that it was time you let Oscar go."

I shake my head. "No. I don't remember. Not at all. In fact . . ." I bite my lip, dropping my gaze to my hands, trapped in Danny's grasp. I want to pull free but fear what will happen if I try. "I don't remember a great many things. There's just . . . emptiness." I force myself to look at Danny once more and let the questions tumble out. "Why am I living in your house, Danny? When did these wedding plans begin? Why is Oscar so angry at me, and who is . . . who is . . . ?" I cannot speak that last one out loud. I cannot ask whose voice is in my head, clearer than any dream or memory. I cannot ask because something about that voice stirs heat inside me that a bride should not feel for someone other than her intended. Am I really so disloyal?

Danny studies me closely, his own expression closed. It's like shutters have slammed behind his eyes. He draws a slow breath before finally speaking. "You've been sick," he says, choosing his words with care. "For weeks. Gray fever. It nearly killed you." He leans closer, cupping my cheek with his warm hand. "I took you home to make certain you received proper care. And then you never went back. You've been with us ever since and . . . and it only made sense that we should wed. As we've always planned to."

His words wash over me, a shower of reason in the desert of my confusion. It all makes sense. Of course I've been ill. That would explain the weakness in my body, the nausea. It would explain the blankness in my head, the great empty space which feels as though it's been hollowed out. So why can't I believe it? Why do Danny's words sound so rehearsed?

I squeeze my eyes tight, pushing into the darkness inside my head. Somewhere in there is my last clear memory. What is it? Where was I, and who was I with? There's something . . . something . . .

The front door crashes wide.

A figure looms in the opening.

Oscar screams. Dad curses, his voice breaking in terror.

"He's dead." I whisper the words. Then slowly I look up at Danny again, my brow puckered with a question. "Dad . . . he's dead."

"Yes, Clara." Danny's cheeks are pale save for two red spots from the cold. "He's been dead for some while."

"How did he die?"

"Don't think of it. Don't try to remember." He reaches out, intending to pull me against him. Part of me longs to give in, to let my head rest on his shoulder, to let my body relax into his embrace.

To take the comfort he so readily offers and let these shadows fade. But I must know. I must remember.

"How did he die, Danny? Tell me. Please."

Danny licks his lips, chapped and colorless. "There was an accident. A bad one. You were there. You saw it happen. Your mind must have blocked the memory, and maybe that's for the best." He takes my hands again, pressing hard, unaware of the pain shooting through my wounded palm. I grind my teeth. "Don't try to remember, Clara. Don't go back to that place. Stay here. Stay with me."

This time when he tugs, I allow myself to go. I lean against his chest, right there in the middle of the busy street, heedless of any onlookers. "I want to help you," Danny murmurs and presses a kiss to the top of my head. I left my bonnet behind, somewhere in the house. I don't even remember taking it off. My hair is flyaway, falling from its messy bun, but Danny doesn't seem to mind. "I want to comfort and care for you to the end of your days. If you can't trust anything else in the worlds, you can trust my love for you."

My heart hitches. That word again—*worlds*. Why do they keep saying it? Danny and Oscar both. What worlds are they talking about? It doesn't make sense. Ice washes through my limbs. I grow stiff in Danny's arms. He must notice, for he draws back and peers into my face again. His expression is gentle, searching. But whatever he sees brings a sharp line between his brows.

Suddenly he leans forward and catches my lips with his. The

kiss is not gentle. It's hard, claiming. I put both hands against his chest, shocked and ready to push away, but then . . . then . . . A scent of ink and parchment and some strange foreign spice seems to fill my nostrils. And the lips against mine aren't hard and rough but full, sensual. Hungry. They move, urging my mouth to respond in kind, and a deep, yawning need awakens inside me. I whimper softly and wrap my hands around that neck, twine my fingers in lengths of long, silky hair as I pull him closer, closer. I don't care where we are or who might see. I don't care about anything in that moment other than my desire for *him.*

Danny breaks away abruptly. "Clara!"

The spell shatters. I stare up into the face above mine. Danny's face. My fingers are not twined in long strands of inky blackness but wrapped around Danny's neck and shoulders. And the eyes gazing down at me aren't intense and violet but blue, wide, and startled.

Danny blinks several times, struggling to catch a breath. Then gripping my hands, he pulls my arms away from his neck. "I wish the wedding was behind us," he growls, his gaze dropping to my still-parted lips. "I wish we were gone from here, on our wedding trip. You shouldn't kiss me like that. Not here, not in a public street! Not when I can't take you home and . . ."

He doesn't need to finish; the burn in his eyes more than communicates everything he isn't saying. Pulling himself together, he rises from the bench and straightens his jacket. Then, all politeness and calm, he offers me his hand and tucks my arm into the crook of his elbow. "I promised Kitty I'd bring you home in time to finish that hem," he says, "and I am nothing if not a man of my word."

So we are back to being ourselves. Danny Gale and Clara Darlington. Strolling through the city. Away from Clamor Street. Away from Oscar. Away from all those dark and dangerous half-memories.

But my heart will not slow its throbbing rhythm. Though I try to listen to Danny's conversation, try to offer intelligent responses, my trembling fingers rise surreptitiously to my lips. And I wonder . . . I wonder . . .

Who exactly did I just kiss?

4

THE WEDDING GOWN IS COMPLETE, THE HEM PINNED, trimmed, and stitched until it just brushes the floor when I wear my white heels. Kitty sits back, pins in her mouth, and smiles, satisfied. "There," she says. "What do you think?"

I look down at myself, clad in this rich satin frock. Kitty has worked wonders on it with all her minor adjustments. An added ruffle here, a new cut to the sleeves, a line of buttons down the back. The overall effect is quite stunning.

"It's . . ." I cannot summon the words. I know what I should be feeling in this moment, a bride on the brink of new life. But I'm numb. "Thank you," I finish lamely and offer her a smile.

Kitty's brow knits. She doesn't pressure me, however, for

which I am grateful. Instead she simply strips me out of the gown, buttons up my simple day frock, and sets me down in the comfortable, overstuffed armchair before the parlor fire. Dinner is already long past, and the hour is late. I'm weary and would love to make my escape to bed, but Kitty presses a handkerchief into my hands and bids me finish the lace trim. I obey listlessly, barely seeing my own stitches, all while Kitty chatters on, keeping up a steady stream of enthusiasm.

Danny doesn't join us until later. When he finally enters the parlor, I find it difficult to look at him. Memory of that kiss we shared sears my brain and stirs strange feelings in my heart. Not the feelings a bride should be experiencing on the eve of her wedding—neither anticipation nor excitement. Certainly not lust. No, it's guilt that churns in my breast. Guilt because I know it wasn't Danny with whom I shared that kiss. I don't know who it was, only that there was someone else, someone standing between us. Someone who inspires fire in my veins.

I really shouldn't be thinking about that kiss. Not now. Not tonight.

"Clara!" Kitty exclaims, dragging my attention sharply back to the present. "You'll mangle it!"

I look down in my hands to find I've crushed the little handkerchief into a ball. Kitty hastily snatches it away along with the needle. "You're going to stab yourself and ruin all your good work in the process." She shakes out the handkerchief and tuts over my awkward stitches. "It'll have to be redone." Lowering the little bit of linen, she looks at me sternly. "Bed," she says with finality. "Take yourself up to bed at once, my dear, and get a full night's sleep. You must be fresh for tomorrow, you know. None of this listlessness."

I nod in mute agreement and rise, avoiding both Kitty's gaze and Danny's. "I am a little tired," I murmur before stepping away from the fire into the shadows across the room.

"Clara, wait a moment." I stop as Kitty hastens to me, catches my hand, and kisses my cheek. "Tomorrow we shall be sisters at last," she says, smiling. "You'll see. We will take care of you, just as you're always taking care of everyone else. Then we'll forget all this darkness and focus only on joy."

Tears prick my eyes. I gaze into my dear friend's face, see the truth limned with determination shining there. As though Kitty can, by sheer force of will, make all this goodness come into being. And maybe she can. Maybe this wedding really is what all of us need. A fresh start. A new life.

"Good night, Kitty," I say softly. I send a swift, half-glance Danny's way but cannot bring myself to speak. So I duck from the room into the unlit hall beyond the parlor's warmth. I take two quick steps for the stairs, my heart inexplicably pounding. Behind me Kitty hisses something sharp. The next moment footsteps pursue me into the hall.

"Clara."

I pause at the base of the stairway, my hand resting on the newel post. Turning, I look back to where Danny stands, a brass candleholder in one hand. Light from the little flame illuminates the lower half of his face. My heart quickens. I wish I could pick up my skirts and flee upstairs to my room. But that would be foolish, ridiculous. And unkind. So I stand my ground, my fingers tightening around the post.

Danny approaches slowly. He smiles, teeth flashing in the candlelight. A low chuckle rumbles in his chest. "I think Kitty is more excited about this wedding than any of the rest of us."

There's hurt in his voice. I hear it loud and clear. When he reaches out and rests his hand on top of mine, I don't pull away. "I'm sorry, Danny," I say, dropping my voice so that Kitty cannot eavesdrop through the cracked parlor door. "It's just . . . I keep thinking about . . . Oscar." It's a lie. But not completely. And it slips out so naturally, it might as well be the truth. "I don't think he'll come tomorrow. To the wedding, I mean. I just . . ." I drop my gaze to our hands, resting together on the polished newel. "I never thought I'd marry without him there."

Danny's fingers close around mine, squeezing gently. "What Kitty said is true. We're going to build a new life. A life without Oscar."

"What?" My eyes flash to meet Danny's gaze. He looks so strange by candlelight. Strange and unnatural and a little dangerous.

"It's for the best," he persists. "You'll see. Oscar doesn't need you anymore. He doesn't want you. It's better to let him go, better to live your life. With me."

I shake my head. "Oscar is . . . Oscar is *everything* to me." Desperation whirls in my breast, a destructive storm, ready to decimate all in its path. I stand in the center of it, clinging to my anchor with white-knuckled determination.

Danny's face hardens into stern lines. "I expect you to make your life here with me *everything*. It's time to give up on trying to save someone who doesn't want to be saved."

"Some people cannot be saved because they do not want to be saved." I shudder as that voice I heard outside the door on Clamor Street echoes through my mind once more. That same harsh truth, spoken with such conviction, like a spear-thrust through the ribs, straight into my heart. The inevitability of it might well break me.

But I cannot fall apart. Not here, not now, not on the eve of my wedding. I cannot do what I long to do—throw myself at Danny, scratching and clawing, screaming at him to take it back. I must hold myself together. Pulling my hand out from under his, I grip my skirts tight. "I'm tired," I say. They are the only words I can summon. At least they're true.

"Here, take my candle. I wouldn't want you to miss your footing in the dark."

I accept his offer. His fingers brush mine as he presses the brass holder into my hand. A chill races up my arm. I start to pull away, but he grasps my forearm, holding me fast for an extra moment. "Clara," he says, his voice raw and low, "tomorrow you will be mine. No one will take you from me. Never again."

There's something ominous in his tone. I stare at him, struggling to see the face of Danny, my friend, my dear one. Cold blue eyes hold mine locked for a count of five breaths. Then I drop my gaze to his hand, latched onto my arm. He lets go at once and takes a step back as I hasten up the stairs. His eyes follow me until I finally duck into the shelter of my room.

I stand a moment, my back pressed against the door as it clicks shut. Then hastily setting the candle down, I bow over the washbasin and vomit once more. I scarcely ate three bites at dinner, but everything burns its way back up my throat. Sweating, panting, I bow over the delicate porcelain until the final spasm passes. Slowly I lift my head, stare at the shadowed reflection in the mirror, faintly illuminated by the candle's glow behind me.

He's not seeing rightly.

My lips move slowly, forming the words in silent echo: "He's not seeing rightly."

A shadowy figure appears at my left shoulder. Long, lusterless hair veils a deathly pale face, marred and misshapen with dark bruises. The eyes are sewn shut in their deep, hollow sockets. Black threads trail down her cheeks, framing her wide, red mouth.

You'll do what you must. You always will.

"I'll do what I must," I whisper. "I always will."

No one understands. Not like we do.

With a sudden moan I turn from the mirror, staring into the shadows behind me. No ghoulish figure stands at my shoulder. I am alone. Just like I've always been.

Fingers trembling, I undress and get into bed. But I don't blow out Danny's candle. Instead I lie for a long while, my head on my pillow, watching the wax melt. Watching the light burn lower, lower, lower. Watching until it finally gutters and goes out.

In the darkness that follows, I become aware of a presence, sitting unseen in the corner of my chamber. It does not move. It does not speak. Neither does it leave.

But when dawn finally creeps through my window, the room is empty.

"Dearest, you're going to burst a seam if you keep tugging on that bodice."

Kitty catches my hand, clenching it tight in hers to prevent me from messing with all the hard work she'd put into remaking her mother's gown to satisfy more current fashions and my current proportions. Apparently I'm not quite as trim in the waist as Mrs. Gale was on her wedding day. Kitty was obliged to insert a discreet gusset, and even so, the maid who dressed me this morning cinched my corset much tighter than I like. The combination worked, and the gown fits like a glove. But I am uncomfortable and perspiring under copious layers of satin and lace.

Kitty's gloved fingers interlock with mine, offering both comfort and support. We're standing together in the foyer of the Chapel of Nornala, the Goddess of Unity. Roses and silver eucalyptus adorn the doorway, symbols of love and good fortune for the bride to pass under. More roses are tucked into my wedding bouquet along with sprigs of pungent lavender.

It's the lavender that makes me nauseated. I'm sure of it. I want to pluck it out and throw it away before I'm sick right on the floor.

"You are so beautiful," Kitty says, as though that's my greatest concern just now. "I think half of Danny's colleagues at Westbend Charity don't believe he really has a sweetheart! Won't they just drop their teeth in surprise when they get a first look at you?"

The knots in my stomach tighten. Beyond the foyer doors is the long aisle leading to the altar where a priestess waits to say the sacred blessings over our heads while Danny and I kneel together, hand-in-hand. The gathered witnesses include Danny's colleagues from work and a handful of social acquaintances, some of whom I knew back before . . . well, back before good society forsook me and all my family. These are the people who will watch me pledge my life to Danny. Strangers and worse than strangers—people who were once my friends. I'll be accepted back into their number now, once I've parted myself irrevocably from my wayward brother and all the scorn associated with my father's name. But I'll never be one of them. I'll never belong.

My chest is tight, my head dizzy. I struggle to draw a full breath. But Kitty peers at me with such earnest concern, and I cannot bear to let her down. So I smile and say only, "It's the dress. That's all. You really did work wonders over it."

Kitty preens at the compliment. Just then music begins to play on the far side of the door, the deep, droning hum of an organ. *Nornala's Processional,* a traditional wedding anthem, seems to fill the whole building, vibrating even through the cracks in the mortar and stone.

The butterflies in my stomach start doing backflips. "Kitty! I don't think I can do this."

Kitty laughs softly. "Nonsense, you goose. It'll all be over in a moment, so just try not to be sick on Danny's shoes before you've said *I do*." She drops a kiss on my cheek then slips my veil down to cover my face. "I'll see you in a moment. Wait for your queue!" With that, she opens the door to the inner chapel and steps inside, marching solemnly in time to the music. Many eager eyes turn to watch her, while others look back to the doorway, awaiting my appearance.

I feel ill. Terribly ill. I haven't seen Danny since last night, since our parting at the base of the stairs. Maybe it would be easier if we'd had a moment together over breakfast, if we'd had a chance to discuss what was said and what is to come. Right now I feel as though I'm about to march myself out there and pledge my life to a stranger.

The processional continues, building up to a grand climax. I take one step toward the doorway, toward that arch of roses and eucalyptus. That step brings me within line of sight with the altar. I see the priestess standing solemnly beneath the image of Nornala wrought in stained glass. I see Kitty just reaching the end of the aisle, taking her place and turning to smile back at me.

And I see Danny. Tall, handsome. Clad in a gray morning suit. In full view of everyone he knows. Looking white as death, his hands clenched firmly before him as though bracing for battle. He swallows hard.

Then he looks up and meets my gaze directly.

A knife of ice stabs through my chest. Gasping, I stumble back from the arch and pivot on heel. I have no reason, no explanation. None of this makes sense in my head. I know only that I must get out of here. Morning light streams through the stained glass adorning the chapel door. I lunge into that light, heedless of how I crush my bouquet as I force the door open and stagger out into the street. Both hands pressed against my temples, I drag great gulps of air into my lungs. Cacophony fills my head, wordless noise without meaning. But wait . . . no. It's not wordless. There are voices in my head. Small, childish voices.

"Mar!"

"Mar!"

"Where are you, Mar?"

"Come back."

"Come back."

"Come back to us."

And underscoring those voices, more intense and dreadful, more beautiful by far, is another: *"Where are you, Darling?"*

"I'm here," I whisper, turning to look behind me. "I'm here, I'm here!"

A burst of light fills my vision, morning sunglow, blinding and beautiful. It seems to gather in front of me, like the sun itself has fallen from the sky and even now approaches along the sidewalk. I throw up an arm to shield myself from that glare even as I strain to discern the figure in the center of it. Fear jolts through my veins, urging me to flee back into the chapel, to fling myself at the foot of the altar and beg the goddess for safety. But I cannot move. The light draws nearer, and that strange, glowing figure takes on more definite shape. An angel? It must be, for what else could explain those widespread, glittering wings? Awe sweeps over me, and I nearly drop to my knees in worshipful wonder. Only a last shred of stubbornness keeps me upright.

The beaming aura fades, and an image of pure glory manifests before me, so shocking, the rest of the world seems to melt away. The chapel, the other buildings, the street, any passersby, all simply fade into unreality compared to this being. This woman. This magnificent creature, taller than any man I've ever met. Great coiling horns like gazelle antlers spring from her forehead, ornately painted in patterns of gold. Her hair is pale and shimmering, wound in a crown atop her head, more beautiful than any diadem. Her gown is pink as new dawn and lightly drapes her powerful form, revealing far more than it conceals behind its translucent folds.

But what draws my eye is the black stone resting between her breasts. It's so dark, so raw and terrible, contrasting to her golden glory. Malevolent energy seems to pulse from its center, somehow both repellent and irresistible.

"Well," the woman says, her voice echoing up and down the street. The sound shocks my senses and draws my gaze away from the stone back to her beautiful face. She looks at me like one might view a drowned mouse discovered in the milk jug. Her perfect mouth creases in a sneer. "Here you are. He told me I would find you at Nornala's door, on the verge of pledging yourself to another. Have you forgotten your Fatebond so soon?"

I gape at her, open-mouthed and silent. Her words ring inside my empty head, sounds without meaning. I simply cannot comprehend this creature, this angel. This goddess? No, for surely no goddess would wear a stone like that around her neck.

The woman laughs, white teeth flashing like daggers. "If only I might let you complete this little farce! It may well be the final blow Castien cannot withstand." Then all mirth vanishes from her face. She is hard, unyielding, and terrifying. "Alas, I haven't the time to waste."

With those words, she takes a single, light-footed step forward and grips my arm, pulling me up so hard and fast, I stand on my tiptoes, almost suspended in the air. I try to struggle, but she snarls, "Be still!" I freeze immediately. It's as though some spell has come over me, an irresistible compulsion. My limbs lock and my breath catches as the woman places her free hand against my stomach. For a moment she seems to be listening, every muscle in her face tense. Then her eyes widen, and that terrifying smile flashes once more. "A heartbeat!" she cries, triumphant, almost jubilant. "Just as I hoped."

Sick horror twists in my gut. I don't understand what's happening, but there's murder in her eye. "Let me go!" I cry, wrenching against her grip.

The woman's lip curls. She takes her hand off my stomach and places it over my face instead, long fingers covering me like a mask, palm pressed hard against my open mouth. "Your groom will have to wait to ravish his bride. I need something from you first. But don't worry! He'll be just as happy to have you back scraped clean of another man's seed."

Shadows close in on all sides. Somewhere far away I think I hear Danny shouting: "Let her go! Let her go, Estrilde! She doesn't belong to you anymore!" There's movement at the corner of my eye. I try to turn my head, to peer through the woman's long fingers. Figures appear at the chapel door—Danny, his fists clenched, his teeth bared; Kitty, white-faced, clinging to the doorway behind him.

Then oblivion crushes in, smothering me in darkness.

5

I STARTLE AWAKE TO THE SEARING STENCH OF AMMONIA burning up my nostrils. My stomach revolts, and I try to roll over in bed, prepared to vomit there and then, no time to make it to the washbasin. But I cannot roll over. My arms are bound.

I turn my head desperately, and my stomach heaves. There's nothing in it, so I gag on air alone, tears sparking in my eyes, limbs shuddering. Slowly, hazily, I drag my awareness to the forefront of my mind. Where am I? What am I wearing? Is this . . . am I clad only in my chemise and corset? Where is my wedding gown? I was supposed to get married today. Wasn't I?

I blink and blink again. Large wooden beams arch overhead, forming a dome with a small circle opening at its peak from which a beam of light shines directly on me. The rest of the chamber is deeply shadowed, difficult to see. It reminds me vaguely of the old belltower of Nornala's chapel. But why would I climb the belltower on my wedding day? And where are the bells?

Once more I try to sit up. But I can't. I seem to be bound to a stone table, which stands in the middle of this strange, cold space. My arms are fastened over my head, and my legs are strapped at the ankle but spread wide. I look down the length of my body. My petticoats are rolled up to my knees, baring my feet and legs. My corset and chemise provide very little covering.

Up until this moment I was too disoriented to feel anything beyond sickness and vague unease. Now panic lances through my veins, jarring me to full wakefulness. Someone stands just out of sight behind my head—the same someone who applied the smelling salts, I would guess. I hear him breathing, though I cannot see him, not even when I twist my head. "Who's there?" I demand, my voice cracking. "Who are you? Show yourself!"

"You are hardly in a position to make demands, Clara Darlington."

A luminous glow draws my eye across the room. A woman appears like a manifesting vision from the shadows. It's her—the angelic being from the street. Her wings are gone; they would not fit in this small chamber. But her skin, her hair, her very being radiates ethereal light as she draws nearer, one careful footstep after the other. She clasps a long, thin knife in her right hand.

"You promised you wouldn't hurt her."

My heart jumps. That voice! It shoots through me, a branching bolt of shock, fear, horror, confusion, dismay—too many feelings all at once. I crane my head again, struggling to see who stands behind me. But I don't have to see him to know. "Oscar!" I gasp, his name a painful rasp in my throat.

He moves into my line of vision. He doesn't look at me but keeps his gaze fixed on that golden woman. He looks so strange, so small, so fragile in this space. His loose white shirt billows about his gaunt frame, the sleeves rolled up to his elbows, revealing all the ink stains smattered like tattoos across his pale forearms. Tousled curls frame his face in a halo, and his eyes stand out very wide and stark, gleaming with a hint of mania.

The woman fixes him with a frigid stare. "It will not be pleasant, what she must endure. But she will survive and she will recover." She takes another step toward me, shedding rainbow fragments in her wake. "If you haven't the stomach for what must be done, I suggest you leave."

I strain against my bonds, legs and arms writhing uselessly. "Oscar!" I roll my head as I try to get a better look at my brother. "Oscar, what are you doing here? Where are we? Please, Oscar, tell me what's happening!" Tears course down my cheeks, and I cannot so much as wipe them away.

Oscar's teeth audibly grind. But he will not look at me. "How long will this take?" he demands harshly.

"Not long." The woman holds up her knife again. "Just until the heart ceases to beat."

"What?" I choke on my own terror. Is she planning to murder

me where I lie? "Oscar!" I cry again, terror stretching my voice into a thin cord. "Oscar, what is she going to do to me?"

At last he turns and looks directly at me. His face is so shadowed, I almost think his eyes are gone, lost in two empty voids of blackness. But then he takes a step forward, and the glow cast by the woman falls across him, revealing an agonized expression. He looks so much older than he is. He's always favored our mother, always boasted her gentle, doe-eyed beauty. But now? Now I see Edgar. Our father. Alive once more, reborn from terror.

"This is your fault, you know," he says, and it's Edgar's voice I hear throbbing in my head. "You're the reason he had to fight. You're the reason he fell. If it weren't for you . . ." He trails off and rubs a hand down his face, pulling at the skin under his eyes. In my addled state, it seems to me as though he's pushing and twisting his own features, warping them into our father's visage and back again. Then he drops his hand and looks at me again, his gaze firmer than before. "I must get him back. Don't you understand? He's the only person who really knows me, the only person who truly cares. I cannot live without him, I . . . I . . ." He sucks an agonized breath through his teeth. "If you loved me, Clara, you wouldn't begrudge me this. One life for the life you so thoughtlessly threw away. It's a fair exchange."

"What are you saying?" I cry, twisting, straining. The chains gripping my wrists, my ankles, and my hips dig into my flesh. "I don't know what you're talking about. This is madness!"

The woman now stands at the foot of the stone slab. The gem at her throat, once black, seems to writhe with living red light in its depths. It casts a hellish glow across her face as she looks me coldly in the eye. "Struggle, and I will not be able to be precise. One wrong move, and you will die. Horribly." She grins, a beautiful, terrifying flash. "You humans are such fragile things."

"Oscar? Oscar!" I scream, watching as she brandishes the long knife once more. "What is she doing? Oscar, stop her! Stop her! *Please!*"

"You must hold still, Clara," Oscar says, coming to stand close to my head. He puts out a trembling hand, nearly touches me, but retracts it again. "It's the only way. I'm sorry."

I scream as the woman bends over the table and my exposed body. Blind panic burns through me. I feel pressure against my inner thigh and then—

A roar fills my ears. The rafters overhead groan, crack, break like matchsticks and blow away under a tremendous whorl of pure power. Bursts of light in colors for which I have no name, heat and sound and dread all explode across my senses as a beam of pure white light falls into the circular chamber and decimates the shadows in a single, heart-stopping instant.

Someone is screaming. Me? No, the woman. Oscar shouts as well, bellowing words I cannot comprehend, for my attention is fixed on the image above me, appearing in the center of that blinding light. A winged man, slowly descending through the now open roof. He wears a crown of some dark stone across his brow. His hair is iron gray, falling in waves across his shoulders. His face is lined but beautiful. So beautiful, so overwhelming that, despite the terror bursting in my head, my breath catches at the mere sight of him.

He looks down at me, his arms outspread as though he has just burst the roof apart in a single great gesture. His shining wings beat the air at his back, holding him suspended overhead. His eyes widen. His expression becomes one of rapt revelation, as though he's just been given a glimpse of heaven itself. I don't understand. I can only stare back, numb, my lips parted.

Then he speaks in a deep, reverent voice: "Darling?"

With a shriek the shining woman leaps across the slab. Still clutching the long knife in one hand, she holds the point of the blade against my temple. "Begone from here at once, Prince!" she cries. "Fly from here, or I will kill her before your eyes!"

Somewhere, in some distant realm of comprehension, I hear Oscar screaming, "No! Don't hurt her!" But I cannot think of that, cannot fathom anything beyond the pain of that knife biting into my skin and the intensity of those two violet eyes lancing down at me and my captor.

"Harm one hair on her head," the stranger says, raising an arm, "and I will blast you to oblivion." Sparks of energy and churning darkness move and play between his fingers. Is this the same power which blew away the roof? Whoever and whatever this man is, he means his threat quite literally.

"Do it!" the woman cries, gripping the top of my head with one hand, her long nails digging painfully into my scalp. "It won't change your fate. When she is dead, you will die soon after, and all Aurelis will fall into chaos without an heir."

"Better than letting it fall into your hands, Estrilde."

"Go on then, Castien," the woman snarls. "If you dare."

Castien. There's something in that name. I don't understand it, cannot begin to comprehend how it burns in my head like living fire. My lips move, trying to form the sounds but cannot seem to remember how.

The stranger lowers his hand. His gaze rips from me, traveling around the small chamber in a quick scan. "And what is it you're trying to accomplish here, cousin?" he demands. "Not murder, it would seem. You've set up a spell. A summoning." His eyes snap back to the woman's face, and his lip curls in a snarl. "Are you trying to bring him back? Because you know my wife's blood will never suffice. It must be mine or nothing. The Rite of the Thorn demands it."

His wife? *His wife?* My heart surges. I stare up at that gray-haired stranger, that beautiful apparition hovering overhead like an avenging angel. I must not have heard right, must not have understood. Fear is addling my brain.

"You think I don't know that?" the woman hurls back. "Not even a Fatebond is strong enough to satisfy the Rite of the Thorn. But the beating heart of your living child will serve well enough."

The stranger rears back in the air as though struck by a blow. His wings beat storms into being behind him. Darkness and power gather in his fists. "What did you say?" he demands.

The woman laughs, a lovely, musical sound. "You could have seen for yourself had you delayed your arrival by another five minutes! I could have introduced you to your child personally."

What? What are they talking about? What child? I writhe, straining in both body and soul to make sense of what's happening. That long knife . . . what this woman planned to do . . . but . . .

"There's been some mistake!" I cry. "I'm not with child! And I don't know who this man is, but—"

"Quiet, Clara!" Oscar barks from where he crouches against the wall.

The winged stranger's gaze shoots straight to him, pinning him in place. "So you're in on this plot too. Are you so deeply enthralled that you would murder innocents for the sake of your lover?" He looks ready to strike my brother dead. I open my mouth to protest, to plead for his life. Instead the stranger turns to the woman once more. "The Rite of the Thorn requires willing blood."

The woman shrugs. "Deathblood is strong. It will serve my purpose."

"It will not."

"That's a risk I'm willing to take."

"You'll not get the chance."

"Perhaps not. Perhaps I'll die here over the corpse of your wife and your unborn child." The woman's grip on my scalp tightens. I choke on a scream. "Unless, dear cousin, you can think of an alternative that may bring satisfaction to all."

The look on the stranger's face is impossible to describe—

somewhere between ravenous hunger and bloodthirsty rage. He seems to be trying not to look at me, but his gaze is drawn back to mine. Those eyes of his capture me, so strangely familiar and yet so wildly foreign all at the same time.

"What do you say, Castien?" the woman cries, twisting her knife slowly against my temple. "Will you give me your willing blood? Will you open the gates to Saalvru and summon Ivor forth?"

"You may not like what he has become, Estrilde," the stranger cautions. "It's been too long. He won't be the man who left."

"Yet another risk I'm willing to take." The woman sneers. "And what about you? Are you willing to risk more than you've already lost?"

The stranger curses. Viciously, bitterly. Then, slowly, he lowers himself into the room, his mighty wings moving with strength and control to ease his descent. The instant his feet touch the stone floor, the wings vanish, and he becomes nothing more than a man. A haggard, gray-haired man. "Let her go, Estrilde," he says.

My captor catches her breath. "Swear you will bring Ivor forth from Saalvru. Swear it to me in blood."

"My word is good enough for you."

"The word of a half-human. The word of a liar." She spits and gnashes her teeth. "I need blood, Castien. Either yours or hers. I don't care which, but I will have it. *Now.*"

The stranger whips out a knife, a delicate little thing, no bigger than a penknife. He opens the front of his robes, revealing the chiseled contours of a warrior's chest, however faded and pale his skin. He pricks the flesh above his heart. Blue blood wells, flows. Next he pricks his right hand in the center of his palm and holds it up to show the red stain. He places his hand against his chest. "I swear on my blood, both human and fae, I will call Ivor forth from Saalvru."

He tips his head forward, those eyes of his like living fire under his dark brows. "Now let my wife go, you bitch."

THE PRINCE

SHE'S HERE.

She's here.

I cannot trust my own eyes. This must be a dream. How many times has my own unconscious plagued me with variations of this same scenario? Clara. My wife. Returned to me from across the worlds. As beautiful and stubborn and terrifying and brilliant as ever. Sometimes in my dreams, she would run to me in a joyful haze of love and renewal. Sometimes she would rage, hurling words of vitriolic hatred. It never mattered. Whatever guise she came in, I would always react the same. I would catch her in my arms, crush her against my chest, and cover her with kisses, drowning out either her joy or her rage until she gave in to me, answering my passion in kind.

But in none of my dreams has she been bound and exposed, stripped to her undergarments, her skirts hiked up her bare legs, her hair wild about her face.

This is no dream. It's a nightmare made real. But I have experience with nightmares.

I stand by silently as Estrilde and that boy cut the bonds holding Clara down to the hideous slab. She sits up, rubbing her wrists, flinching away from Estrilde and reaching for her brother. As though he wasn't equally guilty of the crimes taking place here. Estrilde could never have found Clara without that boy's help. What other crimes has he committed since I lifted that suppression curse I'd placed on him? I should never have released him, should never have relented to Clara's pleading. The sheer power seething in his soul is enough to put whole worlds at risk. If I were wise, I would have slain him in cold blood long ago.

He helps his sister down from the slab. She casts a frantic glance over her shoulder at me, and that single look is enough to cut me straight to the heart. There's no recognition in her gaze, only blankness and confusion. I did that. I stripped all memory of myself from her mind when I sent her from this world. I'd hoped it would make it easier for her to blend back into her old life. Or maybe I was selfish. Maybe I simply didn't want to go on living with the knowledge that she was out there somewhere, beyond the edge of this world, hating me. Now I would give anything for that hatred. Any emotion would be preferable to this absence.

Though every instinct burning in my being tells me to throw Oscar against the wall and take her in my arms, I stand firm. She would not be comforted by my embrace, the embrace of a stranger, of an old man. I know full well how my body has disintegrated over the weeks since our parting. How long has it been for her? After she passed through the gate, I'd seen to it that the portal between her world and mine was broken. This ought to have severed the timeline, allowing her world to progress at its own rate, unsynchronized with mine. What has been weeks for me could have been days, years, or mere hours for her.

She looks exactly as I remember. Still the same beautiful creature I've longed to claim since the first moment I laid eyes upon her. But in my eyes, she could never change, no matter the ravages of mortal time.

Estrilde steps between us. Now that Clara is safely out of her clutches, I fight the urge to swipe that knife from my cousin's hand and drive it straight into her black heart, a worthy punishment for the crime she was prepared to commit. My blood-oath binds me, however, and I restrain myself. "Well, Castien?" she demands, fear glimmering in her eye. "Shall we get on with it?"

"Nothing good can come of bringing Ivor back," I say, my gaze momentarily dropping to the black stone my cousin wears on a chain around her neck. It's the bloodgem necklace, the Obligation price she demanded in exchange for Daniel Gale's freedom. Clara and I gave up a great deal to pay that price. Far more than it was worth. "That man is evil. He cares nothing for you nor anyone else.

He will do anything to further his own ends."

"You are bound," Estrilde snarls, her voice cracking. "You must fulfill your oath."

She's right. I have no choice. I look at Clara one last time, standing there beside her brother, so desperate and confused. How many times will I let my love for her drive me to these dark places? "Very well," I growl. "Let the consequences be on your head."

With those words I step to the stone slab. Estrilde has chosen an interesting site for attempting this spell. Long ago, before my father ruled Aurelis, this tower was used to contain Miphates prisoners brought back from the war. They would be bound to this very slab, the magic drained from their veins, a slow torturous death. It was said some of their fae keepers learned to keep them and their magic alive for long periods of time, their blood feeding great workings of black magic.

I hold my already bleeding hand out over the slab. The Rite of the Thorn is an ancient practice, complex in its workings, strict in its laws. I know it well enough—the blood battle, the sacrifice, the mercy offering. Only I never thought I'd see the day when I would extend such mercy to Ivor Illithor.

"*Ipyrea hyrssean atim,*" I say, the ancient words flowing from my tongue. "*By the Rite of the Thorn. By the blood of my veins. By the blade of Tanatar and the fire of Urym, I call forth my enemy and declare the price of his life paid.*"

Three drops of my blood fall to the center of the slab. Immediately there's a shift. The stone becomes liquid, whirling, bubbling. Then it falls away entirely, and I stand on the brink of another realm, a seething realm of mist and writhing tentacles. So I gaze once more into Saalvru, the Third Hell.

I grimace, bracing myself against the horror rising from that pit. Ivor fell weeks ago, but time itself means little under such circumstances. Hell is not governed by such feeble forces. It would not matter if Ivor had spent weeks, hours, or whole ages of existence in that place. People do not come back from hell unchanged.

I extend my arm again, allow three more drops of blood to fall. Those dark tentacles lash in response, and a deep groan of unspeakable madness echoes up from the depths. The demon of Saalvru does not give up its prisoners willingly.

"Ipyrea hryssean atim." I call again. *"Siandrar."* Then in a loud voice which echoes into those endless depths, "Ivor Illithor, I summon you. Come forth!"

Clara stands just on the edge of my vision. She's buried her face in Oscar's shoulder while her brother holds her almost protectively, as though she has not spent her entire life shielding him from the horrors of the worlds. He stares into the pit, his expression one of desperate hope. Does Estrilde know the true nature of the relationship between Ivor and this boy? Or does she not care so long as she gets what she wants in the end?

"Siandrar!" I bellow again. The demon writhes, uttering a roar beyond description. But the Rite of the Thorn is an ancient law, inscribed into the very foundations of Eledria by the Great Goddess Aneirin Herself. No demon can resist Her will.

I squeeze my hand, send more blood streaming into that pit. I am dizzy, trembling. The long separation from my Fatebound has weakened me more than I like to admit over these last few weeks. Her proximity has reawakened a spark deep inside, but her lack of memory impedes any real flow of magic between us. There's only one way now that I can be restored to full power—and that is not something I can take from her. Not now. Not ever.

"Ivor," I call again, my voice ringing against the stone walls, down into that hell. "Come forth!"

Suddenly a hand bursts through the mist. The skin is mottled purple, covered in pustules and open wounds. The fingers, straight and tense, shake wildly.

"It's him!" Estrilde cries.

Oscar pushes his sister roughly to one side and dives for the pit. He grasps that hand with both of his and pulls with all his might. Clara utters a strangled cry that wrenches my heart as she lunges after her brother, gripping the back of his shirt, fighting to drag him away from that terrible brink. If only I dared interfere. If only I dared grip her arm and wrench her back. But my slowly-dripping blood is the only thing keeping this portal open, and I cannot stop now.

Oscar adjusts his grip, reaching lower to grasp an elbow then a shoulder. Slowly, painfully, a figure swathed in shadow emerges from the mist. There's a sound like sucking mud, trying to draw him back. "Ivor!" Oscar screams through his tears. "Ivor, don't let go!"

With a last burst of suction, the dark figure emerges, tumbling out in a tangle of limbs there on the floor. Oscar pushes himself upright, his arms around the naked, gross, shuddering form as Clara and Estrilde work together to pull them both away from the edge. "I've got you!" Oscar weeps. "I've got you! You're safe now!"

Then Ivor rears back his head.

He's hideous, warped. One eye bulges from a face nearly devoid of skin. The other eye is gone, the empty socket gaping. His flesh is gory, bloody, with a few straggling strands of once-golden hair clinging between the open wounds across his scalp. His mouth is fixed like a skull's grin, and when he opens it, a diabolic rasp tears from his throat. "Sweet Oscar! You saved me!"

Oscar screams, throwing himself backwards into his sister's arms.

I close my fist, stopping the stream of blood and the flow of my power. *"Mita naessyrh!"* I cry, ending the incantation, closing the tear between realities. The demon of Saalvru resists, stretching its tentacles out over the lip of the pit, eager to reclaim its prey. But the price is paid, and the pull of the mist is too strong. With a last, furious cry, the demon sinks, and the pit closes, issuing a last geyser burst of red glare into the chamber. Then it is gone. Darkness descends. I stand before the stone slab, which boasts a spreading, circular crack in its center. Staggering backwards, I hit the wall and press myself against it. Weakness shivers through my limbs. For the moment it's all I can do to keep myself upright. Blood pounds in my ears, dulling all other sounds. That is until Estrilde's wailing cry breaks through.

"You tricked me! You played false on our agreement!"

My swimming gaze clarifies, and her face comes into focus. She stands across the chamber from me, also pressed against the wall. But her eyes are fixed on the ruinous figure of Ivor, crouched on the floor. Oscar, recovered from his own shock, once more grips the broken fae lord by his shoulder, murmuring a stream of comforting nonsense. Clara has turned to one side, dry heaving. But she won't abandon her brother.

I lift a cold gaze to Estrilde. "I may have promised to bring him back," I growl. "But even I can't make him pretty again."

With a wordless cry Estrilde raises her arm, ready to hurl a blast of pure magic straight at me. But I'm prepared; I've summoned a blast of my own, drawing on what reserves of power remain to me. Even weakened, I am stronger than Estrilde. I send a bolt of light across the room, knocking her off her feet. She falls in a crumpled heap, her glamours momentarily evaporated. No longer the glorious princess, she is now a frail, bony hag of a woman with sharp teeth and talon-like nails. She moans, struggling and failing to pull herself up.

I draw three long breaths. Then straightening my shoulders and tossing a lock of hair back from my forehead, I approach Ivor and Oscar. The nearer I come to Clara, the more my breathing eases, the more the tightness in my limbs relaxes, and my blood flows freely. It's incredible what simply sharing her atmosphere does for my wellbeing! But I dare not so much as look at her, dare not face the absence of her memory. The pain would undo me. Instead I stand over my fallen enemy, gazing down at the ruin that was once

Ivor Illithor. Perhaps I should pity him. No living creature should endure what he has endured—and his fate might well have been mine had the gods not looked upon me with mercy.

But I still vividly remember bursting into his bedchamber and discovering him with my wife pinned against the wall. Whatever pity I may have felt evaporates.

"Rise, Ivor," I demand.

My enemy lifts his face. That one bulging eye stares up at me, gleaming with horror. He had not realized my presence until that moment, and now looks as though he would dive back into Saalvru to escape me.

"Get up," I say, my voice cold and cruel, "or I will end your miserable life here and now."

"Don't touch him!" Oscar scrambles to his feet. "Leave him alone!" He steps between us, this slender lad with his brittle bones and delicate features. Features which bear uncanny resemblance to his sister . . . which may explain why I didn't kill him long ago.

"That I will not do," I reply. "I may have brought him back from hell, but he is not free. I intend to throw him into the deepest, darkest cell, far from all light, all warmth, all joy. There let him thank all his gods and angels that I chose to be merciful."

"You won't lay a finger on him!" Sunlight pours once more through the roofless cell, lighting up Oscar's face with manic courage.

"You have no power here, boy," I growl. "For the love I bear your sister, I will not hurt you unless you drive me to it. Now stand aside."

His eyes seem to spin in his skull, so wide, so wild. Then he smiles and holds up his arm. To my surprise, I see a smear of blood across his forearm and realize he's holding Estrilde's knife in his other hand. "No power?" he says, grimacing against the pain. "You're wrong, Prince. It is you who are powerless against me."

My eyes fasten on that wound, that blood dripping down his arm. And I realize what it is: a word, a single word, carved directly into his flesh. "What have you done?" I breathe.

Shadows burst to life all around us, full of churning movement and energy, rushing in, overwhelming. The next moment the sun is blotted out. I whirl in place, stare up through the broken roof.

Up into the face of a vast, dark, twisted nightmare-made-flesh.

CLARA

6

THERE'S NOTHING IN MY REALM OF EXPERIENCE TO HELP me comprehend what I see.

A tremendous being looms above me, twenty meters tall at least. Its frame is gaunt, almost skeletal, but the arrangement of the bones protruding through its paper-thin flesh isn't human. Its hands are enormous, six-fingered monstrosities, with sword-length claws, razor sharp. A demented smile slashes across its face, the teeth protruding from black and bleeding gums. A shadowy tongue laps the air, and more shadows lick from the corners of its cavernous eye sockets. But worst of all is the great hole in its chest. The splintered rib cage, the gaping wound, revealing utter emptiness inside. The size of it, the sheer wrongness of its proportions, the evil of its lines and construction strikes a blow to reason and shatters it into a million shards of madness. I gape up at that apparition in utter horror.

And I know it. I recognize it. For I encountered it for the first time only yesterday. Then, however, it had been safely confined within the pages of a glossy magazine and my own imagination. A real terror, alive and thriving, but bound.

It is bound no longer. The Hollow Man walks unfettered in this world.

The size of him alone would block out all sunlight, but the darkness which surrounds him is more than ordinary shadow. It is a blackness of hellish pitch, permeating mind, spirit, soul, and heart. I crumple to my knees beneath it, my head thrown back, my jaw slack. The emotions flooding me are too great for screams, for flight. This is fear. Pure fear, lancing through every fiber of my being.

Those shadow-filled eyes turn, fixing solely on me. Down in their centers, a red fire burns, twin pinpoints of heat like windows into the deepest hell. That demented grin grows, revealing far too many teeth. One great clawed hand grips the topmost edge of the tower, while the other reaches in, straight for me. That long misshapen arm stretches out, and I cannot hide, cannot fight. I cannot even throw up my hands to shield my face. I can only kneel as darkness billows around me, lost to all hope.

A bolt of brilliant light sears through my head. I scream—a deep, guttural cry, dragged up from the very depths of my soul. Falling backwards, I scramble across the floor. Golden wings beat powerful gusts of air before me. It's the stranger—the gray-haired stranger, the one called Castien. He darts between me and that reaching hand, and my vision seems to split. One part of my mind sees a hazy phantom image of him wielding a book and quill, writing a furious stream of words into the pages. The stronger, clearer part of my mind sees that same man brandishing a flaming sword. He hacks into the monster's outstretched arm, the blade cutting into bone.

The Hollow Man roars. He withdraws his arm, dragging the Prince away with him. As he rears back, sunlight fills the tower once more.

"Out! Out! We've got to get out, now!" I turn my head, seeking the source of that voice. It's the woman—my kidnapper. No longer tall and glorious, but blasted into a scrawny, faded creature with lank, colorless hair. If I'd not seen the transformation with my own eyes, I wouldn't know it was the same being. Even as I watch her, however, a glimmering aura surrounds her limbs, pulling a faint image of youth and loveliness back into place.

The woman catches hold of the hideous man, the one they call Ivor. Grimacing with disgust, she hauls him to his feet. "Estrilde?" the man rasps, looking at her wildly with his single, bulging eye. "Estrilde, what has he done to me?" He clings to her, desperate, shuddering in pain.

"We'll make him pay, my love," the woman snarls. "But first we've got to get you away from here. Now, while Castien is distracted. Here, boy!" she barks, turning to Oscar. "Assist him."

Oscar, recovered from his initial shock, doesn't hesitate to tuck himself under Ivor's arm. I realize with a jolt that he's going to leave with them. He's going to leave me. "Oscar!" I cry, pulling myself to my feet. "Oscar, wait!"

My brother turns. So does the man. His head whips around sharply, that hideous visage a horror of hatred and wrath. His awful, blackened teeth seem to sharpen. *"You!"* he snarls. "You did this!"

The next moment he snatches the long knife out of Oscar's hand and lunges at me. I scream and stagger back even as Oscar throws himself at the man, gripping his arm with both hands. "Ivor, no!" he cries. He's so thin and frail but overpowers the broken man with apparent ease. "We need her. Remember? Remember our plan!"

"He's right," the woman agrees, stepping to Ivor's side and placing a hand on his shoulder. "Everything can still come out right." Her voice is low and dangerous but strangely soothing. She reaches up and unclasps the necklace around her throat then loops it over Ivor's head. The black stone rests against his oozing breast, glittering with its own strange light. "You'll have your throne," Estrilde says, "and I'll have mine. But we must be wise. We cannot waste assets."

The mad monster holds my gaze with his one eye, panting through gritted teeth. Then he shakes his head, and hanks of limp hair fall across his pustuled forehead. "Bring her," he snarls.

Estrilde turns with viper quickness and latches hold of my upper arm. Her grip sends a shock through me. "No!" I cry, prying at her fingers. "No, I'm not going anywhere with you!"

With a wordless growl, Estrilde yanks me toward her. Her other hand closes around my face, fingers latching on tight. "Submit!" she says. Something coils out from inside her, through her fingertips, jutting into my mind, like poisonous leeches, sucking away my will. I try to fight, but resistance saps my energy. My knees buckle. With a quick dart, Estrilde catches me, lifts me up, and throws me over her shoulder. There I hang like a dead carcass, still fighting to keep her out of my mind. "Now," Estrilde says, turning once more to Oscar and the stranger. "To the library."

The world goes dark, obscure, punctured by flashes of golden light. I don't understand what's happening, can neither focus nor concentrate. Some vague part of me is aware of Oscar trailing behind Estrilde, supporting Ivor. That man keeps shooting murderous glances my way, but I cannot find the strength to fear him, not now, not while fighting this influence in my mind. We descend a long, winding stairway and step out into a passage of gold arches. I glimpse incredible sights, images of a glorious palace, like some dreamed-up heaven. Estrilde strides on quickly as though I weigh next to nothing. Oscar struggles more with his burden, and the woman is obliged to pause and let him catch up. We pass others now and then, beautiful people, their faces all strained with terror, many of them screaming. For the moment I can't remember why they're afraid.

Suddenly a shadow passes over the world, darkening the beams of light streaming through those window arches. It's like stepping into another world entirely. Roiling darkness closes in around us, alive and crawling across the floor. Still slung across Estrilde's shoulder, I lift my head, turn to look out the nearest window. He's there—the Hollow Man. With his strange, void eyes, so tall that he seems huge even at a distance. Flashing figures of gold close in around him, angelic beings astride winged horses. They streak across the sky, beautiful and fierce. A jolt of hope bursts in my heart at the sight of them. They swarm the Hollow Man, brandishing swords. But the giant swings out an arm. His razor-edged nails swat the winged horses from the air like flies. Some he catches and stuffs into the hollow of his chest.

Then the giant turns its great head and seems to look straight through this window. Straight at me.

You cannot hide.

A multitudinous voice echoes inside my head. Shrieks, growls, curses, groans. But underneath it all, that thread of understanding, that simple truth, felt but not spoken.

You cannot hide.

I will find you.

I will always find you.

My spirit recoils. I am small, hopeless, and so foolish. I don't deserve to be saved, I don't deserve to be freed. Whatever comes, whatever darkness descends, I brought it on myself. It's only right that I should bow my head, accept my fate. It's only right that I should—

"Mage!" Estrilde's shriek shatters my ears. "Bind it!" she cries. "Bind your monster! Before it slaughters us all!"

"I . . . I . . ." Oscar's eyes roll, shifting from Estrilde to Ivor and even to me, as though I might help him. "I don't know how."

Estrilde bites out a curse. "What use are you then? Perhaps I should kill you here and now." Her wrist snaps, and a knife appears in hand. She points it beneath Oscar's chin, but Ivor catches hold of her forearm.

"No," he says. "Don't touch him."

The floor and the walls vibrate with a sudden *boom*. I look up again, see the Hollow Man turned toward us, moving our way. Each footfall seems to shake the world.

"We've got to move!" Oscar cries.

Estrilde curses again, adjusting her grip on me. Then she turns about and flees down the passage, through an arch into another huge, golden hall. Shadows pursue us, like hounds on the hunt. She comes to a large, double door, shut fast. At a single uttered word, the door flies open, revealing a foyer and a big receiving desk made of living tree roots. Something about it strikes my memory.

"Quick, inside," Estrilde says. Oscar half-carries Ivor over the threshold. She pulls the doors shut behind us, and I get a glimpse into the space we've entered.

It's a library. A vast, golden, incredible library, the most splendid space I've ever seen, with living branches twined together forming arrays of bookshelves many stories high. One has only to breathe in the aroma of words, of ideas, of pure power captured in ink on pages. Even in the midst of terror and confusion, the scope of it nearly stops my heart with wonder.

Then Estrilde is running again. My stomach drives into her sharp shoulder, and I can do nothing but grip the back of her gown, trying to push myself up, trying to find some equilibrium. Oscar and Ivor have picked up their pace now. The urgency of our situation infuses the broken man with unexpected strength. We climb a spiral stair to an upper level and around a set of shelves into a hidden wing of the library. My view extends behind us, and I see the lower library darkening, shadows creeping in along the floor and between the books like ooze.

I will find you, echoes the voice among many voices in my head. *You cannot hide from me, Clara. You cannot escape.*

"Thaddeus!" Ivor rasps. "Thaddeus Creakle, come out to me!"

A door opens. An old man appears from a back room, a quill in one hand, a penknife in the other. He blinks out from behind a pair of square spectacles set on the bridge of his nose. "Lord Ivor?" he gasps. A scream of terror bursts from his lips at the sight of Ivor's ravaged face.

"Silence," Ivor growls even as Oscar draws to a halt. "Thaddeus, you will obey me. I know you know where the gate to Vespre is hidden in this library. Tell me where it is, now!"

The old man backs away until he hits the wall of bookshelves behind him. He shakes his head. "I . . . I am no longer your Obligate, my lord. I belong to the Prince—"

In a few quick strides, Estrilde covers the distance between them, pressing the tip of her knife against the old man's throat. "Take us to the gate, human," she snarls. "Now!"

The poor man's eyes bug from his skull. He catches my eye, and I see a flash of recognition, though I don't know him at all. The sight of me seems to settle something in his mind, however, for he nods and whispers, "This way."

The shadows all around us deepen, licking at our footsteps.

The old man leads us swiftly to another floor of the library, up above the main atrium. It's just a humble little door, one I would guess leads to storage. But the man indicates it with a wave of his arm, the long sleeve of his robe wafting. "There, Princess," he says. "That is your way. But no one can open it besides the Prince."

"We don't need the Prince," Estrilde says. With those words, she *thunks* me down so hard, I stagger and would fall if she didn't catch my shoulder and keep me on my feet. "We have his Fatebound. She can open his gate." I cry out as she forces me to the door and leans down to snarl in my ear, "Open it, Clara Darlington. Open it, or I shall gut your brother and let him bleed out before your eyes."

I don't understand what she's saying, what she wants. I cannot comprehend what she expects to find behind this door. But the look in her eyes tells me she isn't bluffing. She will kill my brother in a heartbeat, and she will feel no remorse.

Hand shaking, I reach out, grip the doorknob. When I turn it, a spark like an electric shock jolts up my arm. I jerk back, trying to let go, but my fingers seem to tighten, dragging the door open with me, revealing a dusty storage room full of boxes and oddments I cannot discern in the gloom. Then the air directly before my face shifts. A sudden sense of falling rushes through my senses. I gasp and stagger back, arms wheeling, and only Estrilde's grip on my shoulder keeps me upright.

"It worked!" Ivor hisses. "It bloody well work—"

The floor shakes. An echoing *boom* resounds through the library, and all the books on their shelves begin to whisper and shiver in dread. Darkness races up the walls on either side of us, an overwhelming flood.

You cannot run.

You cannot hide.

I will find you.

I will always find you.

Estrilde's grip on my shoulder is gone. I am alone. Alone in this place of shadow and darkness. Alone save for . . . I turn sharply, searching. There! Just five paces away, Oscar stands isolated in a patch of pale light. His head swivels, his gaze seeking. When he sees me, his lips begin to form my name.

Then the Hollow Man steps between us.

He is not the vast, towering giant who looked down on me from the broken tower roof. Here in this space, he is a mere seven feet tall, hunched and twisted to fit within the confines of the library. Yet somehow space warps around him, making him enormous beyond comprehension. Dread sweeps over me under his shadow-licked gaze.

There you are, Clara.

I told you I would find you.

"Please," I whimper and drop to my knees. My shaking hands rise in front of me, palms out, as though I might push him away. "I'm sorry! I'm sorry!"

You are guilty.

You are false.

You are small and useless and wrong.

The truth of his words fills me up, burning through my heart, my soul. I feel in the very marrow of my bones my own worthlessness. I cannot run from it, cannot hide from this terrible truth. The Hollow Man steps forward. I hear the thud of a heartbeat inside his broken ribcage but see only darkness in those depths. A swallowing darkness, hungry and devouring. He stretches out one hand, those long, multi-jointed fingers reaching for my face, blocking out all else, all fear, all hope, all reason, all madness. There is nothing but my own inevitable consumption.

You were never enough.

You never can be.

Worthless.

Worthless.

Worth—

A lash of golden light explodes in my vision. I scream, jolted out of my trance, and throw myself backwards, my bare feet scrabbling on the marble floor. Somewhere close Oscar screams as well, but I cannot see him. My vision is filled with confusion. A whip made of lightning seems to wrap around the Hollow Man. My dazzled eyes follow the line of that sparking, burning cord back to its source. To him. The stranger. The Prince, they called him. He holds the whip with both hands, his age-lined face set with a ferocious snarl, his teeth flashing. He yanks, and the monstrous form of the Hollow Man stumbles. His great feet crack the stone floor, and he crashes into a bookshelf, sending pages scattering. The Prince yanks again. The Hollow Man lets out a bellowing roar and topples over, tipping straight toward me. I throw up my arms, expecting to be crushed beneath that massive body.

But the Hollow Man disintegrates. One moment he's there; the next he vanishes in a cloud of dust and foul-smelling ash. Only the voices remain, echoing in aftershock, underscored by an ongoing scream of rage and pain.

Worthless.

Guilty.

I will find you.

I will always find you . . .

You . . . cannot . . . hide . . .

Slowly the echoes clear from my head. I lift my dazzled gaze to find the Prince standing before me, his violet eyes fixed intently on my face. He looks . . . younger. Fuller, stronger, with an inner glow I can hardly explain. Rather than a whip, he holds an open book in his hands. He closes it with a snap and wraps the leather cord around it, binding the cover shut. Dark tendrils lash out from between the pages, trying to escape, but when I blink, that image is gone.

Then the Prince kneels before me, the book tucked under his arm as he grips my hand. "Darling!" His voice is so wracked with inexplicable emotion, it stabs me straight to the heart. I stare into that unfamiliar face, baffled by what I see burning in his eyes. "Darling, are you all right? Did he hurt you?"

"I . . . I'm . . ." I suck in a short breath. "I'm not hurt, I—"

An ear-splitting shriek cuts me off. Both the Prince and I turn sharply in time to see Estrilde pull herself up from the floor. Her beauty has been blasted away again, leaving her hollow and stick-thin, like she might break apart at the least pressure. Colorless hair wafts around her shoulders as she lifts her heavy head, and her eyes stare out from a skull-like face. "Ivor! No! Don't leave me!"

I whip my head around just in time to see both Oscar and Ivor stagger toward that open door. The air under the doorway ripples and churns. It's like all of space and time has ripped apart and funnels out through that opening in a maelstrom of light and energy. And my brother is making straight for it, Ivor's arm draped over his shoulder.

"Oscar!" I scream.

He looks back once. Meets my eyes.

Then the Prince surges to his feet and lunges after them. He takes no more than three paces before Oscar drags Ivor through. Their bodies warp into weird, twisted shapes, then vanish entirely.

A wail breaks from my throat. I collapse on my hands and knees, my body wracked with shock. I cry my brother's name again and again, as though I might somehow drag him back through that doorway, back to me. The Prince pulls up short, turns. His eyes are ablaze, but uncertainty scores his brow.

Then a voice I have never heard before speaks in a tremulous quaver, "What is the meaning of this?"

THE PRINCE

"GODS DAMN IT."

The words slice through my gritted teeth. I shouldn't have hesitated. I shouldn't have let Clara's cry of pain stop me in my tracks. I should have hurtled after Ivor and that thrice-cursed boy, followed them across realities, hunted them down.

Now my father's voice rings in my ears, freezing my blood and stopping me in my tracks. Even now I should turn, cast myself through the portal, pursue Ivor all the way to Vespre, and put an end to his life once and for all. The boy too—the mage, the creator of a Noswraith of such terrible power, I'll never be able to contain it in this flimsy volume. I must wrench its true name from Oscar's throat, bind the wraith, and kill its maker.

But Clara . . . How can I leave her? How can I abandon her to Estrilde and Lodírhal in a world she doesn't even remember?

So I turn in the direction from which my father's voice came. Lodírhal, decrepit, hideous, just clinging to life, stands between two bookshelves. He looks as though he will collapse in a pile of broken bones at any moment. Little of his former glory remains. I'm not even certain how he manages to hold himself upright. But light gleams in his eyes, revealing the power of a fae king—strange, mystical energy, which even the sundering of his Fatebond has not yet fully destroyed.

"What is this?" Lodírhal demands, gazing beyond me to the doorway and the still-churning movement of rippling realities. "Why is there a portal here inside my palace? I did not authorize this."

It's true. Lodírhal never knew this gate existed. And following my mother's death, I took care never to use it; it was a secret she and I shared, a crude passage between Aurelis and Vespre, unsanctioned and not entirely safe. But it allowed her to travel to and from Vespre library without her husband's knowledge, a strategy she often deemed prudent. I had all but forgotten its existence over these last few years. But apparently it was not so secret as I once believed.

My gaze swivels to Thaddeus Creakle, the senior librarian, standing half hidden behind another bookshelf. He stares back at me, his face drained of all color. He was my mother's confidant once upon a time. Did he betray the secret of this gate to Ivor, his former Obliege Lord?

Leaving these questions to ponder later, I turn to Lodírhal once more. "Father, there has been a breakout—"

"I am well aware." Lodírhal's voice creaks like a broken instrument, but he takes two steps toward me, drawing himself up straighter. Power gathers in his emaciated limbs, glowing bright in his veins. "I trusted you, Castien. You vowed to prevent the evil of mortal magic from polluting Aurelis again. You vowed to keep your nightmares safe and contained. So long as you were true to your word, I agreed to not cut them loose into the Hinter."

My eyes widen as realization strikes. "No, Father!" I cry, stepping forward to plant myself between him and the gate. "You can't do this, not to Vespre. The Noswraiths are contained. See?" I hold up the book, which still writhes in my grasp. "This one is bound. I shall carry it back to the library myself and see it locked in the deepest vault."

"You are a fool, my son." Lodírhal shakes his head heavily. "We were all fools to think such beings could be contained, such forces thwarted or turned to good. How many lives were lost in the last hour alone before you got this one under control? No." He draws a deep breath, his chest expanding, his spine straightening as more power, drawn straight from the heart of Aurelis, courses through him. "There is but one choice left. They will continue to break through from Vespre so long as Vespre is connected to our world. To Eledria."

"But this wraith did not come from Vespre!" I persist. "You must listen, Father. It was new, manifested by a newly-fledged mortal mage. The library remains intact, the captive Noswraiths bound—"

"Enough!" My father's eyes lock with mine, burning bright gold with accumulated magic. Magic that will kill him if he holds it in much longer. Magic that will kill him if he dares to use it. I see the death of my father playing out in my mind's eye, and there's nothing I can do to stop it.

"It's time you remembered who you are," Lodírhal growls. "Prince of Aurelis, heir to my throne. It's time you forgot your trolls and your library and became the man you were born to be. Let Vespre go! This was always what must be. It's time to cut the anchors, to let the island carry these monsters away into the Hinter Sea where they can do no further harm."

"What of the people of Vespre?" I cry. "You're dooming them to death and horror."

Lodírhal shakes his head. "Better one city lost than whole worlds." With those words he lifts both hands. The world around him surges in response, the magic that makes up the very essence of Aurelis. Radiant light pulses through his limbs, burns from his eyes. That same power moves through me as well, through every living thing this whole world over. All of us answer the call of our king, sending forth our innate magic to his bidding. In this moment I see Lodírhal as I once knew him—golden and glorious, forever young, mighty, matchless. The beautiful warrior who won the heart of his enemy so long ago. The man who ruled Aurelis for an age of prosperity.

I love him. With all the heartbreak of a son who can never

measure up to the ideals of his father, I love this man, this force of nature. I love him even as I hate him for what he is about to do. For what I am powerless to stop.

He aims a blast of pure magic straight at the Between Gate. The blast strikes with a shock, rippling out from this point in time and space, rippling out across worlds and realities. I am part of it as is every living soul of Aurelis. I feel my own essence channeled into my king, feel the pulse of my blood responding to his summoning. Lodírhal's spirit burns within his physical frame, swelling greater and greater until he dominates all sight and sense. He cannot survive this last great act. I am witnessing my father's death.

The gate crumbles under that blast. And not this gate alone. The magic stretches out farther and farther, catching every Between Gate across Eledria in its sphere. Every magicked portal leading to Vespre rocks under the influence of Lodírhal's might. I always knew he had a failsafe in place—a spell to cut Vespre adrift into the Hinter Sea. Now I watch the very fate I sought to prevent taking place before my eyes. My city. My people. My enemies and friends. All lost. All doomed.

The glare of that destructive blast heats the blood in my veins. With a growl I turn away, my gaze seeking shelter elsewhere. Clara. She stands to one side, her back pressed against a bookshelf, her mouth open. She cannot comprehend what she sees, cannot understand the implications of this moment. I wish I could leave her in her ignorance. It would be easier for her if I could.

But there's no time. And I have no choice.

I stride toward her, catch her upper arms, and turn her to me. Those large brown eyes of hers stare up into my face, horrified. The lack of recognition in her face is like a knife straight to my heart. Her lips part as though she's trying to form a question, but fear binds her tongue. I've brought such terror into her life; yet she is by far the most precious piece of my entire existence. Gods, how I love her! Even now. Even after everything that's happened between us.

I catch the back of her neck, drag her face toward mine. She doesn't fight me. She's beyond all resistance, fully succumbed to fear. But I hold her gaze with mine, willing her to feel what I feel, even if only for an instant.

"Go home, Darling," I say. "Go home and live your life. When you look upon our child, see me again. Hear some echo of my voice reminding you of the truth: I love you. I love you beyond life, beyond death. To the end of all worlds."

I press my lips to hers, pouring all the passion of my heart into that single point of connection. Her body jolts then freezes, shocked in my grasp. Then I feel her shuddering intake of breath, and her arms wrap around my neck, her fingers twine in my hair. Her mouth opens, her sweet tongue dancing across mine. And I know. I know that she remembers me. She remembers us. She remembers and she wants me. She might hate me still . . . but in this moment, she holds me tight and embraces me without barriers.

If only I might lose myself in her embrace. Instead I pull back.

She stares up at me, her eyes blazing bright, all numb unrecognition vanished. "Castien," she breathes. The sound of my name on her bruised lips is almost enough to undo me.

Wrenching free of her arms, I pivot on heel and hurtle for the crumbling gate. Reality ripples, raw, destructive magic lashes in a glaring vortex of destruction. "Castien, no!" Clara screams behind me.

Then I cast myself through that arch and into the unknown.

CLARA

7

I REMEMBER.

I remember . . . *everything.*

I collapse to my knees, waves of memory crashing over me, more than I can bear. Before me the doorway that was a gate lies in cindered ruins. And Castien? Castien, oh Castien! Where is he? Did he make it through to Vespre? Did he survive?

Other names spring to my lips, other faces crowd my mind. "Sis," I whisper. "Calx, Har, Dig." My children. My children! I left them behind, I abandoned them and returned to my own world, and I never even said goodbye. How could I do it? How could I be such a person? How could I . . . how could I . . . ?

Pain slices through my spirit. Crumpling over, my head in my hands, I shudder as great sobs break uncontrollably from my gut. What have I done? What have I become? Oh, children, children! Where are they now? What has become of them? Does Vespre even now hurtle into the Hinter, beyond all reach? If so all connection of time is severed as well. In the moments I've knelt here, a hundred years may have already passed in the Doomed City. A thousand even. My children may be dead and gone. Devoured by Noswraiths.

And Castien. *Castien.* Did the tumultuous void shred his very existence, scattering him across worlds and times? Why did I not go after him? Why did I not cast myself through the crumbling gate in his wake? Why am I such a useless, worthless coward?

They're gone. They're all gone. Gone somewhere beyond my reach. And it's my fault. Every choice I've ever made led me straight to this moment of absolute loss.

A ragged cry erupts in my ears. I drag my head up. Though my eyes are all but blinded by horror, guilt, and shame, my vision clarifies enough to see Lodírhal, the king. He lies on his back in ruin, a burned-out husk. Gasping out his last breaths. My chest tightens. I should go to him. Shouldn't I? He is Castien's father, and he's dying, alone. But I cannot move, cannot make my limbs obey me. Not even when Estrilde approaches him.

Estrilde. Of course—I recognize her now. Her glamours are momentarily withered away, but I would know the cruel lines of that face anywhere. Even as I watch her step across the marble floor, she draws magic to herself, swathing her limbs, disguising the truth. By the time she stands over Lodírhal, she is once more a golden-haired goddess, complete with coiled horns arching from her forehead. She looks down at the broken king, her lip curled in disgust. Then she plants her foot on his withered chest.

"You knew it was supposed to be me all along," she says. Her face is so twisted, not even glamour can disguise its hideousness. "I was meant to be your heir, if only you'd had the foresight to see it. Now?" She sweeps a hand, her pink sleeve fluttering delicately. "Who is there left but me?" She bows over him, pressing more weight into her foot. Bone crunches, and Lodírhal gasps. "Not to worry, Uncle." Estrilde snarls softly. "I will take up the crown of Aurelis. I will fulfill my destiny and reign as queen for a thousand turns of the cycle."

Lodírhal's lips move as though trying to form some last words. But Estrilde presses harder. There's a terrible crack. A last, horrible gasp shudders out from the king's desiccated body. Estrilde stands upright then, throwing back her head and holding wide her arms. She breathes in deeply, waiting to receive the inflow of Aurelis's magic. The power of a queen. It is her right as Lodírhal's only remaining heir. No one is left who can stop her.

But nothing happens. Estrilde's brow tightens. She is so golden and glorious and powerful, but the majesty of Aurelis does not descend upon her. She is no queen. Which means . . .

"Castien," I whisper. He's alive. He must be! And when his father died, the power of Aurelis passed to him. Will it be enough to carry him through the void now that the gate is broken? Enough to get him to Vespre? The searing pain in my heart redoubles with the sudden agony of hope.

Estrilde sucks a sharp hiss through her teeth. She turns, her eyes vicious as they fix upon me. "So," she snarls. "He's still out there somewhere in the worlds." She flicks her wrist, and another long knife appears in her hand. "But there's an easy solution."

I scramble to my feet, backing away. I'm so small, so bare, stripped down to my undergarments, helpless before her.

"If I kill his Fatebound," Estrilde continues, "he will die soon after. The sundering will be too much for him, vulnerable as he is. He will die, and the power of Aurelis must pass to me. A simple fix."

"No, Estrilde!" I protest, raising one hand. The other clamps down around my stomach, an instinct of protection I don't even realize I'm doing. And a mistake.

Estrilde's gaze drops to my hand. "Ah, yes! The little heir. Yes, that one must be dealt with as well. But it's all so easy—"

She breaks off with a cry as something hits her from behind. A book lands on the floor behind her, and she whirls, searching for the source of this missile. Thaddeus Creakle stands behind her, staring up at her through his spectacles, his face pale. "Run, Miss Darlington," he says without breaking Estrilde's gaze. "Run while you can." And he hurls another book straight into the princess's face, knocking her glamour askew.

I have a split second to decide—either I abandon Thaddeus in a bid to save my own life, or I stay, and we both die together. But if I run, perhaps Estrilde will pursue me. It's a faint hope, but in that moment it's the only hope either of us has.

Whirling on heel, I dive in among the library shelves. Estrilde utters a wolfish howl, but I hear nothing from Thaddeus. Did she kill him? Did she gut him on the spot for daring to thwart her? I cannot stop, cannot let myself wonder. I can only flee. I find the spiral stair and descend much too quickly for safety. Estrilde is on my heels, and I haven't a prayer of outpacing her. Survival instinct drives me. I skid on the polished floor of the atrium, aware of just how exposed I am, and dart in among another set of shelves. This library used to be my haven, a place to get away from Estrilde, my cruel mistress, and all her capricious whims. I found shelter here among these volumes and companionship with Thaddeus and the other librarians. Now it is a hunting ground. And I am the prey.

"Come out, little wretch," Estrilde calls, her voice echoing across the atrium dome. "Come out and face me." There's a terrible scraping sound, like she's running her blade across stone. "Are you really such a coward here in your final moments?"

I grind my teeth, my gaze darting in search of escape. Unless I'm much mistaken, Estrilde stands between me and the entrance doors. What other options do I have? This library is many stories high, the windows overlooking sweeping views of the palace gardens. I would need wings to escape. My breath pants in my fear-tightened lungs and seems to echo in my ears. I try to hold it, afraid of giving away my position.

Movement drags my gaze to one side. My heart stops. Estrilde appears at the end of the aisle. She looms seven feet tall, terrifying as a vengeful demigoddess. Madness sparks in her eyes. "I'm going to bleed you dry, Clara Darlington," she says and brandishes her blood-stained blade. "I'm going to hang your husk from the highest gate arch so that all who look upon it may know—"

Her voice is cut off as a sudden burst of brilliant light strikes her in the chest. In the gentle glow of Aurelis's eternal dawn, it's like an apocalypse of flame. Estrilde hurtles backwards, strikes the far wall, and collapses, momentarily stunned. I whirl about, a scream frozen on my lips. Someone stands at the opposite end of the aisle, in the open atrium. Shining wings spread wide from her shoulders, and in her hands, she holds a small, whirling sun. She brings her palms together, snuffing out that light, then lifts her golden eyes to mine. My mouth drops open. "Come, human," she says, her voice cold with disdain, even as she holds out a hand to me. "Come, if you want to live."

Estrilde's ragged laughter bursts behind me. "You're too late!" she cries, picking herself up from the floor and pulling her glamours back in place. "You're too late, Ilusine! Your lover is gone. What loyalty do you owe him now that you would protect his wife?"

The Princess of Solira's gaze fixes on Estrilde. "I owe Castien nothing," she says. "But I will save him nonetheless."

With a shriek, Estrilde throws herself forward, coming at me. I have no choice. I sprint to Ilusine and her outspread arms. She catches me, wraps me close and, with a pulse of her wings, shoots straight up into the air. For a moment I fear we will crash through the glass dome of the atrium. But no—there is an opening, so small, her wingspan cannot fit through it. Just at the last moment,

Ilusine gives a great pulse, tucks her wings close to her sides, and we dart out into the open sky beyond.

I close my eyes. Whirling air and the rush of wings fills my head until I'm sure I'll be sick. Gritting my teeth, I tuck my face into Ilusine's shoulders as she wheels and darts across the rooftops and between the towers of the palace. Somewhere a warning horn sounds. When I dare lift my head, I see the palace guards on their winged mounts taking to the sky, pursuing us. Though their numbers were decimated in the Noswraith attack, there are still so many of them, far more than we can outrace.

"Brace yourself, human!" Ilusine shouts in my ear.

The next moment, we're plunging straight down. I'm sure I've left my stomach somewhere midair, far behind. I dare to look forward, try to see where we are headed with such speed. One of the Between Gates appears before me, the air beneath its arch stirring. I could almost swear I see Lyklor, the old gate guardian, standing by at the dial, gazing up at me with his baleful eyes. Then my vision is entirely made up of churning realities, cracking apart. I just have enough time to wonder, *Where is she taking me?*

The Princess of Solira dives through the gate. Once more I'm plunged into the awful sensation of being skinned alive, shaken out, and reformed inside my own carcass. I scream, my voice spread across worlds and realities. Then we burst through the other side. The princess lets go of me, and I tumble, rolling across a hard surface. When I come to a stop, my vision is momentarily dazzled, bursting with sparks. I blink and blink again and . . .

The chipped face of a porcelain shepherdess looks down at me from the dusty mantel overhead.

Before I have a chance to grasp what's happened, blazing heat explodes at my back. I turn. A portal between worlds churns in the middle of my kitchen, and Ilusine stands before it, arms and wings outspread, a figure of tremendous glory in this small, humble space. Magic channels through her body, sparking from the very center of her being. The void seems to bubble, and something hurtles through, taking on form even as it emerges. A knife, long and sharp, plunges into Ilusine's shoulder.

A burst of white light erupts in my mind. Then the world goes black.

8

THE DARK OF OBLIVION CLINGS WITH GREEDY FINGERS. Part of me doesn't want to resist it. It would be nice to sink back into those black depths and stay there a while. Maybe forever. It would be nice not to face the reality waiting for me when consciousness returns. A reality of both recognition and loss, neither of which I can bear to endure.

Little by little my vision clears. I find myself staring up at the familiar wooden beams of my family home, dust-covered, trailing spider webs. Mama used to keep them polished within an inch of their lives. She would be so sad to see how everything has crumbled since her death. She would be so sad . . . so sad . . .

The truth hits me like a club.

Sis. Calx, Dig, Har.

Lir, Mixael, Khas, Andreas.

"Castien," I whisper.

Their names batter around inside my skull. So many names, so many faces. All so dear to me. And I left them. I left them behind and never looked back. I didn't mean to. I didn't mean to hurt anyone! But does that matter? Do all my good intentions count for a damn thing? Whatever I meant, whatever I felt, I abandoned them all. For Oscar.

A sob thickens my throat. Quickly I press the heels of my hands into my eyes. If only I could press out those images of my brother, standing by while I was bound to that stone slab, and Estrilde prepared to perform her evil rite. He would have let her do it. This boy whom I have loved with my whole heart, for whom I have sacrificed everything and everyone. He would have let her cut my unborn child out of my womb.

I gave up everything for him. Only for him to give me up in turn.

A low groan catches my ear. Blinking through the haze of tears, I turn to see a strange creature lying on her back in the middle of the floor. A small, haggard, undernourished thing with no color in her skin other than purple bruises dotting her limbs and neck and shoulders. Lank hair hangs in patches from a pale scalp. Even as I watch, one skeletal hand reaches up, quivering, and grips the hilt of the knife plunged deep into her shoulder.

"Ilusine!" I gasp. Rolling over, I crawl to the fae woman's side. She breathes fast, her eyes closed and sunken deep into her gaunt face. I reach for the dagger, but when my fingers touch the pommel, her withered lips roll back, revealing a flash of yellowed teeth.

"Don't touch that!"

I jerk my hand away, half-afraid she'll bite. "I've got to get it out."

"And watch me bleed to death? I think not." Her eyes open, bright slits of fury in her skull's head. "Get something to staunch the blood first."

Nodding, I rise. My limbs are unsteady, and it takes a few tottering steps before I am sure I won't topple over. Gripping the table for support, I make my way into the kitchen and search for a rag or towel. One of Mama's old aprons hangs by the window. Oscar certainly hasn't used it in years. It smells a little musty but it'll do.

I stagger back to Ilusine only to find her sitting up and grasping the dagger hilt herself. "You should lie down," I tell her. "It'll slow the blood flow."

"I will not," she answers coldly. While nothing about her looks like the magnificent fae woman I knew, her voice has not altered. "Do you think a little flesh wound can undo me?"

Before the words have even left her mouth, her whole body folds up on itself. She collapses in a heap. I rush to her side and drop to my knees beside her. Her eyes are open but glazed. I reach for the hilt. Her hand latches hold of my wrist. I startle and stare down into her unseeing gaze. "Please, let me pull it out," I urge.

"The . . . knife . . . isn't the problem." Ilusine grimaces and shuts her eyes tight, her eyelids like wrinkled tissue paper over her colorless eyes. "Breaking the gate. I drew on too much power, and . . ." Her words trail off in a slow exhale. She releases my arm, and her whole body goes slack. Is she dead? Fingers trembling, I feel for a pulse at her throat. It's there, faint but present. She's still alive then. For the moment.

I sit back on my heels, dash tears from my cheeks with the back of one hand. "Why did you do it, Ilusine?" I whisper. "Why did you save me?" I'd harbored such bitter jealousy toward this woman. I'd not wanted to admit it, but it's true. Because Ilusine was everything Castien needed and deserved in a wife: a beautiful, powerful princess with the will to fight and the intelligence to maneuver in the dangerous courts of Eledria. What do I have to offer by comparison? Hatred. Abandonment.

Another stab of searing pain shoots through my heart. I cannot let my mind continue down this path, or my body will simply shut down. That won't do Ilusine any good. And I must help her. She risked her life to save me; the least I can do is try to save her in return. I reach for the knife again, not at all certain what to do. I wad the apron in one hand, ready to stuff it into the wound, and—

The front door rattles under the force of a pounding knock. "Clara! Clara, are you in there?"

"Oh, thank gods," I breathe. Dropping my hold on the dagger, I scramble to my feet and fall over myself in my need to reach the door. I yank it open, and a blast of cold air strikes against my bare skin. Only then do I remember that I've been stripped down to nothing but my undergarments.

Danny stands before me. He stares as though coming abruptly

face-to-face with a ghost. Then his gaze drops slowly, and his eyes widen. "Clara," he begins. "Clara, what . . . ?"

I grab his arm and drag him inside. He's still dressed in his wedding clothes. That's good, I think. It means not much time passed while I was away in Eledria. There must be a gate somewhere still linking this timeline with that in Aurelis. Unless, of course, it was the gate Ilusine just destroyed. But I won't worry about that right now.

"Thank the gods you're here, Danny!" I say, slamming the door shut behind him. "You've got to help. She's taken a knife to her shoulder and—"

"Wait, Clara. What happened? Where did you go?" Danny grips my shoulders. His fingers pinch painfully. "I saw that woman."

"You saw Estrilde."

He stops. Slowly, I lift my eyes to meet his, watch the shadow fall across his face.

"You remember her," I say softly. "Don't you."

Danny swallows. Then he drops his gaze to his feet and nods.

"How long have you remembered?"

"All along." He lets go of my right shoulder and rubs a hand down his face, pulling at the skin around his mouth. "I never forgot. But it was such a relief to realize you had. To know everything you'd endured had been wiped from your mind, and we could . . . we might . . ."

"Live a lie?" I whisper.

"No!" He grips me again, squeezing harder, as though afraid I'm going to slip away from him then and there. "It wouldn't be a lie,

Clara. It would be the truth as it was always meant to be."

"So you were going to marry me. Knowing I did not remember. Knowing the version of me you married wasn't me anymore at all."

"She was the version of you I wanted all along. The woman I longed for. The woman who didn't remember . . . *him*."

At those words, I wrench my shoulders, twist my torso. To my relief, Danny lets me go, and I back into the shadowed room, resting one hand on my abdomen. "And my child?" I ask softly, though everything in me wants to scream in his face. "Did you know?"

His stricken gaze drops momentarily to my hand. The corset may have cinched my waist, but it cannot fully disguise the distinct thickening already beginning to reshape my body. "I . . . suspected," he admits. Then he drags his gaze back to mine again. "I thought if I married you, no one would know. You could live your life without that shame, without that burden around your neck."

My throat thickens. I turn away, press my knuckles hard against my teeth.

"Clara," Danny persists at my back, his voice painfully gentle. "Clara, it doesn't make a difference to me. I know how seductive the fae can be. I know what life in Eledria does to a person. I don't blame you, I don't judge you. And I swear I will do everything in my power to . . . to love the child. Like my own." But he cannot disguise the disgust underlying every word. He will never forgive my child for being half-fae. For being Castien's instead of his.

I wrap my arms around myself, shivering and exposed. Then, setting my jaw, I turn again and face him. Determined to look in his eyes when I speak my next words. "I cannot marry you, Doctor Gale."

He takes a half-step back. One would think I'd struck him. For a moment we simply stare at one another, the finality of my words heavy in the air between us. Then his lips pull back from his teeth, a dangerous expression. "Don't say that, Clara," he says, his voice rough and broken. "What else are you going to do? Move back here and live with Oscar?"

Tears spring to my eyes. I draw my shoulders back. "I cannot marry you, Doctor Gale, for I am already married."

"What?"

The single word knifes from his lips, sharp and cutting. But I refuse to back down. "I am the wife of Prince Castien Lodirith of Aurelis, bound to him by cords of fate as ordained by the gods themselves. So long as he lives, I am his and he is mine. I cannot and will not take another husband."

Danny stands rigid before me. Coldness ripples from his very soul, like he's transformed to stone on the spot. Then he lunges. I catch a breath, raising a hand to defend myself, but he grips it tight in both of his, pressing hard, drawing me toward him. "Give this up, Clara. I beg of you. The gates are broken, aren't they? That's what he promised, your Prince. There's no way back. What does it matter if you are married? He's an entire world away! What gods would doom you to such a bond? You are here, and you must survive, somehow. I can help you. I can give you more than mere survival. I can give you a place, a purpose, a home. And love. Because I love you, Clara. Now and always, just as I promised from the start. No one will ever know the difference, and—"

"I would know."

But Danny isn't about to back down. "It's not a real marriage! These fae-bindings, they're nothing but trickery and spells. It's not real, it's not *choice*."

Shaking my head I pull my hand free of his and back farther into the room. "You're wrong. I choose Castien. I choose him now and forever. I will die and be buried in a pauper's grave before I let you or anyone else make me forget him. Not again. Never again."

The desperation in Danny's face breaks into anger like a crumbling mask. "And how will you care for that child of yours? What will you do? Write your little stories? Struggle for publishers? Follow in your father's footsteps?"

Worthless.

Like a murder of crows erupting in a flurry of feathers, so too do the voices burst in my head.

Worthless.

Useless.

Guilty.

I close my eyes tight, press my fists against my temples. But in the darkness of my head, I see the Hollow Man again, looming so great, his massive chest burst open to reveal the empty darkness within.

You are nothing.

You were always nothing.

I'm coming for you.

I'm coming . . .

. . . coming . . .

"Clara?" Danny's voice cuts through the storm, sharp enough to draw me back. "Have you heard a word I've said?"

I drag a breath into my lungs, lower my hands, and face him once more. "I'll find a way," I say, loud enough to drown out the echoes of the Noswraith in my head. "I'll find a way. I'll do whatever I must."

Danny's nostrils flare. He's not giving up this fight, not yet. But his eyes rove over my face, studying me as he contemplates his next move. "Come home with me anyway, Clara," he says carefully. "You don't have to marry me. Just come home. Let us care for you through your confinement. Kitty will love the child, and I will provide for it and for you. What more could you ask?"

"Truth," I whisper bitterly. It feels wrong to say it—nothing about my life has been truthful these last many years. I've clung so hard to delusion, shaping everything, every choice, every hope, every dream around my brother, around my belief that I could protect him. That shattered fantasy now cuts me to ribbons on its razor shards. But I repeat with more firmness. "I ask for truth. And for a life lived and chosen on my own terms."

Danny's eyes are so round, so wide. He looks at me as though I've become his enemy. Perhaps I have. And perhaps that is for the best. "Please, don't do this," he says.

"I've already decided, Doctor Gale." I draw myself a little straighter, my throat constricting. "Now please, leave."

He holds my gaze, battle in his eye and stance. I'm not sure I can withstand him, not sure I have the strength to keep fighting. There's a part of me that would like to give in, a part of me that longs for the safety and familiarity of submission. But if I cannot hold on now, I never will. So I stand my ground. At last he breathes out a long sigh and, wordless, turns to the door.

Just as his hand touches the doorknob, I call after him: "Danny!" He looks back. The hope flaring in his eyes strikes me like a dart. But I step toward him, yanking the amethyst ring from my finger. I hold it out to him. Slowly, reluctantly, he extends his hand, palm up, and I drop the ring into it. "Don't come back here, Danny," I say ruthlessly. "I never want to see you again."

His expression twists with rage and agony. His dear, familiar face becomes something unfamiliar. It kills me to know this will be our last moment, that all those years of friendship have led us here, to a place where love and caring no longer matter. Everything that was good between us has grown so twisted, we cannot help but hurt one another. To try to cling to what was will only cause more harm. I know it—he knows it. But the act of letting go feels like ripping off a limb. Will either of us survive such cruel amputation?

Squeezing the ring tight in his fist, Danny turns, yanks open the door, and slams it behind him so hard, the whole house seems to shake. I stand in the wake of his departure, shuddering in every bone. I wrap my arms around myself, desperate to keep from coming apart at the seams. It's too much. After everything else I've just endured, it's too much.

A little "Oh!" bursts from my lips. I sink to the ground, press my hand over my face. I don't cry. I can't. Crying would be too great a relief, and my body cannot know relief. Not now. So I merely sit there, shuddering, as the burn of guilt, shame, fear, and helplessness courses through my veins. And always . . . *pain* . . .

9

"IT'S NEVER EASY, YOU KNOW."

I'm not sure how long I've been sitting on this cold floor, shivering but feeling no cold. Time lost meaning in the flood which so utterly overwhelms my senses. I don't want to come out again, can't bear to face reality and the pressing needs of the physical world.

But eventually that rasping voice speaks behind me, startling me where I sit. I whirl in place to look back into the room. Oh gods! I'd entirely forgotten about Ilusine. The fae princess sits in the middle of that bare chamber, having propped herself upright. Her sunken face looks at me balefully through straggling locks of colorless hair.

"It's never easy to be the one left behind when the Fatebond manifests," she says, her lips rolled back from her teeth in a grimace.

"You know all along that what you have won't last, that this person to whom you're ready to give your heart will never receive it. But you pretend awhile . . . and sometimes you forget . . ."

Even as her words trail off, she grips the hilt of the dagger in her shoulder and wrenches it out. A little gasp eeks from her lips, and she stuffs the bunched-up apron against the wound. Blue blood immediately soaks through the fabric.

"Oh!" I scramble up from the floor. Turning to the door, I take two steps and stop. I should get Danny. I know I should. I'm not at all prepared to deal with a gory wound, and Danny has experience with these things. He's even treated a fae before. But how can I bear to call him back now with those final words of mine still ringing in the cold air? How can I beg him to treat this woman, this fae, whom he must hate simply for the fact of her existence? I squeeze my hands into fists and bite back curses as a wave of nausea washes over me.

"If you're thinking about going after the mortal, don't." Ilusine's voice is but a faded echo of the strong, confident woman I first met. But the disdain is still there.

I look back at her, my brow knotted. "He's a doctor. He can . . . he *might* help."

"I don't need one of your human physicians." Her lip curls faintly. "I may have used up the bulk of my magic, but there is still power in my blood. I will heal. Though perhaps"—she looks down at her shoulder and heaves a sigh before finishing in a soft voice—"not so fast as I should like."

With a sigh, I return to the kitchen and search out some old kitchen towels and rags, anything that might serve as bandages. Leaving these in a pile before Ilusine, I climb the stairs to Oscar's room to fetch a blanket. His bedding is not fresh, and the stink of mortality will be an assault on Ilusine's delicate senses. But it's better than nothing.

I pause a moment, looking around the room. The haunting presence of Oscar permeates this space. There is his jacket hung on a peg by the wall, mended and patched so many times by my own hand. There on the little shelf are half a dozen volumes of G.H. Godswin's *Adventure Stories for Boys*, thrilling tales we used to read out loud to one another at night, whispering by the light of a single candle. There is his writing desk, covered in evidence of his unleashed creativity, a disaster of pages, pens, trimmings, and spilled ink. And there—lying in a tumble across his bed—the stack of *Starlin* magazines with his own story printed inside.

"His potential was tremendous. And his pain was profound." Castien's words echo back to me, spoken during our last, heated argument. How vehemently I'd attacked him for daring to place that curse on my brother, for blocking his ability to write, to create, to be his whole and best self. I was so firm in my conviction, in the rightness of my stance.

But Castien was right. My brother's potential for destruction was far beyond my understanding. Castien knew it all along, and he tried to warn me: *"That boy's soul is steeped in darkness. If he is ever set free, that darkness will seek to find liberty somewhere. He will put it onto paper, send it forth into the world, and let the combined magic of weaker minds bring it bursting to life."*

Why couldn't I see it? Why wouldn't I let myself see it? I willfully blinded myself, determined to perceive only the reality I desired. A reality in which my brother was an innocent boy, a pathetic victim, my darling and beloved one whom I could protect and shelter and save. I wouldn't see the man he'd become.

Now I've met the manifestation of his darkness face-to-face.

I open the glossy pages of *The Starlin* and find my brother's story once more. There's an illustration on the opening page: a rough sketch in black ink depicting the shadow-wreathed eyes, the leering mouth, the long, pointed fingers, and—worst of all—the gaping hole and broken ribs of the monster's chest. It was a mistake to try to capture it like this. Though the artist is talented, his work is but a pale shade compared to the images conjured by the mind. It was those images—not this—which brought the Hollow Man to life.

I close the magazine, let it drop back into the pile on the bed. I'd truly believed I could prevent Oscar from doing this. I'd truly believed my return was all he needed, that he would let me lead him back to health. But it was hopeless.

How long was Oscar involved with Ivor? I remember coming home to his tales of a new lover and seeing the madness of *rothiliom* whirling in his eyes. And didn't I hear my brother's voice in Ivor's apartments at Aurelis? At the time I'd dismissed it as my own suffering mind playing tricks on me, but the truth is clear. Oscar had traveled to and from Eledria more than once.

There are so many blank spaces in my knowledge, things I can only guess at. Ivor must have learned of my power and potential from Estrilde during their courtship days. Recognizing my magical gift, he sought me out for reading lessons. When I'd protested that the fae cannot learn to read, he'd told me a drop or two of human blood ran in his lineage. The genealogies of the House of Illithor later revealed he possessed significantly more than that. His own father was half-human. Which means Ivor was capable of learning far more mortal magic than he let on during our lessons.

Did he also learn about Oscar from Estrilde? Did the two of them work together to create their own gate into the mortal world so that he might come and go, visiting Oscar undetected? And now the two of them are together. Did they make it through the gate to Vespre before Lodírhal destroyed it? Are they there even now? I cannot imagine for what purpose. They could have fled anywhere in all Eledria following Ivor's reclamation from the pit. Why Vespre? Why the most dangerous place in all the worlds? What is Ivor planning?

"Damn," I whisper so softly the word makes no sound as it tumbles from my lips. I should be there. Right now. With my children, with my fellow librarians. I should be there, and I am not. Because of my own stubbornness. Because of the evil I called *love* and *understanding* and *forgiveness*.

How did I not see I've been feeding a monster all along?

By the time I return downstairs, Ilusine has already helped herself to an old mending basket and is in the process of stitching up her wound. She flinches and curses with every puncture of the needle but persists relentlessly. "You shouldn't be doing that," I say, setting aside the blanket and hastening toward her.

Ilusine flashes me a sharp look. "Do you want to try it, mortal?"

I do not. At sight of that puckered flesh and those ugly criss-crossed stitches, my stomach rebels. I'm only just in time to find a basin and heave into it, emptying whatever is left in my practically empty stomach. When I'm done, I kneel on the floor, faint and trembling. Ilusine casts me a sneer which conveys her thoughts better than words: *Pathetic human.*

I remain where I am until I'm certain my stomach has settled. Then I set to work making a small fire, for the room is like an ice shed. There is at least fuel to be had, which is a blessing; Oscar doesn't usually keep the house stocked with basic necessities. I get a blaze going and, once my hands and cheeks are warmed, turn to Ilusine again just as she bites off the end of her thread with needle-sharp teeth. "What happened?" I ask softly.

She glances up at me, one brow raised.

I moisten my lips. "When you . . . you . . ."

"When I rescued your helpless hide?"

"When you broke the gate. That is what happened, isn't it? You broke the gate between Aurelis and my home. The one Ivor has been using to travel to this world in secret. The one that kept him connected to Oscar and this timeline."

Ilusine looks as though she doesn't want to answer, as though deigning to explain to me is beneath her. In the end, however, she nods. "It takes tremendous power either to make or destroy a gate between worlds. Only those of royal lineage can manage it." She frowns then. "I don't know how Ivor created this portal between worlds. He was Lodírhal's named heir, but that should not have been sufficient."

"He is of royal blood," I answer softly. "The blood of Illithorin."

Ilusine's eyes flash, surprise and revelation mingled in her gaze. I go on to explain to her the discoveries I made in Aurelis library, the truth of Ivor's heritage. Ilusine listens intently and doesn't interrupt once, not even to scoff. "That would explain it then," she says at last when I am through. "Ivor must have used one of the established Between Gates and opened a portal to this point in time, disguising it by layering it on top of the portal already established for you as an Obligate."

"So when my Obligation ended," I answer softly, "and Castien destroyed the way between my world and his as he promised . . . Ivor's portal remained." Which means no more than seven weeks had passed in Aurelis since my departure, the same as my own world.

But then why was Castien so terribly aged? I frown, remembering the gray of his hair, the lines in his face and cheeks. He was still unbearably beautiful . . . but he was not the same man I had left behind seven weeks ago. My stomach knots with dread. The physical effects of our Fatebond are far more intense for Castien than for me, half-fae that he is. Has our separation caused this fading? Will he, like Lodírhal, simply wither away?

Ilusine rises, wincing with pain, and totters over to Mama's old rocking chair. There she eases herself down, breathes out a sigh, and closes her eyes. She looks so different without her glamours, so drained and faded. "It took every last drop of inherent magic I possessed to bring the gate down," she murmurs, more to herself than to me.

I cannot help staring at the once-glorious Princess of Solira. Though her words are still proud and her bearing regal, she looks like a ragged street urchin. The idea that she might never be restored is more terrible than I like to admit. "Why did you do it?" I ask softly. "Why did you do it? Why did you save me? I know you hate me."

"Hate you?" Ilusine blinks and sits up a little straighter in the rocking chair. "I have never in my life felt so strong a feeling for any human. No, little pet, I certainly don't *hate* you. But I do . . . I do love . . ."

Though she cannot say it, I hear the words loud and clear: *I do love him.* I can't blame her for choking on them. She and Castien share history together, the nature of which I don't know entirely. All I know for sure is they had much more time together than Castien and I had a chance to experience.

A knot of jealousy tightens in my gut. It's worse than nausea. I scramble to my feet, leaving the warmth of the fire and stalking to the kitchen table. There to my surprise I discover Oscar's contract from *The Starlin* pinned under a candlestick and a brass snail paperweight. Beside it lies a little box which, upon inspection, contains a gold fountain pen. The editors at *Starlin* really were eager to make my brother their new star. Little did they know what their publication of his work would bring to pass in worlds beyond.

A sob thickens my throat. I turn and, gripping the table's edge with both hands, face Ilusine again. "Do you think Castien is still alive?"

"Yes," she replies at once.

"How can you know?"

"Because Estrilde could not take Lodírhal's power when he died. That power went to his heir. His living heir."

"Will Estrilde be able to take the throne of Aurelis without that power?"

A grim smile twists Ilusine's thin lips. "It won't be an easy task. But I wouldn't put it past her. Unless the heir returns, who in Aurelis would stand against her? For many turns of the cycle now, she's been maneuvering, drawing others into her confidence and clutches. A well-placed gift here, a well-timed bribe there, and she has the support of half the court. The other half fears her and the influence she wields. It wouldn't take much to tip the balance in her favor. But," she adds, pushing to her feet as the rocking chair tips wildly behind her. For a moment I fear she'll tumble to the floor in a heap of bony limbs. Somehow she manages to draw herself upright, assuming a regal stance, despite her wounded shoulder. "But that won't be a problem," she finishes.

"Why not?"

"Because you're going to fetch him back."

"What? How?" I wave a hand, indicating the empty space in the room where, not long ago, a tumultuous opening into the void between worlds had churned. "The gate is broken. *Both* gates. Even if I could find a way back into Eledria, it could land me absolutely anywhere, in any time. How am I to find him?"

"Yes. And all the gates to Vespre were broken by Lodírhal," Ilusine muses, lifting her gaze to the rafters in consideration. "You'll need powerful magic indeed to get you anywhere near where you want to go."

"Can you work magic like that?"

Ilusine snorts and looks down at her small, shrunken, wounded self. "Do I look as though I have the power to rip open portals through realities?"

"No, of course not. But if we were to heal you—"

"Impossible. Not in this world."

"Will you ever recover?"

"Before your mortal air does me in? Unlikely. Judging by the bare traces of magic in this atmosphere, it would take a thousand years to bring me back to what I once was. Something tells me this body won't last more than a hundred, maybe less."

She speaks the words calmly, but there is a slight quaver to her tone. How horrible must it be to find herself suddenly rendered mortal. Did she know this would be her fate when she carried me through that portal? Did she know she would end up far from everyone she knows and loves, trapped in a broken body? She sacrificed everything for Castien's sake.

A sudden upswelling of feeling burns inside me. Not jealousy, not hatred, but love—love for this woman who should be my rival. How can I not love someone who loves my beloved so unselfishly?

Ilusine makes a face. "Don't look at me like that. It's grossly unsettling." She tosses her lank hair over her shoulder. "I'll find my way back to Eledria. It might not be a time I know, and everyone I love may be either dead or not yet living. But I won't end my days in this world, of that you may be certain." She tips her head back then, her withered face set in hard lines. "But first we've got to get you back. And in the right time, or as near to it as we can manage. Otherwise all this trouble will have been for nothing." She tries to take a step, totters, and braces herself, one arm outstretched to grip the mantel over the fireplace, very nearly knocking the porcelain shepherdess from her place. There she stands, breathing heavily, and I don't dare reach out to her. At long last she sighs. "There's really only one thing to be done so far as I can see."

"And what is that?" I ask.

"We'll have to go to the Daughters of Bhorriel."

10

ILUSINE IS LESS THAN PLEASED TO LEARN THAT I'D ALREADY been to see the Daughters of Bhorriel once before. She listens with growing disgust as I relate the bargain I made to receive a way down to Ulakrana, the merkingdom at the bottom of the ocean.

"Three days of pain," I finish softly, staring down at my bare feet on the cold floor. "That was the agreement."

Ilusine mutters a Soliran expletive. "And these three days were supposed to begin in three days' time?"

I nod. "But—"

"But nothing. The crones would not take pain from days you couldn't remember. They must have forestalled their taking until your awareness returned. When was that exactly?"

"Does it matter?"

"Answer the question."

I look out the dirty window, trying to guess the hour. Mid-afternoon sunlight stains the murky glass. Was it really so little time ago that I was walking to the chapel of Nornala, intending to get married? I drag in a shuddering breath. "Two days. One and a half, rather."

Ilusine considers this. Then she smiles a bitter, cruel sort of smile. "No doubt the crones are feasting greedily."

I drop my head, unable to bear the look in her eye. Because she's right; the pain of these last few days has been intense. The dawning awareness that something was missing, the realization that my brother was not who I believed him to be . . . and now this. The knowledge of who I am and what I have done. The agony of knowing that Castien—that the children—that Lir and the librarians and all the people of Vespre are out there, cut adrift into the Hinter. Suffering, possibly dying. And it's all my fault.

I betrayed them. I can no longer hide from the fact. The truth of who I am is laid bare before me. My willfulness. My stupidity. My arrogance. It is truly torturous. Burning poison seems to roil in my veins, in my heart. I feel as though I shall erupt at any moment. Didn't Dad once write a story about spontaneous combustion? About a suffering soul who refused to acknowledge his own evil until it finally—and quite literally—burned him up from the inside. A gruesome tale, a particular favorite among *The Starlin's* devoted readers. I understand it now so much better than I did as a child.

You're not seeing right . . .

I grind the knuckles of one hand against my forehead. "Stop it!" I growl. Gods spare me, the last thing I need is for Emma's voice to pop back into my head again. "Stop it, stop it!"

Ilusine watches me. Flushing, I pull myself together only to realize there are tears streaming down my face. Hastily I dash them away. "There . . . there may be some truth to what you're saying," I admit.

The princess narrows her eyes. "What was *that?*"

It takes me a moment to realize what she means. Then: "You heard her?"

"I saw something. Just for an instant. Like a shadow hunched over your back, its long fingers plunged into your shoulders." Her gray skin pales to a deathly hue. "It was unpleasant."

I briefly consider admitting to Ilusine that I am, in fact, being haunted by my own Noswraith. Just now that might not be the most helpful information to share. "Forget it," I say instead, my voice low.

Ilusine narrows her eyes. Then she shrugs. "Mortal magic," she says and hisses through her teeth. "I sometimes forget just how powerful it can be." With a shake of her head, she drops her shoulders and assumes her incongruously dignified expression once more. "Very well, mortal. We must bide our time. A day and a half remains to the suffering you owe the Daughters of Bhorriel. We must wait it out."

"Wait it out?" I echo desperately. "But every passing hour carries Castien years away. A day and a half might easily pull our timelines irrevocably apart!"

"There's no use in fussing. It will either make all the difference or none at all. We must wait, and tomorrow, just before midnight, we will set out."

"Set out for where?"

"Surely you must know of somewhere in this city where the line between Eledria and this world is blurred. Somewhere that feels a little more fae than it ought? You've dwelt in our world for some time by your mortal count of years. Your senses must have quickened."

I bite my lip, my mind spinning. Then I suck in a breath, and my eyes flick to meet Ilusine's. "I think I know the very place."

And now, after a long, brutal, restless, and—let's be honest—*hungry* night, I face the enormity of the following day.

I sit on the bed in my old bedroom and let my gaze rove about the space, taking in all the familiar details. The clusters of knots in the wood paneling that Oscar and I called constellations, drawing lines in ink between them to complete each picture. The old, dilapidated wardrobe that once belonged to my grandmother, and would have been sold long ago were the mirror not smashed and the bottom drawer broken beyond repair. Even opening it to fetch a musty old gown from inside was taking my life into my hands; I half-expected the whole thing to fall on top of me.

This dress is another memory—far too small now, particularly around my swollen middle. But I remember when Mama bought it for me, the first cast-off I'd ever had to wear following Dad's fall from grace. Mama had embroidered little flowers at the cuffs and collar, determined to make the sad, serviceable garment nicer for her fourteen-year-old daughter.

I run my finger along the bumps and knots rendered in faded silk. Mama tried so hard. She wanted life to be better for me and for Oscar. How desperate she must have felt at times—helpless to save the man she loved from himself or to save her children from him. It was easier to invent a fantasy. One in which she was the devoted wife, the rescuing heroine, the only one who truly understood him. The only one he truly loved. In this story she could break the curse . . . and break it again and again and again if necessary. Even if it meant sacrificing her own children on the altar of her chosen idol.

"You will suffer such pain. *Pain beyond imagining. One for each drop of blood."*

The aged voice whispers in my memory, accompanied by a sudden throb in my thumb, index, and middle finger. I grimace. Three days of pain in exchange for the help I needed had seemed a worthy bargain at the time. What is a little pain after all? But this . . . I'd not imagined this. It's like my eyes have been ripped open and forced to stare directly into the sun. Radiation heat fills my head, boils my blood, hollows me out.

I once saw myself as the hero, self-sacrificing and strong, willing to do anything to protect those I love. I couldn't see the truth: the selfishness, the small-mindedness. The fear. I'm just like Mama. I invented a fairy tale in which I could save Oscar. In which he needed me, and I could be enough. Then I sacrificed everything, including my children, my friends, my husband. I gave them up for the sake of a story. For the sake of a lie.

You're not seeing rightly.

I shudder as those familiar phantom hands weigh down my shoulders. But for once, Emma cannot convince me. It would be a relief to sink back into the comfort my Noswraith offers, the obscurity and blindness. If I could, I would pluck out my own eyes and sew them up tight. Better that than to see the truth: I've failed them. And there's no way to atone for it. I know that with the horrible, stomach-sinking certainty of the condemned.

But it doesn't matter. I might not be able to earn redemption. But I can try to do the right thing. Then the next right thing after that. One after another. I will bargain with the crones. I will pay the price. I will return to Eledria, find my children. Find Castien. And whatever it takes to save them, that is what I will give.

But it won't be enough.

A new voice whispers in my other ear. Not Emma's soft croon. This voice is deeper, darker, and multiplied into a hundred fractured parts.

Worthless.

Pathetic.

Guilty.

Useless.

Just like your mother.

The accusations burn in my body, in my mind, corroding all places of safety to which I might crawl. They hurt because they're true. They're true, and I cannot hide from them anymore. I am what the Hollow Man names me. Lying back on the bed, I curl into a ball, wrap my arms around my middle. I can do nothing but hold on, hold on, hold on. Just a little longer.

Just until midnight.

11

THOUGH IT SOMETIMES SEEMED TO ME THAT THIS DAY would never end, night draws in at last. When the distant chapel bells toll ten deep strokes, I emerge from my room and slip across the little passage to Oscar's chamber. I've already donned an old dress. Now I claim one of Oscar's ragged coats and a leather satchel. Then I turn to his desk. Though it feels wrong to invade my brother's privacy, I go through his books and papers, searching for empty volumes I might use. I cannot journey back to Vespre unarmed. I need books, quills, ink, all the weapons of a mortal mage.

Most of his books are stuffed with manic writing. I open them, one after another, searching for blank pages, not bothering to read the tales of horror within. But one book—a little onion skin notebook—catches my eye. I don't know what it is, for my brother's scrawled hand is almost impossible to discern, but I find myself pouring over the page, my brow furrowing as meaning slowly emerges from the scribbled mess.

Once upon a time, there was a sister and her little brother, and he was very brave. As long as they could be together, they were both very brave, no matter what happened.

My heart stops. I know this story. It isn't Oscar's . . . it's mine. The beginning of a fairy tale I used to tell him when we were small.

One day—it continues—*their mother said to them, "You must venture into the Dark Forest, my children. For your father is sick, and it is up to you to find his cure. But you must be brave, strong, and always loyal to one another, or you cannot hope to survive the journey."*

From there I would vary the tale, inventing new and thrilling adventures for the brother and sister to face on their quest to save their father. It was a story without an end but the same opening and innumerable middles. I never bothered to write it down; that was not the purpose of such a tale.

But my brother's version of the tale unfolds, made up of all the different bits and pieces of the tales I told. Some of it he invented himself. Those passages are dark and twisted, though a childlike sweetness prevails, and the story never plunges into true horror. I keep turning pages, one after the other until I reach the last paragraph.

And so they returned home triumphant, the cure for their father's ailment in hand, only to find the house boarded up and empty. When they asked the neighbors what had become of their parents, they were told, "Your father perished, and your mother fled. She has never been heard from again. You are alone in the world, little orphans. Alone with no one to care for you."

That last line is so badly scrawled, I can scarcely read it. Blurred spots, the size of teardrops, reveal my brother's state of mind as he wrote. A fat tear of my own rolls down my nose and falls on the page, marring the final word. Hastily I close the book and wipe my face with the back of my hand. But I cannot unsee those words. They're burned into my brain.

Alone.

No one to care for you.

Oh, Oscar! Oscar, why would you write such a thing? Why would you take my story and turn it into this? Why couldn't you hold onto hope just a little longer?

But he couldn't. He didn't.

I stare at that book for some moments. Then, impulsively, I stash it into my satchel. A further hasty search, and I finally discover a single empty volume. It isn't much, but it's better than nothing. I add it to my satchel along with several quills, penknives, and a few stoppered bottles of ink. I rue the lack of my own magicked quill, which allowed me to write without having to pause and dip in fresh ink every few moments. But this is the best I can do and better than nothing.

When I finally emerge from the stairwell and step into the living room, I find Ilusine in Mama's rocking chair, gently rocking back and forth. The sight of her is still unsettling, emaciated and colorless as she is. She seems like another creature entirely: not a fae, but some sad changeling gremlin sent to take the princess's place. But the look she turns my way—a perfect mingling of disdain and elegance—could only belong to Ilusine. "You've not eaten, human," she states. It sounds like an accusation.

I place a hand against my stomach. It's true. I've not had a bite, and I'm utterly ravenous! But also nauseated. I can't imagine forcing myself to swallow anything. "I'm all right," I lie.

"Nonsense." To my surprise, she tosses me a still-warm cottage bun. I catch it, blinking in surprise. How did she come by such a treat? She must have ventured out into the streets and . . . "I didn't steal it, if that's what you're thinking," Ilusine says coldly. "I sniffed out a vendor who had a whiff of Eledria about him. Such people are easily recognized if one knows what one is looking for. He was happy to exchange for a strand of my hair." She crumbles the remains of another bun between her fingers. "Under other circumstances I would have killed any man who dared suggest such a thing. But the air of this world has made me soft, and this body needs so much . . . tending. It is singularly obnoxious."

I don't bother to respond. Now that the smell of warm bread is in my nostrils, I cannot resist taking a bite. That mouthful settles in the hollow of my gut, and my body doesn't seem immediately disposed to bring it back up again. I can only hope the little life inside me will benefit.

I've not yet swallowed the last bite before Ilusine asks, "How far is it to this Den of Vipers you spoke of?"

A chill creeps down my neck. I've only been to the Old Docklands warehouse district twice in my life. The first time was a horror I hoped never to repeat; the second time was with the Prince. With Castien. He offered me the protection of his presence, and though I'd not wanted it at the time—and behaved with terrible ingratitude—it had made the experience significantly better. The idea of facing it again . . . alone . . .

"It will take some time," I force myself to answer. "It's a long walk from here, and the streets are not altogether safe at this time of night."

"Walk?" Ilusine's mouth drops open. "You're telling me you intend to go *on foot?*"

I spread my arms. "Humans are not gifted with wings we can summon on command."

"Surely you can call for a litter, a carriage, a steed?"

"I have no money to pay for such things."

Ilusine's eyes travel over my ragged person. She sniffs, as though I've just uttered the understatement of the century. "What about your magic? Your little . . ." She gestures vaguely in the air.

"You mean my writing?"

"Yes. That. Surely you can exchange a spell for transportation."

"My magic doesn't work like that."

Ilusine rolls her eyes but rises from the rocking chair, brushing crumbs from her skirt. "Very well. If we must walk, then we must walk. Shall we get started?"

"Wait." I blink fast. "You're coming with me?"

The fae woman gives me another of those elegantly impatient looks. "Now I've put this much effort into keeping you alive, I'm not about to send you to the crones unattended."

"I'm not sure there's much you can do to protect me from the crones."

"No." She lifts her chin. "But I might frighten off any unsavory souls who might try to impede you on your way."

While I could point out that Ilusine, emaciated, bandaged, and brittle, is hardly the protective force she imagines, I'm too grateful at the prospect of company. So I merely nod.

"Shall we then?" Ilusine asks.

I take a step toward the door, then hesitate. Pulling my lower lip between my teeth, I glance at the table where my brother's contract lies. Before I can talk myself out of it, I stride swiftly to it and catch up the gold fountain pen from its box.

"All right," I say, turning once more to Ilusine, who observes me through heavy-lidded eyes. "Let's be off."

The city is very dark this time of night. Even the gas lamps have burned down low and struggle to pierce the gloom and fog. Ilusine curses softly as we make our way from Clamor Street, picking our way through the shadows.

"Are you all right?" I whisper.

"A strange blindness seems to have come over me."

"Blindness?"

"Yes. Everything is so obscure. So indistinct."

For a moment I don't understand. Then, biting back a little chuckle, I reply, "That's simply how it is in the dark."

"Not for fae it's not."

The superiority of her tone sets my teeth on edge, but I hold onto her elbow, supporting her as we progress. The whole circumstance would be comical were it not so terrifying: me, pregnant, trying not to throw up that bun she made me eat; her, fragile as a newborn fawn, bandaged and tottering and weak. What a picture we must make! Hardly the adventurers suited for such a quest.

"Tell me about this Den of Vipers," she asks after a long silence.

"I don't know much," I admit. "It's a gathering place for disreputable souls, where the desperate may explore their most private, most hidden vices."

Ilusine nods. "Every city has its festering underbelly. But what made you think this one brushes up against Eledria?"

I describe to her what I saw the last time I went to fetch Oscar from the Den of Vipers: the half-crazed men and women, their eyes bright green with *rothiliom* light, dancing in strange patterns and rhythms; the images of trees and flashing sunlight piercing through the reality of the close, smoke-filled space. The mania. The madness. The music.

"Yes," Ilusine admits at last, grudgingly. "That does sound like a fae gathering to me. Like the old Dancing Rings where my kind once lured yours in and made pets of them back in the ages before the Pledge. But what," she adds, stumbling a little and tightening her grip on my arm, "makes you think one of the Blessed Beldames might be close by?"

An image flashes through my mind—a long dark hallway, a simple door. A globe lantern suspended in the darkness overhead. When I first saw it, an almost overwhelming curiosity had filled me. I would have forgotten Oscar entirely and marched straight through had Castien not been on hand to restrain me. Even now just thinking about it, a strange prickling comes over my skin, an inexplicable urge to know what lies on the other side of that door. "Just a feeling," I say quietly.

Ilusine snorts. "You humans and your *feelings*."

With that we both lapse into silence as we make our way through the city streets. Few people are out at this hour. Those who are make a point to avert their gazes. We are a disreputable looking pair, hobbling along together in our ratty garments, heads down against the cold gusts of wind that blow debris off the cobblestones and into our faces. The trek is longer than I remembered. I hear distant bells tolling midnight long before we reach the warehouse district.

We stop at the top of the street underneath a streetlamp,

taking shelter in its wavery light. The way before us is much darker than the way we've come. Rather than streetlamps, torches set in rickety sockets burn here and there, giving the whole street a sinister appearance. Ilusine sniffs the air and curses again. "The atmosphere of this world obscures my senses," she says, "but I'm almost certain I can detect a whiff of Eledria."

I nod. We've come this far; what choice do we have but to continue? Firming my grip on her arm, I lead the way forward into the dark street.

We've taken no more than two steps when three shadowy figures emerge from the darkness before us. I stop short, jerking Ilusine to a halt. Heart thudding, I begin to back up, determined to regain the light of the street lamp. Two more figures block our retreat. My gaze darts, trying to take in all of them at once. The shadows cast by their brimmed hats obscure their faces, but I catch flashes of green eyes reflecting in the lamplight. Gods spare me, they aren't human.

"Stand aside," Ilusine declares and draws herself up straight. The effect is pathetic. Those strange, reflective eyes exchange glances. Behind us, someone sniggers. "You will let me and my companion pass," Ilusine persists, cold and regal.

"And what if we don't?" the foremost of the strangers asks. I glimpse a flash of yellow teeth. "You can put on all the airs you like, but we's masters of this way. You gots to pay the tithe."

"We shall do no such thing, you little vermin," Ilusine snarls, even as I demand, "What tithe, gentlemen?" I hate myself a little bit for saying it. If only I could be more like Ilusine, brimming with command and condescension. But life has taught me to accommodate and pacify when necessary. I learned that lesson early on in childhood and kept on learning it until it was positively ground into my soul. The skill has served me well in the past.

The foremost of the figures turns from Ilusine to me. I can't read any expression in those gleaming disk eyes, but I feel his gaze sliding up and down my body. "From you?" he says. "Nothing much. Just a kiss. One for each of us."

My blood chills. "That is all?"

"For the present, poppet."

Ilusine's nails dig into my arm. "Don't even think about it," she snarls.

I can't bear the idea of kissing any of these men, these creatures. But they have us surrounded. And the fae are bound by bargains once struck, aren't they? Perhaps I can work this to our advantage. "Do I have your word that, with a single kiss for each of you, I and my companion shall pass freely on our way?"

Another flash of teeth that look a little too sharp. "Oh yes, pretty promises, sweet lady."

"Don't trust them," Ilusine says. "Fae who have lived too long in the human world pick up a knack for lying as their blood thins."

"Aw, sweetheart! You're hurtin' our feelings!" another man says, his smile growing so wide, it no longer fits naturally on his face.

My heart thuds harder, fear jolting through my limbs. "Please," I say, my voice quavering. "We don't want any trouble."

"Neither do we," another one says in a slithering, sinuous tone. "We just want that kiss, luv. One wee little kiss."

He lunges. My limbs freeze, but Ilusine moves faster than I would have believed possible considering her frail condition. She dives between me and my attacker and drives one bony elbow first into his face then into his gut. A second man leaps at her, and she whirls like a cat, scratching, screeching. I'm fairly certain she bites the third man in the neck. He howls and pushes her off, and Ilusine spits out a curse before shouting, *"Run!"*

Raw instinct takes over. I pivot on heel, unaware of direction so long as it's away. I take three steps. Long fingers catch me by the hair atop my head. I scream as I'm yanked backwards. That slithering voice hisses in my ear: "Not so fast, little miss. Not without that kiss." My eyes roll, the glare of the streetlamp nearly blinding me.

A tall shape appears suddenly and blocks out that light. I stare up at a looming, featureless figure. My heart stops, overcome with doom and dread. The next moment, a brilliant beam of light bursts in my eyes. I turn my face to one side, squeezing my eyelids tight. The figure at my back utters a howl of agony, and the fingers twined in my hair release. I stagger, fall to my knees. Lifting my head again, I look up at the stranger. He turns in place, shooting that beam of light around at all the writhing, strange forms. I catch glimpses of faces far too pale, eyes far too large, leering mouths full of too many teeth. They scream, throw up their hands, and scatter like rats. Then the lantern-bearer kneels before me, and suddenly, I'm aware of a familiar waistcoat directly in front of my eyes. I've seen it many times, that rich wine red with gray pinstripes.

"Clara, are you hurt?"

"Danny!" I yank my head up. Lanternlight casts his face in strange shadows. But he's Danny. Unmistakably Danny. I've never been happier to see him in my life. I have to stop myself from throwing my arms around his neck. "What are you doing here?" I gasp instead.

His face is stricken. He looks as though he's lived and suffered the agonies of death since last we met, since I told him I never wanted to see him again. Oh gods! How could I have said such a thing? How could I have been so cruel? "I never left Clamor Street," he admits. "I knew you would try something rash like this, damn it. I also knew you couldn't manage it on your own. Not in your . . . condition."

I press a hand against my abdomen. When I try to speak, no words will form. Not with Danny looking at me like this, tipping his head forward so that his blue eyes seem very bright in the glow of his lantern.

"Are you really so determined to do this?" he asks. "To return to Eledria?"

"Yes," I whisper. "I must find my husband."

Pain stabs across his face. But when he draws back and gets to his feet, he holds out a hand to me. I take it, letting him pull me up from the cobblestones. "I might be able to help you," he says.

"She doesn't need any of your human interference."

Danny turns sharply. He spies Ilusine and sucks in a breath. Spatters of blue fae blood stain her mouth, and her eyes gleam strangely as she peers out through a veil of ragged hair. "Who are you?" Danny demands, holding up his lantern once more.

She snorts. "I'm not some Noxaurian who can be chased off by a little glimmer."

I grab Danny's arm. "She is Princess Ilusine of Solira, and . . . and she's a . . ." I can't quite make myself speak the word *friend*. I don't think Ilusine would appreciate it. "She's helping me."

"Princess?" Danny's lip curls as he takes in her distinctly un-princess-like appearance. "I've had some experience with fae princesses. None I should like to repeat."

"I could say much the same about humans," Ilusine replies and spits blood from between her teeth. "But that's hardly the point. What makes you think you can help find a way back to Eledria? Do you know something she doesn't?"

Realization quickens my pulse. Of course! Danny did make his way through to Eledria once before. I never found out how, but he journeyed to Aurelis and then all the way to Vespre library. I should have thought of this before. "Do you know of a gate?" I ask, breathless with hope.

He shifts his uneasy gaze from Ilusine back to me. "I . . . I made a bargain," he says. "There was this old woman, you see. A very strange old woman."

"Do you remember any particulars about her?"

He shudders visibly. "I can't recall her face, only that something about it was unsettling. What I do remember is that she seemed to live in my grandmother's house. Which isn't possible, of course.

Granny never lived in the warehouse district; she kept a cottage in the country. It was demolished for a railway line long ago."

Ilusine and I exchange looks. When I visited one of the crones, the interior of her strange, stilted house had been an exact replica of the Gale family's front parlor. "That sounds about right," I say.

"And you bargained with this crone to get into Eledria?" Ilusine presses. "What sort of bargain were you foolish enough to make?"

Danny casts Ilusine a sideways glance before focusing on me once more. "I bargained to give up my dearest dream in exchange for your safe return home." He closes his eyes briefly. When he looks at me again, tears brim in his lashes. "My dream was always that you and I would wed and be happy, so I knew . . . I *knew*, damn it, that it could no longer come true. Even when I stood at the altar yesterday morning, I knew the price would have to be paid. Part of me hoped otherwise, hoped we'd managed to bypass the bargain entirely. But that only made the dream sweeter, dearer . . . and then to have it taken away . . ."

Ilusine sniffs and crosses her bony arms. "Sounds like crone magic to me."

My stomach twists, sickened by the hurt Danny has endured, sickened at the pain I myself have caused him. But it's also true that he made those choices. He made that bargain. Those decisions, however well intended, were born of his own brokenness. I could not prevent him. Gods, I tried! I had overtly told him not to attempt to rescue me, told him I could not and would not marry him. He chose not to listen.

Just as I had not listened when the Prince warned me about Oscar.

I gaze into Danny's pain-stricken eyes. How much hurt we have caused each other simply by refusing to let go! By holding on to what we thought was love. That love was real at one time; but the poison of circumstance has turned it into a toxic thing.

"Do you remember the way, Danny?" I ask softly.

He nods. "The price will be terrible," he says, his voice raw. "More than you should pay."

"Perhaps," I reply. "But I abandoned my children. Vespre. Castien. I must go to them now and make what amends I can, whatever the cost."

Danny looks deeply into my eyes. I see in his face a glimmer of something that might be resignation and might be relief. But he says only: "I'll take you then."

12

A TALL, SPARE CREATURE IN A RAGGED, LACE-TRIMMED blouse stands at the door of the old warehouse. Catlike yellow eyes with narrow pupils watch the three of us approach through the gloom. We come to a stop before it, and though Danny and Ilusine stand on either side of me, those eyes fix on me alone.

"Password," it demands in a deep, stomach-churning tone.

Ilusine and I both turn to Danny first. He blinks back. "The password I had was from weeks ago." He looks over my head at Ilusine, expectantly.

She stares him down. "Don't look at me. I don't know it."

"But it's fae," Danny says.

"And am I the same as this"—she waves a vague hand at the tall door guard—"in your view?"

Danny lets his gaze run up and down Ilusine's bony frame. He doesn't say a word, but her eyes flash, and I swear the two of them will come to blows if I don't do something right this moment. I take a quick step forward, lick my dry lips, and say, *"Felaadar."*

Immediately the tall guardian steps to one side and pushes the door open with one hand, indicating with the other that we should pass through. Danny and Ilusine stop spatting behind me, both shocked into silence. Then Ilusine grabs my wrist. "What did you say to it?"

I repeat the word, which I once heard Castien say when we came this way together. Ilusine hastily clamps a hand down over my mouth. "That is a word of great power, not one any but the royalty of Eledria might speak. Did Castien give it to you? Of course," she interrupts herself before I can answer. "Of course you are his Fatebound. I suppose that gives you certain rights."

I don't bother explaining to her that Castien never officially gave me the word, that I merely picked it up. Nor do I mention that I've used it before. I suppose there have been indications all along that I and Castien were bound by more than mere Obligation, if only I'd had eyes to see it.

We pass through the doorway and enter a dark passage. A wall of peeling paint stands directly before us. Laughter and song come from our right, beyond a shabby curtain, but I turn left. There a globe lantern burns like a small moon, illuminating a bare board floor, listing walls, and an open doorway into darkness. Everything around that doorway is strangely and subtly warped. I almost can't detect it, but my soul feels the wrongness of that space. Something about it draws me. I approach, both hesitant and intrigued, until I stand on the edge, staring across the threshold into absolute black.

"Is this the way you came, Danny?" I ask, my voice a mere breath.

Danny grunts an acknowledgement but otherwise does not speak. Ilusine heaves a sigh. "Go on!" she urges. "We've come this far; no use in second thoughts now."

These aren't second thoughts. More like tenth or twelfth if I'm honest. After the pain I've endured these last three days, I'm not sure I can bear to make another bargain with the crones.

Danny inclines his head to my ear. "You don't have to do this," he whispers.

His dream still clings to him. The agony of that dream being dragged from his heart is so intense, a powerful, horrible magic. I wish I could stop it, wish I could offer him comfort and relief. But Danny is not my responsibility.

I close my eyes and feel the pressure of Castien's final kiss pressed against my lips, hear again the last words he ever spoke to me: *"I love you beyond life, beyond death. To the end of all worlds."*

I will find him. I will save him. I will save them all.

Drawing a deep breath, I step through the doorway . . . and into my home. Not the rackety house on Clamor Street. This isn't the hovel where we all landed after Dad ruined our family with his excesses. This was our *home*, the beautiful townhouse on Chilworth Drive where we lived at the height of Edgar Darlington's popularity, when money was as plentiful as friends and social opportunities. When all was—on the surface at least—right with the world.

I turn my head slowly, taking in the familiar space. There is the marble fireplace with its frieze of dancing satyrs. Oscar and I used to sit together on that hearth, scribbling away at our own stories or reading juicy passages from the latest G.H. Godswin novel out loud to each other. Later on we would set up games of checkers with Danny and Kitty Gale, listening to the autumn rain pound against the glass outside while we enjoyed our snug security.

It was here, in this very room—while Kitty and Oscar were distracted fetching biscuits from the kitchen—that Danny had leaned forward and whispered "I love you" in my ear. He told me he'd marry me when we were grown up if I would wait for him to finish medical school. Gods on high, how intense my feelings were for that boy back in those days! The kind of intensity which can only blossom in an adolescent heart, still so new to such feelings and sensations. I remember the exquisite thrill of his hand resting on the floor beside mine, of his pinky finger stretching out to just brush the edge of my palm. It had seemed in that moment as though my whole world was on fire.

It all comes back to me in a rush, stopping me dead in my tracks. Then Ilusine runs into me from behind. "Make way, human!" she snarls. I hastily step to one side while Ilusine looks around the pristine space. She sniffs. "I would not have expected beings as powerful as the Daughters of Bhorriel to live so crudely."

Before I can reply, Danny emerges. He takes one look around and inhales sharply. Is he too overwhelmed by the flood of memories? I can't bear to look at him, can't bear to meet his eyes. Not here.

The double doors on the lefthand wall open. Those doors once led to the music room, where Mama obliged me to practice piano every day. I vividly recall slogging my way through a series of resentful chords while Oscar wrestled with the family dog underneath and made fun of each sour note I struck. There's no glimpse to be had of the music room through that opening now, only more of the profound blankness through which I've come.

A hunchbacked little woman appears, all wizened and shrunken as she totters into view. She looks exactly like the crone I met before . . . but this time, she wears one of Mama's gowns, her best violet silk with the bustle and the line of gold buttons down the front bodice. It even boasts the exquisite lacework collar she used to pin on for special occasions. The sight is a jolt to my senses. I want to scream, to dart forward and rip that lace collar off the hideous crone's throat. But I stand firm. She's trying to bait me; I'm sure of it. I won't be so easily manipulated.

Gritting my teeth, I watch her carry a silver tray with mugs of some steaming hot drink. It smells sweet, but not like any sweet I recognize. She sets the tray down on the cherry-wood coffee table and finally looks up. One eye blinks up at us through the rising steam from the mugs; the other empty eye socket sags in a bed of wrinkles.

"Ah!" she cries in a sweet voice. "Three of you! But wait a minute, wait a minute. They'll all want a good look at you." She turns to the mantel where Mama's old stationary box sits. She rummages inside, her bristled fingers searching. Then with another satisfied, "Ah!" she bends over, seems to struggle a moment. An unpleasant *squish* almost makes me turn and vomit into the potted plant by the sofa.

When the old woman faces us again, a many-faceted crystal juts from that eye-socket. She flutters her bristled eyelashes, blinking as her focus clears. "Yes, yes!" she says. "I've seen the two of you before. But you?" She narrows her gaze at Ilusine, the crystal sparkling. "I don't know you, do I?"

"Certainly not," Ilusine answers with offended dignity. "I'm not so foolish as to make bargains with the Blessed Beldames."

The crone *tsks*, shaking her head so that the lace ties of her cap waft about her jowls. "Well, lah-dee-dah. A fine princess, are we? Though not so fine as we once were, I dare say. And nursing a broken heart what's more. Now that is a juicy thing. We might make something of it, if you're willing."

Ilusine's nostrils flare, but the crone turns from her to Danny. "And you! Welcome back, dear boy. You must be pleased to see your bargain so nicely fulfilled. And that dream of yours? *Mwha!*" She kisses the tips of her fingers before licking her lips lasciviously. "Such a fine morsel."

At last she turns to me. I want to hide from that crystal, from the observation of I-don't-know-how-many sisters, gazing at me through those stone facets. Can they sense my fear, my shame? I lift my chin, determined to meet her horrible gaze without blanching.

"And you," the crone purrs. "That pain of yours—three days of it, wracking your soul. We did not care for the delay, but when it came . . . yes, indeed. So sweet. So succulent. My sisters and I will enjoy the benefits for months to come."

She turns then and waddles to the rocking chair. Mama's rocking chair, the very one which remains at Clamor Street, only here it has plump velvet cushions attached to its spindly bars. The crone takes a seat, leans forward far enough to select a mug from her tray, then rocks back gently in perfect comfort even as hot liquid spills over her fat fingers. "I'll be happy to bargain again with either of you," she says, smiling from me to Danny. "Sit down, please. Tell me why you've come to see me. Have a drink?" she adds.

I shoot Danny a glance and catch him eyeing me as well. We both know exactly how dangerous it would be to eat anything this woman has to offer. Ilusine, by contrast, sits her bony self grandly in the wingback armchair across from the crone, selects a mug, and takes a loud sip. The crone rolls her eyes, the crystal flashing, before turning her gaze back to me. "Most people," she says, "don't come bargaining a second time, particularly not hard on the heels of their last bargain. You must be desperate indeed."

She says it with such an air of greed, warning bells go off in my head. But I haven't any choice. "I need to get to Vespre," I say.

"Vespre has been cut off from the worlds." The crone takes another sip before adding, "Mostly."

That one word—such a simple word, yet it sends such a surge of hope racing through my soul. "You know a way to get there?"

"Well, of course I do. It's all a matter of price."

"Name it."

"Within reason," Ilusine adds with a growl, "or we're walking."

The crone laughs and kicks up her little feet, offering a glimpse of thin, scaly ankles and long toes ending in talons. She tips so far back in Mama's chair, she nearly goes over. "It's too late, little princess!" she cackles, wiping a tear from the corner of her crystal eye and flicking it into the fire. The flames flare green for an instant. "The mortal has already revealed her hand. She must reach Vespre, and she'll pay any price to manage it." She leans forward again, sets her mug down with a *thunk* and a slosh before steepling her fingertips. "Hmmmm, but what should I ask for? How about your firstborn child?" Her gaze shifts to my abdomen. "You could hand it over here and now if you wanted. I won't make you wait until it is born."

I wrap a protective hand over my stomach. "No." I say firmly. "Not that."

The crone sneers and settles back in the rocker again. "You love that little dab of nothing more than the rest of your children then?"

A stab of guilt pricks my heart. For an instant my troll children's faces flash across my mind's eye. But I shake my head. "I would give anything for them, anything that is mine to give. This life . . . it doesn't belong to me. It is merely mine to guard and protect for a short while."

"Tut," says the crone. "Too fussy for my taste, but fine! Fine. We'll move on." She taps her fingertips again. Her mouth crooks in a nasty smile. "What about your heart?"

"What?"

"I'll get you through to Vespre where you can perform your

mighty deeds of heroism. But in exchange, you leave your heart behind. Here, with me. There's nothing more powerful than a beating heart full of love."

I blink stupidly. "How can I do anything without a heart? I'll die!"

The crone snorts. "I find most people can live heartless for a long, long while. Sometimes mighty deeds are easier to accomplish without such a burden. After all," she adds, pointing a long finger at my chest, "your heart has led you astray time and again. That brother of yours . . ." She clucks, her forehead puckering over the crystal eyeball. "Just think: without a heart, how much easier will it be to deal with him and the horror he even now unleashes?"

My throat tightens. I want to demand what the crone knows, to beg her to tell me what Oscar is doing in Vespre. An image of the Hollow Man looming large and terrible in Aurelis seems to fill my vision. Is that nightmare even now rampaging through the streets of Vespre? Without its true name, how can Mixael and Andreas hope to bind it?

"Beware," Ilusine warns softly. "This devil is devious. She'll say anything to get what she wants. Remember, the crones are not fae. They can and do lie."

"That is true, little princess," the crone replies with a shrug. "But in this instance, I speak only the truth." The crystal rolls around in her head before finally fixing its strange, multiplied gaze on me. "Give me your heart, and I'll see you arrive in Vespre all in one piece."

"Will you make certain I arrive at the same time as Castien?"

"Castien Lodírith?" The crone shakes her head. "He is beyond my range of vision. I cannot tell you where he is or in what time."

My knees tremble. I want to sink to the floor, to utter the sob that even now struggles up my throat. She doesn't know where he is. Does that mean he's dead? Gone beyond the range of even the Blessed Beldames' far-seeing vision? Sorrow wells inside me, ready to drown me in its depths. But I cannot let it have me. If I'm to have any chance of seeing him again, of seeing any of them, I must keep pushing ahead.

"Oscar then," I say, my throat so tight I can scarcely get the words out. "Will you make certain I arrive in the same moment as my brother? It won't do me any good if I get there a hundred years too early or too late."

The crone smiles nastily, as though the thought had occurred to her. "With the gates broken, I cannot promise such precision. The best I can do is within three days, either before or after his arrival."

Three days. It could work. If I arrived three days early, I could put the other librarians on alert, make certain everything is ready before Oscar and Ivor burst through from realities beyond. I might even be able to prevent the gates from being broken at all, might be able to get a message to Castien in Aurelis or . . . or . . .

Or it could be three days later. Three days too late.

"Do we have a bargain?" the crone asks, leaning forward in her chair, closer and closer. Her unblinking gaze seems to fill my vision. I am lost in the glittering facets of that crystal, ready to be fractured and cast into a thousand pieces, scattered across worlds. I have no choice. If I'm not willing to give up my heart for the chance to save

Castien, to save Vespre, then what good am I? This is what they need. This is what I must do. My atonement, my sacrifice, my—

"Take mine instead."

Something snaps inside my head. I draw back with a gasp then whirl and stare up at Danny. He stands over the crone, his fists clenched. "Danny, no!" I gasp.

"What?" he demands, whirling on me. His face is lined and dreadful. "I already gave you my heart, Clara, and you didn't want it. You tossed it back to me again, and what good is it to me now?"

"Your heart is the best part of you." I reach out, try to catch his hand, but Danny takes a step back out of reach. Tears spring to my eyes. "Whereas mine . . . mine is the worst. Your heart has led you to pursue a life of healing and help, while mine has only led me to hurt and betray those I love. If either of us deserves to be heartless, Danny, it's me. It's me."

"You're not helping your case, little human," the crone chuckles with glee. "From the sound of it, your heart isn't worth all that much, while his sounds more and more tempting."

"No!" I turn to her, clasping my hands over my breast as though I might even now remove the wretched organ and place it in the crone's claws. "No, please! You can't do this!"

"Don't be a fool," Ilusine hisses. "You'll be no use to Castien heartless. For what you must do, you need to be whole and strong." I look down at her, my eyes swimming, my vision blurred so that I cannot discern any expression in her gaunt features. I can only see her head slowly shake. "Let him do it," she says. "Let him have his moment of heroism." There's a certain bitterness to her voice; bitterness and understanding combined.

I turn to Danny again, my protests silenced. Tears stream down my cheeks. I can do nothing but whisper his name. He steps toward me, cups my face with his hand. "Clara," he says, "I love you. I always have. But the truth is, I'm not sure I can bear to go on loving you. Not like this. I'll be a better doctor, a better brother, a better man if I don't."

I want to protest. I want to tell him how false this idea is, how foolish. But I cannot form the words.

"I've made my decision," he continues, no longer gentle but firm. "As my heart is worthless to you in every other way, let me use it now to help you. To let you be with the man you love. I only—" For an instant his voice breaks. He draws a painful, steadying breath. "I only hope you will think of me kindly now and then."

Then he turns from me and steps across the little room to stand before the crone. It is so strange to see him here, in this room that was once the setting of our blossoming love. To see him standing over that wretched creature, to watch how she grins up at him so greedily. It's too horrible, and I half-lunge to interfere. But Ilusine is on her feet and catches hold of both my arms, restraining me with surprising force. "Let me go!" I weep.

"I think not," the princess hisses. "If this is what it takes to save Castien, I, for one, am willing to pay the price."

I cannot tear my eyes off Danny. I feel him slipping away from me, fading into a mist of time and obscurity and unfathomable distance. Blood pounds too loud in my ears—I can no longer hear what the crone says or what Danny answers. She places one gnarled hand against his chest, and all my awareness seems to center on that single point of contact.

There's a burst—not of light, but anti-light. It's blinding, painful. I turn away with a cry, tuck against Ilusine's shoulder. The inside of my head throbs with the aftershock, rendering me temporarily senseless. Then I hear my own ragged breath again. Slowly other senses return. I pull away from Ilusine, peer into the room again.

Danny lies on the floor, collapsed and still. The crone stands at the mantel, settling the lid of a blue-and-white porcelain jar. She chuckles with satisfaction as she places the jar in the center of the mantel. Without a spare glance for her victim, she steps to a door which has appeared suddenly beside the fireplace. It doesn't belong there, doesn't belong in this chamber of my memory. The crone opens it, revealing another portal into absolute blackness.

"Follow the center path and step through the gate at the end of my garden," she says. "The way to Vespre won't last long. Not even such a bargain can generate enough magic to keep a rift between worlds open. But it'll get you through, and you'll arrive within three days of your brother."

"And Castien?" Ilusine demands.

The crone shrugs. "I have no idea where that pretty man has ended up. Our bargain is complete, and he is beyond my range of detection. But the cords of fate will surely draw them back together."

Only now does Ilusine release her grip on my arms. I dart

forward and drop to my knees beside Danny. He lies face-up, so still and so pale. For a heartbeat I fear . . . but, no. He's breathing. Light and fast, but audible. "Danny!" I cry, reaching out to touch him, desperate to wake him, to speak to him.

Ilusine snatches my wrist. She crouches on the other side of his fallen form, glaring at me. "He did what he had to do. As did I." Her thin lips twist, and her hollow cheeks tighten. "No one deserves the poison of unrequited love. But I hope you find Castien. I hope you make something of this mess you've created."

Tears fall from my cheeks, spattering Danny's waistcoat. "What about him?"

"I'll see that he gets back to his people safely."

"But what will happen to him now?"

"That is not your concern." Ilusine rises and drags me to my feet. "You've made your choice. Your path is set and it no longer involves this man." Her fingers tighten painfully. "Give Castien my best."

With those words, she lets go, steps back, and crosses her arms over her emaciated chest. I look at her, uncertain what words of farewell are appropriate in a moment like this. I cast a last look down at Danny, wishing I could do something, say something. There's already such a change come over his face. Though his features are unaltered, the expression is different. He looks like a stranger now.

I dash tears away with the back of my hand. Then, adjusting the strap of my satchel over my shoulder, I turn and face the crone. She leers at me, her one good eye blinking while the crystal remains fixed and focused. "Hurry, little one. The magic won't hold much longer."

Dragging in a short breath, I hasten to the door. As I step past the crone, she makes a slurping, satisfied noise with her lips. When I look at her, horrified, she grins. "Sometimes the dregs of despair are the sweetest," she says and tilts her head. "A pleasure bargaining with you, my dear."

I cast a last glance back at Ilusine. She crouches over Danny once more, holding his hand with her bony little fingers. Her golden eyes hold my gaze hard. Then she nods. Stifling the sob in my throat, I wrench away and stride through the open door, out of the crone's house. I pass through the darkness and stumble out onto her front porch.

Glaring light burns against my eyeballs. I throw up a hand to shield my vision, blinking until some of the pain recedes. Then, peering out through my fingers, I look once more upon the Desolation of Gorre.

The sky overhead churns.

Castien told me Gorre exists too close to the *quinsatra*—the dimension of pure magic. As a result, storms of magic wrack the land, permeating the flora and fauna. Nothing can live here but monsters. I stand on the porch of the crone's weird little house, overlooking what she calls her garden. Everything about it is strange and twisted, home to any number of unholy mutations, both plant and animal. A rabbit hops into the center of the main path, its side gaping with a ghastly wound from which fungus sprouts and spreads. It turns eerie lantern eyes my way before scurrying into the shelter of a broad-leaf plant that oozes puss from every leaf.

My stomach flips. It's a good thing I've grown used to living with nausea over these last few days.

Gripping my skirts with both hands, I descend the porch steps. The crone's house balances on a pair of enormous chicken legs, which shift in place, making the whole porch rock like a storm at sea. It nearly casts me down in a heap of broken limbs, but I manage to reach level ground in one piece. Soil squelches underfoot as I follow the center path, keeping well away from any bushes and shrubs. Some of them look altogether too hungry for comfort.

By some miracle, I make it to the end of the garden unmolested and approach the ramshackle gate arch. It's covered with black fungus and looks ready to topple over, but is still recognizably a Between Gate. The air beneath the arch shimmers and ripples, veils between realities thin. A stone dial stands beside the arch, marked with symbols of all the different locations throughout Eledria to which this gate may lead. I find the mark for Vespre—a single eye. A crack runs through it, nearly obscuring the symbol entirely. Evidence of Lodírhal's destructive spell, no doubt. Even as I look, it seems to crumble more and soon will vanish entirely. The crone was right; I haven't time to delay.

I turn the dial. Sparks and energy erupt beneath the arch. Freezing terror rushes through my limbs, fixing me in place. This is it: my last chance to turn back. Even now I could retreat through that hideous garden, mount the porch steps, pound on the crone's door, and beg to be let back in. Back to my own world, my own life and existence. Beg to undo the bargain for Danny's heart and put everything back together as it should.

"There's no going back," I whisper and press my dry lips together. Whatever happens next, I am committed. To finding Castien. To reclaiming my children. To rescuing Vespre.

To facing my brother.

I place a hand against my womb and close my eyes. If only I was far enough along to feel the life inside me, to know I'm not alone. It would be nice to have that little reminder to give me courage. Instead I just feel more nauseated. "All right," I whisper to my child, the words soft in that magic-stricken air. "Let's find your father, shall we?"

Then I stride forward and hurl myself through the gate into the void between worlds.

13

I'VE TRAVELED BETWEEN THE REALMS AND REALITIES OF Eledria more times than I can count. While one never fully gets used to the experience of one's essence being broken down and remade again, at the very least, I know what to expect when I cast myself through one of the gates.

This is not like that.

At first it's the same skin-scraping sensation I know, like the outer layers of my existence are being sloughed away by a very fine, very precise razor. Then the pain increases. It no longer feels like just the outermost layers are being pulled away. It's more like reality itself is trying to rip down inside of me and rend me to pieces. I cannot seem to find myself, cannot hold onto my center of being. There's nothing but tearing, ripping pain, and I don't even have a body with which to feel it. My essence has become nothing but agony, and then—

I tumble out into a blur of light and shadow and suddenly re-formed limbs that flop uselessly around me. Coming to an abrupt stop, I lie on my back, staring up at nothing, knowing nothing, seeing nothing. Feeling too much of everything to know what I feel. Some vague part of me is aware of whirling void spinning in the air some feet away. I try to turn, to look at it, but can't seem to remember how necks work. Or eyes for that matter. It's a strange thing to be embodied again. Everything is so heavy and sluggish.

The void closes with a snap. The pressure in my head pops suddenly, and my lungs seize, dragging in a desperate gulp of air. Now at last the rest of reality settles in around me. I can blink. I can breathe. My heart *thunks* several times as it relearns how to beat. Then, slowly . . . I frown.

Wherever I've landed, it's dark. But of course, this is Vespre, isn't it? It must be. Vespre is one of the Umbrian Islands, which exist in a state of perpetual twilight, so I didn't expect to arrive in blazing sunshine. But something feels off here, if I could just put my finger on it.

Groaning, I sit upright. My eyes strain as I try to take in more of my surroundings in the gloom. There are plants everywhere. Dead, skeletal plants. I shake my head, look again. Very little vegetation grows in Vespre, which is a realm of rock and crystal. Why would there be plants here, even dead plants? Did the crone play me false? Did the gate not work? Have I ended up in some wildly different part of Eledria?

Slowly my memory fills in missing pieces. "The solarium," I whisper. Of course it's the only explanation. Castien made the solarium for his mother, Dasyra—a mortal mage with an affinity for plant magic. He'd used a powerful spell to channel light all the way from Aurelis and funnel it into this chamber. It had been a little piece of the Dawn Realm, just for her. But now the gates are all broken, including this bit of magic-working.

I suck in a sharp breath. How long has it been? My gaze, somewhat adjusted to the dark, roves across the chamber, taking in the dry fountain, the skeletal trees, the rot and ruin. The last time I was in this chamber, all was lush and green, a veritable jungle of thriving life. This ruin couldn't have happened overnight.

A slither of movement makes me startle and turn sharply where I sit. My vision strains, peering into the deeper shadows. I am no fae; I cannot see in the dark. Perhaps I'm imagining things. Perhaps the shock of travel through the gate has made me jumpy. But no . . . Something creeps through a tangle of dead hydrangeas. The desiccated flower clusters bob like so many heads on spikes, stirred by that subtle movement. Otherwise all is still, silent.

My heart kicks against my breastbone. I knew there was something off, something wrong with this darkness. It's not normal gloom at all. That twisting energy in the deepest shadows can only mean one thing: the Nightmare Realm has infiltrated my head.

Before the thought fully clarifies, my hands are in motion,

ripping open my satchel, dragging out the little notebook and that damned fountain pen. No sooner are they in my grasp than a snake-like limb lashes out, darting for my leg. I'm not fast enough; a vine, thick as a man's arm and covered in thorns, wraps around my ankle and yanks me hard. I scream as I'm dragged across the ground through stalks and dead stems and dried out flower husks straight toward a writhing tangle of briars that looks like a mouth opening and closing. Harsh red light burns deep inside, causing the thorns to stand out stark and black as they churn hungrily, ready to devour me.

But I've not entirely lost my skills in the last seven weeks. I flip open the volume—aware that somewhere, in another layer of reality, I'm lying on a stone floor littered with dead leaves, not being dragged toward that hideous maw. If I can remember this, if I can hold onto that knowledge, then I can just manage to scrawl a few lines of text into the little notebook. It doesn't take more than a few lines.

In this reality an ax appears in my hand.

With a bellow, I hack at the vine, little caring if I hew into my own leg. My blow lands true; the vine shudders. Somewhere in the midst of that snarl, a woman's voice screams in pain. I shake off the vine, which flops like a dead thing, and pull myself to my feet. More vines close in around me, crawling down the walls of the solarium, slithering along the paths, swarming over the dead plants and trees. "Stand your ground," I whisper, both in this reality and the other where my physical self writes as fast as she can. "Be brave and stand your ground."

Then, heedless of my own advice, I turn and run like hell. I'm not thinking straight. If I were, I'd remember that it's never a good idea to run from a Noswraith. They cannot resist a chase. But this wraith is far beyond anything I was prepared to meet so soon upon arrival. If I don't get out of this chamber, I'm going to turn into plant food.

A woman's voice sings through the vines around me: *"Red blooms the rose in my heart tonight, fair as the dawn, new as the spring."*

Brilliant roses burst into life on all sides, blood-red and flaming. The Thorn Maiden. That's who this is—one of the Greater Noswraiths, created by one of the most powerful Miphates mages of all time. She's hungry, violent, insatiable, and somehow she's escaped her vault and is loose in the palace. What is her name? Gods spare me, I've memorized reams of Noswraith names in my time, but I cannot remember what the Thorn Maiden's true name is. Without that name, she cannot be bound.

I put on speed. The solarium door stands partially open. Rose canes shoot out at me from all sides, but I swing my ax, hacking into them, perfectly aware that my physical body doesn't possess enough muscular strength to hew through such dense growth. So long as I can write it, I can will it into being here in this parallel realm. Still even my imagination can only do so much. And the Thorn Maiden is hungry after her long imprisonment.

"Red blooms the rose in my heart, tonight," she sings, her voice coming from everywhere all at once.

I leap for the door just as the briars reach it. Heaving my ax, I carve through those grasping, hand-like thorns and burst into the stone passage beyond. It's dark here, but not the writhing dark of the Nightmare Realm, not yet at least. Dropping the ax, I whirl, grab the solarium door, and haul it shut with a resounding *boom*. The Thorn Maiden shrieks on the far side and bashes the doors again and again.

Then all goes still.

I let out a slow breath. I'm back in my physical body, beyond the reach of the nightmare. For the moment anyway. I squint down at the scrawl of words covering the pages of the little notebook. It's a potent spell, but it will never hold. I have hours at most, perhaps minutes before the Thorn Maiden breaks out. Grimacing, I slam the book shut. I could almost swear I feel thorns and vines moving under the cover, ready to tear free. What will I do if I meet another Noswraith? I only had this one volume. There are pages left, but I'm not sure it would be wise to try to contain more than one wraith within a single book.

Great gulps of breath heave from my lungs. I look up and down the stone passage. All is quiet. That's not unusual; the palace has always been sparsely populated. But this quiet feels more significant. It feels like emptiness. As though the whole place is abandoned. How long has it been? How long have I been away? Oh, gods, *how long?* I shove the notebook into my satchel. I must find them—all of them. My children, my fellow librarians.

"Castien," I whisper.

"I will come to you."

My senses quicken. That voice, that memory inside my head . . .

it's haunted me all along, even before my awareness returned.

"*From anywhere in all the worlds, I will come. Just call my name.*"

I could not remember before, even as my heart and soul longed for him. Now it flickers like a spark inside my head. His true name. His fae name. The name of power which I used to summon him to me once before. If he's still alive out there somewhere, he will hear it. He will come.

I draw several deep breaths. The air around me is cold, dank, and reeks of nightmares. Perhaps it won't work. After all Vespre has been cut off from Eledria, set adrift in the Hinter. There might not be enough natural magic left in the atmosphere to activate the Fatebond. If I try, and it doesn't work, I'm not sure I'll survive the disappointment. But I've got to try.

"*Lianthorne,*" I whisper, breathing the name out into the air. I can almost see it, curling and delicate as it drifts from my lips. "*Lianthorne,* if you can hear me, please co—"

A hideous squelching sound pops in my ears.

I know that sound. I don't know how I know it, but something in me remembers. Slowly I turn.

Something crawls around the corner at the end of the passage. It's the size of a large dog but shaped vaguely like a man dragging his body along by two sharply-angled arms. One of those arms ends in a stump, while the other boasts a long-fingered hand. The body itself is squat, slug-like. A heavy head hangs from the end of a skinny neck. Everything about it sags, oozes, drips. The Melted Man.

I back away, watching that hideous thing make its aimless

way along the passage. It doesn't seem to be aware of me yet. Is it tracking me? Does it sense my presence? I can't move, fearful of drawing its attention. My fingers tighten around the fountain pen. I know this one's name—*Yinzidor*, a demon from ancient Valaayun mythology. A minor wraith, but deadly after his own fashion.

And I can't very well stuff him into the same volume as the Thorn Maiden. While I might be able to hold him by the power of his true name, the Greater Noswraith would surely take the opportunity to escape.

The Melted Man dribbles and slurps his way up the passage, his dripping head close to the ground. I hold my breath. If I run, he will see me and he will pursue. If I don't run, if I stand my ground, is there a chance he'll turn off into one of the side passages before he reaches me? I don't have long to decide. He's getting closer . . . closer . . . soon it will be too late . . .

He looks up. His eyes—one half sunken into his head, the other dripped halfway down his cheek—fix on me. He opens his mouth, long streams of slime parting like teeth.

I take off running. I don't look back, not even when I hear his gurgling roar and the *plop-plopping* sound of his pursuit. Everything in me focuses on flight, on putting some distance between me and this monster. Maybe I can find another book? A loose piece of parchment, something, anything I can use to write on. If not I'm completely at the mercy of this nightmare. I need to reach the library, but I can't remember the way. All these halls and passages are unfamiliar, as though it's been a hundred years since last I walked them. I simply cannot remember, not with the Melted Man gaining behind me.

Thunk.

I round a corner and run directly into a wall. Only this wall reaches out and catches me with two strong arms. I'm stunned, dizzy. Shaking my head, I look up and vaguely recognize the shape of one of the troll house guard helmets.

"Noswraith!" I gasp, hardly able to get the word out, too stunned from impact. I point wildly, waving my arm. If those big stone hands weren't holding me upright, I'd topple over. "Noswraith! Behind me!"

"*Korkor.*" The growling troldish voice cracks oddly around the word. "There's lots of wraiths crawlin' about the place these days."

Then those strong arms lift me clear off my feet. My unexpected companion sets me behind him, angling his body protectively as he faces down the hall where the Melted Man should appear at any moment. "Wait!" I cry, clutching my would-be rescuer's arm. "You can't fight it! You haven't the means!"

The helmeted head turns and looks down at me. He's got a small moonfire lantern hung on a chain around his neck, and its pale light illuminates his big, craggy, rock-hard troll face. Small square teeth flash like diamonds when he smiles.

"Don't worry, little *Mar*. We're not alone up here."

My breath catches in my throat. "Calx?"

14

IT'S HIM. IT'S ABSOLUTELY HIM. THIS MOUNTAIN OF A TROLL man with shoulders the size of a bull ox and arms as big as trees, yet I would recognize that face anywhere. That ugly, beloved, dear little face of my troll son, not quite lost in these mature, craggy lines.

"Calx, you've . . . you've grown!" All thought of our imminent peril flees my mind. I lift a hand, touch his cheek under the helmet. My heart shivers in my breast, tangled in a snarl of emotions. I don't know if I'm relieved to have found him, glad to know he's alive and well and here, or devastated. Devastated at this evidence of just how much I missed. So much. Too much.

"Well, yes," he answers, tipping his massive head to one side. "It's been seven turns of the cycle, you know."

"Seven?" I echo. Images of that skeletal garden flash through my mind. Every week I was away in my own world has been a full turn of the cycle here in Vespre. I cannot wrap my mind around it, cannot grapple with the loss of those years. Years in which my children grew up without me. Grew up and . . . *up*. "You're so big," I choke out, only just now realizing that tears course down my cheeks.

"Ah, well." The boy—my boy—rubs a platter-sized hand along the back of his neck. "You should see Har and Dig. They're much bigger! But I'm catching up quick."

"Are they well? And Sis? Where are they? Are they here in the palace? Do they know about the Noswraiths? Are they—"

"*Hisht!*" Calx holds up a big hand in a silencing gesture. He turns from me, peers back down the hall, his small eyes narrow. "He's coming, little *Mar*. Best get ready."

I peer around Calx into the passage faintly illuminated by the glow of moonfire. The Melted Man oozes into view. His head lolls strangely, long streams of slime dripping from the gash of his mouth. He shakes his head, ungodly noises issuing from his throat.

"Calx, I can't bind him," I whisper, gripping my boy's elbow.

"Oh, don't worry, little *Mar*," Calx says just as the Melted Man lifts his head and those awful, dripping eyes fasten on me. "Time to run!"

The next thing I know, I've been scooped up in a pair of massive arms, tossed over an enormous shoulder, and whisked away through the palace. All the breath is knocked from my lungs, and I can't seem to draw another. I want to shout, to order Calx to put me down. I came all this way to save him, not to be born like a burden, putting him at greater risk.

But the Melted Man slavers just at our heels, his strange, angular arms crawling too fast, his weird, slug-like tail wriggling as he propels himself in short bursts. Gods, have I dropped my book? I still grip the fountain pen in one hand, but it will do me no good unless I find something to write on.

Calx turns a corner, surprisingly lithe and graceful for his bulk, and we enter a snarl of threads which crisscross every which way. They hum gently together, pulsing with an ancient form of magic far beyond my comprehension. A glow suffuses the atmosphere, shimmering and delicate. For a moment I'm convinced Calx and I will both be inextricably tangled in those threads, but he weaves his way in and out without disturbing a single one. The Melted Man, however, dives straight in, heedless, only to utter a dismal, moist sort of cry as the threads stick to his hide, pulling around him, wrapping him up.

"*Wut garek, Sis!*" Calx cries as we reach the far side of the thread-strewn passage.

"*Korkor!*" a high, piercing voice shrieks. A slim figure, all ghostly white and clothed in a gauzy slip of a gown, appears in the windowsill on our right. She swings down from a suspended cord and lands in the middle of the floor in front of us. The Noswraith lets out another wet howl. The threads binding its limbs tighten, hauling him up from the floor into the vaulted ceiling overhead. He hangs suspended, struggling, screeching, as more and more threads wrap around him until he is nothing more than an unrecognizable lump.

"*Rhozah!*" that bright, small voice cheers. "I got him! I got him, I got him!" She whirls on her little bare feet, pointing at Calx, "That's three altogether, and—" She stops. Her gaze fixes on me.

"Hullo, Sis," I say softly.

Seven years have only added to her already painful beauty. She stands before me, all gawky angles, elbows, and knees, and positively luminous. Her long silver hair hangs below her waist, held back from her face in tight braids woven with little bits of bone. Her face is fierce, fire burning in the depths of her moon-wide eyes. For a moment she stands completely frozen, and I have time enough to wonder if she, at least, hates me for what I've done, for the choices I've made. I deserve it. I deserve her hatred even as I long for her love, for her forgiveness. My dry lips move, struggling to speak. "Sis, I—"

A wordless shriek bursts from her lips. She flings herself straight into my arms. The wildness of her overwhelms me, sends me staggering back and sitting down hard on the stone floor. We crash together, her arms around my neck, and a stream of troldish words erupt in my ear. I don't understand a single thing she says, but I hear the tears in her voice. Wrapping my arms around her, I hold her tight as I can. "It's me. It's me, Sis. I came back. Oh, my precious girl, I came back for you!"

Calx looms above us. His eyes shimmer with tears in the moonfire glow. He smiles, rubs the back of his neck again, and says, "You got 'em good, Sis. But we need to keep moving. There's more of these nasties about, and your gubdagog is full."

"Did you spin this, Sis?" I ask, pushing her back just enough that I can sit up and look into her exquisite little face. "Is this your work?"

Sis sniffs and wipes her nose with the back of her hand. She starts to speak troldish, stops herself, and starts again. "I'm the best gubdagoglir, Mar. The low priestess says I'm the best she ever did see!"

I clasp the girl's cheeks and draw her to me, pressing my forehead to hers. "You are a miracle, my little Sis," I say. "You always were."

"Sorry, kurs Mar," Calx rumbles above us. "Time to go. It's not safe up here."

I nod. Taking Sis's hand, I scramble to my feet and let her guide me as we both follow Calx. He leads us away from the writhing gubdagog. I cast a glance back, half-afraid the furious Melted Man will break free. But profound magic vibrates from those threads. Sis's skills have grown over the last seven years. Could she weave something strong enough to catch the likes of the Thorn Maiden? I don't want to wait around to find out.

"Where is everyone?" I ask as Calx guides us through the passages, peering carefully around each bend before continuing. Now that I know to look for them, I spy dozens upon dozens of gubdagogs strung up all over the place—in windows, along the ceiling rafters, tucked away in corners. Whole passages are filled with nothing but massive tangles of thread and debris, like some giant and eclectic spider has taken up residence. Many of the gubdagogs hum with captive Noswraiths. So, so many of them.

"They're down in the low temple," Sis explains eagerly, squeezing my hand. "We had to run away when the big breakout happened."

"Breakout?" My heart drops to my stomach. I seek Calx's eye, but he is busy scanning the next passage. He beckons, and Sis and I hurry after him, crossing a small courtyard under an open, starlit sky. Swirling nightmare energy draws my eye to one corner of the yard, but we make it across and enter the stone gallery across the way.

"Yes," Sis says, much too eager for comfort. "All the nasties in the library! They broke from their books and are getting into everything. If not for my gubdagogs, we'd all be ugdth."

"Not just your gubdagogs, Sis." Calx rolls his eyes. "There's lots of gubdagoglirs in the palace these days."

"Really?"

"Yes." My big boy smiles down at me. "The palace and the low temple have been working together to keep Vespre safe since the gates all broke. We managed pretty well until about three days ago."

My stomach plunges. They've been floating in the Hinter alone for seven turns of the cycle but have managed to survive, even to thrive. What changed three days ago? I already know the answer: Oscar. But where is he then? Somewhere in this wraith-invested palace? Is he still with Ivor? Or have they both already perished?

Calx leads us out a side door. We finally leave the palace proper behind and enter the city streets. It's a relief to escape those haunted halls, but we've not gone far before I spot signs of wraith activity in the streets as well. Buildings caved in. Roads ripped apart. And absolutely everywhere gubdagogs strung across ruins and rubble. Some are broken and drifting in the breeze, the magic long gone from them. Some are full, thrumming with the angry beings trapped within their spells. Others pulse with quiet energy, waiting to be activated.

"Is everyone safe?" I ask as I trot after Calx and Sis. "Lir? Mixael and Andreas? Captain Khas and . . . and . . ." I cannot bear to ask after Castien. But surely he must be here. How else could they have survived seven years on the Hinter Sea, with just two librarians on staff and a handful of gubdagog weavers?

"I told you, they're all down at the low temple," Sis says, bouncing with excitement. "They're gonna be so glad to see you!"

We turn onto another street when Calx puts out an arm, halting our progress. I peer around him and see a hulking, hunched figure making its way at the end of the street, dragging nightmare shadows in its wake. I don't recognize it from a distance. It wouldn't matter if I did—even with its true name, I don't have the means to bind it. But there's a gubdagog strung up between two buildings on either side of us. It must generate a protective barrier, for the Noswraith never once looks our way. It lumbers on, stalking prey in the night. I can only hope the rest of the city folk have found shelter.

"All clear," Calx says and beckons us on. I hate to leave the gubdagog arch behind, but I can't very well stay crouched here. Calx strides forward, so strong and so confident. My heart swells with pride. It's hard to believe this big troll man is still the same sweet, hard-headed, big-grinned little boy I knew.

Grateful to follow his lead, I fall into step behind him, Sis still clinging to my hand. "Why were you two up at the palace?" I ask.

"The low priestess said you was up there," Sis answers, utterly unconcerned with lowering her voice. "She asked for anyone brave enough to go fetch you." She grins enormously, teeth flashing in the moonfire glow. "I said me first!"

"What?" I look from Sis to Calx again, totally confused. "How could she have known? I only just arrived, and I wasn't there all that long . . ." Even as the words leave my lips, I realize it may have been longer than I thought. I encountered the Thorn Maiden immediately upon arrival, and she dragged me into the Nightmare Realm. Though it had seemed as though our fight took mere minutes, it may well have been several hours.

Sis shrugs. "We found you," she says, unconcerned by my bafflement. "We found you before everyone else. That's what counts."

We move on to another street. I stop dead in my tracks, eyes widening. The destruction here is horrifying. Houses are decimated, lying in rubble, the street broken and strewn with debris. There's blood everywhere. And bodies.

Even Sis sobers up at last. Her hand tightens around mine. "Some of the big nasties got out," she says softly. "Gubdagogs don't do much against them."

Calx leads on through the debris. I have no choice but to follow. It's all so terrible, so gory, so undeniable. How could this have happened? How could Mixael and Andreas have managed to contain the library for all these years only to lose control within the last three days? Did Oscar summon the Hollow Man and set it loose on the city? I simply cannot fathom it. What could he or Ivor possibly hope to gain?

Whichever Noswraith had wrought this ruin must be temporarily sated and gone back to the Nightmare Realm, for I see no sign of it as we pick our way across. But it will return soon enough. Hungry, eager to feast on the fear of its victims.

We come at last to a street so positively swathed in gubdagogs, I cannot see the buildings from which they are strung. Were it not for Calx leading the way confidently forward, I would have been lost in the snarl, as thoroughly trapped as any wraith. As it is I cling to Sis's hand and let her help me navigate the winding threads and bits of brick-a-brack, intensely aware of the profound thrum of magic in the air around me. There are Noswraiths caught in parts of this tangle, most of them fairly minor but all potentially deadly. One toothy phantom lunges, trying to snap my head off. Sis yanks me back in time, and the gubdagog tightens, subduing its captive.

Just when I despair of ever getting free, we emerge into a pseudo courtyard, surrounded by gubdagog snarls rather than bastions and balustrades. Across the space are little pale fires around which hunch large, boulder shapes. It takes me a moment to recognize them as trolls; whole families of trolls, taking refuge within the shelter of the gubdagogs, so many of them, packed into this space. Their small boulder children, all wide-eyed and fearful, look up at us as we emerge, but the adults don't move. Maybe they've entered into deep jor, a trance-like meditational prayer.

Calx stumps forward between the family groupings. Occasionally he calls out in troldish, lifting a big hand in greeting. No one answers and no one interferes with our progress. Soon we stand before a cave mouth which I recognize as the entrance to the low temple. Two hulking guards stand before it, stone clubs resting on their massive shoulders. They are so still and solid, one might easily mistake them for statues.

But it isn't the guards who arrest my attention. Instead it's the tall, broad, and dangerously beautiful troll man standing between them. He is one of the throwback trolls, a remnant of ancient days before trollfolk became more one with the stone of their world. He wears troldish garments, culottes of hugagug silk and a broad collar that emphasizes the width of his powerful shoulders. Long white hair falls in silky braids down his back, and a silver band rings his brow. He is Anj—the terrifyingly beautiful leader of the Hrorark.

His cool gaze takes me in as we approach. He growls something in troldish to Calx, who responds in kind. It all sounds so harsh and aggressive, I wouldn't be surprised if he suddenly commanded the two guards to lunge forward and brain me with those great clubs of theirs. I glance sideways at Calx but cannot read his expression. Sis smiles broadly, which isn't terribly comforting.

Finally Anj turns to me again, his brow stern in the glow of moonfire lanterns. He raises both arms. "Hail, Clara Darlington, the savior of Vespre."

I could not be more surprised. I gape at this man, my enemy . . .

or at least, not my friend. Then, with a little shake of my head, I gasp, "The what now?"

Before I can utter another word, a whoop echoes from inside the cave. The next moment there's a streak of silver hair and long white limbs, and I find myself caught in a powerful embrace, pressed hard against a soft bosom. "Oh, Mistress!" a gentle voice sobs in my ear. "Mistress, Mistress, I knew you'd return! I just knew it!"

15

I PUSH BACK ENOUGH TO LOOK UP INTO LIR'S FACE. MY DEAR friend, my former maid, here and alive and standing before me. I cannot find words to speak. Lir is talking, but Sis jumps, claps, and squeals so loudly as she dances around us, I cannot understand a word. It doesn't matter. Because Lir is here. She's still the same stunningly beautiful woman I've known since my arrival in Vespre. My first friend in this world, my confidant and confederate.

A second look, however, and I realize there is something different about her. Despite the horror of the situation, the peril even now holding her city captive, Lir projects a confidence and strength I don't recall seeing in her before. Though she's not altered physically, the change in her spirit is profound. I'm not sure

I would have even recognized her from a distance.

She turns suddenly and snaps at Sis in troldish, finishing with, "And do *stop* shouting my ear off, child! I can see perfectly well for myself that she's here, thank you very much. If you've quite finished pestering, go find her something to eat—something *humans* can eat," she adds.

Sis pouts and turns to go, but Lir calls after her in troldish. The girl stops, looks back. To my surprise Lir drops a kiss on the top of her head. Sis rolls her eyes but looks pleased even as she pretends to rub it off. With a last half-grin my way, she scampers off to do as Lir asked. I've never seen Lir behave with such affection toward the children. But there was something altogether natural about their interaction, and . . .

Lir catches my eye. Her face goes still for a moment, as though she's reading my expression, reading something I'm not certain I can even name. "Mistress," she says quietly, "when you left—"

Anj steps forward, interrupting whatever she meant to say. Lir turns to him, a smile breaking across her face. She speaks swiftly in troldish, and he responds, his tone solemn. Am I mistaken in thinking there's a certain attentiveness to the way he listens to Lir? As though every word she says is a drop of pure gold. I remember all too vividly when Anj confronted us in the streets of the lower city; when Lir threw herself at him in my defense and tossed him into a lava pit. It would seem things have changed somewhat between them since I've been away.

"We are glad you have joined our ranks, Miss Darlington," Anj says, addressing me again at last. He speaks the common Eledrian tongue very smoothly and eloquently, and the sounds transform in my ear, heard as though spoken in my own language. "It is you we must thank for the harmony which now exists between the city and the palace. Because of you, we were better prepared for the terrors we have faced. Now that you're here, you can join the other librarians and bind these nightmares again."

"Other librarians?" I turn to Lir. "What others? Who is here?"

"Both Mixael and Andreas escaped the palace during the outbreak," Lir says. "They are within the temple, working on rebinding broken spells. Neither of them has stopped since we came here. That was three days ago."

"How many Noswraiths broke out?" I ask. "Do we have a tally?"

Lir shakes her head. "No one knows for sure. Many. Too many. And we suspect more every day."

Anj speaks to Lir again in troldish. She acknowledges him then turns to me. "Come," she says, taking my hand. "The low priestess has asked to see you the minute you arrive. We must go to her now."

I nod. Though my legs are numb from all the running around I've been doing, and my body positively shakes with the need for food, drink, and rest, I push all these things aside. I did not risk everything to get back here only to be a liability to those I came to save. These people need me. I owe it to them to give whatever I have left to offer.

I turn to follow Lir into the temple entrance when Calx's deep voice calls from behind. *"Mar?"* I turn to face him, opening my mouth to answer, but he continues speaking in troldish. His gaze is fixed not on me but on Lir.

Lir's face goes stern. She answers Calx sharply, and he seems to persist. Lir interrupts him, holding up one hand, but chews her lower lip with concern. Finally she turns to me. "He's worried. About his brother. All three of the boys volunteered to go up to the temple with the *gubdagoglirs* when the low priestess said you were there. Har returned not long ago, but Dig hasn't yet."

"I'll go find him," Calx insists, his rock brow deepening over his eyes.

Lir takes hold of his big arm, squeezing. Though she's slight compared to his massive bulk, she has true troll strength and she's not afraid to use it. "You will stay. There is plenty of time for Dig to return. Patience, my *borug.*" She pats his cheek. "Go find some *xurl* stones to chew. You look famished."

Calx shrugs and huffs a deep breath but turns to me and offers a half-grin. "Glad you're home, *kurs Mar.*" With those words, he stumps away, disappearing among the refugee fires and stone folk deep in *jor.*

I turn to Lir. "He called you *mar.*"

Her eyelids drop for a moment, long lashes veiling her gaze. "They were devastated," she says softly. "When the gates were broken, and you were on the far side. Vespre was cut loose on the Hinter Sea, and the children believed they would never see you again. I . . . I never thought I would do it, but . . . I remembered all you had risked, how hard you fought against the Prince and the powers of the low city to give them a home, to provide for them. I knew I couldn't let you down. Or them either." She lifts her face then, meeting my gaze steadily, though tears swim in her eyes. "I told them that I was their *mar* now. Until your return."

I stand there, my knees locked even as dizziness tries to overwhelm me. It's too much. The children don't know the truth. They don't know that I abandoned them, left them long before the gates were destroyed. Part of me is glad they've been spared the pain of that knowledge . . . but I don't deserve it. I deserve their anger, their disappointment, their disgust.

And Lir. She's been their mother now for seven turns of the cycle, while I was their mother for a few mere months. Their love for me may have endured, but their need for me is long gone. I missed those important years. I missed everything.

All because I wouldn't let Oscar go.

My body begins to shake. I fear I'm going to fall to pieces. What was it Anj had called me? *The savior of Vespre.* They think I'm some sort of heroine—a bringer of peace and union, a champion of the small and helpless. They don't know the truth. They don't know what I really am. I want to cave into myself, to collapse and be crushed under the weight of this guilt and remorse. But to do so won't help these people. Perhaps I'm not the heroine they believe me to be. But I owe it to them to at least try.

Lir's eyes brim with concern. "Mistress?" she says, squeezing my hand. "Mistress, what can I do?"

I cannot spill these thoughts and feelings on Lir. Not now.

Much as I want to confess my sins, Vespre is hanging by a thread. There will come a time when I must honestly communicate what I've done. But not yet. Not now.

Instead I look up at Lir. Suddenly the question I've been longing to ask bursts from my lips: "The Prince? Is he here?"

Her mouth parts in a silent, "Oh." Then she presses her lips in a firm line and shakes her head. "I'm sorry, Mistress. He was also on the far side of the gate when it broke. We have not seen him these seven years. We all hoped you were together."

Tears sting my eyes. I sniff and drop my head, then shake it. "No. We parted and . . . and . . ." I don't know how to continue. I can't begin to explain all that has happened. My hand moves unconsciously to my abdomen, and I wish again that I could feel the life inside, could feel that connection to Castien. I just feel alone.

As though reading my mind, Lir places her arm around my shoulders and draws me closer. "Don't worry, Mistress," she says gently. "You're with us now. We will help you. We will help each other. And somehow we will find our way through this."

Her gaze is so clear, so confident. She certainly has changed these last seven years. Gone is the timid, uncertain maid. This woman is a leader, a mother, a fighter. A woman who can be leaned on in times of trouble. A woman I can only aspire to be like in days to come.

"Thank you, Lir," I say and straighten my shoulders, tossing a lock of hair out of my face. "All right. I'm ready. Take me to the low priestess."

Umog Grush sits on her throne in the middle of a vast cavern. The throne itself is like an island in the center of a lake of darkness. I don't know how deep that darkness goes, but judging by the echoes in this chamber, I would guess many fathoms.

I cross the rickety rope bridge slowly, feeling my way mostly blind. The only light in this whole huge space is a tiny glimmer from the stone on the end of the low priestess's staff. It glimmers off flecks of mica in her hide, offering some faint definition to her boulder-like shape. I know she's watching my approach. But she does not call out a greeting.

Gubdagogs hang suspended from stalactites overhead. The last time I came this way, they contained a single captured Noswraith. Now many nightmares writhe in the tangled threads, moaning, snarling, hissing. Some lie still, and they are the most terrifying, biding their time, awaiting the right opportunity. But the magic generated by the *gubdagogs* is tremendous, evidence of the low priestess's power and skill. Is she strong enough to bind one of the Greater Noswraiths? I hope I never have opportunity to find out.

I stagger the last few steps across the swaying bridge, convinced my stomach is on the verge of leaping right up my throat. The last time I came this way, Castien was with me. He'd insisted on holding my hand, claiming to be afraid of the dark. How irked I'd been with him at the time! It was becoming more and more difficult to disguise my growing feelings for him. That simple contact of his palm against mine was almost too much for my façade.

He's not here now. He's not returned to Vespre. I've risked so much, traveled across worlds, left behind everything. And he's not here.

I grind my teeth. Now is not the time to think such thoughts. I step off the swaying bridge onto the stone ledge beneath the low priestess's throne. The light from her staff intensifies. I drop to my knees and lower my head, closing my eyes against that glare. "Umog Grush," I say and place a hand against my heart, "I have come at your summoning."

"Well." The low priestess's voice rumbles like the first murmurs of an earthquake. "Greetings to you, little *kurspari*. The stones of Umbria sang out when the portal between worlds opened and you stepped through. I'd set them to watch for your return and the return of your Prince. I must admit, I had long since given up any expectation of meeting you again." She leans forward in her throne, grinding the end of her walking staff into the dirt. "I cannot say I was well pleased to learn they had successfully fetched you back from the palace. Not after you so unceremoniously abandoned us."

Shame floods my cheeks with heat. While the others might assume the best, trust Umog Grush to discern the truth. I swallow hard. "I . . . I wouldn't have been gone so long by choice."

"Wouldn't you?"

My heart drops. But what's the point of trying to lie my way out of this? She will know. With an effort of will, I lift my gaze, meeting hers under the steep ledge of her brow. "You're right," I say softly. "I chose poorly. But I will choose better going forward. I will do whatever it takes to make up for the wrongs I have done."

"Fine words." The priestess settles back in her seat. The lines of her face harden into a foreboding scowl. "Both you and your Prince abandoned Valthurg in its hour of need. Then again, perhaps it is better for troll kind to be cut off from the worlds. We've never been a particularly social lot." She chuckles darkly, spinning the staff in her hands. "But these nightmares . . . these Noswraiths . . . they must be stopped."

I nod, even as my stomach tightens. "I will join Mixael and Andreas at once. I will help them rebind the—"

"No." Umog Grush's voice cuts like a sword. "No more bindings. They must be stopped. Destroyed. Ended."

For a long moment I can only gape up at the troll woman. I simply cannot find the words. Then, with a gasp, I blurt, "That's impossible."

"Nothing created by humans is intended to last forever. The gods themselves ordained it to be so."

"Yes, but . . . but Noswraiths have been around for hundreds of years. Thousands perhaps! In all that time, no one has ever discovered a means to destroy them."

"Then you must be the first."

She holds my gaze long and hard. Neither of us speaks for some time, but I feel the crushing weight of everything in her eyes. The success of bringing the palace and the low temple together—the shock of Vespre's sundering—the wrongness of my abandonment of them all. It's all there. The good. The bad.

Both what I have accomplished and what I have failed to honor.

"All right," I answer at last, my voice low and firm. "I will do it. If it can be done."

Umog Grush's eyes narrow to glinting slivers, studying me, searching for the lie in my words. "Go," she says at last, flashing her diamond teeth in a snarl. "Get on with it then."

Without another word, I rise from my knees, turn, and hasten back along the swaying bridge over a chasm of endless darkness. Overhead, Noswraiths writhe and gnash their teeth, watching me go.

16

"MISTRESS, I'M HERE. REACH OUT AND TAKE MY HAND."

I nearly whimper out loud with relief at the sound of Lir's voice. With her troll senses, she can see me well enough as I pick my way blindly along. I do as she bids. Lir's strong fingers close around mine and draw me the last few steps from the bridge and back into the closeness of the tunnel. It's not exactly comforting to find myself once more hemmed in by a thousand tons of solid rock, but at least I'm no longer alone.

"I'll take you to the other librarians," Lir says.

I nod, deeply relieved when she doesn't ask after my conversation with the priestess. I'm not sure I can bear to recount it. Not yet. Not with this new and impossible task now weighing on my shoulders.

"They will be so glad to see you after all this time," Lir continues, "and very glad of the reprieve." She tugs me along a few paces. I'm completely dependent on her, helpless in this pitch black. Only after we've progressed for some moments do I realize we're not alone. There's a third set of footsteps.

"Who's there?" I demand.

"Oh! I forgot your human eyes can't see in here," Lir says. "Captain Khas has joined us."

A little bloom of warmth unfurls in my chest. I'd feared something might have happened to Khas during the outbreak. Valiant defender that she is, she would not have fled the palace willingly. "I'm glad," I say, tears choking my voice. I swallow them back; Khas is not one for excessive emotion. "Are you well, Captain?"

A moment of silence. Then: "Yes, Miss Darlington. I am well."

Her words are followed by a strange, gurgling coo that makes absolutely no sense to my ears. I frown, uncertain what to say. Then Lir leads us around a turn, and the dense darkness of the temple lifts, illuminated by a series of moonfire lanterns. "The low priestess agreed to let Mister Silveri and Mister Cornil have light in the southwest quarter," Lir says. "Some of the priestesses complained; it is considered sacrilegious to bring light into the temple of the Deeper Dark. But under the circumstances, most agreed it was a priority to give the librarians a protected space to go about their spellwork."

While she's speaking, I turn and look back at Khas. The captain, as tall, muscular, and beautiful as ever, steps into the light, and I lose my breath entirely. "Khas!" I exclaim. "Why . . . I didn't . . . I never . . . Oh!"

A chubby baby is bound to the front of Khas's torso, facing out to watch the world with a curious gaze. Its bone-white skin and silvery eyes look very like its mother, but a mop of red curls adorns the top of its head, a colorful contrast. It grins up at me, displaying a full set of stumpy diamond teeth.

I drag my gaze from the babe back up to Khas then down again. "A boy?" I ask at last.

Khas grunts. A faint blush stains her cheeks.

"What is his name?"

"Sor," Khas replies, then adds, "Soran. But Sor is more troldish."

Soran. After Mixael's father, Mage Soran Silveri. As if the red hair hadn't already given it away! Once again tears prickle in my eyes. Gods, I can't seem to help weeping at the least thing these days. "I . . . I've missed so much."

Khas shrugs one muscular shoulder. "After the gates broke, everything was . . . very dire. We did not know how much time we had left." She looks down at her child and strokes his glossy curls. "Every day has been a gift." Then her eyes flash, catching and holding mine. "But now you're here, maybe . . ."

The hope in her face is terrifying. Why does everyone seem to think I have the means to set everything right? Anj, the low priestess, now Khas. Do they really believe I'm some sort of savior? They don't know what I really am. They don't understand.

Worthless . . .

"What word do you have of the Prince, Miss Darlington?" Khas's voice breaks through my thoughts, dragging me back to the present.

"Hush!" Lir says sharply, her eyes on my face.

"No, Lir." I put out a hand, my throat constricting as I force back another sob. "No, I'm all right." I turn to Khas again. "The last I saw Prince Castien, he cast himself through the gate to Vespre even as it collapsed. I hoped I would find him here."

Lir and Khas exchange looks. Khas's jaw tightens. They were both counting on the Prince's return at Vespre's darkest hour. Khas wraps a protective hand around her little one. "Well," Lir says, glancing my way, a determined smile on her lips, "he must be on his way. Now that you're back, I mean. He'll be guided here straight away."

"How?" Khas demands, her voice rumbling.

Lir shoots her a look. "Oh, come now, don't be a *uggug*, Khas. Their Fatebond, of course!"

"What?" I blurt, my eyes rounding. "You knew about that?"

"Now I do." Lir laughs outright. "I merely suspected before. But it's true, isn't it?"

Helplessly caught, I can do nothing but nod. My hands once more press unconsciously to my stomach, a slight gesture, but both women notice. To my tremendous surprise, Khas reaches out and places her hand on top of mine. "*Wut kharzug borugabah,*" she says with surprising gentleness.

"What does that mean?" I ask.

"It's difficult to translate," Lir says. "I suppose it's something like: *Our lives belong to our children.* It means we will give everything we must for their sakes."

I meet Khas's gaze, solemn and stalwart. "Thank you, Khas. Thank you for . . . for reminding me." Stretching out my hand, I stroke little Sor's soft cheek. He snaps, his diamond teeth chomping just inches from my finger, hard enough to break bone. Khas smiles proudly.

"Mar! Mar!"

Sis's voice echoes down the stone passage. I whirl about, shocked all over again to see the girl, so tall and grown-up. A pang stabs through my heart . . . only to increase ten-fold when I realize she's not addressing me. Sis skids to a halt in front of us, and though she tosses me a quick glance, it's Lir to whom she pours out a stream of troldish far too fast for me to discern more than a single name: *Dig.*

"What's wrong?" I demand. "What's happened?"

Still speaking troldish, Sis turns to me, but Lir talks over the top of her. "The *gubdagoglir* who went with Dig up to the palace has returned without Dig. They were separated."

My heart judders. "Dig is alone? In the palace?" A palace crawling with Noswraiths for which he is totally unprepared and defenseless. I don't stop to think about my next words; they simply spill from my tongue: "I'm going."

"Me too!" Sis cries.

"Don't be rash, either of you." Lir takes hold of Sis's arm as though to prevent the girl from darting off that instant. "It's dangerous."

"*I'm* dangerous!" Sis snarls.

"Sis has a better chance of finding the boy than anyone," Khas inserts. "She has the skill."

"No!" I take a step forward, my fists clenched. "I don't need a *gubdagoglir*. I'm a librarian, remember?"

Lir looks from me to Sis to Khas. Her naturally alabaster skin is gray in the dim light of the hall. She presses her lips into a hard line, then says only, "I will speak to Anj."

"*Rok!*" Anj growls the harsh word accompanied by a vehement shake of his head. I don't need to know troldish to understand his meaning. Standing in the courtyard just beyond the temple entrance, he looks fierce and dangerous by the low moonfire light. His eyes flash as he stares down Lir, and I momentarily wonder if I was mistaken about the nature of his feelings for her.

Then he turns to me, speaking common Eledrian but with that same rough, growling accent. "I cannot risk the safety of our people. We have so few defenses against these foes. We need every *gubdagoglir* here, guarding our barriers."

Sis lets out a little shriek and stamps her foot, tears rolling down her cheeks. She's already boldly declared that she will go, with or without permission. Thankfully Har and Calx stepped from the shadows to restrain her. Har is, as Calx mentioned, taller than his brother. He's absolutely massive, even by troll standards. The sight of him fills my heart with pride. He shoots me a shy smile, more reserved than his brother and sister at our reunion.

I turn to Anj, putting my shoulders back as I meet his ferocious gaze. "I agree. And I don't need a *gubdagoglir*. I will go alone."

"No, *Mar!*" Sis cries. It nearly breaks my heart in half to hear her use that name for me again. Perhaps I've not been wholly replaced in her affections. Calx joins his sister, saying, "It's dangerous, *kurs Mar.*"

"Yes," I answer. "And Dig is in the thick of it."

"He knew the risks," Anj says. "He is no child; he is a guard of Valthurg. He made a choice when he volunteered."

"Yes," I agree, "and now I am making a choice. He is my boy. I am his chosen mother. It is my responsibility to save him."

"You are not his only mother," Lir says softly. "Not anymore."

"What?" Anj turns sharply, slipping back into a stream of angry troldish.

Lir lifts her chin, her eyes shining with reflected fire. "I am a weaver of *gubdagogs*, trained by the low priestess herself. I am more than prepared. I will go with Clara Darlington to save *our* son."

Anj lunges, grabbing her wrist and dragging her toward him. Their faces are mere inches apart, his fierce with desperate anger, hers serene and strong and unyielding. In that moment I'm not certain if he's going to kiss her or bite her or some combination of the two. Lir never flinches. At last Anj growls, "*Guthakug!*" through bared teeth. Lir's lips twist in a smile. She responds softly, reaches up to trail a finger along his cheek.

Then she wrenches her arm free of his grasp and turns to me. "Let's go, Mistress," she says.

17

"SO," I SAY AS CASUALLY AS I CAN MANAGE, FOLLOWING Lir through the snarl of *gubdagogs* surrounding the temple yard. "You and Anj?"

Lir casts a cool glance over her shoulder. "Hmmm?"

"You seem . . ." I stop. I was going to say *friendly* but that is decidedly not the right word to describe the scene I just witnessed. "You seem to have a dynamic."

She sniffs and shrugs prettily. "Anj is head of the *Hrorark*. Since the gates broke, and Vespre was cast out into the Hinter, he stepped up as leader of the whole city, under the low priestess's eye, of course. As both Mixael and Andreas were quite caught up in the cares of the library, they needed a troll to serve as go-between for the palace and the city folk. That became my role. Anj and I have learned to work together."

She says it all so easily, as though it was perfectly natural for an orphaned outcast and former housemaid to take on such a vital position. I give her a narrow look. "You do remember he tried to kill us, don't you?"

"It doesn't pay to hold grudges in Vespre," Lir retorts, shifting a *gubdagog* thread just enough to allow us room to pass under. "Besides he could have killed me many times during that altercation and didn't. Which was rather gentlemanly of him if you think about it."

None of that so-called gentlemanliness was directed my way. Anj absolutely would have crushed my skull if he'd gotten close enough. But under the circumstances I probably shouldn't hold it against him.

Lir guides us smoothly through the snarl of *gubdagogs*, rescuing me from becoming hopelessly entangled numerous times. My satchel weighs heavily on my shoulder and against my hip, supplies borrowed from Mixael and Andreas's stash. It's good to have something more substantial than Oscar's notebook to write in, but I don't know if they will be enough against the nightmares I will face. "Who created this *gubdagog?*" I ask as we skirt a captured Noswraith, which eyes us menacingly through the winding threads.

"All of us," Lir answers. "Me, Sis, the priestesses of the low temple. Even Umog Grush herself. *Gubdagogs* gain strength the more people work on them together. We've spent the better part of these last three days creating this one."

I wish I could say something, express my wonder at the extent of Lir's skill. Mere words don't seem sufficient, not for a creation understood outside of words. Words are the domain of librarians, and they are incredibly powerful, but this is something more. Something even Noswraiths cannot breach. Well, most Noswraiths.

We come to a portion of the barrier where something large has ripped right through. Threads strung between two buildings hang black and broken, and the buildings themselves are crumbled ruins. A cluster of priestesses work to restore it, retying the threads and reestablishing the spell of protection. Lir catches my eye. "It was a Greater Noswraith," she says to my unanswered question. "It broke through those threads like they were nothing. The only reason it did not destroy the entire *gubdagog* was that it seemed to be distracted, intent on some other goal."

"Which one?" I ask.

"I did not recognize it. Granted I do not know all the Noswraiths, but my adopted parents trained me to recognize all the Greater Wraiths. This one I have never seen before, never heard of. It was tall, like a giant, with a great hole in its chest. You could see the broken ribs. And its eyes were full of living shadows."

My blood runs cold. The Hollow Man. That's what she's describing. Of course she does not recognize it; no one in Vespre has seen this nightmare before. No one is prepared to face it, not the priestesses, not the librarians. Maybe if the Prince were here we'd have a chance, but without its true name, we're helpless.

Lir continues silently, and I follow her from the shelter of the *gubdagog* into the open streets. We progress like furtive shadows, alert to the slightest movement or sound. Here and there whirling nightmare shadows erupt in dark corners, driving us to change our route. The journey from the low temple to the palace is long already, but the circuitous route we are obliged to take adds precious minutes. I feel the time keenly. Every moment puts Dig at greater risk. I can only hope he managed to find some safe haven within the infested palace.

With a little hiss of breath, Lir puts up an arm. Something is coming toward us down the shadowed road. The starlight isn't bright enough for me to get a clear view, but Lir grabs my arm and drags me around a corner. We press our backs against a stone wall. My heart races. "What is it?" I whisper.

"I don't know." Lir's pale eyes are very wide. "It . . . it looked like . . . a bird? But with a serpent's tail."

"*Ichneu*," I whisper, recognizing her description. "The Cockatrice. Not a great wraith, but if you look it in the eye, it will turn you to stone."

I reach into my satchel, withdrawing one of the books and the gold fountain pen, but Lir stays my hand. "Allow me," she says and takes a ball of string from her own satchel.

I watch, fascinated, as she deftly weaves some complicated thing I don't understand at all. "Isn't it too small?" I hiss.

"It isn't so much about size with *gubdagogs*," Lir replies. "In fact they're easier to make when large. But small ones, well-woven, will work just as well if the weaver has the skill." She looks up, her tangle suspended between both hands. "Stand back, Mistress."

Then she leaps out into the street, her head turned to the side, her eyes closed, holding her *gubdagog* out before her. A raucous shriek echoes across the stone, and a shadow seems to fill the street, roiling with nightmare energy. I stand with my pen poised above the page, ready to dive into battle, ready to defend my friend. Pressure pops in my ears. There's a strange, squealing sound, a sense of fracturing in my head. Then Lir's *gubdagog* snarls up on itself, becoming a tight, wriggling knot in her hands.

"You can come out now, Mistress," she calls.

I step out from hiding, mouth ajar, and watch as Lir suspends her little, wriggling tangle from her belt like a trophy. "How long will it hold?" I ask.

"Long enough for me to return it to the librarians," she answers with a satisfied smile.

Most *gubdagogs* are not intended as lasting prisons for Noswraiths. They will work for a time, but eventually break down. Umog Grush managed to snare and contain the Striker for over a year, but that was an unusually potent spell. The fact is, not even the greatest, most intricate *gubdagog* can offer a solution to the Noswraith infestation. Like the books I use, they must and will eventually disintegrate. For these nightmares to be truly ended will require something else entirely.

"They must be destroyed," the low priestess's voice echoes in the back of my mind. But I can't think about this now. I must concentrate on saving Dig. The rest will just have to wait.

At long last we approach the palace gates. They hang from their hinges, broken and sagging. Writhing shadows fill the courtyard, far too dense to be safely navigated. Lir and I peer inside, and my heart drops to my shoes. "How are we supposed to get through that?"

"Here, Mistress." Lir holds out a little charm suspended on a metal chain. I look more closely and see an intricate weaving, not unlike the *gubdagogs*. A faint vibration of magic emanates from it, but it feels different from the tangles somehow. "It repels Noswraiths," Lir explains, noting my questioning look. "They sense it and avoid it. It won't last for more than an hour, but if you pull on this string"—she demonstrates, holding up the charm to show the little dangling thread—"it will activate the spell."

I accept the offering gratefully and hang it around my neck. "How many do you have?"

"Only these two," she admits. "They take time to make, and the weaving is very precise. Whatever we do manage to create are distributed immediately."

"Does Dig have one?" I ask hopefully.

"Yes. All of the volunteers had one when they set out. But," she adds, her brow puckered, "as I said, they only last about an hour."

I know what she's saying—Dig surely used his up long ago. But I won't let that thought discourage me, not after we've come so far. "Let's find our boy," I say.

We pull the strings to activate the protection spell. A hum of magic surrounds me like a protective cocoon. The Noswraiths react to it immediately, a series of hisses, yelps, growls, and groans erupting beyond the broken gates. When we step through, the shadows retreat to all the deepest corners. Unseen eyes watch us with hatred and deep suspicion. Walking side-by-side, Lir and I hasten across the courtyard to the front steps. We climb swiftly to the door, which stands ajar. I peer through into the vaulted front hall and scan the echoing space. Across from me, a hunched, half-man, hound-like thing appears in a doorway. He stops, turns, looking at me with glowing green eyes. Then he turns and lopes off. Lir's necklaces seem to be working. For now.

"Where to, Mistress?" Lir asks. I'm surprised at her deference. She has been a leader in Vespre for the last seven turns of the cycle. I don't feel at all prepared to take charge now. But I am the mortal mage of the two of us, a librarian of Vespre, endowed with special power. I can't shirk this duty.

"My old room," I answer decisively. Lir gives me a questioning look. "They came up here to find me, right? Perhaps Dig tried to reach my old rooms. It would be a reasonable place to search for me."

"Maybe," Lir replies, considering the idea. "The children's rooms are also close to your old chambers. They're all heavily warded with *gubdagogs*. It would be a good place to take shelter so long as the *gubdagogs* aren't full."

Or torn down, I think but do not say. That image of the ripped *gubdagog* around the temple is still vivid in my mind. Such a powerful spell—yet the Hollow Man passed through it like it was nothing. I suppress that thought and urge Lir to take the lead. She guides us through the winding palace, our every footstep careful and precise. Phantoms waft just on the edge of vision, but the spells in our necklaces keep them at bay.

We step into one passage that skitters and crawls, every inch covered in insects. I peer through the swarm to see a young woman in a lace dress with a bright crimson rose tucked behind her ear. She sits at a little table, sipping from a delicate teacup. She catches my eye and smiles. Insects crawl out of her mouth and nose. I shudder, recoiling, but when I look again, she is gone. The insects scatter up the walls on each side and vanish into the shadows among the ceiling stalactites. Lir and I hasten on our way, and when we reach the far end of the passage, buzzing erupts behind us. We exchange glances but neither of us can bear to look back.

"How did you all survive?" I whisper. "After the break-out, I mean."

"We had an escape plan prepared," Lir answers. She holds a woven *gubdagog* out in front of her like a weapon, the strings wafting with every step she makes. "After the gates broke, Mixael and Andreas spent all their time managing the books, and the rest of us started to prepare. We knew it was just a matter of time before breakouts became more frequent. *Gubdagogs* were strung across the palace and used to temporarily bind any escaped wraiths. It was a good system! It worked well for a long while. But it was too good to last." Her expression goes dark, haunted by recent memory. "We lost good people that day."

We turn a corner, and I recognize the old hall where my own bedchamber once lay. Only now it is absolutely snarled with *gubdagogs*, many of them full. A few broken tangles show evidence of escaped wraiths, but others writhe and shiver, the monsters inside securely bound. There must be dozens of them, both big and small, none of them great.

"This was Dig's room," Lir says, leading to the third door on the right. A writhing *gubdagog* hangs suspended over the doorway, but she ignores it and peers into the chamber. Then she shakes her head and backs out again. I wish we had time to go in, to make a more thorough inspection, but our protection spells won't last much longer. It's not as though Dig is small enough to hide under the bed anymore anyway.

We check each room by turn. It's all so hauntingly familiar. I come to the door of my own room and hesitate. Somehow I can't quite bear to open it, can't bear to face this space of so many memories, so many precious moments, all of which I threw away without a thought.

"Mistress?" Lir whispers behind me.

I draw a short breath and, gritting my teeth, push the door open. A single moonfire lantern illuminates the shadowed space. A lantern which hangs around the neck of a burly troll guard. "Dig!" I cry.

He's crouched against the wall beside the fireplace, his head tilted to one side, his eyes glassy. His left arm is mangled, his stone hide cruelly carved into and covered in streaks of blood.

I fly across the room to his side, kneel, touching his broad face and calling his name over and over again. "Dig! Dig, it's me. I'm here. I came back. Dig, can you hear me?"

Lir crouches beside him and inspects his arm. "It's not good, Mistress," she says, her voice thick with grief. Then she takes Dig's face between her hands, turns him toward her, and barks in troldish.

"Aw, *Mar!*" he growls, and I jump out of my skin at the sound of his voice. He tries to shrug her off. "*Gurat, Mar, gurat!*" But Lir won't be put off. She presses him, jostling his big solid body until he answers her in a series of short, grunting words.

Lir's teeth flash in the moonfire. "How could you be so foolish?"

"What? What happened?" I demand.

"He tried to lead Boney Long Fingers away from Umog Hith, the pretty priestess he was paired with on the rescue mission." Lir curses harshly in troldish. "I should have known better than to let him go with her. She's quite turned his head, and now he's gone and been *gutha* stupid!"

I look at Dig again. It's not the time, I know, but I can't help the dart of pain which stabs my heart. My little boy is already old enough to have developed a soft spot for a pretty priestess. I've missed so much. Far too much!

I turn my attention to his wounds. Boney Long Fingers dug deep. Biting my lip, I reach for my pen and book.

"What are you doing, Mistress?" Lir demands.

"A wound like this won't heal without spellwork," I answer,

opening the book to the first blank page. "I don't know if I have the skill to perform such a spell, but if I don't . . ."

Though Lir looks tense and uncertain, she says only, "Do it."

I touch the tip of the fountain pen to the page and start to press. But before I can form a single word, something stirs in the atmosphere. My body recognizes it before my brain has caught up. My blood turns to shooting ice, and my limbs become numb blocks of dread. I lift my eyes from the page, looking around the room. The shadows are alive, writhing. The Nightmare Realm. It's here. Something is coming, passing right through the protective *gubdagogs*.

There's no time to try to heal Dig. We've got to get out of here. Now.

"Can you lift him?" I ask, looking up at Lir, my pen still poised over the page.

Lir blinks, surprised. Then she glances around the room, suddenly aware of the encroaching nightmare as well. Sucking in a sharp breath, she nods and gets her hands under Dig's massive arms. Her strength is truly tremendous despite her delicate proportions, and she lifts him to his feet. Dig, not fully unconscious, staggers, sags. Lir pulls his arm over her shoulder and looks to me. "Lead the way."

I nod. I don't know how much time we have, how close the Noswraith is. But it's coming; of that I'm certain. And it's a big one. I step to the door of the chamber, peer up and down the hall. All is dark, but with that strange darkness of the Nightmare Realm which allows one to see *just* enough. No sign of the wraith yet. I beckon, and Lir hauls Dig to the doorway.

Suddenly the *gubdagogs* at the end of the hall begin to sway and writhe, and the Noswraiths inside start shrieking. A lance of pure ice bolts through my heart.

Then a voice appears in my head. No, not *a* voice—many voices.

Worthless...

Useless...

Pathetic...

"Run!" I choke and grab Lir's arm, trying to spin her around. "Take Dig and go!"

"No, Mistress," Lir protests. "I won't leave you."

But Lir is not prepared to face this foe, not with her *gubdagogs*, no matter how well woven. I look up into her face, holding her eyes fast. "I'll cover your retreat. Please, Lir, trust me. Trust me and ... and save our boy."

Lir's eyes meet mine, studying me, reading me. In that moment I think she understands— there was more to my story than a mere broken gate. There was a choice: a bad choice, an evil choice. One I can never unmake. She sees my guilt, my shame, written across every line of my face.

Then, very softly, she says, "I'll save him, Clara. I promise."

To my utmost relief, she turns and retreats up the hall, opposite the way we entered. Dig manages to lift his heavy head, to look back at me. His eyes catch mine briefly, and I think there's recognition there. He opens his mouth as though to speak, but Lir carries him around a corner, out of sight. I can only pray to all the gods that Lir will get them both out safely, that whatever protection is left in her *gubdagog* necklace will be enough.

I turn to face the coming nightmare. My pen is poised, the nib pressed against the page. I take a breath. Then, not waiting for the wraith to show himself, I begin to write. Scribbling out words as fast as they will come, a furious scrawl. As I write, the shadows pull back, revealing that which they have hidden.

The Hollow Man stands at the end of the hall.

18

ALL THE CAPTURED NOSWRAITHS SCREAM AND WRITHE in their bonds. Do they too feel that overwhelming dread? That cloud of despair, that helplessness, that terror? They shriek, struggle, desperate to get free, but the Hollow Man has no use for them. His shadow-flickering eyes stare straight through the snarling threads, fixed on me.

A wave of *smallness,* of absolute *nothingness* washes over me. I want to curl up and die then and there. Anything to avoid that gaze, anything to avoid being seen and known for exactly what I am. Because that's what it feels like—as though the truth of my soul has been dug up from beneath all layers of pretense and spread out in plain view.

Worthless.

Small.

Useless.

He takes a step. His great arm swipes away *gubdagogs* like they're spider floss, all their humming magic meaningless against his greatness. The Noswraiths, liberated from their chains, skitter away, hissing and shrieking, eager to escape this greater being. But I cannot move. Not even to write the first word on my page. I stand frozen in the center of the hall, watching my doom bear down upon me. Multiplied voices dance inside my head.

You're nothing. You always were.

Nothing.

Nothing.

I feel it and know it to be true. I deserve what's about to happen to me. I deserve whatever pain he brings. The world around me melts away into writhing darkness. The hall, the door, the bedchamber sink and vanish, and suddenly I'm down in a claustrophobic coal cellar, damp and cold and trapped, trapped, trapped. There's no escaping this place. I don't deserve to escape this place. Shame, guilt, fear wrap around my senses like strangling vines, binding me. I huddle on the ground, my back to the wall, and know in the depths of my vile little heart there's no escaping the justice to come.

My gaze fixes on the cellar stairs, illuminated in a harsh red glow pouring through the doorway. A shadow appears, silhouetted and sharp. Then footsteps. Heavy, inevitable.

I'm coming for you.

I'll always come for you.

You cannot hide from me.

He is much too huge to fit into this small space. Reality is forced to bend around him, to make space for his malice, which extends beyond all physical boundaries. All reason, all thought, all will seem to rush out from my body and mind. I crouch, making myself smaller, hands over my head. If only I can become the nothing I am, small enough, inconsequential enough. It's my fault after all. My fault when those long fingers wrap around me, squeeze my body, crush my ribcage.

Shadows dance from the Hollow Man's eyes. He will swallow me. He already has—my soul, my spirit. This last act, this last atrocity is hardly the worst. He drags me inevitably toward that gaping hole in his chest. He will stuff me inside, fill his emptiness up with everything I am, his unique form of devouring. And I am helpless, useless to stop him. I'm not sure I even want to.

I know his name. In that moment, when all other thought has fled, that one spark of knowledge takes light and burns with absolute clarity. I know his name, but what good does it do me? What use is such knowledge when I cannot even wield a pen?

A pen.

A pen.

I look down at the fountain pen in my hand, glinting bright and gold. I haven't lost it. The awful dark of that cavernous chest yawns before me. A blast of foul stench fills my nostrils. I am ready to succumb, almost too weak to fight, and yet . . .

With a last gasp of defiance, I draw my hand back and fling

Oscar's pen straight into the hollow. It turns once, twice, shining with its own light. Then it vanishes between those open, broken ribs and into that black center.

The Hollow Man stops. His body shudders. His massive head tilts, looking down at his chest cavity. Though his face is too hideous to register expression, a sense of *shock* emanates from him. His grip on me loosens, and I slip through his fingers, landing hard on the stone floor. Then he paws at the hole, fingers scrabbling, as though trying to reach inside to snatch the pen back. Black blood oozes, spurts.

The Hollow Man throws back his head and roars.

By then I'm on my feet. The spell broken, my frozen veins are on fire once more, driving me to action. I turn and run. The images of the cellar walls are faded, misty, and I plow through them, back into the solid reality of the palace passage strung with *gubdagogs*. Some vague part of my awareness remembers that I need to give Lir and Dig time to escape, so when I reach the end of the passage, I don't take the turn that would lead to the front entrance and out into the city.

I turn toward the library.

I'm not sure what drives me. There's no conscious thought, only one instantaneous decision after another. I simply run, heedless of all other wraiths. Perhaps Lir's necklace hasn't lost all its power yet, or perhaps the other nightmares simply part ways to make room for the Hollow Man. They scatter before me, tattered shadows and high-pitched keening. I never slow my pace.

Heart throbbing, I turn a corner, expecting to arrive at the vaulted hall before the curved stairway leading up to the library doors. My feet skid on polished stone, arms wheeling as I come to a halt. This isn't right! Damn it, there are no stairs rising before me. The palace melts away, and I'm standing before the open cellar door. The stairs lead, not up, but down into darkness.

I know what waits below.

Pivoting on heel, I retreat through . . . not the palace. Gods spare me, I'm in the Nightmare Realm again. It looks dangerously like my old home. I cross the living room, past Mama's old rocker, ignoring the way the walls shiver and the shadows churn. I've got to get out, back into Vespre and the waking world. I can't linger here. The stairwell yawns before me, and I race toward it, thinking to climb back to awareness. But the stairwell doesn't lead up like it should. It points down, back to the cellar. I choke on a scream, bracing my hands on either side of the doorframe, just stopping myself from tumbling. Red light and mist roil below.

You're not seeing rightly.

My heart stops. "Emma!" I breathe.

Of course.

Of course she's here.

The Eyeless Woman. Unleashed like the rest of them.

He's in pain.

He just needs your love, your understanding.

The mist churns, beckoning. Long-fingered hands clamp down on my shoulders from behind, and cold breath hisses in my ear.

You just need to see him as I do.

Then you'll know.

Then you'll understand.

She pushes. A small pressure at first, but harder and harder, until I feel the pull of that fall, feel my hands starting to slip. The absolute swallowing hunger of that mist calls to me. Death awaits, but it's tempting. I want to . . . I want . . .

A shriek rips through my ear, down into my brain. I scream, and my grip slips. I tumble forward, but a hand clamps down hard around my wrist. I stagger, stumble, and sink to my knees, but not on the cellar stairs. I'm back on solid stone floor. The writhing shadows of the Nightmare Realm shred and disperse, and even the red mist in my brain filters away.

I drag a painful gasp of air into my lungs. Though I'm stationary, my body still feels as though it's toppling, tumbling out of control. I press a hand to my throbbing heart, but my other wrist is still gripped fast. I turn sharply, eyes focusing on a withered, age-spotted hand and long fingers, so gnarled and thin. I drag my gaze along the length of an emaciated wrist and arm which protrudes from a tattered satin coat of faded purple and gold. From there I lift my eyes to a cadaverous face. Gray skin stretches taut across a prominent skull from which only a few long white hairs hang limply. Beneath a heavy, wrinkled brow, a pair of eyes gleam down at me. Violet eyes, shocking and brilliant in that hideous setting.

"Well, well, Darling," an ancient voice creaks. "Fancy meeting you here."

19

IT'S HIM. IT'S *HIM*.

Castien. My husband. Standing right in front of me. Here in Vespre, sharing the same space of existence as me.

But oh! Gods on high, he's so disastrously warped. So hideous. This is not the gray-haired, beautiful stranger I saw in Aurelis. This is far worse, far beyond anything I'd imagined. The very sight of him fills me with such loathing and dread even as my heart soars in my breast. The conflict is so great, for a moment I cannot move, cannot think, cannot react.

I know what's happened. I remember the slow creep of age and decay that came over King Lodírhal after his Fatebound wife perished. Over the five years of my Obligation in Aurelis, he seemed to rot away before my very eyes. But it happened over time. Shocking and terrible, yes, but a slow progress that gave one time to adjust. This? This is much worse.

"Castien!" I manage to breathe, my voice a strangled whisper. "Castien, you—"

"A moment, if you please," he says and releases my hand. He turns a little away from me, his hunched, withered body bowing over the book in his hand. I watch a quill feather bob as he scribbles out a last few lines. The volume seethes with the power of the spell it contains, red mist eking from between the pages. But the Prince finishes writing in a quick, mad scrawl, muttering, "And the name!" just as he reaches the end of the page. With a last flourish, he slams the book shut, and the mist evaporates entirely. Then he turns and holds it out to me. "I believe this belongs to you."

Mutely I accept the book and lower my gaze to the cover. The Eyeless Woman inside struggles and rages at being imprisoned, but the Prince, withered though he may be, is no less brilliant than he ever was. The binding spell will hold for a little while at least. Slowly I lift my gaze back to his. It's horrible to see those striking eyes set in that death's mask of a face. Rot has set in. Bits of his cheek have fallen away, leaving awful, raw wounds. He's missing one ear and most of his lips. There's nothing but a hole where his nose once was. If I didn't know better, I'd think he too was a Noswraith.

But he's not. He's Castien. My Castien, my Prince. Alive . . . if only just.

Something moves in the passage behind him. My heart jumps

to my throat. "The Hollow Man!" I gasp.

The Prince casts a look over his shoulder, every movement stiff and precise. Then he extends a claw-like hand to me. "Come, Darling," he croaks. "Let us make good our escape while yet we may."

I dare not put any weight on his offered arm for fear of breaking it in two. But I scramble to my feet and take his hand and elbow, supporting him up the long stairs. Every moment I expect the Hollow Man to appear, to descend upon us, to devour us. And there's nothing I can do. My one, pathetic defense is now used up. As for the Prince, he exhausted whatever strength he had on the Eyeless Woman.

But for reasons I cannot fathom, the Hollow Man does not appear. Was he distracted by some other prey? Did he simply lose interest in me the moment I was out of sight? Or perhaps he did not wish to confront the Eyeless Woman. Noswraiths rarely interact, never by choice. He might view her as a threat to be avoided, like two tigers carefully eluding one another in the depths of the jungle they both terrorize. Whatever the case may be, we reach the top of the stairs, and I force myself not to drag the Prince along in my haste. As we draw nearer to the top and the library door, however, my footsteps slow and my heartrate quickens. "Isn't it dangerous?" I whisper, thinking of all those books of nightmares lining all those shelves across all those floors.

Castien chuckles, a dry, painful sound. "One might think so, mightn't one? But as it turns out, the liberated wraiths were all so keen to get out, they vacated the library premises as soon as they possibly could. It's all but empty now. Just a few sad little frights still floating mournfully about the lower levels. Many of the books slumber, as yet unaware their prison doors stand ajar."

We step across the threshold, and I'm immediately struck by a huge wave of emptiness. It's hard to describe, even to myself. The library has always brimmed with latent, barely-suppressed power, danger, and twisted life. Now it echoes like a carved-out husk.

I blink, looking about the upper story beneath the crystal dome. It's all so familiar. There is the guard rail circling the well down the center of the citadel. There is the big drafting table where the Prince once held meetings. There are the desks in their stone cubicles, the spiral stairs leading down to the seemingly endless levels, the book lifts which Nelle insisted were not meant to be ridden, but which the rest of us always used when she wasn't looking.

A wave of homesickness crashes over me. It makes no sense, and yet how can I deny it? I was dragged into this world against my will, forced into a war for which I was wholly unprepared and hopelessly ill-equipped, all with the inevitability of doom hanging over my head. But I was happy here. I was full of drive and eagerness. Even when the days and nights of perpetual twilight bled together, and I was so weary I feared I would drop, I loved the sense of belonging. As though I'd finally found both home and purpose.

It wasn't just the library, nor the work, nor even the people beside whom I labored. They were all important, yes, but . . . in the end it was *him*. Just him, him, always him, pushing me, prodding me, frustrating me. Driving me to the absolute brink of violence! Then a word, a look, a single gesture would set my heart dancing and my world ablaze. Because I belonged with him. Even when we both fought it with everything we had, even when that resistance made us enemies, that one truth remained.

"This way," the Prince says, leading me across the empty floor, past the drafting table and my old desk. I cast a longing glance that way, wishing I could step into it, refamiliarize myself with its contents. The Prince continues doggedly forward, his footsteps determined if tottering, his breath labored. He staggers, and I grasp his arm, just preventing him from tumbling headlong.

"Please!" I place a hand on his bony spine. "You must stop. Rest in one of these chairs, catch your breath."

He sighs and casts me a sideways glance from under his sparce brows. "It's not safe out here. My office, however, is heavily warded. We can regroup there."

He leads on, and I have no choice but to follow. I've never been to his office; it's always been his private haven, one I've not dared intrude upon. I used to avoid it, sensing strongly that he fled there at times to get away from me. Sometimes the draw of our Fatebond was too great, and he could not bear my proximity. I felt it too. Of course, I did, though not as strongly, not without fae blood driving my senses wild. All I knew was that it felt safer at times not to breathe the same air as him . . . though any atmosphere he did not share always seemed thinner, less satisfying.

Deep shadows surround the doorway leading to his office, but none of them writhe with nightmare energy. The Prince fetches a key from his pocket and unlocks the door. It creaks when he pushes it open, and a strange frisson of magic ripples in the air along the doorframe. The wards he spoke of? I'm not sure. Something feels off about it, though I can't say why. Apparently oblivious, the Prince steps through. He lights a little moonfire lantern and hangs it on a hook before calling back over his shoulder, "Shut the door behind you, Darling."

I hesitate, peering into that space which has always been off-limits to me. It's exactly what I would expect of Castien's office—an untidy disaster, but with a sort of care in the chaos that leads one to suspect he knows exactly where each item is. A tall bookcase full of unwritten tomes lines one whole wall, a rolling ladder reaching to the highest shelves. Tall, pointed windows with diamond panes offer a splendid view of Vespre City spread out below.

With a little shiver, I step across the threshold. The hair on the back of my neck rises as I pass under the lintel; if I didn't know better, I'd say it reminded me of passing through a Between Gate. But that doesn't make any sense. Hastily I pull the door shut and turn the latch with a click.

I turn just in time to see the Prince bow over the desk. He looks ready to collapse. "Castien!" I leap to his side. One quivering hand grasps mine weakly, and he allows me to help him around to the tall, velvet stuffed chair. Sinking into it with a heavy sigh, he tips his haggard face back and breathes out through tattered lungs. "Not as spry as I once was," he says and chuckles darkly.

I stare down at him, destroyed at the sight of his ruin. Of all the evils I've wrought through my stubbornness, my ignorance, my willful blindness, this is the worst. I want to sink to my knees, to let my head fall into his lap as I weep and beg his forgiveness. "What . . . what happened to you?" I ask instead in a whisper.

He opens one eye, peering up at me. His rotted lips twist, but his expression is strangely soft. "You, my dear, don't look a day older than the last time I saw you."

A knot tightens in my throat. "It's been two days."

He shakes his head and heaves another rattling sigh. "Not for me." His eyes drop shut again, his features slack save for a tight line between his brows. Though I study him intently by moonfire light, I can find no trace of the beautiful man I once knew. It's simply not there, not when his eyes are closed. He's a wreck, a gross approximation of a living thing. Yet somehow my heart still calls to him, desperate and starved.

"When I made my daring dive through the collapsing gate," he says at last, each word as labored as his breath, "it dumped me out in the middle of the Hinter Sea. Vespre was already cut loose and had disappeared from the horizon. I nearly perished swimming back to the shores of Noxaur. Since then, I've been searching the Hinter far and wide. Seven long turns of the cycle."

My eyes widen. "Seven years have done *this* to you?"

"What?" He cackles bitterly. "Am I not carrying my age well?"

My knees are weak. The nausea which has abated since my arrival in Vespre returns in a rush. I sink down on the edge of the desk, shaking. "I did this to you," I whisper.

"Well, yes. But not intentionally, I trust." He peers up at me again. Those terrible, beautiful eyes of his like knives to my soul. A claw-like hand, several fingers rotted away to stumps, moves as though to take mine, but he thinks better of it. Instead he folds both hands in his lap and blinks at me blandly. "It's the Fatebond, you see. The moment you were beyond this world, I began to fade. That one stolen kiss before the collapsing gate did wonders for my restoration, but then you were gone again. Beyond the boundaries of Eledria. The fading set in once more and steadily ate away my life force every day, every night, every hour."

Tears race down my cheeks. "How did you survive?" Memories of Lodírhal appear vividly in my mind's eye. "Your father . . . he lasted only five years."

"Ah, but you were not dead, my dear. So I could not die." He grimaces, his gums black and gaping. "I admit, sometimes I wished I could. I may have even contemplated taking matters into my own hands . . . but then I would think of you out there in the farther worlds. You and the child you carried. I would wonder if you were both alive still, and if my death might affect you. One can never predict how the Fatebond will react. So I clung on. Day by day, hour by hour. Moment by bloody moment." His grimace slowly twists into a smile. "Imagine my surprise when, mere hours ago, I suddenly heard your voice in my head, calling out my name. My true name."

"You heard me?"

"Of course I heard you. I told you I would, didn't I? And the power of your call led me straight here, straight to this damned island for which I've been searching all these damned years."

I can't even begin to guess how he managed to come so quickly, by what magic or what means. I can only look at him, both horrified by what he has become and humbled that, after everything I've done, he would still honor that vow, would speed across worlds and realities straight to my side, only to save me again from the monster of my own creation. To give me one more chance to fight, to survive, to atone for all I've done.

But what will it matter if, at the end of all my fighting and striving, I am to lose him?

"Castien," I say softly, wishing he would look at me, wishing he would give me the relief of his beautiful eyes. Instead he sits so still, I could almost believe that desiccated form has already given up its last gasp of life. "Castien, what will become of you?"

"Oh," he says, his brow puckering slightly, "not to worry, Darling. Now that I'm back in your lovely presence, I've already begun de-aging."

"What?" I blink, unable to disguise my surprise. "You have?"

He laughs weakly. It's nothing but a shade of the warm, bitter-chocolate laugh I know so well, the one that never failed to set my blood on fire. This laugh is cracked, sharp-edged, and grates on the ears. "Would you believe I looked significantly worse than this not two hours ago?" he wheezes. "Fewer teeth, less hair."

I shake my head. It simply doesn't seem possible. "Will you recover now that I'm here?"

All traces of laughter fade from his face. He looks up at me again at last, his eyes clouded and uncertain. "Not rapidly, I fear.

Not without . . . assistance."

I press my lips together. Then: "What sort of assistance?"

He lifts a hand, waves it feebly. "That's not for you to worry about. We have more pressing concerns at this moment."

That's when I know. I know exactly what he needs, exactly what kind of magic it will take to restore him. A shudder creeps up my spine. Because he is truly horrible, hideous. A ghoul sprung straight from the Nightmare Realm.

But those eyes of his . . . Those are the same eyes I know so well.

Something sparks within my chest.

I slide from the desk, standing before him where he sits, huddled in his chair. His shirt hangs open, revealing every protruding bone of his chest, all held together by paper-thin skin. I take a step nearer, stretch out my hand, and rest my palm against his heart. It beats wildly, frail and fast, like a dying bird in a snare.

His eyes flash, catching mine. "Please," he whispers hoarsely. "Please, Darling, I'm . . . I'm not sure I can bear it."

"You've borne a great deal, my love," I whisper. "I think you can bear a little more."

I lean over him. His eyes take up the whole of my vision, bright and burning, desperate. I will not see the rot, the ruin. I will not smell the decay emanating from his every ragged breath. I will only look into those eyes and see what I know is true.

Then I press my lips to his.

20

HE'S SO COLD, SO STILL. IT'S LIKE KISSING A CORPSE. MY body trembles at this proximity to decay, yet I refuse to recoil. I hold that kiss, hold that connection for as long as I can bear, pouring everything I have into that small point of contact between two bodies and souls.

At last I draw back, my eyes still closed. "Darling," he rasps, as though I struck him a blow.

"Hush," I whisper and cup his cheek. Then I lean forward and kiss him again. The spark in my chest flares brighter, stronger. It seems to rise from inside me, flowing up my throat, across my tongue, burning on my lips. I hold this kiss longer, until he gasps in sudden shock and perhaps a little pain. But when he starts to draw back, I grip his face harder, this time with both hands. "Castien," I whisper, "kiss me."

He obeys. His lips move against mine, molding and urgent. They're already fuller than they were at first brush. One of his thin hands touches my cheek. I press my own palm against it, holding it there. It's cold as ice, but I send the warmth of my soul into it.

In my head a clamor of resistance fights even now. All the pain of the angry words I hurled at him at our parting storm inside me, threatening to break us in two. I let them go—the hurt, the pain. Everything I caused and everything he withheld. They don't matter. Not here, not now. Neither betrayal nor anger nor abandonment nor any other hurt we've inflicted on one another. Here, in this moment, we are two broken hearts longing to be made whole again. It is terrifying—that gut-plunging terror one feels when standing on the brink of a cliff.

But I will not shrink from this fear. I will take the plunge. With him.

Suddenly he grips my shoulders, pushing me back. I look down into a face still old, still lined. But now I see him again—my Castien. Iron gray hair flows from his head in glorious waves, brushing his shoulders, framing features marred with pain such as one never sees revealed in the ageless fae. That pain only makes him more beautiful in my eyes. He rises from his chair, towering over me. He is like a great king of legend, no longer in his prime, but on whom the mantel of true majesty rests. He takes my breath away.

"You left me," he breathes, his voice hoarse and hard.

"You sent me away," I reply in little more than a whisper.

"You told me you hated me."

"I did."

He takes my face between his hands. "And now?"

I wrap my arms around his neck, drag him down to me. I don't care that he's not the youthful man I once loved and loathed. I don't care for anything except the knowledge that he is my Castien, my beloved, my Fatebound. Let the nightmares close in on all sides and devour us! I will have him. Here and now.

The energy between us changes. I'm no longer on the offense but suddenly the recipient of everything he feels, everything he needs. His lips against mine are savage, demanding. He's taken charge, and I am utterly helpless against the force of his passion. His hands are in my hair, gripping at the roots as his mouth devours me. His tongue slips between my teeth, ravishing, and I receive him with a moan that only excites him more. He tastes of salt and wide, lonely skies, and it awakens such a deep hunger in me I fear can never be sated.

He backs me up, away from the desk. I reach behind me, uncertain and unmoored. My hand grasps the cold bar of the rolling ladder attached to the bookshelf. I wrap my fingers around it, my arm up over my head to brace myself. His right hand catches hold of my wrist, pinning me there even as his other hand slides to my throat, fingers resting over my pulse. His knee parts my thighs, and I feel the swell of him pressed up against me, a pressure that calls to the ache in my core.

"Clara, my darling," he growls against my temple, breathing in my scent. His hand slides down lower, lower, molding over my curves. I arch into his touch, my eyes half-closing as I moan. For me it's been mere weeks since we were last in each other's arms, since our flesh became one. But it feels like a lifetime. His mouth explores my ear, my jaw, my throat, kissing, tasting, nipping. "I've burned for you," he says, releasing his grip on my wrist. I hold fast to the library ladder as he runs his hands over the shape of my body, his palms hot through far too many layers of fabric. I could scream for need of his skin against mine. "I've burned with a fire that could know no relief all these years."

"Forgive me," I plead, only just now realizing there are tears on my face. "Forgive me, my love."

He draws back, looks down into my eyes. The expression sparking in the depths of his dilated pupils sets my heart racing. He's changed again. His hair is raven black, streaked with threads of gray. His face is harder, sterner, older than the one I once knew, but so beautiful it hurts. "Forgive you?" His breath rachets hard and fast. "Oh, Darling! I forgave you long ago. My only hope now is that you can bring yourself to forgive me. For withholding the truth. For being a coward. For—"

I place two fingers against his lips. "It's forgotten," I whisper. "Forever. There's only you and me. There's only this moment." Taking hold of his hand, I press it against my beating heart. "My gown . . . it fastens up the back." I flick my lashes, peering up at him again. "Will you help me?"

With surprising gentleness, he turns me around. All the wild passion of his initial embrace gives way now to a lingering, luxurious precision that drives me wild. He unfastens the buttons, peels away the fabric, revealing the lacy chemise and corset underneath. Finally he slides my bodice away, and I feel the touch of his fingers against the curve of my neck and shoulders. Lava roils in my gut.

I yank the rest of the bodice away, drop it to the floor. With shaking fingers, I unfasten my skirt as well and let it fall in folds of fabric at my feet. Then I turn to him again, my breasts rising and falling, still caught in the restricting embrace of my corset.

Castien breathes out slowly, his gaze drinking in every inch of me before finally returning to my face. Playful light glints in his eyes. "And do you want my help this time?"

Heat flares in my cheeks. For a moment I flash back to the first time I'd stripped in front of the Prince, standing on a cliffside above a frigid sea. I'd refused to ask his assistance with my corset then but struggled with the troublesome laces on my own. He remembers as well by the look on his face. He stretches out one hand, running one finger lightly along the edge of my corset, toying with the lace, lightly brushing my skin so that it prickles deliciously in response. "You don't know," he murmurs, "how badly I wanted to rip off those remaining few garments and take you then and there."

"I wish you had," I answer breathlessly.

His eyes flare and his lips part in a smile so brilliant, it sheds years from his face in an instant. "And what would prim and proper Clara Darlington have thought?"

I know the answer—she wouldn't have thought at all. She would have absolutely given in to anything he tried, anything he offered. She would have devoured him with a desperate hunger she scarcely understood but which nearly consumed her every hour, both waking and dreaming.

But she is not here. That version of me is gone forever, everything I believed I was, everything I stood for, everything I thought I needed. And who is left? Just this poor excuse of a woman, her heart full of both remorse and hope. Hope that I may someday be worthy of the love this man freely offers.

He steps forward, unfastens the laces, and pulls the corset free, while I slip my hands under his ragged, wine-colored shirt, which now strains across the breadth of his chest and shoulders. I slip it off and caress his glorious, golden skin. Leaning forward, I kiss his chest, right above his heart. Then I kiss up to his throat and jaw, until he growls and claims my mouth once more. He pushes me back against the library ladder, his clever hands finding their way beneath my petticoats, sliding up my thighs until he finds my center. I gasp, my head thrown back as his fingers move in rhythm, toying with me, calling my heat to life. His mouth burns against my neck, my shoulder, down between my breasts.

"It's been too long," he sighs even as he rips open my chemise, heedless of the laces. "I feared I would forget the taste of you." He takes my nipple between his lips, sucking and teasing with the tip of his tongue before kissing his way over to the other. All the while his fingers play with me, and I can do nothing but cling to the ladder, propping myself in place. Fire builds in my stomach, ripples through my body.

"I dreamt of you," I whimper as though confessing a sin. "Of your touch, your kiss. I dreamt of . . . of . . ."

"Of what, my love?" he asks, his lips smiling against my skin. "Tell me your dream."

I tilt my head, looking down into his eyes as he kneels before me. My lips part, but I cannot make a sound. My breath is too tight, too fast, too eager. A lock of dark hair falls across his forehead, gleaming in the moonfire light. "Ah!" he says. "I know that dream well. It has haunted me these seven years." He pushes my petticoats up higher then kisses the inside of my knee, my thigh. His teeth scrape against my sensitive skin, sending thrills through my core. "Perhaps," he whispers, "we can bring that dream to life."

His tongue trails up, farther, farther, until he once more finds my center. I bite my lip, struggling to strangle my cries. A moan vibrates in my throat, and I grip the ladder hard, moving my hips in time to his rhythm. My fire, already stoked to fever pitch, mounts higher and higher with every stroke he makes.

"Castien." I let my head fall back as he licks and kisses with a ravenous hunger. "Castien, more. *More.*"

"Everything, my Darling," he answers. "Everything I have. All that I am."

I grasp the hair atop his head, twining my fingers in those dark locks as I sling a leg over his shoulder. He deepens his angle, devouring me like a starving man fallen to his knees at the banquet table. My body erupts as he takes me over the edge. His name bursts from my lips before vanishing in a wordless cry. I'm alive, every atom of my body singing in a magnificent symphony of sensation, of joy, of regeneration. In this moment I no longer care that we are in the depths of the Doomed City, surrounded on all sides by terrors and death. This dream is real. Real and bright and beautiful, beyond the reach of any grasping nightmare.

THE PRINCE

WE LIE ON THE FLOOR ATOP THE PILE OF HER DISCARDED skirts. Clara rests on her back, one knee drawn up, while my head lies gently against her stomach. She looks down at me. Me—her lover, her husband. She looks at me the way I once only dreamt she would look, with a light in her eyes I thought I should never see again. Reaching out one hand, she runs her fingers through my hair. "Is your glamour not fully restored?" she asks musingly.

Frowning I pluck the hair, pull it away from my face to focus on it. The moonfire glow reveals streaks of silver still wound through the black. It will take more glamour than I have the energy to expend to disguise it. "I don't know, I think it gives me a roguish edge," I say and smirk at her. "Wouldn't you agree? Do you not find me all the more irresistible with a grizzled edge?"

She quirks an eyebrow. "There is nothing about you that's *grizzled*. But . . . I do like it," she admits, stroking my hair again, swiping it back from my forehead.

"Then I'll keep it. For the time being." I roll over and kiss her stomach, so smooth and soft and gently curved under my mouth. My lips linger for a moment, before I murmur, "I feared the passage of time. Feared what it might mean for you and for . . ."

My words trail away, too terrible to be admitted. But Clara slips a hand down over her stomach, her fingers gently splayed. "It's been no more than two days for me, Castien. Two days since last I saw you." She shudders then, inexplicable pain in her eyes. "An agony, but a short one."

"And our child? Did Estrilde . . . ?"

She shakes her head. "I don't know. I believe . . . I hope . . . Oh, Castien!" Her voice breaks, but she struggles on bravely, catching my hand with hers. "Before the idea terrified me. Just one more impossible responsibility, one more small being dependent on me for everything in a dark, dangerous world. But now you're here, now we're together . . ." She drags in a ragged breath, tears sparkling in her lashes. "I want a chance to bring this life into this world, however dangerous it may be. I want a chance to drive back the darkness with the sheer audacity of life! But I don't know if our little one is still alive. I don't know if it survived traveling between worlds, being unmade and remade. I simply don't know. And I'm afraid."

I rest my head against her stomach, closing my eyes. At first I feel nothing but her tension, her terror. The pulse of her blood, the knot of pain and anxiety in her soul. But when I send my awareness down deeper, there is more to be discovered. Something small but bright and burning. An infinitesimal speck of infinite wonder.

"Keep that hope of yours alive, my Darling," I say, lifting my head and meeting her eyes again. "There's little more we can do. But maybe hope is enough."

The shadows in her face momentarily lift. She strokes my cheek with her delicate hand. "So . . . you didn't need . . . well, um." She flushes, lowering her lashes. Then: "You didn't need *more* to restore you?"

I prop up on one elbow and trail a finger along her bare skin, tickling around her breast and one hard, pink nipple. "What more did you have in mind?"

She bites her lip, that pretty flush deepening. "I think you know."

"Yes, I think I do." I bend over and kiss her bare stomach again, lingering and a little regretful. "But in fact, no—it would seem I do not need that particular pleasure to restore me." I sit up, rest one elbow on my updrawn knee, and gaze down at her. Gods, but I could indulge in this view for an age and never grow weary of it! In all those years of lonely searching, I had often tried to call to mind this very image. As time passed, and my life force drained, the memory faded to nothing more than an impression, a feeling. I'd held it fast in my heart, locked away as a final defense against despair. I'd long ago ceased to believe I would bask in her presence again.

But here she is. Bared before me, not just in body, but in spirit.

The change in her is remarkable, and while darkness yet simmers in the depths of her gaze, there is new understanding as well. I caress her gently, glorying in the way she moves and responds to my touch. "Oh, my Darling," I sigh. "I should love nothing more than to lose myself in you again and never to return. But I fear we haven't time." So saying I take her hand and help her sit up. She leans naked against my arm, rests her head on my shoulder, and I would give a kingdom to remain thus with her for a little while. "I'm sorry," I say, turning and murmuring the words into her hair.

"Sorry?"

"I should have told you about the curse on your brother. I should have told you before I allowed things to progress further between us."

She nods, not in agreement so much as acknowledgement. After a moment she says, "If you had, I wouldn't have been able to forgive you. We would have missed what little chance we had." She lifts her head from my shoulder, her doe-soft eyes holding mine captive. "You were wrong. But I am glad nonetheless. And I forgive you." Even as she says the words, those shadows in the depths of her gaze darken, as though in that instant, she relives terrors, choices, and losses beyond speech. When she finally speaks again, her voice is raw. "I'm sorry too. For my blindness. For everything I've put you through. Oh, Castien, I—"

Her voice breaks in a flood of grief and regret. She sobs incoherently, and when I put my arms around her, she tries to pull away. But I am too strong for her. Firmly I pull her to my chest, let her tears dampen my skin. "Feel it, Darling," I say. "Feel all of it. Let it come and let it go."

She trembles in my embrace, so fragile. Yet I know for a fact she has the strongest, truest heart of anyone I've ever met, if only it can be freed from that clenching fist which has so long held it captive.

"I don't deserve your love," she whispers at last, choking on the words.

"I don't deserve yours either," I answer, my mouth against her soft hair. "It's damn lucky for us love isn't about deserving."

She lifts her tear-streaked face to mine, allowing me to stroke hair back from her face. Then my lips find hers. This kiss is different from those we shared in those hot, hungry moments. This is a kiss of knowing and healing, of bitter experience and sweet acceptance. A kiss of reclamation. She has begged my forgiveness as I have begged hers. We have given and we have received. Our bond is stronger than it ever was before.

Strong enough to withstand the battle that lies ahead? That remains to be seen.

Slowly, reluctantly, I push her back enough that I can look into her eyes again. I don't want to say these next words, knowing the pain they will usher in. But we've stolen more time than we should already. "Oscar is here."

To my surprise she nods. "I know. I saw the Hollow Man."

My chest tightens. Memory of that monster passes through my mind's eye, and I feel once more like the old, doddering wreck I was less than an hour ago. "It would seem Oscar and Ivor arrived not long before you and I. When the gates were broken, the two of them must have been caught in the ensuing shock."

"Yes," Clara says. "The crone promised to deliver me to Vespre within three days of Oscar's arrival."

"The crone?" I frown. "You went to the Daughters of Bhorriel? Again?"

"It's all right," she hastens to assure me, though the expression on her face tells a very different tale. "Danny paid the price for me."

My blood freezes at mention of that name. If there was ever a man I came close to hating in this or any world, it's Daniel Gale. Not even Ivor holds that distinction in my jealous soul. "And what price was that?" I ask coldly.

"His heart."

"What?"

She tells her story, simply and softly. I listen with some resentment, not caring to have my opinions altered in the face of such revelations. My impression of her former sweetheart was of a small-minded, stubborn man. That he would make so great a sacrifice for the woman he loved, knowing all the while that she could never be his? Perhaps I misjudged him. Somewhat.

"That was well done on his part," I admit grudgingly when she tells of his interaction with the crone. "I would have done the same in his place."

Clara lifts her gaze to mine. "Ilusine paid a price as well."

"Ilusine?" Now that was not a name I expected to hear. Nor could I have prepared myself for the next part of the story she tells. Ilusine and

I had been close once, but we had parted on tenuous terms at best. I never would have thought she'd risk so much to save my beloved. Not for my sake. I'm not sure what I feel in that moment. Gratitude. And perhaps a little shame that I did not treat her better, that we had not managed to be kinder to one another in the end.

"I confess," Clara says as she finishes her account, "I had only one thought when I returned to that horrible house: reaching Vespre. Finding you, finding the children. Now that I'm here, though, I . . . I don't know what to do."

"That's simple enough," I say, smiling into her worried eyes. "We must figure out what in the nine hells Ivor has planned, then thwart it all costs." I lean back against the bookshelf, heaving a sigh. My thumb runs up and down the back of Clara's hand, over the delicate ridges of her veins. "But I have no idea what he's planning."

Clara's brow knits in that thoughtful expression I know so well. "Estrilde," she says after a moment. "Estrilde gave Ivor the bloodgem necklace."

"What?" The word bursts sharply from my lips. I fall silent then as Clara recounts those panicked moments after the Hollow Man attacked Aurelis, when Ivor, Oscar, and Estrilde made their mad flight to Aurelis Library. At the time she'd not understood what she saw, but now she remembers that necklace and its significance.

I listen grimly to the end of her tale. "That would explain a few things," I say darkly. "When I first arrived, I went down to the vaults. It looked as though the source of the initial outburst was the Eight-Crowned Queen. She must have escaped when Ivor ventured into her realm, trying to take control of her as Vokarum once did." I grimace, teeth grinding. "Hopefully she slaughtered him in the attempt. But it would make no difference. Idreloth is so powerful, her escape would have set off a chain-reaction. Mixael and Andreas alone would have no hope of containing the outburst. It's a miracle anyone got out of the palace alive."

"A miracle," Clara acknowledges, "and the *gubdagogs*."

"Why yes. I did notice an awful lot of those eyesores strung about the place." I squeeze her hand again then raise it to my lips and kiss her knuckles. "My mule-headed wife. Your stubbornness may have saved them all in the end."

"Perhaps," she smiles back. "Temporarily. But I don't understand." Her brow darkens once more. "Why would Ivor want to control the Eight-Crowned Queen?"

"Why do you think? Conquest. He fancies to set himself up as High King of all Eledria."

"Of course!" Revelation dawns on her face, followed swiftly by horror. "Of course he is Illithorin's heir! He must have been plotting all this time, back even when he first begged me to teach him how to read. He intended to take control of one of the Noswraiths. And who could stand against him if he succeeded? There are no great mortal mages left."

"Well, maybe one or two," I remind her.

"Yes," she acknowledges. "Oscar. Ivor must have learned about him from Estrilde. He must have set about seducing him just as he tried to seduce me."

"And if he'd succeeded, he would have had two Noswraith-creators at his beck and call, a formidable force indeed."

Clara shudders, seeing visions of terror and darkness sweeping across all Eledria. No corner of the fae realms would be safe. "It doesn't matter though," she persists. "The gates were all broken. Vespre is cut off from the worlds. Ivor can do nothing now."

"That's where you're wrong."

"What?"

I rise, leaving her cold and shivering on that pile of garments, and step to the door. Though it is locked and warded, we both know what a feeble barrier it provides against the Noswraiths. But other power shimmers around it, alive and responsive to my touch. I reach for it and feel the magic reaching back. My own magic . . . and my mother's.

Clara pulls her feet under her and closes her chemise across her breast. I'm very aware of her studying gaze on me. She is so sensitive to magic, particularly that of her own kind. Frowning, she rises, slowly approaches the door, and reaches out a hand, not quite daring to touch it. "What is that?" she asks softly. "It's not a ward, is it?"

"No."

"It feels like . . ." She hesitates, as though afraid to name her suspicion, afraid to let herself hope.

"It is the last remnants of the gate between this library and the library in Aurelis," I supply. "The one Ivor and Oscar passed through. The one Lodírhal destroyed when he set off the reaction that broke all other gates to Vespre as well. But when it came to this one, while he certainly broke it down, he did not have the means to destroy it. Not entirely. It was not his creation. He did not even know of its existence until he discovered it that day."

"How could Lodírhal not have known about it?"

"Because my mother and I kept it secret," I answer with a grin. "We worked together to make this gate as a means to visit one another without my father's knowledge. An innocent enough intention; he was so disapproving and protective of his Fatebound wife. He did not care for her to frequent Vespre more than absolutely necessary, but she enjoyed her time in the library among the other librarians. Besides she felt responsible for the denizens of the city as well as the dangerous books collected here."

Clara runs her palm up and down the door frame, never quite touching it, simply feeling the reaction of magic against her skin. "Does it still work?" she asks. Those big eyes of hers turn to me, shining with sudden hope.

"No. But I believe I could get it to open one last time. Vespre is so far out in the Hinter now, I'm not sure how long I'll be able to hold it." I grip her shoulders, my words low and urgent. "Clara, this is the only chance for the people of Vespre, and a slim chance at that. But if you can get as many of the city folk as you can up here to the library, I will open the gate and send them through to Aurelis."

I can almost see the images passing through her mind—the faces of her children, those scallywags she fought so hard to claim, to protect, only to abandon. Her need to save them is strong, far beyond any instinct for self-preservation. "How many?" she asks. "How many do you think you can send through?"

"I'll hold it open for as long as I can. Now that we've spent the last delightful hour together and my vitality is restored, I hope I can maintain the connection for some minutes. Even so, it must be done soon. The farther Vespre drifts, the harder it will be." I tip my head, holding her gaze, needing her to hear and understand my last words. "It may already be impossible."

She nods. Her complexion is very pale by the moonfire glow, and dark circles ring her eyes. But her brow tightens in that determined knot I know too well. "I'll do it," she says. "I'll bring them up. But you will come with me, won't you?"

My heart twists. "I cannot. I must remain and guard the gate. If Ivor is still out there, I cannot risk him finding it and getting through to Eledria."

"But surely he cannot open it! He is no king."

"He bears the blood of kings in his veins. With a simple gate like this, all he would require is someone on the far side listening for his call."

"Estrilde," Clara whispers.

I nod. "So you see, I cannot risk it."

"But for all we know, Ivor is dead already." She takes my hand in hers. "For all we know, the Eight-Crowned Queen devoured him."

"Let us hope so."

But we both know we cannot count on such a stroke of luck. I see the understanding in her face, even as she wants to fight me. I can't blame her; the last thing I want after everything we've been through is to part from her again. I want to take her in my arms, to hold her fast, to never let go.

Instead I set about packing her satchel with blank books and fresh quills. Then I assist her back into her dress, taking my time over the buttons, kissing the curve of her neck and shoulder. She responds to my touch. I feel the heat spark within her, and it's all I can do to keep myself from ripping these garments away once more, from losing myself in the delight of her closeness. The final button fastened, I wrap my arms around her from behind, and pull her against my chest. "If you would let me, Darling," I whisper, "I would open the gate now and send you and our child through. It would be a relief to know that you are safe." She stiffens, protests forming on her tongue. "But I know you would never allow it," I continue hastily. "I know you won't leave your other children behind."

"Not again," she responds firmly. "Never again." I nod and kiss her temple. Then I turn her to face me. "Castien," she says. Her eyes shine fearfully in the moonfire light. "Castien, there's only Mixael and Andreas left. The *gubdagoglirs* will do what they can, of course, but—"

"There is another."

She gazes up at me blankly. Then understanding comes over her in a flash. "Vervain!"

"Unless I am much mistaken, she's still in her tower cell," I say. "She is a strong magic-wielder. She can help you lead the others back here. If you can get to her. If she is still alive."

Clara grips my forearms, her fingers tense. "I'm not sure I can reach her. The tower . . . it's on the opposite side of the palace. There are Noswraiths around every corner, and the Hollow Man is still out there."

She's right of course. It's a deadly game we play. But we need every player to our advantage if we're going to have any hope of success. "I have an idea," I say. Gently pulling free of her grasp, I step to the window, lift the latch, and push it open. Leaning out into the cold air, I whistle softly. Movement stirs among the rooftops of the lower palace. The unsuspecting might think it another Noswraith, attracted by my call. But it's not a nightmare which takes to the air on broad, white wings. It's a dream.

My wyvern circles in the air before us, every line of its body a poem brought to life. Clara gasps. The next moment she steps to my side, gazing out at the exquisite being. It draws in close to the window and catches hold of the outer wall with its hind legs, balancing there, its delicate head level with the sill. It ruffles its feathers in greeting, large eyes blinking. Clara reaches out to scratch the beast under the chin. "Is this how you made it to Vespre so swiftly after I called your name?"

"Yes." I step back from the window to my desk and open one of the lower drawers. "We have been searching far and wide across the Hinter Sea for the better part of these last seven cycles. That fellow has been my constant and often only companion all the while."

My hands find a little box buried beneath sheets of loose paper. Withdrawing it, I lift the lid. There on a bed of silk rests a crimson quill. A mage's quill—my mother's. Carefully, reverently, I pull it from the box and hold it up to the moonfire light. How vividly I remember when Clara first arrived in Vespre Library, carrying this quill with her. Fury filled me when I saw her with it. After all, her own written creation had been the cause of my mother's death. Back then I could not have imagined where our story would lead. I certainly could not have imagined doing what I do now.

"Here," I say, holding the quill out to Clara. She gapes, mouth open, eyes round. "You must be armed for battle, my valiant librarian."

She doesn't even breathe. She simply stands there, motionless, staring at the quill held so lightly in my fingers. Slowly she lifts her gaze to mine. "I can't, Castien."

"Of course you can, my Darling. Prove your mettle here and now. Rescue Vervain. Bring the children up from the low temple." I take a step toward her, grasp her hand, and press the quill into her fingers. "Let us undo what we can of the evil we brought into this city."

To my relief, she doesn't fight me but tucks the quill into her satchel. I give her the key to Vervain's cell as well, then take her trembling hand and guide her to the window. Her breath quickens, and her fingers tremble in mine. "You must take care," I urge. "There are airborne Noswraiths aplenty out there. But my friend here is swift and will carry you safely across the palace."

Clara swallows hard then turns those big eyes of hers up to me once more. "How can I bear to leave you behind? I only just found you."

"I know." I cup her face gently, pressing my forehead to hers. If only there was some other way. If only I might go in her stead, leave her here to guard the gate. But the risk is too great, and we both know it. "We will see each other again. I swear it."

Her lips find mine in a kiss so sweet, so hungry. I respond in kind, eager for her touch, for that connection, eager for everything she is. She tastes of tears and delirious hope, wild and intoxicating. I could feast upon such kisses for a lifetime and never crave any other.

But it ends all too soon. She pulls away, pinching her swollen lips between her teeth. Without a word she turns to the window, climbs onto the sill, and swings out onto the wyvern's neck. The dream-beast holds still, balancing carefully until she is settled in place. Her face is pale and tense, her satchel slung across her breast and resting against her hip. She looks at me over a shoulder of white feathers.

"Remember, Darling," I urge her, "you are more powerful than you know."

She nods. Then she buries her face in the soft feathers of the wyvern's neck just as it pushes off from the tower and launches into the sky.

CLARA

21

NOSWRAITHS SWARM THE PALACE BELOW. FROM MY PERCH astride the wyvern, I see them climbing the walls and towers, lurching along open parapets, hanging out of windows. Leering, hideous shapes, unnatural and brimming with malice. I don't spy any sign of the Greater Noswraiths just now, however. They seem to have gone dormant for the time being. But they're out there. I know it.

The wyvern soars over the palace rooftops and darts among towers, using them as shelter. I wish it would simply make a sprint for it, but this is probably safer. Best not to attract attention. If only I could take out my book and quill and be prepared to write in case of attack, but it's all I can do to grip handfuls of feathers, bow over the white beast's long neck, and pray this flight will be over soon.

More than anything I long for Castien. To have found him again and reclaimed him is a blessing far beyond anything I dared pray for. It took every bit of will I possessed to leave him again, and even now I must force myself not to turn the wyvern around and fly with all speed back to his study window.

Movement in the tail of my eye draws my attention. I turn sharply and catch my breath. A dark cloud rises from one of the towers, whorling wings carving patterns against the star-strewn sky. Terror surges in my heart. "Frights!" I hiss. I've seen them before. Small nightmares, but deadly, they'll strip the living flesh from your bones while you scream. Have they spotted us? For the space of three breaths, I dare to hope otherwise.

Then the swarm banks in the air and rushes our way.

Choking on a cry, I wrench my satchel open and grab one-handed for my book. I've barely pulled it out before the cloud of churning malevolence is upon us. The wyvern utters a fluting cry and darts forward. I latch hold of shoulder feathers again, and the book drops away, fluttering uselessly into darkness below.

The next moment frights surround us, tiny, bat-sized bodies like hunched little men with elongated limbs and lantern eyes. Viper fangs gnash ravenously at the air. Several bury those fangs into the wyvern's neck, its head, its wings. I let go with one hand, try to brush them away, but the wyvern banks, and I nearly fall. Shedding frights, my mount wheels through the air. I can do nothing but cling to its back, unable even to breathe.

With a sudden powerful propulsion, the wyvern breaks free

of the swarm. I have a dizzying view of a balcony and an open doorway before me, and some part of my brain comprehends the wyvern's intention. It puts on speed, creating distance between us and the frights, then pulls up sharply in midair and hovers over that balcony. I have mere moments to act.

Releasing my hold, I slip from the dream-beast's back and fall ten feet onto hard stone. The landing knocks the wind from my lungs, but I spring up, adrenaline burning in my veins, and race for the open door. I don't have time to worry if more nightmares wait in the shadows on the other side; the frights are a much too present danger. I dart into the shelter of the building, then turn and look back, lips parted to call for the wyvern. But the beast banks again and leads the frights away. It speeds across the sky, a streak of daydream beauty in the midst of nightmare darkness, a shining, angelic being, silhouetted against that endless backdrop of stars.

The frights close in. Shrieking, tearing. Shredding, devouring. I stuff my knuckles into my mouth and choke back a cry. There's nothing I can do. I'm too far away and too late. I can only watch as little bits of parchment paper float down from the devouring cloud of claws, teeth, and wings. They flit in the air like delicate snowflakes and waft away on the breeze.

The swarm seems to turn in search of their next victim. They'll be upon me in a moment. I step inside, haul on the heavy door, and shut it fast. Leaning my back against it, I cover my face with my hands. My heart throbs as though the fright's savage fangs had bitten into it. That dream, that beautiful dream! Castien's dream, the product of his beautiful mind . . . torn to shreds in an instant.

Despair wells in my chest. I'm alone. Trapped in this Noswraith-infested palace. Though I reach into my satchel and wrap my fingers around Dasyra's quill, what good will it do me? I couldn't save the wyvern. Who's to say I can save anyone else?

"Remember, Darling, you are more powerful than you know."

I close my eyes and see Castien's face again as he stands there with his mother's quill in his hand. His eyes, bright with the renewed force of his own magic, glowed with such love, such trust. I never deserved it. I still don't. But he entrusted me with this mission, and I must keep fighting. For him, for the children. For all of Vespre.

Dragging in a harsh breath, I straighten and dash the tears from my cheeks with both hands. The wyvern dropped me in the west wing of the palace unless I'm much mistaken, not far from where Vervain is housed. There's little light to be had in this echoing chamber, but at least the shadows don't writhe with nightmare energy. That's got to count for something.

I hasten from the chamber and out into a long hall with floor-to-ceiling windows. There's no glass to shield me from the outside elements, but enormous *gubdagogs* fill each empty frame, many of them twisting with captured wraiths. I step out into the passage and all but run to the door at the far end, wrench it open, and peer up the spiral stair. It's been some time since I last visited Vervain. She was such a sorry, haunted creature then. Her own Noswraith had nearly overcome her, and her mind had broken doing battle against it. The Prince, in his mercy, had given her safe haven in her little tower cell, keeping her far from all books, pens, and writing implements. But that was seven years ago. What has become of her since then?

I take a step into the stairwell. In that same moment, all the *gubdagogs* in the windows behind me tense suddenly. I feel the tightening of their strings, the sudden vibration of magic in the air. A frisson ripples up the back of my neck. Heart in my throat, I whirl on heel and stare back into the hall. There's nothing there. Not even in the deepest shadows. No sign of the Nightmare Realm closing in. No sign of an approaching wraith.

I remain frozen for a count of five. Then, with a firm push, I force myself to face the stairway again, to begin that climb. I've got to get to Vervain. I've got to get out of this palace. I can't just stand around waiting for some monster to get around to gulping me down. Taking the stairs two at a time, I pause only to peer through barred windows into the little cell rooms on my way up. Each chamber is darker and more forlorn than the last. "Vervain?" I try to call, unable to push more than a breath of sound between my lips. "Vervain, are you there?"

A patch of warm light gleams up ahead, just around a bend in the stairs. Not pale moonfire light, but a warm, reddish glow, shocking in the perpetual gloom of this unbound island. Heart leaping with hope, I hasten around the last turn and see the final cell door at the very top of the tower. Light streams through the window bars.

My footsteps slow. I press a hand against the stone wall and lean heavily, my breath tight in my lungs. The last time I saw Vervain, she was a ruined version of herself, halfway succumbed to madness. Our interaction was terrible, and I'd fled her presence, fled her manic laughter, and vowed never to return. Memories of that encounter return in a rush—the bony woman in her bloodstained and torn nightgown, sitting on the cold floor. The wildness of her hair, the lunatic burn in her eyes.

"What is your betrayal, little girl?" she'd asked me, spitting the words through her teeth. *"From whence does your darkness flow?"*

I shudder. My feet seem to fasten to the stone floor. Now that I'm here, I'm of half a mind to turn back, to make my escape from the palace and return to the temple alone.

A soft hum reaches my ear: low, rich, and warm as the firelight flickering through those bars. It's a lullaby, one I recognize from my own childhood. Mama used to sing it to me long ago. I stare at the door and draw a steadying breath. Then I creep forward and peer through the window into the cell.

It's not at all what I expected to find.

A cheerful fire burns on the grate and casts a cozy glow across the little space. A neat bed piled with quilts and pillows stands against the wall, and an upholstered chair sits close to the hearth. These are all the same furnishings I'd seen last time I was here, but the tapestries that once lined the cold walls are gone. Instead every inch of wall space is covered in intricate patterns. Handprints, I realize on close inspection, creating exquisite mandalas, so complex and interwoven with one another, it dazzles the mind. They seem to move and turn gently in the firelight, a riot of dancing colors, a visual harmony to that gentle, hummed song.

I swivel my gaze, searching. There, in the corner of the room where I'd last seen her is Vervain. But this is not the hunched, bony creature I remember. Her hair is pulled back and tied with a neat ribbon. Rather than a nightgown, she wears a simple gray dress, the sleeves rolled up to the elbows. She perches on a stool, pots of paint surrounding her. Even as I watch, she wipes blue pigment from her hand onto a much-stained apron, picks up a pot of orange, dips two fingers. Then she bends forward and, with careful precision, begins to add to an already intricate pattern, two dots of color at a time.

I watch in silence, captivated. Is it not a risk to let Vervain have paints in her cell? She might just as easily choose to scrawl out the name of her Noswraith and free it from its bonds. Someone—Mixael perhaps, as head librarian—must have decided it was worth the risk, decided it was time to allow the latent genius of Vervain Keldi some means of expression once more. From this angle she does not look wasted and frail as she once did. Still thin, yes, but possessed of a certain energy which harmonizes with the delicate patterns surrounding her.

"Vervain?" I call softly.

She doesn't startle. She merely draws her hands back from the wall, conscientious not to mar her work. Slowly she turns on her stool, lifting her gaze to the cell window. Her eyes widen slightly. "I know you," she says after a long silence.

"I am Clara Darlington. I am . . . I was a librarian. Along with you."

"Ah, yes." Vervain blinks once. "The Prince's little poppet."

Though there's no malice in her tone, my stomach clenches. I lift my chin. "The Prince's wife."

"Indeed?" Vervain picks at a fold of her apron, carefully wiping the orange from her fingertips. "Things have progressed these last few turns of the cycle."

I grip the cell window bars tightly. "Do you know what's happened here in the palace?"

"You mean the breakout?" A soft chuckle vibrates her throat. "I am aware."

A swift glance back around her cell reveals no visible *gubdagogs*. Which doesn't make sense. A determined Noswraith seeking prey could have easily found a point of access to this cell, yet Vervain seems unscathed. "Have you seen any sign of nightmare activity?" I ask.

"No," she admits. "My guardian has driven away all who might have tried to reach me."

"Your guardian?"

A small smile twists Vervain's lips. *"Madjra."*

I shudder and draw back from the window. I remember that name—the true name of the Hungry Mother, the Greater Noswraith who escaped her vault soon after my initial arrival in Vespre. I participated in her re-capture and was horrified to discover the fiend was Vervain's own creation. It had hardly seemed possible at the time. Since then I've learned a thing or two about Noswraiths. And their creators.

"Madjra wants me for herself," Vervain continues, turning in her stool to face the wall once more. She tilts her head, contemplating her complex array of patterns, and I'm obliged to strain my ears to hear her next words. "When we go back down that winding stair, she will come for me."

A pit seems to open in my gut. I remember how vicious the Hungry Mother is, how terrified and small I felt in her presence. My career as a Vespre librarian was nearly cut short the night she got loose. If she is truly stalking Vervain, it would be better to leave her here. But I can't abandon her. She is alone up here, with no one left to help her, no one even to bring her fresh food and water. To turn away now would mean to leave her to a slow death by starvation. Better to take our chances against the wraith.

I fetch the key from my satchel and, before I can change my mind, unlock the cell door and push it open. It creaks loudly, startling Vervain. She turns, her eyes wide and staring as though she'd forgotten I was there. At sight of me, however, her face calms once more. "Come," I say and reach into my satchel, producing both a book and a quill. "You'll need these. The whole palace is crawling with Noswraiths."

"The Prince forbade me from touching pen and ink."

"The Prince sent these for you now. So that you may join the fight. So that you may help us save this city."

She studies that quill. Then very slowly she stretches out her hand and approaches the open doorway, like a captive bird uncertain whether or not she should fly through the open window. Just as she reaches the threshold she stops. Her gaze moves from the quill to my abdomen and fixes there. All the color drains from her cheeks, leaving her pure white. For a moment she stands not breathing, not moving.

Then her eyes flash, catching mine. Light from the fire reflects off a sheen of tears. I remember suddenly the history Nelle related to me—the tale of how Vervain's Noswraith came into being. The fear, the pain. The impossible choice she was forced to make, the loss she suffered. All so many years ago. Yet it haunts her to this day.

Her mouth opens, closes. Then she swallows and straightens her shoulders, plucking the offered quill and book from my hands. "Let us go, Miss Darlington," she says at last in a clear, calm voice. "Let us face what must be faced with courage."

I lead the way back down the winding stair. We progress slowly, for Vervain is timid and weak following her long imprisonment. When we reach the base of the tower at last, I push the door open and peer out into the long hall. The *gubdagogs* in the windows shimmer like spiderwebs, but there's no sign of roiling nightmares in the deeper shadows. "The way is clear," I whisper and step out, motioning for Vervain. We proceed silently, Vervain's bare feet making no sound on the flagstones. My senses are on alert, ready for anything.

Yet I am entirely unprepared for the darkness which erupts suddenly all around us. It's like an explosion but soundless, heatless. Nothing but pure energy, writhing with malice, crawling down the walls, rolling across the floor, permeating the humming threads of the *gubdagogs* as though they aren't even there. I leap back and grip Vervain's arm. "Stay close!" I hiss, pulling her to my side. My other hand plunges into my satchel. I drag out both book and quill and flip frantically to the first page, but before I can write a single word . . .

Mama's here.

The voice fills my head, oozing down into those deepest crevices of my mind, those primal spaces of thoughtless instinct, of unmitigated fear.

Mama's here, my sweetness.

Come to Mama.

I turn slowly in place. I'm so small. My whole spirit is contained in a tiny, frail form, tottering and unbalanced. I lift little hands, far too clumsy to hold a pen, to write a line of text. These hands are meant for clasping, holding, clinging. Needing. I need, oh! I need! I need safety. I need warmth. I need strong arms wrapped around me.

"Mama?" I say, my voice small and trembling.

A shadow falls across me. I turn, unsteady on my feet, and tip my head back, looking up and up and up some more into the face looming high above me.

The Hungry Mother smiles.

22

SHE'S HUNCHED OVER SO FAR, THE PEAK OF HER SPINE IS the highest point of her body. Nevertheless she towers ten feet above me. Sparce black hair wafts from her skull, hanging over her face so that all that shows is her wide, ravenous mouth. Naked, sagging breasts distended, limp belly flopping to her knees, she is indeed a nightmare to behold. But when I look at her, I love her. Love her with the absolute love of a child.

"Mama!" I cry, lifting my hands.

Yes. Mama is here for you, sweetling.

Her lips don't move. Her mouth remains fixed in that wide grin, and her voice simply appears in my head, soft as shadow. She lurches toward me, her overlong arms dragging on the paving stones, trailing blood from her fingertips. She takes three paces toward me, and I take two, hastening to meet her.

Then a hand clamps down around my wrist, yanking me hard. "Miss Darlington!" Vervain's voice snaps in my ear. It's just enough to jar me back into awareness, back into my own adult body. It hurts, and part of me wants to resist. It's better to be a child, better to hold out my arms to that mighty power, secure in my own helplessness. Now I must face that horror for what it is—looming death, dragging itself toward us.

I look down at the book in my hand, the pages blank. My mind seems to scramble, unable to conjure a single word now that I need it. But a humming of magic draws my attention, and I turn to the window nearest me where a *gubdagog* hangs, unfilled and waiting. I lick my lips. "I have an idea."

"Better be a good one," Vervain replies as that nightmare closes in.

I don't know if it's good or not, but I haven't a moment to waste with doubt. Springing into action, I leap for that window and the single long cord hanging from the sill, just in reach of my hand. I grab that cord and yank with all my might, half afraid the entire tangle will simply disintegrate there and then, dropping bits of debris on top of me.

Instead the *gubdagog* seems to launch from the window into the hall. It falls across the Hungry Mother's bent spine, drapes over her head, her shoulders, her awful, dragging limbs. I yank the cord again, and the tangle tightens. With a roar, Madjra is wrenched off her feet, wrapped up in the snarl of threads.

I don't wait to see more. Grasping Vervain's hand, I drag her after me down the hall. The Hungry Mother's bellows echo behind us. "That troll spell will never hold her!" Vervain cries.

She's right. Even in that brief glimpse, I'd seen how the *gubdagog* struggled to grasp her flailing limbs. She's simply too powerful. She must be bound with words or she'll be upon us again in a moment, stalking our footsteps through the palace and into the city streets.

We reach the end of the long hall, duck through the doorway into the chamber beyond. Only then do I skid to a halt and turn around, book and quill in hand. "What are you doing?" Vervain pants, gasping beside me, hands on her knees.

"What does it look like I'm doing?" I flip the book open. Before I can write a word, however, Vervain's hand comes down on top of the page. Startled, I look up into her wide eyes. They shine with a strange light, like the energy of the Nightmare Realm, only brighter, stronger.

"Madjra will not be bound again," she says.

She turns from me then, steps back through the open doorway into the hall. I try to cry out her name, but the sound dies on my lips. When I attempt to reach out, to catch her shoulder, I find I've lost the ability to move. What is happening? Am I in the Nightmare? Is my consciousness split? Is there a part of me which stands in the real world, writing out a spell? Or is this Vervain's spell, Vervain's work? I can't tell. I can't do anything except watch Vervain progress into those churning shadows, away from me.

She does not have a weapon in hand. She is so small, so delicate and fragile, with her bare feet and her simple gray gown. She makes for the twisting, writhing *gubdagog*. The Hungry Mother sees her coming. Her awful mouth leers into view between spell-threads. With a powerful wrench, she pulls a distorted arm free, reaching out for her maker.

Mama's here.

Her voice burns in my brain, dark and terrible.

Mama will hold you.

I want to scream and beg Vervain to flee. But she does not stop. Neither does she crumble into childlike fear and innocence. I blink, narrow my eyes, struggling to see. Because it seems to me that Vervain is . . . growing, somehow. Though the physical frame of her body is as small as ever, something about her shifts, as though her spirit pours out through the seams of her being and fills up the echoing space around her. Energy thrums, like the strange musical hum of the mandala patterns she painted on her walls. A song of peace, a serenity of soul. Beautiful and simultaneously inexplicable.

The Hungry Mother roars, her free arm tearing at the *gubdagog* threads. They snap, strain. The spell won't hold much longer. But Vervain never hesitates. She draws nearer, holds out one hand toward the monster, fingers relaxed.

"I see you, child," she says.

With a snarl and a last vicious twist, the Hungry Mother rips free of the *gubdagog* and lands on the floor in a pile of limbs.

Pulling herself upright, she looms higher and higher, towering over Vervain. Lashing out with one hand, she smashes into the stone wall. Broken rock falls in a shower, and dust fills the hall, whirling with the nightmare darkness.

"Vervain!" I cry and try to run, whether to her or away, I cannot say. It doesn't matter. I simply cannot move, cannot tear my gaze away from the two of them.

Vervain stands unmoved in the face of Madjra's slavering rage. "I see you," she says again. "I see you and I know you."

The Noswraith rears back her head, awful hands ripping at the straggling strands of hair hanging from her scalp. Her cruel, long-nailed hand strikes at Vervain's face, razor nails missing by inches. The wraith recoils, sags into herself and the *gubdagog* threads still hanging from her limbs. She rips more of them away, shredding her own flesh in the process. Raw, open wounds cover her breasts, her belly, seeping ribbons of black blood.

Vervain steps closer. Now she is within easy range of those awful hands. One more swipe, and the Hungry Mother can crush every bone in her body. She can lift her off her feet, bite her head clean off her shoulders. But Vervain doesn't hesitate. She keeps moving forward, one foot after the other. "My darling," she says. "I see you." Then she puts out both hands, reaching for the monster's face. "I see you, Vervain."

My stomach tightens as though I've been punched in the gut. All the air escapes from my lungs in a single burst.

The Hungry Mother roars again, but she's smaller suddenly.

Smaller and shrinking rapidly. Still snarled in *gubdagog* threads, she collapses into herself, a horrible sack of bones wrapped in loose skin with lank hair. That awful, rictus mouth gnashes viciously. Nightmare shadows whirl up from the floor, obscuring her in a dense, dark veil.

"Vervain!" I try to call out. But Vervain walks straight into that maelstrom, out of sight. I cry her name again and again and, finding my feet, manage three lunging steps forward. I cannot seem to make myself go farther. Fear binds me, fear of that darkness, that storm. I look down at my hands, struggling to discern whether or not I hold a book and quill. I can't tell. I don't know if this is my real body or merely my projected form. I'm trapped between the two states, utterly helpless.

Suddenly the darkness parts like a curtain, revealing a strange tableau. It's not the gruesome vision I would have anticipated, but a most unexpected sight: a woman, kneeling, holding a small child against her shoulder. The child weeps as the woman strokes her hair, murmuring words I cannot understand.

"Vervain?" I say again, taking another step closer. But the darkness enfolds them again, deeper than before. It whirls up around my ankles, spreading too fast for any thought of flight. I open my mouth to scream, but the nightmare overcomes me, pours into my mouth, my nose, pours into my body—

I blink. Drag a deep gasp of air into my lungs.

I'm lying on the cold stone floor. It's dark all around, but the shadows are quiet, not alive and churning. Faint starlight gleams through windows strung with *gubdagog* threads, which waft gently in a breeze.

A cry rising to my lips, I scramble upright and cast about for my book and quill. They lie a few feet from me, and I crawl to them quickly, snatch them up, and turn the pages of the book. They're all blank. I never wrote a word. Slowly I look around the hall. Everything is back to the way it was. The broken wall is mended, the torn *gubdagog* reestablished in its place. There's no sign of either the Hungry Mother or any of the damage she wrought. But Vervain . . .

She's there. Kneeling in a pool of starlight, her back to me. Alone. One hand hangs limp at her side, numb fingers wrapped lightly around a white quill pen.

I rise unsteadily and clutch my book and quill against my stomach. When I try to call Vervain's name, no sound will come. I approach her slowly. She doesn't turn, not even when I stand at her shoulder, close enough to peer down at the book in her lap. It lies open, displaying blank white pages. No nightmare energy emanates from inside it, no sign of magic or containment. Did she not bind the Hungry Mother? Is the wraith still free and on the hunt?

"Vervain," I say softly. Summoning my courage, I place a hand on her thin shoulder. She startles, lifts her head, and looks up at me. I let go and take three steps back, shocked. Shocked because her face is so . . . calm. So serene. Even as tears course down her cheeks and fall to her breast, an expression of peace shines from her eyes. "Vervain," I gasp and shake my head. "What happen—"

Her eyes widen. *"Look out!"* she cries.

Propelled by pure instinct, I throw myself to the ground. A whistle of cold steel rushes through the air just overhead. I land hard and roll. When I come to a stop, I pull myself upright, every muscle tense, every vein pumping with adrenalin.

Throwing back my head, I look up into Ivor's leering face.

23

THIS IS NOT THE BEAUTIFUL FAE LORD I ONCE KNEW—THE image of golden perfection, a godlike being of majestic glamour. This is the creature that returned from the pit. The being Estrilde and Oscar were willing to pay my child's blood to retrieve. Nothing but a faint echo of his former beauty lingers in his face. Instead he is warped, grotesque, with his bulging eye and his raw, puss-filled, open-wound skin.

Gone too is the way he once looked at me, all admiration bordering on adoration. There is only hatred in that one-eyed gaze.

"Well, well, Clara Darlington," he says, his voice a ragged rasp. "We meet again at last. Do you know me? Please tell me that cursed oblivion has faded from your mind. It would not be so satisfying to end your life as a stranger."

I rise slowly, standing on the balls of my feet. I offer no answer, but Ivor smiles, that horrible, lipless mouth peeling back from blackened gums. He looks like a Noswraith himself, a creature born of wrath and sorrow. "I see the truth in your eyes," he says, taking a step toward me. He brandishes a sword in one shaking arm. Its sharp edge glints in the starlight. "You know me. You remember the lovely times we shared. Do you recall as well how you betrayed me? How you thought to send me to my doom?" He widens his stance, throwing open his arms. "A destiny like mine is not so easily thwarted. Not even by you or your precious prince."

Movement catches the tail of my eye. I glance to one side, see Vervain rise, pen and quill in hand. But what use are such weapons against a physical sword? Ivor shoots a disdainful look her way, his awful eye rolling. He takes her in and dismisses her in an instant, focusing his attention back on me. "Your brother," he says, "my sweet Oscar tells me I should keep you alive. He claims you will be useful to me in the days to come." He tips his head to one side. It looks so unnatural, like his neck ought to break but doesn't. "It seems he was right. You found a way back into Vespre when all the gates have been broken. If you found a way in, there must be a way out."

I cannot let my face reveal the truth, so I fall back on a trick I've learned since childhood—a smile. Bland, meaningless. A disguise for anything else my face might like to betray. "I'm sorry to disappoint you, my lord," I say, my voice calm and measured despite the leaping of my heart, "but the way I took was one-use only. Unless you're willing to make another bargain with the Daughters of Bhorriel, you'll not find it again."

Ivor's eye narrows. He bargained with the crones once before, when he convinced them to place a blood-curse on Castien. Whatever price he paid must have been terrible indeed. "You're lying," he snarls.

"I am not."

"You're human, through and through. You lie as you breathe."

"Not about this."

He raises his sword, arms trembling. "Tell me the truth, Clara Darlington. Is there a way off this island?"

I don't hesitate, not for a moment. "All the gates are broken, my lord."

Something in my voice must give me away, for Ivor laughs. He angles his sword, pointing the blade at my throat. "There!" he cries. "A lie. A perfect, exquisite lie. Now tell me—"

He breaks off with a strangled cry, falling backwards. It takes my dazzled eyes a moment to realize Vervain is latched onto him from behind, her arms wrapped around his throat. He cries out as she wrenches him back, and the edge of his sword nicks my jaw. I tumble to the floor, stunned. Vervain is stronger than she looks. Not long ago, Lord Ivor would have crushed her like an insect without a second thought. Now, broken as he is, he struggles to fend her off. She yanks his arm, and he drops the sword. Quick as a cat, she swipes it up and stands with the tip of the blade pointed at Ivor's heart.

"Get behind me, Miss Darlington," she says, puffing and winded. A strand of graying hair falls across her forehead. I scramble to my feet and hasten to her back. Her arms, holding that sword upright, begin to tremble. If she doesn't act now, if she doesn't run him through, he will get away.

"He's the enemy, Vervain," I hiss. "He means to invade Eledria with Noswraiths, to set himself up as High King."

Ivor's eye flicks to me. "So you know about that, do you? Did your brother tell you?"

"I figured it out for myself."

"Another lie," Ivor sneers. "You're trying to protect your brother. You don't want me to punish him for betraying my confidence."

"Believe what you like." I lift my chin, meeting his gaze over Vervain's shoulder. "It makes no difference. You will never rule Eledria. You will never leave this island. You, like the rest of us, will perish at the hands of the monsters you yourself have unleashed."

A slow, dreadful smile rips across Ivor's ravaged face. "Oh, is that what you think? That I, like the rest of you, should be cowering in my boots, arms over my head, praying to all the gods who have long since forsaken this place?" He reaches a hand inside his ragged shirt, his one eye sparkling. "I have no need of gods or prayers. Nor will I cower, not for monsters, not for nightmares. Certainly not for the likes of you."

He draws out the black gemstone hanging on its chain around his neck. With a single tug, he breaks the chain and holds the necklace out. The stone swings back and forth, a hypnotic rhythm that captures my gaze. Everything else fades away, until that gemstone dominates all existence. That stone, and the dark spell it carries. A spell of deadly love, of suicidal passion. Of pain.

"There is not one of your man-made monsters that does not fear my Beloved," Ivor purrs. "She will protect me."

As the words leave his mouth, roiling darkness gathers around the stone. Suddenly that darkness solidifies into a towering form, pale-skinned and exquisitely sculpted. A siren, a seductress. Her long hair hangs in glossy waves down her back, and between her bared breasts, the bloodgem necklace glints with its own spell-light.

I recognize her. I've seen this face before. But then the head was severed and stuck on a metal spike, displayed in Lord Vokarum's dining hall. Even then I had been struck by her beauty, though it was nothing compared to this. She is terrifying and totally consuming. The mere sight of her sets my body on fire with a lustful need I cannot comprehend. My mouth drops open in dumb wonder and longing.

But she takes no notice of me. She bends, catches Ivor by the front of his shirt. For a moment I believe she will devour him as Idreloth devours all her husbands—biting off his head and guzzling his blood. Instead she lifts him off his feet and plants her lips against his, a sensual, devastating kiss, her plump lips drinking in his horror-ravaged mouth.

Then she lets him go, turns, and faces me. I want to drop to my knees before her, to beg for such a favor, for one such kiss. The urge is so great, I take a step toward her without realizing what I do.

Vervain puts out a restraining arm. "Beware, Miss Darlington!" she says. "Remember what she is."

Startled from my fog, I shake my head and look again. In that moment I see Idreloth, the Eight-Crowned Queen, as she truly is, as the old song once told:

> *The lover, the loner, the mother, the crone,*
> *Sister and slayer, the flesh and the bone.*

All of her is visible to my eye at once, all eight terrible personas. The Prime Head is at the center, long black teeth gnashing, dripping with blood. The others surround her, flashing in and out of view. She steps toward me, moving with sensual grace on eight sets of limbs that overlap each other, blending in and out of perception. One instant, she is beautiful, the next horrifying, then heartbreaking, all within the space of single heartbeats.

Tell me, my sweet, a voice of pure silk and knives whispers in my head, *have you come to taste of the pleasures I offer?*

I stagger back, reaching for book and quill. But I don't have them. I am fully in the Nightmare Realm now, trapped in this space of reality with Idreloth. There is no protection from this being, this great and terrible darkness. I stare into her eyes, all sixteen of them, and know that I am lost.

A burst of flame erupts before me, blinding my eyes. I scream, throw up my hands, and stagger back. Blinking with pain, I peer out through my fingers to see a silhouette carrying a flaming sword step between me and that oncoming wraith. At first I cannot make sense of it. Then she looks back. Vervain's wide eyes stare into my own. In a flash of clarity, I see her standing before me, book open, writing a counter spell with a swift, sure hand. I blink. The image of the nightmare closes in again, and Vervain is there, wielding that sword.

"Run, Miss Darlington," she says.

"No!" I cry, even as my feet carry me three paces backwards. "I won't leave you!"

Her eyes flare with spell-fire. "You must think of the life inside you now," she says and angles her sword in an arc of red flame. "Go. Save your child. Save all the children."

Then she turns and raises her defense just as the Eight-Crowned Queen descends upon her. She swings her blade straight for the nearest of those eight necks. There's a flash of light, a burst of heat.

I turn. And I run. Run in such a blind panic of terror, if the gods were not with me, I would easily leap right into the arms of another Noswraith. I simply cannot be cautious, cannot find the strength to care. Terror pulses in my veins, driving my footsteps across the paving stones. I leave the hall behind, escape into the next passage, and plunge into shadow. But it's not the living, moving shadow of the Nightmare Realm. This is real shadow, real darkness, and that gives me hope. I speed on, faster than before, my heart thundering in my ears.

A scream echoes across the stones behind me—a human

scream, cut short in agony.

Tears stream down my cheeks. Vervain! After all this, did I drag her from her cell only for her to die at the hands of such a monster? I should have stood my ground, should have found my quill and book. I should have tried to help. But I cannot stop my flight now.

A stairway yawns before me. I grasp the banister, only just keeping myself from falling all that long way down and breaking my neck. Half leaping, half flying, I take the treads four or five at a time. I recognize where I am; below me is the front entrance hall, and that door leads out into a courtyard riddled with nightmares. I don't care about that. Not now, not with Idreloth at my heels. I can think of nothing but escape.

I leap the last several steps, land hard on the floor below, take three paces, and . . . my feet sink to the ankles in black swamp muck.

24

"GODS BLIGHT IT!" I CRY AS MY BODY PITCHES FORWARD. My hands splat into mud, sinking elbow-deep. For a moment I can do nothing but remain where I am, down on all fours, frozen in place and staring into mire so deep and so dark. My heart pounds in my throat. This is just what my rational mind tried to warn me against—run too far, too fast, and you're sure to run straight into another Noswraith. I should have slowed, I should have watched my step.

It doesn't matter now. I know exactly where I am. This is Dulmier Fen, and I have no weapons, no defenses. No way out of this.

"Blight and damn!" I curse again. With a wrench I manage to pull my hands free and sit up onto my heels. But I'm still stuck fast in this mud. When I try to get to my feet, I flounder, flop, and topple forward again. My own dark reflection stares up at me from the wavering pool of water just inches from my nose. I stare back, as though seeing myself for the first time.

"Failure," I whisper.

Castien sent me to rescue Vervain. We needed her, needed all the help we could get in this last, wild hope of saving the children. But I failed. Vervain is dead.

I close my eyes but cannot escape the memory of Anj's voice in my head. *"The savior of Vespre,"* he'd called me. And they'd all looked at me as though I was some sort of heroine, returned in this final, desperate hour to turn the impossible tide. I was supposed to make a difference. Instead what has my arrival caused? I've only put more people in danger. Dig is wounded because of me, may have already perished. Dead like Vervain. Dead like the wyvern. Dead like we'll all be soon enough. Dead, dead, dead.

And it's my fault.

I feel their approach long before I see them, wavery figures, indistinct in the mist. Some close. Some far. Surrounding me. When at last I lift my heavy head, I cast my gaze across the broad, flat, empty expanse of the fen, endless on all sides and full of ghosts, each standing in his own dark pool. Young men and old, faded, thin, hollow-eyed. All alone. Desperately alone.

"Amelia."

I suck in a short breath. Turning slowly, I look over my right shoulder to see one of the ghosts drawn nearer than the rest. He's a young man with captain's bars on the shoulder of his ragged uniform. I know him. I've read this story before—read it and bound the wraith within. I've walked in this man's footsteps and encountered him face-to-face. He helped me once.

Some small, rational, librarian part of my mind protests this idea. Helped me? He's a Noswraith. This whole world is a Noswraith—the fen and the ghosts which inhabit it. A spell of tremendous power, born from a mind in tremendous pain, and brought to vivid life by the imaginations of those who read the original tale, who felt the truth of it in their bones. Only horrors can be wrought of such magic. The Miphates proved that truth long ages ago.

Yet there's something about this ghost, this young man who approaches me now. He doesn't move in steps but in a fluid, floating grace, like a low cloud moving above the surface of the fen. The lower half of his legs vanish beneath stagnant water and tall grasses. One hand presses to his abdomen, catching the guts that spill from a gory wound. His face is drained of all color, corpse-cold, but his eyes are bright as he looks down at me.

"Amelia," he says again. "Amelia, you came back."

He remembers me. He doesn't know my true name, of course. He can't. He can only know what was written into his creation, which includes a memory of the sweetheart he left back home. He's mistaken me for that sweetheart, but he remembers her and remembers that we met here once before.

It's not what I would expect from a Noswraith.

I push to my feet. I cannot flee—the mud holds me fast. Soon the fen will pull me under, and I too will be a ghost alongside the rest of these wandering souls, while my physical body, somewhere back in Vespre, lies on the stone floor at the base of the stairs. Drowned without a drop of water in sight.

But I'm not dead yet.

"They must be stopped. Ended. Destroyed." Umog Grush's imperative voice rings hollowly in the back of my head. I shake that thought away, however, and instead call to mind a different, more recent memory, that brief vision I'd glimpsed through the roiling darkness surrounding Vervain and the Hungry Mother. That strange, terrifying, beautiful image.

"I see you, Vervain," she'd said to her own creation.

This is the truth. The truth I've known for some time, though I've not fully understood it.

"Let me see you," I say, gazing into the captain's dead eyes.

"Amelia," he repeats, drawing nearer and nearer. He lets go of his abdomen, and his guts spill forth, trailing behind him as he stretches out both hands to me. "Amelia, Amelia, I should never have left you."

Horror rises in my heart. I feel the pull of the fen, but I force myself to look into his face, to look into his eyes. To search for what is truly there, not this grim apparition of death.

"Let me see you," I say again. "I know you're there."

He stops. His wavering form solidifies before me, or perhaps my vision sharpens. I see him, no longer wounded and dead, but alive.

His uniform is bright and new, a line of silver buttons adorning his proud chest. He sports a little mustache that must have taken him an age to grow, and there's a scar beneath his eye, a fine line of white skin that only one intimately familiar with his face would ever notice. He is everything he was meant to be, a bright young officer, full of optimism and arrogance, brimming with potential. But this is not the truth.

"No." I shake my head. "Let me see the real you."

His pretty face puckers, petulant and stubborn.

"Please," I urge. "What reason have you to hide from me? We are in this place together. Our own choices led us here. Why should there be any pretense now?" I tip my chin, wishing I could reach out to him. He's close enough, I might be able to take his hand if I tried. But I can't quite summon the courage. So I say again only, "Please."

He bows his head, his face momentarily hidden from me by the brim of his plumed hat. Then, slowly, he looks at me again. Hat and uniform melt away, along with all traces of youth, replaced by, not a phantom, but a man, very old and on the brink of death. Life drains from him in a river of pain that cannot quite sweep him away. He sways, his thin lips drawn back from gaping gums.

Then he whispers: "I failed them all."

"Who are you?" I demand. "Tell me your name."

"Amelia." His faded eyes flicker with understanding. "You . . . are not Amelia."

My heartbeat quickens. I know better than anyone how swiftly

Noswraiths turn violent when provoked. "No," I answer softly. "But Amelia would want you to tell me. She would want me to know." His solid form flashes back to the wafting phantom clad in that tattered uniform, cold and frightened and dead. Have I pushed too far? "Tell me," I urge, forcing myself not to look down at his gory death wound. "Please."

We are Dulmier Fen.

The voices whisper from every one of the ghosts surrounding me. They've closed in while my attention has been fixed on their captain. I glance around at all those dead soldiers, so pale, so stricken with horror and grief. I feel the pull of the hungry fen once more, feel myself sinking into the mud. Hastily I focus my gaze on the captain once more. "But who are you?"

We are endless.

We are desolate.

We are alone.

"I know you're in there," I persist. "This burden you carry is terrible. Was it a relief to put it down in words? Was it a relief to open your heart and let this pain flow out from your pen onto the page?"

The phantoms do not answer. They merely look at me. The fen mud is cold and lapping at my calves. I force myself not to struggle, knowing I will only sink faster. "I know you're there," I say. "I know because . . . I know what I felt when I first put everything down in ink and words. When I first let the page carry what was in my heart. It was like lancing a boil, painful and disgusting and such relief! I remember." I tilt my head to one side, gaze into the eyes of the young dead man, struggling to see what I now know lies on the far side of that image. "I remember. And I think you do too."

He doesn't answer. He blinks and looks down at the wound in his abdomen, pressing his hand into the opening, pushing his intestines back inside.

"Who are you?" I urge again. "Tell me your name."

He closes his eyes. The muscles in his hollow cheeks tighten. Then finally the ravaged face of the young man melts away again, along with his uniform. Now I see a man past his prime but not so old as he was before. In place of a uniform, he wears a dark dressing gown of forest green, the cuffs stained with ink. An iron-gray beard flows like a waterfall down a great barrel chest, and slightly darker hair sweeps back from a broad, intelligent forehead. Huge eyebrows form a formidable ledge above eyes so bright, keen, and full of pain.

A shuddering breath escapes my lips. Somehow I feel as though I know him, though I've never met him before. "What is your name?" I ask again.

"My name doesn't matter," he says in the rough tones of a heavy smoker. He lifts his head, drawing a breath through his teeth as he turns to look across the endless fen, taking in the phantoms around us. "What matters is their names. My brothers. Who died."

I try to move, but the clinging mud holds me fast. So I stretch out one hand and find I am just close enough to take hold of his. His fingers are cold and, like his cuffs, stained with ink. Writer's hands; I recognize the signs. "Your name does matter," I persist.

"Will you tell me? Your true name?"

But he will not meet my gaze. He stares into the face of the nearest phantom, one I recognize from my first experience with this Noswraith: Sergeant Guntor. He died of red fever, and his ghost bares all the ravages of that disease. He tips his head to one side, his eyes great death-hollows, deep enough to swallow a man whole. But his author does not flinch from that horrible gaze. "So many died," he says, his voice a terrible growl. "Why not me? Why should I be spared? They perished, one by one... yet I was cursed to live on."

"Please," I whisper, squeezing his hand. "Your name. Tell me."

He shakes his head sadly. Were it not for my grip on him, I believe he would reach for the phantom of Sergeant Guntor. I don't know what would happen to him then. "I suppose," he says, "I never really left this place, did I? For here I am. And here they are. Together, as we were meant to be. Faithful to the end and beyond, just as we vowed."

The author himself must have died a long time go, whoever he is. The cut of his dressing gown looks like something my great-grandfather would have worn. Yet here, within the bounds of his own creation, he lives on, forever tormented, trapped in the story born from the deepest wounds of his heart.

"It's time for you to rest." I don't know if it's the right thing to say. Perhaps there is no right thing. But I remember that glimpse of Vervain embracing the child. I remember how Vervain named herself when she looked at the Hungry Mother. For that's what Noswraiths are in the end—pieces of their creators' souls. The miracle of life belongs to the gods. Humans cannot make life from nothing as gods can. They can only use what the gods have given them—their own lives, their own spirits, their own divinely-inspired passion, all fallen, twisted by the sins of life and the shocks of pain and suffering.

Tears stream down my face, hot against my cold skin. "You must forgive yourself," I say, nearly choking on the words. "You must forgive and let them go."

"Never!" The man turns to me, his eyes fierce, his expression more frightening in that moment than any ghost or ghoul. "I can never forgive myself for the unpardonable sin of surviving."

I shake my head. "You've punished yourself far too long, and in the process, you punish them too." I sweep a hand, indicating all the sorry phantoms. "If you cannot show yourself compassion, then do it for them." He tries to pull his hand free of my grasp, but I refuse to be shaken off. "They're trapped here. All of them. With you. They cannot be at peace until you let them go."

To my shock, tears course down his face. As they fall, they seem to melt away beard and wrinkles and aged-lined skin. The big, barrel-chested, swollen man shrinks into a younger, fitter self. He doesn't look like the young captain of the story, though he's not unlike him either. He sports the same sparce mustache, the same fine uniform, almost brand new, the silver buttons only a little tarnished. He looks at me through his tears, desperate and sad, but also painfully hopeful. I clasp his hand in both of mine, holding onto him like a lifeline. "Tell me your name."

"Godswin," the youth says, and breathes out a shuddering sigh. "George Godswin."

The name hits me like a thunderclap. No wonder I felt that I knew him. How many hours did Oscar and I spend together, curled up before the fire, reading G.H. Godswin's *Adventure Stories for Boys?* Thrilling tales, which I certainly enjoyed as much as any boy, reading aloud all the scariest parts with dramatic gusto that made my little brother hide his head under his hands. Though hardly a figure of literary renown, G.H. Godswin left his mark on the world. His flowery prose, ridiculous plots, and on-the-nose moralizing never won him much acclaim.

But this story—a ghost story, tucked away in some magazine and forgotten—it had carried the truth in his heart. Truth enough that those who read it responded to it, and the joint power of human imagination brought Dulmier Fen to life.

Before he was G.H. Godswin, he was just George: a young officer ready and eager to do his duty, to serve his country, to win himself a little honor. One of only three survivors of the Battle of Brass Hill.

"I see you, George Godswin," I say, my voice a mere breath. I'm so out of my depth, so unprepared, so inadequate. But I'm all he has, here in this space of reality carved into being by his pain. "I see you and I . . . I absolve you."

When I move toward him, the sucking mud relents unexpectedly. I find I can draw nearer to him, as have all the ghosts. They press in on every side and, one by one, lay their hands on his shoulders. Those who cannot reach rest their hands on each other's shoulders. Some stand at my back, reaching over me. I feel the pressure of them, the weight of their pain, their loneliness, insubstantial though they are.

I gaze up into George's young, horror-wracked face. Leaning forward I lift onto my toes and plant a kiss, ever so soft and gentle, on his brow. "Be at peace, soldier," I whisper, my eyes closed, my lips a breath away from his skin. "You and all the ghosts you bear."

He sighs. When his eyes open, I see for a moment, not George, but the young captain once more. He looks down at his gut, at his death wound. Only there is no wound anymore, only a gash in his coat and a visible, puckered scar across his abdomen. No more bleeding. No more pain. His head shoots up, and he catches my gaze, his face lighting up with a smile. "Amelia!" he cries.

A burst of white light erupts in my face. I cry out, my hands grasping. Despite everything, I try to hold on—to him, to George, to all the phantoms and the fen. But they slip away through my fingers, one after the other, lost in that radiance. In the end I'm left standing alone, my eyes too dazzled at first to see anything. All I know is that I'm cold, but I'm no longer wet. Am I not in the fen? I turn slowly in place as my vision adjusts to the gloom. There's just enough starlight to illuminate the stone entrance hall of the palace. No fen, no stagnant pools stretching on for endless miles. Just tall walls and the long staircase before me. Even the shadows are quiet, no sign of the Nightmare Realm churning in their depths.

The Eight-Crowned Queen has not pursued me. Yet.

I dash tears from my cheeks with the heel of my hand. I'm still shaking, overcome by everything I just experienced. Was that . . . was that the end of a Noswraith? Is Dulmier Fen no more, released from the spell of its creation? Have I actually found a way to stop these horrors once and for all?

There's no time to dwell on any of this. I must go. I must return to the temple, bring the children up, send them through the gate. Castien is waiting, and I won't let him down. Gathering my skirts, I turn and dart for the open palace door. I'm within three paces of it when a figure steps into view, silhouetted in the opening. I stop. My heart lurches to my throat in a surge of pain and fear. But this is no Noswraith who blocks my path.

"Oscar!" I gasp.

25

"WHAT ARE YOU DOING HERE, CLARA?"

I take in the sight of him, standing before me like a ghost stepped straight from my own past. He holds a moonfire lantern in one hand, and its soft light illuminates one side of his face. That side is so innocent and boyish, it could break my heart. The other side is harsh beneath deep shadows. The green light of *rothiliom* whirls in the centers of his pupils, but even that drug-haze cannot hide the fear shining in their depths.

I draw a steadying breath. If he's afraid, good. I can use that. And I cannot let him know how frightened I am. "I think the better question is what are *you* doing here?" I answer coldly. "You don't belong in Vespre. You don't belong in this world."

He blinks. For a moment I see that vulnerable child I knew, not the man he has become. But when his eyelids rise, his expression flashes defiantly. "I will go anywhere with Ivor," he says. "Into any danger, into the deepest of the nine hells. I love him."

Summoning all my courage, I take a step and hold out one hand. "Dearest," I say. "Dearest, please, believe me. I know this man. I know what he's done. You don't know everything he's capable of. He's enthralled you, and—"

"No, Clara." My brother's voice snaps like a whip, and I can't help recoiling several paces. "For the first time, I know what true love is. Not the awful, pathetic, nasty thing called love our family shared. Ivor has liberated me. Ivor has let me become my true self, and no one—no one, Clara, not even you—will stop me from being my true self. Never again."

His words echo hollowly inside my chest, in that carved-out space where once I felt only warmth and love for him. How have we come to this? How could a brother and sister, so devoted, so dependent on one another for happiness, end up at such desperate odds? Part of me still doesn't want to believe it. Part of me still wants to fight, even in the face of each terrible revelation. "Was this your plan all along then?" I sweep an arm as though I might encompass the whole city in a single gesture. "To come to Vespre and unleash nightmares on the citizens?"

"What?" Oscar blinks and shakes his head. "No, we don't care about any of that. Ivor has a plan. He is the High King of the fae— did you know that? He is Illithorin's heir. But to claim his rights, he will need to claim all four of the Eledrian crowns in one fell swoop." He takes an eager step toward me, overwhelmed by passion for his subject. The hand holding the lantern shakes, and the pale glow wavers. "Fae cannot stand against these nightmare monsters. Ivor explained it all to me. He took control of the Eight-Crowned Queen using the bloodgem. She is a great weapon, greater than anything the fae are prepared to face. He had a plan that involved you and me and Princess Estrilde too, of course. With the Eight-Crowned Queen and the Noswraiths you and I wield, he could take all Eledria before they even knew the attack had begun. It was all coming together . . . until you betrayed him."

Dismay churns like heated stones in my gut. The boy is deluded and determined to cling to his delusion. But the truth is there, behind the manic drug-light in his eyes. He already knows the monster he created is far beyond his or anyone's ability to control.

"Oscar," I say, "you must believe me, I never betrayed Ivor."

His teeth flash in the lantern glow. "It was your fault he was thrown into that pit! It was your fault he is what he is now!"

"No." I take another step toward him, careful, like approaching a rabid dog. My heart races, but I keep my voice gentle. "His glamours are stripped away, that is all. But he was always just as he is now: twisted and ugly. Monstrous."

"You lie!"

"No, Oscar. I'm telling you the truth. If you could just see—"

A growl rumbles from above, in the passage beyond the stair. Oscar chokes on a scream, and I whip my head about, staring up into that darkness. Unless I'm much mistaken, the shadows are living, churning. The Nightmare Realm closes in. I turn to Oscar again, breathing hard. His eyes are wide, white-ringed with terror. "Clara," he gasps, sounding so young once more. "Clara, it's not too late. You can still join us."

"No, Oscar. I can't. I won't."

He bares his teeth as though biting back either a curse or a sob. "I never wanted us to be enemies."

The heartbreak in his voice tears me apart. "Come with me then," I say, holding out my hand to him. "Come with me, Oscar. Now."

"Why? So your husband can put another curse on me?" I withdraw, and he barks a bitter laugh. "Yes, Clara. Ivor told me that little detail as well. And he told me you knew. You watched me suffer in torment for years, the best part of myself stripped away, and you did nothing."

"I didn't know—"

"Really? You do now. What will you do with that knowledge? Will you turn from the man who did that to me? Or will you cling to your beloved Prince?"

My heart aches, heavy and throbbing in my breast. But the image of the Hollow Man is too clear, too hideously real in my mind. How can I deny the wisdom of Castien's decision to block Oscar's abilities? It was cruel, it was hard. But it was necessary. And can I blame him for not telling me? No, for I would have done exactly as I did—I would have refused to see the truth, would have hated and blamed him instead of placing blame where it belonged:

on the shoulders of my brother. My beautiful, beloved, damaged, desecrated, adored brother.

But I am not the woman I was even three days ago.

"I will love Prince Castien until the day I die," I say. "And when I am dead, I will love him from beyond the grave."

Oscar sneers even as tears gleam in the corners of his eyes. "So which of us is truly enthralled?"

Another roar echoes across the walls, rippling from stone to stone. Shadows twist and writhe on either side of us. The nightmare will overwhelm us both in another moment. By the look on his face, Oscar knows it as well. "It seems we have both made our choices," he says, lifting his chin. "When we meet again, it will be as enemies. You must know, Clara, that I will do everything in my power to help Ivor. I will see him ascend where he belongs."

"And I will stop you," I answer softly.

"You will fail. Ivor will bring this whole city to ruin before he gives up his dream."

"And what about the people, Oscar?"

"What people?"

"The families. The fathers and mothers. The children. They are suffering, they are dying, all for the sake of Ivor's ambition."

His brow knits. "They're just trolls, Clara."

With those words, some last tether—some delicate thread still binding my heart in a snare I once thought impossible to escape—snaps. The pain is so sharp, so unexpected, I nearly stagger, nearly drop to my knees.

Instead I stride forward three paces and slap Oscar across the face. Pain spikes up my palm, my arm, and explodes in my head, but I do not back down. He doubles over, shocked, horrified. Then he whips his head around staring up at me, his mouth open, his eyes wide. I slap him again, harder. He cries out, cupping his cheek with one hand. When he looks at me this time, it's the same look he used to give our father.

All the wind goes out of my lungs. "Oscar," I breathe. "Oscar, I—"

"Go," he snarls, his teeth clenched and bared. "Go now. Before I change my mind."

Another roar quakes my bones. Darkness thrashes all around us, a nightmare we've both shared and never escaped, not in all the years of our life together. But Oscar steps to one side, clearing my path. Though the last thing I ever wanted was to leave him behind, I gather my skirts and flee down the palace steps into the haunted courtyard. Minor wraiths scatter before me, terrified of whatever looms behind me in the palace. I don't look back to see if my brother watches my flight or if he hastens to make his own escape.

I simply run.

26

EVEN WITH DASYRA'S QUILL AND TWO BOOKS LEFT IN MY satchel, my frame of mind is so distraught, I'm not sure I could survive a Noswraith if I meet one during my mad flight back through the city. But it's almost as though the Noswraiths have scattered before me, scurrying away into buildings and alleys. Though I feel their watching eyes, their malevolent stares, feel the intense hunger churning in their twisted hearts, none move to interfere with me.

I don't try to guess why this is. I simply press on, sticking close to any *gubdagogs*, trusting they will provide at least some protection. Many of them are torn and damaged, and I wish I understood their workings enough to make repairs. But they are as baffling to me now as they ever were, and any interference on my part will surely only make matters worse.

At one point something enormous passes overhead. I duck beneath the nearest *gubdagog*, hunched and terrified. I can't get any solid impression of the nightmare. It's simply too big, with enormous stalk-legs that support a body hidden in clouds overhead. It could either crush or devour me without once breaking stride, and if it takes notice of me now, there's nothing I or these flimsy threads of spell-weaving can do to stop it. It continues on its way, however, unhurried and massive, making for some distant destination without particular malice. It may not be hungry just now. But it will grow hungry again soon.

And when it does, the children need to be far from this place.

The wraith's footsteps echo away into the distance. I force myself to breathe out slowly, closing my eyes. *Castien,* I think, and even let my lips whisper his name. I'm more tempted than I like to admit to call his true name, his fae name. He would come for me in an instant if I did. And oh! How I need him! Need his strength, his comfort, his reassurance. But my needs aren't what's important right now. I must get to the low temple, and I must—

Silence.

It's so sudden, so absolute, it knocks the breath from my lungs. The city was quiet before, caught in the stillness of shivering terror. Now it is truly silent, like a smothering blanket has fallen across this street, blocking out all sound. My other senses are dulled as well; my skin feels heavy, my eyesight blurred, my tongue sluggish and thick in my mouth. I recognize this sensation. All around me the shadows writhe with the living energy of the Nightmare Realm. A Noswraith stalks me, is even now closing in.

Slowly I turn, peer through threads of my sheltering *gubdagog* back up the street. There it is—the Silence, crawling along the walls, slithering over and under and around *gubdagogs* as though they aren't even there. I don't see it so much as *feel* it, an impression of existence. Long, jointed limbs, a smooth flat forehead, no eyes. Great curving horns and batlike ears, and long claws which pierce through stone like silk.

"*Nahual.*" I mouth the name, unable to produce sound as the wraith skitters ever nearer. It's the old Vaalyun word for *silence*, and this is an old Vaalyun Noswraith brought into being. I've encountered him before and survived. He's not terribly strong, despite his size. I slide Dasyra's quill and a book from my satchel, preparing to write a binding. I can deal with this monster. A few quick strokes of my pen, and suddenly I stand in the street with a sword in hand, braced, prepared for battle. I'll trap this nightmare in the pages where he belongs, and then I'll—

Prrrrlt.

I whip my head to the right. A pair of glowing green eyes blink up at me. I only just have time to register that I heard that sound, that it should not have been able to penetrate Nahual's silence.

Then Bheluphnu, the Black Cat, launches straight at me.

I turn, raising my sword, but the wraith hits me in the chest with all four paws. Though he's the size of a housecat, the force of that blow knocks me to the ground. My weapon falls from my hands and clatters in the street, further breaking the silence of Nahual. Bheluphnu stares down at me, his demonic eyes spinning in his head. He utters a deep yeowl, and his mouth opens wider, wider, a cavernous maw, big enough to swallow me whole. A serpentine tongue licks at my face, and the *gubdagog* overhead vibrates uselessly. I scream, throwing up my hands.

White fire flashes. For a moment, I don't understand what I'm seeing; it all happens too fast. A brilliant, burning cord wraps around the Black Cat, snakelike coils constricting. Bheluphnu's huge mouth shrinks, and he utters a startled, *Mew?* Then he's yanked off me in a blur of light and yeowling.

I push myself upright, shaking strands of hair out of my eye. "Mixael!" I cry.

He's there—Mixael Silveri, the head librarian of Vespre, standing beneath the *gubdagog*, grasping the handle of a long snake whip. The Black Cat struggles in its coils, but Mixael has it well in hand. He casts me a quick look and flashes an incongruous grin. "Get behind me, Miss Darlington!" he cries. His voice sounds soft and faraway, and I'm obliged to read his lips to understand him, for the Silence is suddenly deafening once more. I scramble to my feet, but rather than do as he said, I cast about for my dropped sword. It lies in the middle of the street. I reach for it.

In that same moment, Nahual, clinging to the side of a building partway down the street, turns his bony head and fixes all his sightless attention on me. He spreads his wings, leaps. I haven't time enough to react, to raise any defense. But it doesn't matter, for another figure steps into the space between me and the approaching nightmare. Light from a moonfire lantern glints off his spectacles as he plants his feet, aims a crossbow and, with an absolute coolness that borders on uncaring, fires off a silver-headed missile. The bolt flies true, piercing straight through Nahual's protruding breastbone. The nightmare crashes to the road, cracking stone where it lands.

The next instant both Noswraiths vanish. I find myself standing in an empty street, beneath a canopy of *gubdagog* threads, between the last two remaining Vespre librarians. They are scribbling away in open books, Mixael with furious zeal, Andreas with a lazy, looping scrawl. They reach the end of their binding spells simultaneously and clap their books shut before lifting two pairs of eyes to focus on me. "Well," Mixael says, lighting up the gloom with his enormous, heart-melting smile, "looks like we arrived just in time!"

He's aged in the last seven years. The air of Eledria kept him forever young, but now that Vespre floats out into the Hinter. Time seems to be catching up to him along with the strain of his position. There's gray in his hair, lines under his eyes, and grizzle on his cheeks. But when he smiles, his beauty shines through. "You seem to have gotten yourself into a bit of a pickle," he says. "A little out of practice with the pen, are we?"

I shake my head and can only manage to answer, "What are you doing here?"

"No time to chat." Mixael tucks the sealed book containing Bheluphnu's new binding into the satchel at his side. "We're close to the temple. Shall we go? I'll tell you what I know on the way."

I nod and fall into place between the two librarians. Mixael keeps up a steady stream of whispered talk: "Lir burst into our workroom and said you two were parted up at the palace. I confess, it was all a bit of a shock. But once she explained it, Andreas and I knew we'd all have a better shot at survival if you were alive, so we asked Anj to let us risk going back to fetch you. Old Anj didn't want to let us go but technically he doesn't have any right of rule over librarians, so . . . we came anyway." He lifts an eyebrow, casting a wary glance back up the street, currently free of nightmare essence but crawling with shadows. "My wife might just kill me. But look! Here you are, and I barely had to step beyond the barriers. No harm done in the end."

Andreas maintains his customary reserve throughout this speech, but when I turn his way, he smiles vaguely and offers a mild, "Welcome back, Miss . . . ?" He blinks uncertainly. He never could quite remember who I am.

"Darlington," I supply. Then I bite my lip. "Actually, that's not true. I'm not Miss Darlington anymore. Technically speaking, I'm Mrs. Lodírith."

Andreas's brows rise slightly, but Mixael stops dead in his tracks and slaps a hand over his mouth as though to prevent an outcry. He swallows, blinks, then slowly drops his hand and says, "Are you kidding me? No, wait, don't tell me now, Miss—Missus—

Whatever you are! Let's get you back to the temple before you go dropping anymore gob-smacking revelations. I can't watch for Noswraiths and take in all this gossip at the same time."

As it turns out, we weren't more than a street away from the beginnings of the *gubdagog* barrier. In my fear I hadn't realized how close I was and might very well have missed the temple entirely. But Mixael and Andreas guide me through, and when we reach the courtyard on the far side, Lir is there to greet us.

"Mistress!" she cries and flings herself at me, catching me in her arms. "Oh, Mistress, I was so worried!"

"Did you know she's Mrs. Lodírith now?" Mixael asks.

"Of course she is," Lir snaps, glaring at him over my head. "Those of us with any sense saw it coming ages ago. Now go find your wife, Mister Silveri! I believe she's currently arming herself to go out in search of you, and she might have found a helmet small enough to fit Sor's little head."

"Right." Mixael grimaces and darts away at once, Andreas following behind at a leisurely stroll, as though we aren't all in imminent peril.

I grasp Lir's hands in mine. "Dig?" I ask, my voice trembling.

"He's all right," she assures me. "Umog Grush is with him, drawing poison from the wound. It'll take a little spellwork to get it all out, but he should recover. He's resting in the temple now, and the others are with him."

Relief floods me in such a rush, I almost sink to my knees. Lir senses it and grasps my elbows, keeping me upright. "Are you hurt?" she asks.

I don't feel well. Not at all. Now that the immediate danger has relented for the moment, I'm suddenly exhausted, nauseated, overwrought, and on the verge of full-blown panic. But there's no time for any of that. "I'm all right, Lir," I say, though my hands shake as I grip her forearms. Then, because I don't know what else to say, I simply blurt, "I've seen the Prince."

"The Prince?" Lir gasps. "He's here? In Vespre?"

In a mad tumble of words, I tell her about the gate in the library which the Prince even now guards, ready to open. When I start to mention Ivor and Oscar, however, my throat closes up. I can't bear to admit what my brother has done. Besides, Ivor isn't our greatest threat. He's nothing compared to the massive host of Noswraiths between us and the library, all of whom will be immediately attracted by a mass exodus from the temple.

"I tried to get Vervain," I tell her, my voice threatening to break. "She could have helped us, but . . . but . . ."

Lir nods her understanding. "You did what you could, Mistress," she says gently. "Vervain was a lost soul in any case."

Lost soul . . . Her words echo inside my head. I close my eyes, and for a moment I'm standing back in that cold stone hall. I see Vervain as she kneels in the center of a nightmare storm, holding a small child in her arms. I see as well the image of George Godswin, standing in the fen, surrounded by phantoms. Lost souls. Like me. Like Oscar. Like all those who, in their desperation, turned to the darkness of our own creation for relief.

But were they truly lost in the end?

Lir is still talking. I drag my attention back to the present, and her words clarify in my ears. "Anj will not be easy to convince," she says. "He wants to believe we can hold out here until the Noswraiths are all rebound."

I shake my head firmly. "Once the Greater Noswraiths realize we're here, they'll break through the *gubdagog* barrier without a thought. We've got to get everyone up to the library, as many as we can."

Lir nods, her lovely face scored with hard lines. "Yes," she says. Then she firms her jaw. "The gods themselves sent you to us, Mistress. They sent you to show us the way." She smiles, a fierce, determined expression. "We will save our children."

I nod, even as tears brim in my eyes. "Yes," I whisper. "We will get them out."

Lir was right—Anj is not easy to convince.

The two of them argue vehemently in troldish, right there in the courtyard under the wide, terrified eyes of the refugee families surrounding them. I watch, helpless and unable to follow any of the dialogue being exchanged. I can only study their faces, try to read their expressions. In Anj, I see desperation, in Lir, conviction. Both terrible forces, battering each other with rough, growling words.

I look around at the families. Most of them are parents, some with very small children held in their mother's arms. They are so vulnerable, so helpless against the forces of darkness assailing them. Many of them won't survive a journey from the temple to the palace . . . but none will survive if we don't at least make the attempt. And they know it. I see the truth dawning in their hard, stone faces.

Anj works up into a frenzy, raising his fists over his head. Sudden movement at the temple entrance interrupts whatever he's about to say, however. All heads turn, all eyes fix on that cavern opening as the two guards part, and a procession of stone-hided priestesses pour from the darkness within. They carry complicated *gubdagogs* in their hands and wear *gubdagog* necklaces across their broad bosoms. They keep their eyes downcast but form two neat rows, a path between them. I hold my breath, knowing who is about to emerge.

Umog Grush appears. She is so vast, not only in her size but in her sheer presence. Lichen clings to her shoulders, a strange natural mantel that somehow only lends greater majesty to her terrifying form. She rolls out from the shadows, hunched over her walking stick and yet somehow more regal in bearing than any of the Lords and Ladies of Eledria I've ever seen. She proceeds between her loyal priestesses and across the courtyard until she stands directly in front of Anj. She pins him with a cold stare.

"*Kaurga-hor, gruaka-hor,*" she growls.

Anj draws a sharp breath through flared nostrils and takes a step back. The low priestess addresses herself to Lir next, speaking another series of rumbling words that mean nothing to my ear. Lir drops to her knees, her head bowed as she responds. To my great surprise, Umog Grush places her hand on Lir's head in what looks like a sort of benediction. Something solemn is taking place here. Whatever comes next will depend on the low priestess's words.

Umog Grush lifts her heavy head, casting her gaze about the courtyard. At her people, gathered here for shelter from the storm. Shelter she cannot provide. Not for long.

Her small eyes narrow. *"Drag!"* she barks.

Lir springs to her feet. "We leave for the palace at once," she declares, before turning to Anj. She speaks a few words to him, still in troldish, but in a different tone than their argument. He shakes his head, distraught. She reaches out, touches his arm, but he recoils from her and turns away, barking orders.

The courtyard erupts into action. Families gather themselves, putting out their small fires, piling their belongings on their backs. There are some grumbles, questions, and protests, but on the whole, the trolls work in silence. They trust Anj, their leader; but when Anj glances my way, I see nothing but deep distrust simmering in his gaze. Can I blame him? So far I've not done anything to merit better. I can only hope that, in the next few hours, I'll be able to prove myself to him and all these vulnerable souls.

All is chaotic to my eye, though Lir and Anj work to bring some form of order to the chaos. Calx and Har emerge from the temple, Dig slung between them. Sis dances at their heels, eager as ever, weaving a *gubdagog* with her nimble fingers. The priestesses of the Deeper Dark form protective lines on either sides of the vulnerable families, their *gubdagogs* humming with awakened magic.

A shock of red hair catches my eye. I turn to see Mixael and Khas in heated debate. She looks furious, but he reaches up, grabs the back of her head, and draws her forehead down to his. He closes his eyes, and she closes hers. They stand like that for a moment, breathing each other's air. Little Sor sleeps in the front pack of his mother's breastplate, his head flopped to one side, his fat cheek smooshed.

"Miss?"

I turn to find Andreas approaching me, a stack of books in his arms. He offers them to me, and I realize they are empty spellbooks. I accept them, grateful to refill my satchel. "Do you have a pen?" he asks.

"Yes, thank you, Mister Cornil," I say and hold up Dasyra's quill.

He starts to turn away but pauses and looks back. "It's good you came, Miss," he says, blinking from behind his spectacles. "Things were a bit . . . tight in your absence. I hope you can make the difference."

Coming from Andreas, it's an impressive monologue. I smile softly. "I hope so too."

He nods and wanders off in that vague way of his. I look down at my satchel full of empty books waiting to be filled with binding spells. If I can write them fast enough, that is. The Noswraiths will be drawn to this great crowd. The moment we're beyond the *gubdagog* barrier, they'll—

Sudden tension disturbs the air, a tightening in the atmosphere

I can't quite explain. It shivers across my skin, drawing my gaze once more around the courtyard. What is it I'm sensing? I can't explain it, but . . . are those shadows expanding around the corners of the courtyard? My stomach drops.

"Noswraith!"

In that exact moment the cry bursts from my lips, a massive figure crashes through the *gubdagog* wall to my right. Screams explode all around me, but I can only stand, frozen in horror as the tall, terrible figure steps through. A nightmare so beautiful, so dreadful, shifting between her eight aspects all within the blink of an eye. One moment she is the mighty queen, the next, the devouring demon. In a strange way, I feel as though I see all eight of her selves at once, like a hydra with multiple long necks and heads twining in and out of each other. An impossible horror, born from the depths of a depraved mind.

She followed me here. And now the Eight-Crowned Queen will feast.

Trolls hurtle bodily against her, flinging themselves between the nightmare and their children. None of them can stand against her. Their strength and their weapons have no effect. She is a figure of spellcraft and pure malice, and there's only one way to fight her.

I snatch a book from my satchel, open to the first page, and begin to write. The next moment, a spear appears in my hand. In the real world, I wouldn't have the first idea how to wield such a weapon, but that doesn't matter here. My pen flies across the page, and my dream-self steps boldly forward. "Idreloth!" I cry.

She turns. Once more, I have the strange impression of all eight heads looking my way, of sixteen awful eyes fixed upon me. I cannot defeat her as I defeated Dulmier Fen. There's no finding her truth, her center, no reaching her creator and sending this nightmare to ultimate rest. There can be only binding.

I heave the spear straight between her bare breasts, putting all the force of my spellcraft into that missile. It whistles straight and true for its target. But Idreloth is no small fright. She catches the spear easily in one hand and bites off the head. It gleams between her long, black teeth before she spits it out again. Then she lunges at me, and her long fingers close around my throat. I don't even have time to scream.

Just as she wrenches me from my feet, a net falls around us. It's like threads of music, snarled and complex and humming with tremendous magic. It wraps over her eight heads, her numerous limbs, a tightly-woven mesh of moth silk and dew drops and mushrooms and memories, all rolled into a great chorus of magic.

Idreloth rears back, losing her grip on me. I drop to the ground and roll away across the paving stones. Yanking back my head, I look up at her massive, multiplied form as she dances and shrieks, struggling to get free of that binding. She cannot escape; it's too huge, too complex, like the vastness of mountains, the distance of stars. It's a story and a song, it's a whole living history caught in the threads of the most complex *gubdagog* I've ever seen. I don't understand it, and yet visions burst in my brain—visions of cataclysm and fire and destruction, visions of lands torn apart, islands scattered across the Hinter Sea. Visions of Vespre, beautiful Vespre. The last of the great troll cities.

Now Idreloth is part of that story, part of that history. Those threads now contain her, binding her with a strength I've never before seen. She's trapped in this moment of time, this moment of story.

Strong hands grip my shoulders, yanking me back from the *gubdagog*. "You all right, *Mar?*" Calx's voice growls in my ear as he sets me on my feet.

I gape up at him, too dumbstruck to speak. Then I turn my blinking eyes and see what I was not able to see before. Umog Grush stands before the Noswraith, holding the threads of that complex *gubdagog* with both hands. Pure power pulses from her hard stone frame, feeding those threads, feeding the spell she has woven. It will tear her apart.

"We've got to help her!" I cry, gripping Calx's arm. In the same moment, a small, pale figure darts forward and clutches at the priestess, nearly pulling her off kilter. Idreloth lurches, ready to break free of her containment, and Umog Grush lifts her gaze to me.

"Take your daughter, librarian," she growls. "Take her and go!"

Her voice snaps me back into reason. She doesn't want our help. She's giving us a chance and she expects us to use it. We cannot waste whatever time she manages to steal.

"Help me, Calx," I cry, and the two of us take hold of Sis and drag her away from her beloved teacher. The girl screams and kicks, much too strong for me. Calx restrains her, slinging her over his shoulder. She shrieks a stream of troldish curses, her small hands reaching out for Umog Grush as though she could catch hold of her and pull her away from this nightmare. But the low priestess has chosen her fate, and we will honor her for it.

Anj bellows in troldish from somewhere across the yard. The crowd of troll families turns to him like a guiding star. He steps through the torn barrier, and they file after him, the priestesses with their *gubdagogs* acting as flank guards. "Come on, *Mar*," Calx rumbles. "Time to go."

I grip my quill and book fast. Then, without a backward glance, I hasten after the refugees into the haunted streets of Vespre.

27

MY PEN NEVER STOPS FLYING.

No sooner do I bind one Noswraith than another creeps, lurches, or ravages its way up a dark alley, out through a gaping doorway, over the edge of a listing rooftop. Though I never would have attempted such a feat before, I stuff three bindings into a single volume in quick succession, knowing perfectly well they will soon escape. My only hope is to give us time to get to the palace, to get through the gate.

Discarding the squirming, twitching book, I drag another from my satchel. Mixael and Andreas are writing as furiously as I, and the three of us lead the way through the city streets. The *gubdagoglirs* surround the vulnerable troll families, weaving their spells with frantic precision, but these are more deflections or deterrents, not powerful defenses. Here and there, one of the priestesses runs ahead to fix a fallen *gubdagog*. I see one such woman make this brave attempt only to be skewered on the end of razor claws suddenly emerging from a darkened window. The woman lets out a single scream before she is dragged into the house and the roiling nightmare within. We hurry on. We cannot stop, cannot try to save her. To do so would be to split our defenses, and those are feeble enough as it is. We must guard the children. They are our only priority now.

I try to keep track of my own children. At one point I glimpse Sis, still weeping over the fate of Umog Grush even as she works frantically on a small *gubdagog* of her own. Lir is close by her, and they have a cluster of little trollings between them. Where the parents are, I cannot guess. They may all be *grakanak-balja*—orphans, belonging to the Deeper Dark. But Sis and Lir both know something about that, and they will not forsake them.

I look ahead up the street. Though we have made good progress from the low temple, the palace still seems so far away, and still more Noswraiths close in on us now, leaping from rooftop to rooftop. "Watch out!" I cry to Mixael, who turns and, spelling a sword into existence, hacks through the reaching limbs of a shadow monster.

Something long and low shoots between my feet. I look down to glimpse a serpentine slither, pale and faintly luminous. It snakes between the legs of several trolls, as though fixated on a single mark.

It's heading straight for Sis, and she doesn't see it coming.

"*Sis!*" I scream, even as my fingers fly, trying to write a knife into existence, something, anything I might use to catch that nightmare, to pin it in place. I cannot seem to make the words answer me. Numb terror floods my veins, slowing my reality, my perception. I can only watch in horror as that hideous thing shoots toward my daughter.

Andreas steps in the way.

The wraith rears up like a cobra, hissing and waggling its coiled body. Andreas's glasses gleam. Part of me sees him as he is in the waking world, standing there with book and pen in hand, writing with that familiar lazy script of his. Most of my awareness, however, sees him as he is here in the Nightmare Realm. He holds a long knife in his hand and slashes at the wraith, cutting it neatly in half. The two halves flop on the ground only to twist about and lift themselves upright again. Then they dart for his legs, two snake-like entities winding up his limbs, his body, his neck. Before I have time to register what's happening, they burrow into his ears and vanish inside his head.

Andreas stares. For a heartbeat, his gaze meets mine. Then he screams. Writhing and jerking unnaturally, he falls to his knees. "No!" I shout and rush toward him, my quill at the ready. But what do I write? What spell can I offer? I don't know this wraith, don't know its name or any means of binding it. "Andreas!"

He drops to his hands, to his face. His body contorts, goes still.

Then he lifts his head, and two black, slithering things emerge from his eye sockets, bursting right through his spectacle lenses. They wave like antenna from his head. His body begins to jerk, pulled upright as though propelled by some outside force. He lurches to his feet, and for a moment seems to regard me with those antenna eyes.

Then he turns to the children.

Before he can take a step, Mixael is there, a spell-sword in both hands. In a flash of white light, he cuts the heads off those squirming back writhers. They drop to the ground, and Mixael grinds them under his boots before, in a single, smooth arc, he strikes Andreas in the head with the hilt of his weapon. Andreas topples backwards, landing face up to the starlit sky.

For a moment the Nightmare Realm retreats. The librarian lies there on the stones, no writhing wraiths protruding from his eyes. He looks almost peaceful, save that his spectacles are shattered.

"Andreas?" Mixael cries and kneels over his friend. He's weeping, tears rolling down his cheeks. But we don't have time for mourning.

"Mixael, we must go." I grab his arm and pull with all my might.

"It was his," Mixael chokes and turns to look up at me through swimming eyes. "*Shusolor*, the Mind Worm—it was his wraith." He bows over Andreas again, his teeth clenched, struggling to hold back a sob. "They always get their makers in the end."

Cold washes over me. I've always known Andreas was a Noswraith creator. Like me. Like most of the librarians brought to serve in Vespre, punished with lifelong exile for the crime of bringing such horrors into being. But Andreas had always seemed so mild, so gentle. Part of me had never believed him truly capable of such sorcery. I look down into his empty face, into those glassy, staring eyes. Is he at peace now? Will any of us ever be?

Khas steps in beside her husband. Little Sor, no longer asleep, lets out a pathetic wail from his pouch. This seems to galvanize Mixael. He lets his wife help him to his feet then puts his shoulders back. "I've got this, love," he says, looking into her silvery eyes. "Come on. It's not much farther now." He turns to me and says, "Quills up, librarian. I'll guard our retreat."

I offer a salute with Dasyra's quill then hasten to the head of the line where Lir waits with the children. Our company is drastically reduced since leaving the temple. Several of the families peeled away into side streets, unwilling to remain with such a large group. I don't blame them, but I also know they cannot survive for long on their own out there. Now there are scarcely six families left along with the orphan children. Will they be the last of the trollfolk? Exiled from their own world, doomed to wander Eledria in search of a haven to call home? Is this the end of the mighty people of Vespre?

"Keep close behind me," I tell Lir. Anj stands beside her, helpless against the Noswraiths. He's got a child in each arm, another on his back, and this alone warms my heart to him for the first time. I cast him a flashing glance before fixing my attention back on Lir. "Last push," I say. "Get ready to move."

Then I stride forward up the street, writing a flaming sword into existence. It illuminates our way, a warning to all Noswraiths. The nightmares must sense something in me now, some determination, some passion. They cringe away from that light and retreat trembling into the shadows. I glimpse flashes of glowing eyes, of slavering jaws, of long, needle-sharp fingers. But they skuttle back into the alleys and buildings, hissing, spitting, cooing, weeping. None dare approach.

We move as fast as the smallest child on foot can run. It seems like forever, but suddenly we reach the courtyard of the palace. There are so many Noswraiths here, but we've come this far, I'm not about to back down. Without hesitation I stride forward, hewing left and right with my sword, knowing full well that each shadow I cut down will reform and attack again soon if not properly bound. It doesn't matter. I just need to get these survivors through to the library. That's all.

Lir, Sis, and the remaining priestesses spin their small *gubdagogs*. I hear screams behind me and know people are being cut down, taken. I forge onward, my sword bursting with radiance as I plunge it into the leering mouth of a shadowy wraith. There was a time when even one of these nightmares would have been enough to send me cowering in terror. No longer, not after everything I've been through. They are but obstacles between me and my goal. I will not let them stand in my way.

We reach the palace steps. I dare to cast a glance back, to see who is still with me. The children are here, shielded by Anj, Calx, Dig, and Har, all of whom are useless against Noswraiths. A handful of the parents and seven priestesses remain, all with *gubdagogs* strung from their nimble fingers. Sis and Lir stand on either flank, Sis so small and ferocious as she faces the nightmares. Khas is at the vanguard, one hand shielding her baby's face as though to spare him from encroaching terrors. It's such a useless and yet maternal gesture, it breaks my heart.

Mixael is behind us, battling a creeping foe. For a flash, I see him in truth, standing there with a book and quill, scribbling down spells as fast as his mind can conjure them, pouring magic into the ether as he creates realities with words. He is a master of his craft indeed.

I look down at my own book. It's stuffed—every page scrawled over in tight, messy script, only just enough to temporarily contain the ravening wraiths. Hurling it aside, I reach for the last volume in my satchel even as I turn to mount the palace steps.

A sharp sting at my cheek. I put up a hand, feel the warmth of blood. My eyes dart to the side in time to see a thorny cane ripple across stone. I just have time to register what I see, to grasp what it means, before a voice coos in my ear: *"Red blooms the rose in my heart tonight, fair as the dawn, new as the spring."*

The next moment a whirling, churning mass of thorns and briars appears at the top of the steps, blocking the palace doors. In the center of that churning stands a woman made of thorns—a glorious, cruel creature. She smiles, and red roses burst into bloom all around her.

I stagger back a step, even as thorns lash around my ankle and yank me off balance. Dasyra's quill drops from my fingers. I scream, scrabble to retrieve it, but the Thorn Maiden yanks me up from the ground and hangs me suspended, upside down. She draws me toward her monstrous center. The stench of rotten roses fills my nostrils, and I stare into a face made of petals and thorns. Her jaw opens wide, thorn teeth gaping, ready to swallow me whole.

Then she gasps, chokes. A cord of gold wraps around her neck, yanking her off balance. She turns, looks, and sees more such cords wrapping around her innumerable limbs. They burn bright, and her canes begin to smolder. The Thorn Maiden screams as large chunks of her being break off and fall charred to the ground. The limb holding me breaks. I fall in a heap on the palace stairs. Luckily I don't break my neck but manage to scramble upright and stare through the mass of brambles and glowing cords. The Thorn Maiden shrieks and writhes, but beyond her . . . beyond her . . .

"Castien!" I cry.

He's there, standing in the hall behind the Noswraith. His dark hair streams behind him like storm clouds, and his purple robes billow as though in a high gale. His head is thrown back, the light of his kingly glory ablaze in his vivid eyes. He holds tight to a multi-tailed whip, a spell of exquisite craftsmanship. He is a mage beyond compare, a conduit of tremendous magic drawn straight from the *quinsatra*, all funneled through ink and pen and page in a terrible flood of power. Even a nightmare as ferocious as the Thorn Maiden must tremble before him.

I've never seen him more beautiful than he is in this very moment.

With a final shriek, the Thorn Maiden disintegrates, vanishing from this reality. The Nightmare Realm retreats, and Castien turns to me, his spell-whips gone. Instead he holds a book across his arm and writes the last few words of his binding with a flourish of his quill. Then, snapping the cover shut, he flashes me a most devastating grin.

"Welcome home, Darling. I missed you. Had a busy day of it then?"

I cannot find words. It doesn't matter. He swiftly descends the stairs to me, pulls me to my feet and presses me to his heart. I rest there a moment and listen to the *thrum* of his pulse. Though he looks so calm, cool, and collected, that frantic heartbeat reveals a great deal. I close my eyes, allowing myself to revel in his closeness for the space of three breaths and no more.

Then pushing back, I turn and look down at our little party, clustered at the base of the stairs. One of the priestesses lies dead. Another is wounded, supported by Dig, who is himself still recovering from his Noswraith encounter. Is she the pretty priestess he risked life and limb to protect earlier? I hope so.

"So few," Castien murmurs, taking in the assembly. Devastation underscores each word, but when I look up at him, his face is bright and determined. "Come along," he says. "We've got to get them through. Fetch your quill, my Darling, and hurry!"

28

THE WAY THROUGH THE HAUNTED PALACE IS WORSE THAN the city. Noswraiths crawl out from every crevice, reach from every shadow, hungry and unable to resist the lure of so many vulnerable victims. But Castien is with us now. Quick and sure, he dashes off spells with an ease I scarcely comprehend. In all my time serving in Vespre library, he suffered under the blood-curse, which prevented him from using his power to its full extent. Now, with the curse broken, and our proximity having restored him to full strength, he is a wonder to behold.

He leads the way, and I guard the middle, while Mixael continues to bring up the rear. Our party has dwindled so much, it's easier to manage, but we also have fewer *gubdagoglirs* to aid us. Dig supports his wounded priestess, whose eyes are wide and staring, her expression fixed with horror. I don't know if she will survive, but I can't bear to tell Dig to leave her. Sis rides on Calx's shoulders, exhausted but still spinning *gubdagogs* as fast as her fingers can fly.

We reach the library stairs, and here the Noswraiths abruptly thin out. They are still reluctant to go anywhere near the site of their former imprisonment. We hasten up to the top floor of the library and step into the open space beneath the crystal dome. It's strange to pass through that doorway and feel some measure of safety. What used to be the most dangerous place in all Vespre—possibly in all the worlds—has become our unexpected haven.

Mixael and I stand on either side of the door, pens at the ready, until each member of our party is through. Then we shut the door fast and drop the bolt. "Go," Mixael says, turning to me. "Help the Prince. I'll stand guard."

I open my mouth to answer, but it's Khas who speaks instead. "No," she says, reaching out to take his hand. "You come, Mixael."

He lifts his blue eyes to hers, soft and yet fixed with resolve. "Khas, my love, you must carry our son through the gate. You must be the warrior Sor needs."

She nods, her jaw firm, her expression fierce. "Yes," she says, "and you will come with us." She looks in that moment as though she will sling her husband over her powerful shoulders and carry him away with her.

But Mixael shakes his head. "I am the last librarian of Vespre," he says. "It is not a role I sought, but one to which I was born. I cannot abandon the people of Vespre. I cannot abandon the library." He draws a steadying breath. "I will remain until every last Noswraith is bound once more or I will die in the attempt, as befits a Vespre librarian."

A low growl rumbles in Khas's throat. "Then I will remain with you."

"No, Khas. I'll guard your retreat, but I cannot protect any of these others where you are going. They will need you. Sor will need you."

For a moment I fear Khas will fight him, that she will stand her ground and utterly refuse. And what could Mixael or I or anyone do to persuade her otherwise? But Mixael is right, and she knows it. Wherever the troll refugees end up, they will not be received with warm welcomes. They will need whatever protection they can get, and no one is better suited to that role than Captain Khas.

She bends her head and kisses her husband. I have to turn away for fear the sight will bring me to tears. I cannot afford tears. Not now. Not yet.

"*Grakol-dura, ghorza,*" Khas says, drawing back from Mixael, the words rumbling harsh in her throat.

He smiles, touches her cheek. "My shining diamond," he says. Then he kisses his weeping son, their two red heads momentarily blended under the starlight. "Now go," he urges his wife. "Go quickly! Lead the others."

Khas wrenches away and marches across the upper floor of the library to where the rest of our small party already gathers outside

Castien's office. Mixael turns to me then and nods. "Help the Prince," he says. "I'll stand guard."

I nod. "Give a shout if you need me."

He flashes a roguish grin, which momentarily transforms his face back to the young man I first met upon my arrival in Vespre. "Consider my next bloodcurdling scream your official invitation."

With a quick salute of my pen, I turn and hasten across the upper floor. The family groups have gathered into clusters, surviving parents holding their children tight. The orphans cling to Lir and Anj and my own grown children, but they do not weep. They are too stricken for tears. Everyone stands as still as the stone from which troll myth claims they were born. I feel as though I'm weaving through a cemetery as I make my way to my husband.

Castien stands in a little clear space before the door, which is open to reveal the messy room on the far side. For an instant I let my memory return to the stolen time we shared together there, and my skin burns with warmth. But there's no time to dwell on such pleasures. Castien holds out both hands, his fingers moving in a pattern I don't understand as he summons magic. I feel the flow of energy answering his call and feel how he directs it into that empty space beneath the doorframe. The air ripples, shifts, the same phenomenon I've witnessed beneath the great Between Gate arches. But something isn't right. There's resistance.

I turn to Castien. He looks strained. He's expending a tremendous amount of energy, and his wellspring isn't limitless. As the trueborn King of Aurelis, he was endowed with great power at the moment of his father's death, but that power is also linked to Aurelis itself, and he is far from his kingdom now.

Finally Castien utters a little curse that might be a prayer. I catch my breath, peering into the whirling space under the door once more. "Did it work?" I ask, uncertain. To my eye, it looks like an ordinary doorway; I can no longer detect the ripple of realities.

"It's been so long, and the connection is strained," Castien says, shaking his head. "We need someone on the other side to come through first in order to establish the opening."

My heart sinks. "It's hopeless then," I whisper. There's no one left on the far side of this gate who could possibly help, no one left who cares for Vespre or its people.

But Castien casts me a glittering smile. "Not so hopeless, Darling. I do still have friends in Aurelis."

"Who?"

A sudden surge of energy beneath the doorway draws my gaze. Bursts of golden light, like dawnlight pulled directly from Aurelis, shoot in stray beams from across the worlds, illuminating the library gloom. The trolls gasp and shield their sensitive eyes. I hold up a shading hand as well, but peer through my fingers into that swirling vortex.

A silhouette appears. The perspective is strange, making it seem both impossibly far away and simultaneously as though the figure stands in Castien's office, right in front of his desk. It walks toward us, closer, closer, hazy and warped as though seen through rippling veils. My heart lurches, and I grip my quill and book, half-convinced it's a Noswraith speeding toward us.

Then the figure steps out through the doorway—a man in a well-tailored household uniform, gloves on his hands, his hair slicked back from his plain, freckled face. He looks mildly around at the huddled trolls, at me with my pen, and brings his gaze at last to the Prince. "You summoned me, sir?"

Castien steps forward and claps his Obligate on the shoulder. "Good man, Lawrence! I knew you wouldn't let me down."

"I do endeavor to oblige," Lawrence responds with a hint of a smile.

"There's no time to lose." Castien indicates the gathered refugees. "We've got to get these folk through to Aurelis. What will they find on the other side?"

"Better than Noswraiths but not by much," Lawrence admits solemnly. "Princess Estrilde has taken over rule of Aurelis. She does not, however, pay much mind to the goings on in the library. Your friends' arrival will not be immediately discovered."

Castien catches my eye. We both know Estrilde will not welcome any Vespre folk into her bosom. But what other choice do we have? "It'll have to do," Castien says. He turns and barks for Captain Khas. She steps forward and salutes, an incongruous sight with her baby on her breast, cooing and blowing spit bubbles. Castien's eyes widen—after everything we've endured, everything he discovered upon returning to Vespre, *this* has taken him aback. His gaze flashes to meet Khas's once more, and there's even the ghost of a smile on his lips. It fades at once under the grimness of her returned stare. "You will go through first," Castien says. "Make certain all is safe."

Khas salutes. She draws her sword, sets her shoulders, every line of her warrior's build tense for action, even as Sor kicks his fat legs and babbles. She does not look back at Mixael, but I do. He stands guard at the library door still, book and quill at the ready. His gaze fixed on the back of his wife's head. My heart breaks for him, for them. For all of us.

Castien commences the spell, however, and the gate begins to open. Beams of golden light shoot through from the far side, and the trolls once more turn away, shielding their faces. But Khas does not flinch, though surely that brilliance must hurt her troll eyes as well. She merely covers little Sor's face with one hand and adjusts her grip on her sword. At the Prince's signal, she steps through. For a moment her silhouette stands poised in the opening. Then the vortex swallows her from sight.

"Darling!" Castien says, turning to me. "Get the others ready. I can't hold it open for long."

I nod and turn back to the rest. My eyes are met by Sis's fear-limned gaze, and my heart plunges with the sudden realization that I'm about to send my children through. That despite all my bold declarations to never leave them again, I'm about to be parted from them, perhaps forever. And there's no time for goodbyes.

"Har!" I cry, turning to my oldest boy. "You first. Help Khas if she needs it."

"*Korkor, kurs Mar,*" he responds with a flash of diamond teeth. Hastily I arrange the rest of them. Sis is ordered to hold the hands of two small children, and Calx takes up position behind her. Dig cradles his unconscious priestess against his shoulder but offers me a nod when I touch his big hand. The rest of the children and families line up in swift silence.

"Now!" Castien commands, and they begin to file through, Har first, the others marching swiftly behind him. I stand to one side and watch them go. All the things I wish I could say burn on my lips. Sis pauses at the opening, casting me one last agonized look, and for a moment, I fear she won't do as she's told—notoriously stubborn little thing that she is. But then she turns and dives through the veils, and Calx and Dig follow close behind. As each of them pass through, I feel pieces of my heart breaking off and going with them. Will I ever feel whole again? I doubt it. I hope not.

Someone steps to my side, watching the file of refugees pass by. I turn to see Lir, very solemn and still. "Lir, you must go too!" I say, touching her hand. "You must go with our children. They need you. They need their *mar.*"

She smiles and shakes her head, even as two tears trail down her cheeks. "Our children are brave, Mistress," she says. "Brave and bold. They will have each other, but . . ." She turns, and her gaze fastens on Anj. He is helping to direct the refugees through the gate, murmuring both comfort and commands to the smaller children. "He won't go," Lir says. "He won't leave his people behind." She draws a shaky breath. "He has no one else."

I take her hand. While part of me wants to urge her and argue, I offer instead my understanding. Whatever strife lies between her and Anj, they need each other. If I can't understand that, who can?

"We will fight," I say softly and squeeze her fingers. "We will fight with everything we have and reclaim this city. Then maybe we'll see our children again. Someday."

The words have scarcely left my mouth when there's a sudden knock at the door. It's such an unexpected sound, hollow and echoing. Though Castien maintains his focus, holding the gate open with all his strength, the rest of us exchange startled glances. Mixael backs away from the bolted door, his brow furrowed, his pen poised. But Noswraiths don't knock, do they?

Another knock. I let go of Lir's hand and, quill at the ready, hasten to Mixael's side. Whatever is there, I won't let him face it alone. "Courage, Miss Darlington," Mixael murmurs, though I suspect he's speaking more to himself than to me. "Steady now. After all we've faced, what's one more ghoulie, eh?"

Then a voice calls from the other side. A human voice, small and a little muffled.

"I know you're in there, Clara."

All warmth seeps from my blood. "Oscar," I breathe.

I turn to look back at Castien, wishing I could catch his gaze. But his entire concentration is fixed on keeping that gate open, and there are still so many left who need to go through. He cannot help me. He cannot support me.

Whatever happens next, I'm on my own.

"Clara? Clara, I know you can hear me."

His voice sounds sweet and scared. Like the little boy I once knew.

"What's going on?" Mixael whispers out of the corner of his mouth. "Is it a Noswraith?"

I shake my head and exhale a slow breath. "I'll handle this. Leave it to me." Closing my book and lowering my quill, I step to the door. My heart thunders against my breastbone, and my limbs tremble with dread. Strange how I was so confident in the face of all those nightmares, but the prospect of confronting my brother again? That is true terror. Slowly I lean forward, rest my ear against the door, poised, listening.

"I'm here, Oscar," I say softly. "I'm here with you."

He is silent for a long moment. Does he stand with his ear pressed to the other side? Just as he used to when Dad locked him in the coal cellar, and I would sit and whisper through the cracks in the door, letting him know he wasn't alone.

"You know what Ivor told me?" my brother says at last, breaking the silence between us. Though the door is thick, his voice sounds very close. "He told me that each man has a weakness at his core. A bad seed which must be rooted out with violence and vengeance if he is ever to be the strongest version of himself."

My lip trembles. "Dad used to say something like that too."

Oscar bites out a bitter curse. "Don't change the subject! This isn't about Dad. This is about you and me."

He is quiet again save for ragged breathing. Is he in a manic episode? Or has the *rothiliom* carried him too far into its green depths? Perhaps it is just the natural terror any soul must feel to be trapped in the Doomed City. I hate that he's on the far side of that door, hate that he's out there with all those nightmares, unprepared, unprotected. My hand unconsciously strays to the doorknob. I wrench it back with a force of will.

"Do you know what my weakness is, Clara?"

I close my eyes. I do know. And I don't want to hear him say it.

"It's you. It's always been you. I've always believed that you would save me, that you would stay with me. I believed I could depend on you even when everyone else failed me." The door vibrates suddenly, as though a fist pounded just where my ear rests. I wince but do not draw away. "You kept me weak! You held me back! You made me less than I could be, pathetic and loathsome. But Ivor taught me better. He showed me how to cut out weakness. How to be a man."

Tears stain my cheeks. There's darkness in his voice, as deep as the Nightmare Realm and equally as twisted. It pulses from inside him, drawn up from the deepest well of his soul. The child I know is gone, replaced with someone cold and cruel, but still terrified. Always terrified.

It's not Oscar's voice I hear—it's Edgar's. If I didn't know any better, I'd think my father stood just on the other side of this door.

"Open up, Clara," he says and pounds it again with his fist. "Let me in now."

I shake my head. "No."

"I'll break it down if I have to. You know I can do it, you know I have the means."

I do. I know what destruction he can bring about in the next few moments with a single flick of his pen. "You don't have to do this," I beg. "You can let these people go. Just let them leave Vespre, and don't hurt them."

Then another voice speaks in the darkness on the far side. A voice once golden, rich, and beautiful, now ravaged with pain, disappointment, and deadly triumph: "How exactly do they plan on leaving Vespre, Clara Darlington?"

I jerk back from the door, my eyes widening. Ivor. Ivor is there with Oscar. And I just revealed . . . what? What did I reveal? Too much, too much, too—

The door crashes open. The force of the blast knocks me off my feet, sends me skidding across the floor. I lift my head, vision spinning, and see twisting shadows pour in through the doorway and swarm the upper floor. Standing in the center of those shadows, too large to fit in this space, is a giant, an all-encompassing horror: the Hollow Man.

For the space of a single breath, his shadow-licked eyes stare down at me, and I see the twin pinpoints of red light gleaming in their depths. Then he turns his heavy head slowly, casts his gaze to the gate, which the Prince still holds open for the remaining refugees.

"*Castien!*" I scream. "Break the gate! *Break it now!*"

Castien stands in a whirling cloud of magic, which he channels from the *quinsatra* and sends in a steady pulse to the gate itself. I can barely see him through the glare, but I feel the moment when he looks my way, feel his desperation. He'd hoped in the end to convince me to pass through as well, to carry our child to safety and away from Vespre and its horrors. Even now if he could, he would urge me to pick myself up and hurtle through the portal.

But there's no chance of that. And there's no time. With a twist of his arms, he begins to break down the spell.

The Hollow Man lumbers forward. His huge feet shake the floor, the walls, rattle the cracked and broken panes of the dome overhead. Trolls scream and scatter, terrified, but his attention is focused on that portal, on escape. I cast about, but though I still hold Dasyra's quill, I've dropped my book. I have to write something, I have to craft a spell, a binding, anything.

Before I can take action, Mixael jumps in the Noswraith's path, his whip of white fire brandished high. He lashes out, wraps the coils of the whip around the Hollow Man's leg, and yanks. His spell-work is good; the wraith utters a gut-churning roar and crashes down hard. Mixael springs out of the way, narrowly avoiding being crushed, and sets to work lashing the Hollow Man's flailing right arm. Lir steps forward as well, a *gubdagog* between her hands. She throws it over the Hollow Man's face, and the nightmare begins to shrink. I can scarcely believe it. Between the two of them, they have him down, pinned. Mixael will bind him, and even without his true name, we can get him contained.

The thought has scarcely crossed my mind before Ivor is there. He strides into the room, hunched and warped and hideous, his face set in a rictus grin. He heaves a sword, lunges . . . and I watch the blade pierce through Mixael's abdomen.

I scream. Wordless, wild. As though the blow was dealt to me instead.

Mixael gasps. His eyes widen. He looks down at the blade protruding from his body, sinks to his knees.

Anj is already in motion. He throws himself straight at Ivor. His big troll hands close around the fae lord's shoulders, and he hurls him across the room. Ivor hits the rail around the central well of the citadel. It cracks, and for a moment I think he will break through and plummet. But he doesn't. He pulls himself upright, and his smile is like a devil's in his warped marred face.

Mixael's binding spell disintegrates, the white whip vanishing to nothing. The Hollow Man shakes free, rises up, ripping Lir's *gubdagog* from his face. He fixes those terrible eyes of his on the gate again, his goal unchanged, his purpose fixed.

And I know then what I must do.

I'm on my feet. I'm running, diving for my old writing desk. Ivor lets out a shout. He sees me and surges in pursuit. Distantly I hear Oscar's voice screaming my name and know my brother has also entered the library. I ignore him, ignore Ivor, ignore everything. My entire focus is on that cubicle and what I know I will find there. I dash open a drawer, yank out a blank book, throw open the cover. Drag Dasyra's quill across the empty page.

The Nightmare Realm closes in around me.

29

I SIT UPRIGHT IN BED.

My bed. The one with the bonnet lady quilt and the cold iron headboard. The one I lay in so many sleepless nights on Clamor Street, straining my ears for telltale sounds down below, for the haunting presence of my own father. The bed of my childhood, my young adulthood.

My fingers curl into fists, gripping handfuls of quilt. It all feels so real, so true. I know I'm not really here but somewhere back in Vespre. Vulnerable. Writing for dear life while enemies close in upon me, ready to cut my physical body down where she stands. But if I don't deal with the Hollow Man now, no one can. There's no one else left.

Soft sobs catch my ear. My heart lurches as though stabbed straight through. "Oscar!" I whisper. In that same moment an overwhelming cloud of doom comes over me. Absolute dread breathes in the very walls, like a hundred voices, screaming, whimpering, weeping, laughing, and moaning all at once.

He's coming, he's coming.

He's coming now.

He's going to find you.

He's going to hurt you.

He's coming, he's coming . . .

I leap from the bed, my bare feet hitting icy floorboards. I'm a child—a young girl just on the brink of womanhood, all elbows and knees. And I'm so afraid. But Oscar is out there, and he's crying. He needs me.

I hasten from my room out into the passage, a passage I both recognize and don't. It isn't the upstairs hall that I know, for it stretches on and on and on, with doors on either side. The only light source is the streetlamp shining dimly through the far window, casting the space in a dull reddish glow.

He's coming.

He's coming.

Dragging in a ragged breath, I leap to the first door, the one beside mine, the one that should lead to Oscar's room. When I fling it open, there's nothing but absolute blackness and . . . far head, as though at a distance but drawing nearer . . . two burning eyes. I slam the door shut.

He's coming.

I dart to the next door, fling it open as well. More of that same blackness, only this time, the eyes are closer. Panic floods my limbs. I slam that door, turn, fling myself to the one on the opposite side of the hall. Each door I open reveals only more of the same, but Oscar's weeping increases in frenzy until I can hear words among the sobs. "Clara! Clara, where are you?"

"I'm coming!"

He's coming.

I spin in place, my hands in my hair. I have moments, mere moments, before it's too late. Where is he? Where? I look back to the room I vacated. My own room, my bedroom. Feet pounding on the bare floorboards, I retrace my steps. The hall feels impossibly long, and a weird sluggishness weighs down my limbs. Somehow I reach the doorway, pull myself inside, and drop to my knees. I lift the edge of the bonnet lady quilt and there! There, under the bed—a tear-streaked face, a pair of enormous eyes, framed in floppy dark curls.

I reach under, grab Oscar by both hands, and drag him out. He sobs uncontrollably, his whole body trembling. "He's coming! He's coming!" he cries, joining his voice to the whispers in the walls.

"Hush." I hold him close. Though he is a small, thin, bony little boy, I am no longer a child, but a woman. Myself. Clara Darlington as I have become, warrior and librarian. He pushes back from me, looks up at me with wondering eyes. I can't tell if it's his child's face I see or the adult he's become. He's just Oscar. Oscar my darling, my beloved.

"It's my fault!" he whimpers. "I shouldn't have done it. It's my fault, and now he's coming. He's going to punish me. He's going to make me pay."

"No." My grip on him tightens. "I won't let him touch you. Never again."

A shadow falls across the floor. I twist in place, looking up. There in the doorway is that same darkness that lurked within all those chambers, and those twin pinpoints of red light, drawing nearer, nearer.

Something burns in my breast. "Get behind me, Oscar," I say and push him gently from my lap before rising to my feet. I step in front of him as he clings to my skirts, shuddering with dread. But I'm not afraid. Not anymore. Somewhere, far away in another world, another lifetime, my physical body writes. Perhaps she has moments left to live. Perhaps Ivor's sword even now descends upon her in a deadly arc.

But I will fight. Until the end.

I raise my hand. A burning sword appears in my grasp, lighting up the room, lighting up the darkness, lighting up the silhouette of the Hollow Man, who looms large in my doorway. He morphs reality around him, filling up that space but never contained by it. He's an idea—terror given flesh and form but unbound by either limitation. He is as great as the emptiness inside him, a yawning hunger, an unfillable vastness. The gaping hole in his shattered chest could swallow worlds and still not be filled. The well of his soul is devouring and unsatiable and endless.

I know him. The only monster who could ever spring from

Oscar's mind and heart.

"Edgar," I snarl.

The Hollow Man looks straight at me. In his gaze I feel the absolute smallness of myself, the worthlessness. A wave of contempt rolls out from that hollow center in a noxious cloud, and I know in his eyes I am nothing, less than nothing.

But I have Oscar to defend.

"You won't have him!" I cry, leaping forward. "Not this time!" I swing my sword, a whistling arc of light and steel and hack straight for his head. The Hollow Man rears back, surprised. His head smashes through the ceiling, which splinters and falls all around us. The walls shiver and fall away too, disintegrating into darkness. I don't pause. Not when my house crumbles, not when the ground underneath my feet breaks and plunges. I lunge again, swinging my sword, and the Hollow Man backs away three paces. With each retreating step, he grows, becoming more terrible, more horrible in my sight. The great looming vastness of Father, who cannot be fought, who can only be submitted to on bended knee. I feel the compulsion of my childhood, the compulsion to bend, to bow, to let him overwhelm and devour. It's so great, this terror, this awe, this love, this need freezing my limbs.

"I'm not the child I once was!" I scream into the face of the nightmare. "I'm no longer at your mercy. And I will save him this time."

The Hollow Man swings at me with one great arm. I bring my sword up with all my might and slice right through the wrist.

Black blood spurts, hot and thick and rotten. I dodge the flood and swing at his leg, hewing clean through bone. The Noswraith roars and comes down hard on one knee.

His heavy head turns. His eyes focus on me.

I dodge his swiping arm, drop to the ground, and roll, nimble as a cat. When I come up, I wrench my hands apart, splitting my sword into two glowing chain links. As the Hollow Man lunges, I throw first one than the other. They wrap around his arms, so heavy, so tight, weighing him down. He shrinks beneath them. I twirl my hand, and another chain appears, spelled into being by my fast-writing pen in another reality. I wrap this chain around his neck, pull him smaller, smaller, until he is nothing but a hunched little bag of creeping bones, bowed before me in this landscape of shadows.

I stand over him, tall and strong. Now it is I who gaze upon him with contempt.

"You are nothing," I snarl. "You wanted to make your name great across the nation. You would sacrifice anything to your ambition, but what did it bring you in the end?" I create another chain, bind him faster, tighter. He roars, straining, but he's helpless in my grasp. "That legacy of yours? Forgotten. Everything you cared about is nothing but rot and ruin now. Like you."

He shudders, bowed down before me, straining against his chains but unable to break them. A Greater Noswraith? Hardly. He's nothing but a minor fright, a pathetic joke.

"You never were anything," I say, standing over him. "You are hollow, Edgar. Empty, weak. Puffing yourself up on our misery because you always knew there was nothing real inside you."

His head rears back. Those living shadows pour from his eyes, from the hole in his chest, struggling even now to reach me, to claim me, to draw me into their depths. I jerk the end of the chain, and the monster roars and rattles, helpless in my grasp. Bending over him, I spit in his face. "When you died, the whole world breathed a sigh of relief. You were not mourned. You will not be remembered. You are nothing."

His raging eyes gape up at me, twin windows into hell. For a moment—a terrible moment, that sends my heart plunging—I see him. Edgar. With his prominent brow and the shaggy, overgrown beard, his collar pulled askew, his tie hanging limp from his neck. I see him, this man I loved and feared and wanted so desperately to please and to emulate. My father. My idol. My god.

You're not seeing rightly . . .

He's in pain . . .

A ragged cry bursts from my lips. I draw my arms back, and a sword forms from nothing an instant before I bring it down, straight through the Hollow Man's neck.

His head tumbles. Hits the ground. Rolls.

Trailing a river of black blood.

I stand above him, breathing hard. And I'm no longer in the formless dark of the Nightmare. I'm on Clamor Street, gazing down on the moonlit body of my father. My dead father, who lies in ruin beside me, unable to hear my screams. Only I'm not the one screaming. I'm the one holding the sword. I'm the one who ended him.

I stare at that broken body, the blood, the death. My own screams, disembodied, disconnected from me, echo in my ears. I am the slayer, and I am the mourner. I am both and neither at once.

And Edgar lies dead at my feet.

"Dad?" I whisper, my voice choking. "Dad, what have I done?"

A piercing scream.

Not my own voice—Oscar's.

I whirl on heel toward our house. My brother stands in the doorway, staring out at me. Only it isn't the child Oscar but the man, and he isn't standing in the doorway of our wretched house on Clamor Street but the entrance to Vespre library. The library comes into focus all around me, the chaos, the starlight, the hard, painful reality. I stand in my cubicle, looking at my brother over the spell-scrawled pages of the book in my hands.

"Clara!" he cries, stretching out his hand to me. "Clara, help me—"

A sudden gout of red mist billows up from behind and envelops him, even as a subtle voice whispers in my ear: *He really loves you, you know.*

Then pale arms wrap around my brother and jerk him back from the doorway, back into that mist.

"*Oscar!*" I cry.

30

SOME DISTANT PART OF ME IS STILL AWARE OF THE WORLD around me. Aware that I'm still standing in my cubicle with the volume containing the Hollow Man's binding clutched in my hands. Ivor grapples with Anj, while Lir kneels beside Mixael's fallen body. Castien stands at the gate, working to break it, power flowing through and around him.

It's been no more than a few seconds since I entered the Nightmare Realm.

It's also been a lifetime.

I stare at that open doorway, writhing with mist. No one else seems to have noticed the arrival of a new Noswraith. No one else realizes what this means, who she is. But I know.

The Eyeless Woman has Oscar.

My own nightmare, my own creation. And she's taken my brother.

With a roar I snatch another blank book from the desk, wrenching open the cover to a fresh page. Immediately I plunge back into the Realm of Nightmare, surrounded by churning shadows so thick, they obscure all view of the library. I don't care. I fling out my arm, and my flaming sword appears once more. Springing out from the shelter of the cubicle, I race to that doorway. But it's no longer the entrance to the library.

Instead I look down into the Clamor Street coal cellar.

Red mist churns below, consuming the rickety stairs. I hesitate for no more than a breath before diving through that doorway, plunging down those stairs, straight into the mist. Heedless, reckless. What should only take ten short paces stretches on into twenty, fifty, a hundred. I hurtle faster, careless of my own safety, of whether or not I'll miss my footing and break my neck. The mist roils around me, burning, creeping into my nose, my lungs.

Oscar screams.

Screams of pain. Of fear. Of hopeless horror.

Oscar, Oscar, *Oscar*.

Suddenly the mist parts like curtains as I reach the final step. I stagger but swiftly bring my sword up into a defensive stance, ready to hack the Eyeless Woman in two. But there is no wraith. Even the mist evaporates now. There's nothing but the frigid coal cellar with its low ceiling and one grimy window looking out at the world on street level. A little hunched form huddles in the farthest corner.

"Oscar," I breathe. Dropping my sword, I leave it burning on the floor and race across the cellar. I fall to my knees beside the boy and grip his hands. His cold hands. I touch his face, roll him toward me. He's so cold, too cold. "Oscar, please! Answer me!"

His head lolls to one side, an unnatural angle. His eyes, staring out from those hollowed-out sockets . . . they're glazed over. Dead.

"No," I whimper. "No, no, no!" Then I throw my head back and scream. Scream to the high, echoing, stone ceiling of the palace hall below the library stairs. Scream until my voice fills all Vespre. The coal cellar is gone, as is my sword. There is nothing but a discarded book with a few scrawled lines and a red quill pen lying beside me. And Oscar. Broken on the floor. Every bone in his body smashed, his collarbone sagging at a weird angle, his neck limp, his head crooked unnaturally.

Oscar.

Oscar.

I gather him in my arms, plead with him to speak, to say my name, to give me one last word. I press his bloodied, battered face to my breast, sobbing into his matted hair. "I'm sorry!" I wail, the words thick and broken and useless on my tongue. "I'm sorry, I'm sorry! I'm sorry I couldn't save you, sorry I couldn't be what you needed. I'm sorry for everything, everything . . ."

He can't be gone. It was too soon, too abrupt. I'm not ready. Gods damn me, I'm not ready.

Mist coils around my knees. I peer out through my tears, watch the red, glowing tendrils. They crawl out from every corner of this dark chamber, creep down the walls, ooze out through crevices in the stone, filling up the atmosphere. Slowly, I lift my face from Oscar's battered form and turn to look across the hall.

There stands Emma. Clad in her white nightgown. Barefoot. Small. Long dark hair hangs in straggling strands across her shoulders and covers her face. But then she lifts her head, revealing the sewn-up eye sockets and the black threads dangling against her smiling cheeks. She holds out both hands in gentle supplication.

He really loves you, you know.

My teeth set on edge. Carefully I lay my brother down on the floor and reach for my quill. The instant my hand touches it, it becomes a flaming sword in my grasp. "All right, Mama," I say softly. "I took care of Dad already."

I rise to my feet, brace myself, and raise my sword up high.

"Your turn."

31

I HURTLE STRAIGHT AT THE NOSWRAITH. SHE HISSES, looking more monstrous than ever, and raises hands like claws as though to ward me off. I hack through those hands, sword sizzling. The stench of rotten flesh fills the air.

Then mist whirls up around me, blinding me. I angle my blade, slicing through coils which replenish at once, denser than before. I've stood in this mist before. I know what's coming. A battle cry on my lips, I whirl, carving at nothing. My sword passes uselessly through vapors.

The first blow nearly knocks me off my feet.

I gasp, stagger, the breath driven out of me. Recovering quickly, I whirl and lash back, striking once more at emptiness.

You're not seeing rightly.

Emma's voice echoes all around me. I scream and thrust my blade, only for another blow to knock me to my knees.

He needs us. He's in pain.

A third blow cracks the bone in my arm and sends my weapon flying. I collapse to all fours, scrambling around in the mist, searching for the sword, frantic. Another blow catches me in the ribs, sends me skidding across the paving stones.

Dearest, you must come. Come and see for yourself how much he loves you.

Another blow batters my head just as I'm trying to pull myself upright. I go over backwards, my hands flailing. But no—no! I'm not going to take this. I'm not going to give in and let my own wraith destroy me. With a savage cry, I stretch out one hand. No grappling in the dark, no searching—I am a mistress of my craft, a mage, a wielder of ancient magic. I will not be undone by my own damned spell.

So I extend my arm, and the sword appears, flaming bright, burning away the mist. I take hold with both hands and slash wildly upward. The blade makes contact with something I cannot see, something huge, which bellows and backs away on heavy feet. I don't hesitate. I lunge, striking out again and again. I hit something and smell burnt flesh. I'm utterly blind, but I don't care. Pure rage drives me now.

You're not seeing rightly.

You're not seeing rightly.

"Damned right, I'm not!" I bellow and raise the sword over my head, hewing downward in a powerful stroke. The mist parts before me.

I stop.

A picture appears: a vignette seen as though through a foggy glass but slowly clarifying. I see a warm hearth, a dancing fire in the grate. I hear the gentle *creak-creak-creak* of a rocking chair, the click of darning needles. And voices. Low, sweet, giggling voices. Those come from the two figures on the floor in front of the hearth. Children, a boy and a girl, seated together. The boy's head rests on the girl's shoulder, and she holds up a book which obscures her face, but which gives me a clear view of the title: *Adventure Stories for Boys* by G.H. Godswin.

A breath shudders from my lips. Slowly the rest of the image comes into view: Mama, rocking away in her chair, focused on her handwork, while her two phantom children giggle and read together. I cannot hear the words, only the tone of their voices. But I can see them clearly now. I see the bruises on Oscar's face. I see the tension in Clara's jaw and around her eyes. I see the careful smile on Mama's face, the smile which reveals no true emotion, that refuses to let any unwanted expression stain her careful mask.

"He suffered because of you, you know."

I inhale sharply. When Mama speaks, her voice is clear, unlike the voices of the children on the floor. She goes on rocking, but I know she's aware of me and my silent observation. The rest of the image seems to fade, as though she and I are the only two real things in this place.

"He suffered because of you. You didn't protect him." She lowers her work, lifting her face and turning toward me. "You should have been stronger, Clara."

She isn't Mama.

She wears Mama's soft lavender gown, her brown hair coiled in a neat bun at the base of her neck. But her face is deathly white, and black threads dangle down her cheeks from the raw, bloody stitches sealing her eyes shut.

"I know you," I whisper.

"It's your fault he's dead," she says, still smiling, still rocking. "You weren't enough for him in the end. You failed him."

"I know you," I say again. "And . . . and I see you."

The apparition's smile grows. "You're not seeing rightly," she says gently. "You've never seen rightly."

"I know," I answer. Tears form in my eyes, spilling out onto my cheeks. "You're right. I never have. I never saw . . . *you*."

The image around the fire fades more and more. Red mist closes in around us, enveloping the children, muffling their voices as they read together. But the woman goes on rocking, her features hollowing out, melting away into the haggard, monstrous creature with the lank black hair and the sunken cheeks.

But I shake my head. "No, this isn't right either."

I drop my sword. It melts away into nothing the instant it leaves my grasp. Unarmed I step forward, kneel before the rocking chair, before the hideous Noswraith. She hisses at me, revealing bloody teeth. I don't flinch. Not this time. I reach out a steady hand and slowly, delicately, begin to pull the stitches from her eyes.

He really loves you, you know.

No one else understands him.

We have to care for him. Who else will if we don't?

The words echo in my head even as the wraith's mouth remains bared in a terrible grimace. I don't respond. I pluck those stitches free, one after the other. The Noswraith's face screws up with pain.

Finally her eyes blink open. Two large, brown eyes, surrounded by pin-prick wounds that seep beads of blood. But the face is no longer hollow, pale, and haggard. It's a young face, full-cheeked, with a round little nose and a rosebud mouth. A face far too young to bear such fear, such guilt, such shame. She's a child. Just a child. Trapped in this house, believing if she could just find the right thing to say, the right thing to do, the right way to be, she might be able to fix what's broken.

"It's time to see rightly," I whisper. "It's time to see who you really are. *Clara.*"

Blood and tears pour down the child's cheeks. She shakes her head.

"You are strong," I tell her. "You are brave. And you were placed in an impossible position. You've made many wrong choices, for there were no right choices to make. There was nothing but survival, day after day. Survival and the choice to love those who did not deserve it. To love and to pretend to be loved in return. Because as long as you pretended, you could go on surviving."

I reach out then, take the child in my arms, pull her from the rocking chair and into my lap. "You don't have to pretend anymore. I'm here now." I press a kiss to the top of her dark head, which rests against my breast. The child is so tense in my arms, so uncertain and afraid. But I hold her tight. "I love you, Clara. I love you, and I'm proud of you, and I will protect you. I will fight for you. You don't have to keep on fighting. Not anymore." I close my eyes, tears falling freely. "I wasn't ready before. But I am now. I'm ready to be what you need."

Tension melts out of the child's limbs. She begins weeping, softly at first, then loud, hiccupping sobs. Tears and blood soak the front of my bodice.

"We are so much stronger than we know," I say, rocking her back and forth. "And we will learn from our mistakes. We will break the cycle and we will grow. We won't stay here in this house. It's time to come out."

Time to release shame.

To release fear.

To release guilt.

Time to release . . . *me*.

I get to my feet, the child cradled in my arms. Red mist parts around me, and I see that I'm no longer in the pretty front parlor of our old family home. No, we're back in the coal cellar. But this time it isn't Oscar I hold and comfort in the dark. It's my own small, trembling, frightened self. I turn to the cellar steps, begin to climb. The mist coils around me, trying to hold me back, but it has lost its power over me now that I know my Noswraith's true name.

Not Emma.

Clara.

White light pours through the doorway above, warming my face, warming my soul. I climb higher, still murmuring words of encouragement to the child. Just as I reach the topmost step, the figure in my arms melts into my chest, into my heart. I feel her enter and become one with me again. I feel the wholeness inside me where a piece has been missing. This is powerful magic—the magic of pure creativity rejoining my soul.

The Noswraith is gone. Healed. Whole.

With a shout akin to laughter, I burst through the open door and stagger out into the white light. In that moment I'm more powerful than I've ever been, powerful enough to vanquish all foes. But the light around me is blinding, and I cannot see where I have come. I put up a hand, shading my face.

Worthless.

A long black shadow falls across me. I gasp. Fear jolts through every limb as I whirl about and look up, up, up.

Up into the leering face of the Hollow Man.

32

HE CAME BACK.

Of course he came back. Because chopping off his head couldn't bind him. Not for long. No Noswraith is bound for long. Time is a meaningless concept to beings such as they. Words and ink and stitched spines, what do such things matter to nightmares? They will wait them out and escape to the ravaged minds of mortals, filling them with their malice, their hatred, their horror.

All the glory of my victory vanishes in an instant, overwhelmed by the sheer vastness of this darkness before me. The same darkness which haunted me and my brother since before memory—the great power, unstoppable, almost deified in its might. There is no escape. There is no hiding. There is nothing to be done but to love, to adore, to bow one's head, to accept the suffering that must come upon beings as worthless as we.

Worthless.

Shameful.

Guilty.

Pathetic.

The multitudinous voices echo in my soul. I bow my head, kneeling and broken, succumbed before him. I close my eyes, squeeze them shut, expecting any moment for the death blow to fall, for the Hollow Man to swallow me up in his echoing emptiness. But as I crouch there, I press my hands to my heart and . . . and there's something there that was missing before. That piece of my power which had gone out from me for a while, but which is now restored.

The child hidden safe and close in my soul.

Suddenly I remember. I remember what Vervain taught me. I remember what George Godswin revealed. I remember what I just experienced for myself and now hold as truth in the very core of my being. I remember.

And I look up into that awful face.

"Oscar?" I say.

The Hollow Man rears back as though struck. Shadows ripple from his eyes, pour from his broken chest, pulsing like blood. He is hideous and fantastic, a true nightmare made flesh, and yet . . . and yet . . . I recognize him. He isn't Edgar. He never was. No more than the Eyeless Woman was Emma. Our parents are dead and gone and lost. These, their haunting phantoms, are the images our own hearts created. They belong to us.

"Oscar," I say again, "Oscar, my dearest." I hold out my arms.

The Hollow Man, massive as a mountain, giant and twisted, roars. He lunges at me, his broken cavern chest gaping to gulp me down. But I close my eyes, refuse to see what my mind is trying to make me see. Instead I focus on the truth, reach out with both arms, and catch him in my embrace. He is unbound by time and space, an impossibly huge monstrosity of churning shadow. Yet I hold him, writhing, squirming, struggling to get free. I hold him, press him to my heart, even as he bites and claws my flesh. I hold on fast.

But this time I know I cannot hold on forever.

"Let go of him, Oscar," I say, speaking into a head of dark, curly hair while the wraith contorts in my grasp and rips at my soul. "Let go of this shadow. He needn't haunt you anymore." The being in my arms shakes its head, desperate to break my hold. But I won't relent. Though Oscar is dead, I embrace the last living vestiges of him, this hideous creature born from his heart. I embrace it because it *is* Oscar. The last, final, horrible truth of my brother's existence. And I will say my piece and it won't be too late.

"You always drove yourself to beat him. You thought if you could make yourself stronger, better, bigger, then he couldn't hurt you anymore."

The wraith shudders, howls, slavers . . . and becomes a child, beaten black and blue. A child with no recourse against a terrifying father save to become that which he feared most. Which is what he did. Following in the hated footsteps of his worst nightmare, destroying himself every step of the way. Failing to rise above, failing to defeat, only to become.

Hopelessness throbs in the heart of this little boy. Hollowness, an empty void that could never be filled, not by the love of a brutal father nor the love of a weak mother. Not even the love of a desperate, clinging, stubborn sister. Nothing. Nothing could fill that void. Because it was never meant to be filled.

"Oscar," I whisper. "Oscar, you've already won. You won long ago. Don't you understand?"

The Noswraith draws back, peering up at me from its dark, twisted, shadow-writhing mask. But behind the shadows and the hollow eyes, I can just discern my brother.

"Edgar is gone," I say. "He died, and everything he was died with him. He is unmourned and unloved. But you?" I cup his awful face in my hands, feel the soft round cheeks beneath the hard ridges. "I will love you until my dying day. And love like that never ends. It lives on through eternity, long after we are dust. When our names, our faces, our deeds are forgotten, still that love endures." I lean forward, press my lips to his savage brow, then rest my forehead against his. "You defeated Edgar long ago. For I will mourn you, dearest brother, as he was never mourned. And I will hold my love for you forever in my heart."

When I look again, Oscar's large brown eyes gaze back at me. "Clara?" he whispers.

"Give him up, Oscar," I whisper. "Let him go."

For an instant I glimpse twin points of light in the depths of his pupils, the flame of genius which always burned there, feeding on hatred, passion, and fear. That light flares again, bright torches in the depths. But even as I watch, it transforms into a white, shining radiance.

Oscar closes his eyes, tilts his head back. The apparition in my arms dissolves into little points of light, floating away into the air. I kneel in this space outside reality, kneel in the street of my family home, watching him drift into the distant night sky. I press my hands to my heart, holding the warmth in its center.

"Let him go," I whisper.

And finally . . . I do.

THE PRINCE

THE POWER INSIDE ME IS OF SUCH DESTRUCTIVE FORCE, one wrong move, and I will bring this whole palace crumbling to dust.

A distant part of me is aware of the mayhem all around—of Noswraiths and battle and blood and death. But I cannot turn my attention to it. If I do, I will look for Clara. In that moment, I will be done for. I'm not strong enough to resist throwing myself completely to her defense or rescue.

No, I must trust her to fight her own battles. After all I cannot save her from everything—particularly not the monsters which haunt her soul. If she does not choose to save herself, there's nothing I can do. I learned that lesson seven long years ago.

So I concentrate on the gate and the spell of unmaking. I'm not as strong as I would be if I stood on the other side of that portal, in the realm of my kingship. Some of that raw, Aurelian power funnels through realities to reach me, but if anything, that makes it harder to reverse the spell, to break the gate, to cut myself off from that great wellspring of magic. But I won't risk Ivor escaping into the worlds beyond.

The gate crumbles. The vastness of too many realities opening at once ripple, surge, and spurt out magic in bursts. The doorway cracks, stone falling in a showering stream. Then, with a last expulsion of energy, the portal collapses.

The blast strikes me straight on, sends me hurtling against the wall. I fall to the floor, momentarily stunned. Shaking my head to clear the pulsing magic still moving in my brain, I look up. Before me stands the doorway to my office. The frame is cracked, but otherwise all looks as it was. No gaping void, no churning vortex. Just a simple doorway opening into a chamber crammed with books and shelves and a too-large desk.

I let out a short breath. It's done then. Vespre is truly sundered from the worlds.

As though doors and windows are suddenly flung open, I become aware of the noise all around me. Blinking away the last of the daze, I take in the sights. My gaze lands first on Mixael, gasping for breath as he lies in a pool of blood, his hands pressed to a gash in his side. Anj grapples with Ivor, the two of them intent on carving each other to ribbons with their swords. Anj is so great and terrible, and Ivor such a small, wretched thing, yet he does not give ground. His madness has made him ferocious, and even the powerful troll warrior falters beneath his blows.

As though my gaze alerts him, Ivor turns abruptly and fixes his mad, rolling eye on me. Then he looks beyond me to the gate. Broken, empty. His face seems almost to rip in half as his jaw opens in a horrible roar. With a last vicious twist, he knocks Anj's sword spinning from his grasp. It lands with a clang, but rather than run the troll through, Ivor pivots on heel and flees the library.

I'm on my feet in an instant, snatching up the big troll sword as I go. Some instinct tells me that even now, with the gates closed and his plan foiled, I dare not let Ivor out of my sight. I rush from the library to the top of the stair and look over the rail to see Ivor descending at lunatic speed. At first I think he merely flees me. Then I spy a figure kneeling on the floor below: Clara. Cradling a broken body in her arms.

Ivor comes to a halt, staggers, and grips the newel for support. His ravaged voice chokes out a single word: "Oscar?"

Clara startles and looks up. When she sees Ivor standing above her, sword in hand, she does not react. She merely presses her brother's corpse closer, her expression filled with raw pain and yet, simultaneously, a strange serenity.

Ivor utters a wordless roar. Then he points that long blade directly at her face. "You never understood him," he snarls. "You never believed in him, never saw what he could be."

Clara does not answer. She looks Ivor in the eye, along the line of that blade.

"This is your fault!" Ivor continues. "You stubborn, willful bitch. Everything would have come about right, everything would have been made what it should be. I would be king! Ruler of a united Eledria! I would have risen to my destiny, acclaimed by all."

Clara shakes her head slowly. "You are so small, Ivor. Small and mean and . . . in the end . . . nothing."

Ivor stares at her, his sword arm trembling. For a moment he cannot speak, cannot move, struck utterly immobile by her disdain. Then he roars, draws back his arm, his blade angled to take off her head.

But I'm already there. Plunging over the banister, I fall to the floor, land lightly, and bring the troll sword down hard and block that blow. Fae steel rings against the troll crystal blade. Ivor whirls about, shocked. When he sees me, hellfire blazes to light in his one remaining eye. All the hatred that exists between us ignites an inferno in the atmosphere as he hurtles toward me, blade flashing. I receive his blows, parry, lunge, deflect.

Then, in a single fluid thrust, I drive my blade straight through Ivor's heart.

He gasps. Staggers back. Stares dumbly down at the weapon protruding from his chest. A flicker of glamour comes over him, sparked into being in this last moment of life. The hideous visage that escaped from the pit vanishes, replaced once more by the golden and glorious fae who once held the whole court of Aurelis in the palm of his hand. He lifts his head, tosses shining hair back from his shoulders, and gazes at me from two brilliant, hate-filled eyes. He smiles. Blood flows from his mouth, dribbles over his chin. "Hail king," he says, choking on the words.

Then he falls to the ground. The last heir of Illithorin. Dead.

I turn to Clara. She has not moved but still kneels on the floor, holding her brother's broken body. She looks numbly at Ivor, as though she doesn't even realize what has happened. Slowly she lifts her gaze to meet mine. "He's gone," she says.

She doesn't mean Ivor.

I drop to my knees beside her, wrap my arms around her, and pull her to me. She rests her head against my shoulder and utters a shuddering sob. "Darling," I croon, unable to find words of comfort as she weeps. I can do nothing. I can only anchor her here in this world, with me. "Clara, my darling."

All around us the shadows writhe with nightmare life. But they are far too afraid to draw any nearer.

CLARA

33

"LET ME SEE IF I'VE GOT THIS RIGHT. YOU'RE TELLING ME you effectively *destroyed* two Noswraiths? As in *permanently?*"

I smile down into Mixael Silveri's disbelieving face. He lies in his own bed, beneath a tangle of empty *gubdagog* threads, bandaged, pale, unable to sit up. But alive.

The palace has been quiet ever since the gate was closed. A hush has fallen across the entire city. If I didn't know any better, I would think word of the Eyeless Woman and the Hollow Man's demise spread through the Nightmare Realm, and the rest of the Noswraiths fled into hiding, making themselves small and unobtrusive. Not one report of a Noswraith attack has reached the palace in three days. People are starting to come out of hiding, starting to look ahead with something like tentative hope.

Castien has been ceaseless in his labors. He's down in the city streets more often than not, a stack of blank books in his arms, hunting out each and every wraith, both big and small. They put up little resistance against him, empowered as he is. When he's filled every book to the brim, he returns to the library and turns them over to me to sort and shelve. I would like to be down in the streets with him, but for now allow him to persuade me to stay in the palace, to guard the library, and to oversee Mixael's recovery.

The head librarian has not proven the easiest of patients. He knows better than anyone how understaffed we are and wants to be out on the hunt with the Prince. But he's in no condition to do more than sit upright in his bed, sipping the occasional bowl of gruel. It's unfair, I know; with his wife and child sent through the portal, he longs for nothing more than distraction from his loss. I offer him both company and sympathy as often as I can. When I entered his room today and saw the color just pinking his pale cheeks, I decided it was time to tell him of my recent discoveries.

"Three, actually," I say in answer, modestly smoothing my skirts. "Dulmier Fen wasn't exactly a powerful wraith, but it gave me the experience I needed. And I couldn't have done it at all were it not for Vervain."

Mixael shakes his head in baffled wonder. "You know, Miss Darlington," he says, and I silently forgive him for forgetting my new title, "my mother always did say you would make the difference. I don't know how she knew, but somehow she thought your arrival in Vespre was the beginning of a new era." He grins a little sadly. In that moment he looks very like Nelle Silveri, right down to the glint in his green eyes. "She would be proud of you, I think."

"She would be proud of *you*," I respond and press his hand in both of mine. "And you will go on making her proud. After all you're still head librarian of Vespre, aren't you?"

He snorts and makes a rueful face, looking down at his bandaged body. "I suppose so. And I suppose you'll have to start teaching me this new method of yours. Do you think it's possible it'll work on all of them?"

It's difficult to imagine. How could one ever hope to find the true name at the heart of a creature like Idreloth or the Melted Man? "It will take time," I answer after some consideration. "Time and practice." Then I squeeze his hand and offer another smile. "But we have time now. And we have each other. Who knows what we might accomplish together?"

There's a knock at the door. "Come in," Mixael calls, and Lawrence enters the room. Castien assigned his manservant to the head librarian's care, a duty which he has taken on with tremendous solemnity.

"Time for your dose, sir," Lawrence says, setting a silver tray down on the table by the bed. "We cannot heal without consistency, now can we?"

Mixael mutters but releases my hand. I slip from the room, leaving him to Lawrence's ministrations. In the passage beyond Mixael's apartment, *gubdagogs* swath the pillars and walls. They are all empty—Castien and I have already removed any wraiths caught in their tangled spells and safely ensconced them back into books. Anj and Lir sent a *gubdagoglir* up from the city to place more protective spells all over the palace. So far none have been needed.

I sigh as I make my way to the library. After all the terror I experienced here, one would think I would hesitate to walk by myself in these silent halls. Instead I feel an overwhelming sense of homecoming tinged with deep melancholy. In my mind I still hear Sis's manic laughter, the shouts and bellows of her brothers. Theirs is the primary haunting presence which clings to these cold, familiar passages now. While my heart is lighter knowing they are safe, knowing they are far from this drifting island . . . I ache for them. Ache for the children they were but are no longer. Ache for the years I missed. Ache for Lir, who misses them as brutally as I do, even as she is caught up with helping Anj reestablish order in the stricken city. We succeeded in our mission. But we lost much in the process. I'm not sure we will ever fully recover.

The library feels very large and full of whispers when I arrive. The Noswraiths in their grimoires chatter softly to one another until they sense my approach. Then they cut off abruptly, tucking ever more deeply into their binding spells, as though afraid to draw my attention. Perhaps I'm only imagining it—there are those who claim my imagination is far too vivid for my own good—but the sensation persists even as I ride the book lift down to the lower levels and the vaults of the Greater Noswraiths.

Castien is in the vault containing the Eight-Crowned Queen and all her many volumes. He is sealing up a final binding, and I wait in the doorway until he is quite through. He shuts the book then turns and smiles at me, as though he was aware of my presence all along. "Quiet as a lamb, our queenie," he says, stepping down from the pedestal and exiting the chamber. He shuts the door and seals the lock. "I have to say, my Darling, you've truly put the spirit of fear into these monstrosities. I've never known nightmares to be such a load of wet blankets!"

I smile through a shudder. But my smile drops away entirely when Castien reaches into the front of his jacket and produces the bloodgem. He holds it out to me like a present, but I recoil and shake my head. "Wise choice, my love," he says, tossing the gem once and catching it in his fist. "Some treasures are simply not worth the trouble." He strolls to the central rail above the citadel well and looks out into the seemingly endless darkness below. "Would you like to do the honors?"

I decline, vehemently. He shrugs and quite simply flicks the gem out into the void. I watch it wink and vanish from sight, and my heart lightens with relief. So much pain was caused over that gem, all born of the ongoing, foolish desire to somehow control Noswraiths. And to what purpose? It certainly hadn't done Ivor any good in the long run.

Castien leans his elbows on the rail, gazing out at his library, his eyes lifting to the upper levels and the dome high above. I lean with him and rest my head against his shoulder. "What happened to Umog Grush?" I ask after a little silence. "Did you find her?"

He grunts. "The low priestess gave her life to bind Idreloth. Quite a pretty binding it was too! The Noswraith hadn't yet worked her way free when I came upon her. Yes, those troll spell-weavings are a sight to behold, and old Grush was a mistress of her craft. But her heart gave out with the effort."

I nod. It was as I expected but . . . another loss. A tear escapes and runs down my cheek. I wipe it away absently. "I wish she'd held on a little longer. I would have liked to have told her."

"Told her what?"

"That I did as she commanded. That I found a way to end the Noswraiths once and for all."

Castien turns to me then, his expression contemplative. "And are you ready yet to share your secret with me, Mage Darlington? Because I still cannot fathom how you managed it. I know what a wonder you are with the pen, but to have succeeded where all the Miphates of history have failed? That is unexpected even for you, my brilliant wife."

I smile softly but shake my head. "It was Vervain who saw it first. It's all in the naming—the true name. We used their names for bindings, but those names were not true enough. They did not capture the essence of the wraiths. Only their true names could do that. Only recognition and release."

Castien nods slowly and takes my hand. He walks with me back along the hall of vaults, and we both feel the pressure of the spells contained behind those doors. All those angry creations which, one by one, must be faced, named, and set free. "It won't be easy," he says after a long silence.

"No," I agree. "But we will do it in the end."

I stop at the book lift, ready to climb aboard. Castien catches my wrist. "Now, now, Darling, you do recall the library rules, do you not? Book lifts are for books, or so Nelle Silveri once insisted."

I indicate my abdomen. While I can't claim to have grown significantly in the last few days, I feel the swelling and the weight and would even swear I have the beginnings of a legitimate bump. "And do you expect me to take the stairs, my Prince?"

He pulls me into his arms, presses my head to his chest. "I'd offer to carry you myself," he murmurs, his lips in my hair. "Though I don't know if I can bear this tremendous bulk any better than the lift."

I smack his arm and start to pull back, only for him to scoop me right off my feet and kiss me soundly. I kiss him back, my hands in his hair, strangely aware of all the haunted books watching us from their shelves and through their vault windows. But I don't feel unsafe. The library is peaceful, the Noswraiths subdued. If I didn't know any better, I'd say the atmosphere was distinctly hopeful. As though they know they will soon find rest, though they will fight with everything they have to resist that rest. But that fight can come later. For now I kiss my husband. Kiss him with all the joy and passion of seven lost years. Kiss him until I'm drunk and silly on his love.

Castien lets me come up for air at last. I gasp, clinging to the front of his robes, and lean my forehead against his neck. "I feel so selfish," I admit.

"Why is that?"

"Because you are here. Our baby is here." I place a hand on my stomach. "Here with me." I sigh and shake my head. "I was just with Mixael before I came to find you. His wife and child are in another world entirely. I don't know how he can bear it."

"No doubt he is relieved to know they are both safe."

"Safe? Are any of them safe?" I've not wanted to consider the question too closely, and I've certainly been kept busy enough to keep such worries at bay. Nonetheless the image of Estrilde encroaches on my mind. "Lawrence warned that your cousin would not be a welcoming hostess."

Castien curses softly but offers me a gentle smile. "No matter how bad Estrilde is, she doesn't compete with a horde of ravening Noswraiths."

"I'm not sure I agree." I look up at him again, gaze into his vivid eyes. "Is there no chance of repairing the gate, my love? Of opening a way back to Aurelis, of retrieving my children and our people? Now that the library is stable once more and the city is relatively secure, would it not be better to bring them home?"

He shakes his head sadly, setting me back on my feet at last. "I haven't the power. I'm too far cut off from Aurelis and cannot access the fullness of my magic. Besides we're so far gone into the Hinter now, to reconnect with Eledria would take a tremendous act of magic, the kind of magic you only see when a fae monarch first comes into power . . ."

His voice trails away, and his gaze drifts from mine, staring into empty space over my head. I sigh heavily, and my fingers toy with the embroidery on his lapel. "I suppose we must start getting used to life out on the Hinter then. And I hope—"

Castien lets out a whoop and swoops me off my feet, whirling me in a flurried circle of petticoats. "Darling, you genius!" he exclaims.

I'm still dizzy when he sets me back on my feet, kisses my forehead, and darts for the stairs. I watch him go, jaw slack, wondering what in the name of the seven gods just happened. With a sigh I turn back to the book lift. It's all well and good for him to go racing off at a moment's notice, but I'm not climbing ten stories in my current condition, thank you very much.

34

LIR STANDS CLOSE BESIDE ANJ BENEATH THE CRYSTAL DOME of the library. She does not take his hand, but there's something protective about her stance, as though she would like to place herself between him and Castien. I don't know who she is more concerned for—the *Hrorark* leader or the Prince of Vespre. They have not exactly been allies over the last many turns of the cycle. While the events of the last few days may have drawn them temporarily into uneasy cooperation, they have every reason still to look upon one another with suspicion.

Three days have passed since Castien's burst of inspiration down in the lower vaults. Though he sent a summons immediately, it has taken this long for Anj to respond. The restoration work in the city has consumed the troll leader, and in the end, I suspect he would have ignored the summons entirely. So I took matters into my own hands and, against Castien's express wishes, ventured into the city myself. I sought out Lir, however, not Anj, and explained the Prince's plan.

That did the trick. Her eyes wide, Lir stared at me like I'd grown an extra head before light dawned in her gaze. Then she clasped my hands in hers. "I'll find him," she declared. "I'll bring him. I'll drag him up by his hair if I must."

Whether or not she resorted to such extremes, Lir was true to her word. Now Anj stands in the library once more, looking simultaneously confused and perturbed, his arms crossed over his huge, bare chest. He does not bow when Castien emerges from the stairwell leading up from the lower library and hastens toward him. His face is a hard, stone mask.

My husband, by contrast, offers a brilliant smile. "Anj, my friend!" he exclaims, his long coat billowing behind him as he approaches with long-legged strides. Though I vividly remember doing up each and every button of his shirt myself at the start of our day, somehow half of them have come undone, and his silk shirt hangs open rakishly. Even now, married woman that I am, the sight brings a blush roaring up my neck. How is it that an unbuttoned shirt works such a profound effect on me when Anj's near nakedness leaves me utterly unmoved? Some ongoing effect of Castien's glamour perhaps.

He catches my eye as he draws near, takes note of the color in my cheeks, and quirks a knowing brow before turning his attention to the tall troll. "What do you say, old man?" he asks, jutting out one hand. "Are you ready to become King of Vespre?"

Anj stares at that extended hand hovering in the air between them. His expression remains utterly blank at first but slowly morphs into one of such deep confusion, I would almost think he didn't understand what was just said. He turns from Castien to Lir, who smiles broadly. She touches his arm and nods, murmuring something low and urgent in troldish. The line of his jaw tightens. "You said ten turns of the cycle," he says at last, addressing the Prince. "Ten turns before you returned the rule of Valthurg to the people of Valthurg."

"Under the circumstances, I think we can all agree seven turns is plenty." Castien takes another step forward, hand still outstretched. "Come now, Anj, we both know you still hate me with every fiber of your being. Don't you want to get rid of me once and for all? This is your best chance. Take the kingship and all that it entails. When the power of ancient Valthurg flows in you, use it to reopen the first gate between this realm and Eledria. You can use this very gate—the bones are still there, even if the connection is broken. Reestablish that connection and send me through to my own realm. Once I have secured my rule, I will work together with you to reestablish this island in conjunction with the rest of Eledria. Together, we can drag Vespre back from the Hinter, make fast the anchors, and save us all."

Anj's expression looks more and more horrified as the flood of

Castien's enthusiasm washes over him. Lir, by contrast, is positively giddy and scarcely waits for the Prince to pause for breath before she jumps in. Speaking in rumbling troldish, she squeezes Anj's arm. Anj turns to her and shakes his head, uttering protests I don't understand. I don't need to know the words to see the disbelief in his eyes. The magic Castien describes is on such a massive scale, far beyond anything Anj ever hoped to wield.

"Don't worry," the Prince says when Anj finally turns from Lir to face him again. "Once I've reclaimed my kingdom, my own strength will increase tenfold. I won't say it'll be a simple matter to rebuild the gates on my end, but I will do it. And I will find all the trollfolk we sent through and return them home. Moreover I swear that from this day forth you will have an ally in Aurelis for so long as I and my heirs shall live."

Finally Anj nods, though his face is still wary. "And the books?" he demands. "The Noswraiths?"

My chest tightens. Of course this must be his first concern to see these dangerous spells removed from his shores. When Vespre was subjugated to Aurelis and the rule of King Lodírhal, they'd had no choice but to accept the Noswraiths into their midst. But no king would willingly harbor such a library in his kingdom.

Castien, however, has already considered this. "They cannot be moved all at once," he says. "Not safely. But I give you my word, within a hundred years, Valthurg will be free of Noswraiths. I will see new vaults created within Aurelis library under the supervision of my head librarian." He indicates me with a sweep of his hand.

"There are still nightmares wandering our streets," Anj growls. His arms remain crossed, Castien's offered hand still hovering between them. "My people cower behind their *gubdagogs*, frightened of shadows."

Castien nods. "I will personally see to it that every Noswraith currently loose in the city streets is rebound. Mixael Silveri will remain in Vespre to manage the library from this end until the grimoires may be safely transported to Aurelis."

"I have your word on this?" Anj demands.

"As one king to another."

They go back and forth, detailing terms and conditions. I don't follow half of what is said, for my mind remains fixed on the Noswraiths themselves. This is not the solution I would prefer. Lodírhal was right in one respect—Vespre is far less densely populated than Aurelis, and outbreaks are more easily contained. But the people of Vespre have suffered under the threat of doom for so many generations. We cannot ask more of them. It is time Aurelis shouldered the weight of responsibility once more.

As for me? Will I truly be able to bring about the end of each wraith? The prospect is daunting. But if this is the atonement the gods have set before me, how can I refuse? And I will have Castien at my side every step of the way. I will learn; I will grow. I will get stronger with each new Noswraith I face and bring to rest. I doubt very much the task will ever get easier, but I will gain both confidence and understanding, and I will train others to do the work with me. Someday I hope there will be no

Noswraiths left anywhere in the worlds.

In the end Anj agrees to the terms. But when Castien brightly declares, "Excellent!" and extends his hand once more, the troll man hesitates yet again. He stares at that offered hand like it's a poisonous spider, his expression grim. "I'm not sure I'm ready to be king," he admits in a low, rumbling growl.

"Neither am I," Castien answers, his voice solemn. "We will both of us have to learn as we go, won't we? And depend on the support of our queens and the friendship of our allies."

Lir blushes at the mention of *queen* but makes no protest. She simply squeezes Anj's arm again, and when he looks at her, murmurs something soft and urgent in troldish. Anj nods. Finally he clasps the Prince's hand. They shake, and I brace myself, expecting some sudden onrush of fae magic to erupt around them. Nothing happens. For a moment we all look at each other, mildly perplexed.

"Ah!" Castien says, with a toss of his head. "How silly of me. These things require a touch of ceremony, don't they?" He darts into his office. Lir and I exchange baffled glances as a series of bangs, shuffles, muttered curses, and clatters sound within. At length, however, the Prince returns, carrying his stone crown in both hands. I've seen him wear it many times, though I certainly had no idea he kept it stashed in his office.

"If you wouldn't mind kneeling, Anj old boy," Castien says. "This won't take but a moment."

Anj mutters something that doesn't sound very kingly but at Lir's urging drops to his knees before Castien. The Prince of the

Doomed City lifts the crown on high and boldly declares, "By the power of Lamruil and the Deeper Dark, by the grace of the Great Goddess Aneirin, and by the authority vested in me as the once-prince of Vespre City, I declare you, Anj, King of Valthurg, Master of the Umbrian Isles, and Sovereign Ruler over the trollfolk."

The crown fits exactly across Anj's broad, pale brow. As it settles into place, there's an immediate change in the air, a prickling of tension like the oncoming sweep of a great storm. Anj gasps, feeling the effects more profoundly than the rest of us. Castien steps back quickly, takes my hand, and puts himself between me and the new king. I peer around his shoulder, staring at Anj. It's impossible to look away. Light ripples out from the crown and pours over him in a shining flood that sinks into his skin, into his bones. He rises to his feet, arms extended as though to receive it. His eyes open wide in wonder. The air around him warms and ripples, and I could almost swear I feel the *quinsatra* itself open wide and rain raw magic down upon him.

Abruptly Anj pivots on heel and faces the office door. I don't know how he knows what to do, how to channel that magic and manipulate it to his will, but he holds out his arms and, much as Castien did, begins to shape and manipulate the air with both hands. Magic, not truly visible, sparks across my senses as it erupts from his fingertips and flows through the ether, touching the broken spell which still clings to the doorframe. The air beneath the mantel begins to twist, churn. With a sudden burst, it opens. Radiant beams of dawnlight shoot through a portal much broader and clearer than the last time I peered through realities. The veils are so thin, I can see directly into Aurelis library on the far side.

A glad cry on my lips, I lunge forward. Castien catches my hand, restraining me, and I turn to look up at him, desperation in my face. I must get through, must find my children, must bring them home. But he shakes his head. "It might be dangerous."

"Yes," I answer and adjust my grip on his hand, intertwining my fingers with his. "It might be. Which is why we will go together."

He looks deeply into my eyes, reading the determination that simmers there. In the end he smiles that dangerously heart-melting smile of his. "All right, Darling. Together."

So we turn to face the shining portal and step through worlds hand-in-hand.

35

TWO GLORIOUS WINGED GUARDS BAR THE WAY AS I approach the doors to Biroris Hall. They cross their lances and look down at me, sneering. I can hardly blame them. Small, human, clad only in my simple work gown, I'm hardly an impressive sight.

I come to a stop in front of them and slowly cast my gaze from one to the other. One stares back without flinching, but the other narrows his eyes slightly. Perhaps he senses something in me, some inner truth that is only becoming more real the longer I breathe the air of Aurelis.

I draw my shoulders back and speak with cold clarity: *"Felaadar."*

A shadow passes over both their faces. They exchange looks, their cheeks paling. Without a word they both bow deeply and step aside, folding their wings tight at their backs. I pass between them to the great double doors, tall and solid gold and wrought in intricate patterns of roses and dancing deer. Raucous sounds rumble on the far side, and I know the fae are deep in their revels. All the powerful Lords and Ladies of the City of Dawn will be gathered within, and Estrilde has had ample time to cement their loyalty to her.

It's too late for second-guessing now, however. I'm here. Whatever comes next must be done with swiftness and certainty if we're to have any hope of prevailing. Besides, what is a host of drunken fae compared to all the ravening hordes of Vespre?

Steeling my spine, I push at the double doors. Though they are huge and heavy, they move easily at my touch, opening just a crack so that I may peer through at the scene taking place within the golden hall. I see it all in a couple of heartbeats, my jaw slowly gaping.

If I did not know any better, I would think I had somehow stumbled into Under—the dark lower levels of Aurelis City, where the basest depravities of fae kind are put on display, and the Lords and Ladies venture to indulge their most vicious vices. All the glory of Biroris remains—the carved pillars like great tree trunks, the arched roof like spreading branches alive with living gold leaves that shimmer in the dawnlight. Yet everything is stained with an atmosphere of gross indulgence and untamed wickedness that casts a pall over everything that was once fair and good in this place.

The long tables have all been pushed back from the center floor, and the fae lounge about them, clad in shining raiment that does little to clothe their naked limbs. They laugh together, tossing back food and drink, their eyes shining with tell-tale *rothiliom* gleam. In the center of the hall is a ring of space where the floor is stained in blood, both red and blue. As I step into the hall, I see a great furred body dragged from the center, trailing gore in its wake. The onlooking fae cheer uproariously.

I've seen this before—these displays of violence and cruelty all for the entertainment of bloodthirsty onlookers. In Lodírhal's day such things would not have been permitted in the upper palace. While he could not fully suppress the darker addictions of his court, he neither welcomed nor celebrated them. But Lodírhal is no longer sovereign of Aurelis.

I lift my gaze from that bloody floor to the high seat on the dais directly across from me. There sits Estrilde, draped in gauze and diamonds, her magnificent figure on prominent display. She boasts rings on every finger, bangles on her arms, legs, and neck. Gilded antelope horns curl from her forehead, neatly curving around her shining crown. Her long golden hair falls in rivers across her shoulders, pours over the arms of her throne, and spills to the floor in gleaming pools. She is wondrous and beautiful, the perfect portrait of the seductive fae queen straight out of fairy tales. But there's a certain desperation gleaming in the depths of her eyes. I can sense it even from across the hall. Without the magic of Aurelis at her fingertips, she holds onto that crown by a thread. For now she keeps her courtiers pacified, indulging their every whim. But she knows it cannot last.

A shifting movement draws my attention from Estrilde down to the pale figure seated at her feet. My heart stops—Sis! My sweet Sis, clad in an ornate gown, a bejeweled slave's collar gripping her throat. The poor child winces in pain, her eyes and skin unsuited to the light of this world. Has she seen me? Does she know I've come for her? I want to cry out, want to raise both hands, waving for her attention.

But in that moment a chant goes up from the crowd, drowning out all other thought: *"Khas! Khas! Khas!"* they cry.

I lift my gaze to the minstrel's gallery where I myself once hid, waiting for my turn to be summoned forth for the entertainment of the Lords and Ladies. The curtains are gone, the figures standing in that gallery on full display to the hungry gazes of the Dawn Court. My heart jumps to my throat. My boys! Calx, Har, and Dig. They're all lined up on display, massive stone figures, completely out of place in this setting, their eyes downcast. But another figure is dragged out from behind them and forced to march down the stairs. Clad only in rags, her wrists and ankles heavy with shackles, Khas walks nonetheless with her head high, refusing to flinch under the glare of light. She carries baby Sor in her arms.

"Bring the little one to me!" Estrilde calls out as Khas reaches the bottom of the gallery stairs. "It's a pretty thing—I'd like to make a pet of it."

I watch in mounting horror as a long-fingered fae pries the

baby from Khas's arms. Danger flashes in the troll warrior's eyes, and the fae hesitates. But when the crowd jeers and crows, urging for bloodletting, Khas relents. She won't let her baby be caught in the middle of a fight. The fae carries Sor and offers him up to Estrilde. She smiles like an angelic dream and sets the baby on her knee, bouncing him up and down. Then she looks around at her gathered court.

"Your champion is here, my loves!" she cries. "Now, who among you would like to test his mettle against her? Whoever wins the match will win this child. How is that for a prize?"

The fae laugh, tossing back their heads and raising their wine glasses in salute. Some elbow their friends, trying to convince them to throw their fate into the hands of the gods and step onto that floor across from Khas. No one has the courage to try.

"What, no takers?" Estrilde feigns surprise, her eyes wide and blinking. "Come, my dears, the babe is sweet, is he not? Surely someone among you is willing to risk life and limb for such a delectable little *ibrildian.*"

Sickness churns in my gut. More than anything I want to take up the quill and book I've brought with me from the library and scrawl out the name of the worst Noswraith I can conjure. Idreloth perhaps. Or the Thorn Maiden. Let a true nightmare rip through this crowd and end once and for all their manic laughter. Only the knowledge that my children would be at equal risk stays my hand.

"Very well," Estrilde sighs theatrically and beckons with one hand. "Bring forth the Skull Crusher. Let us see how our beauteous troll damsel fairs against him!"

The crowd goes wild with enthusiasm, parting to make way for the tall, hooded figure that approaches. His features are completely obscured in the folds of his long black cloak, but he carries an enormous battle ax in one hand which drags along the floor, making sparks. The Lords and Ladies *ooh* and *ahhh* at his appearance. Some blanche and draw back in fear. Khas watches him with a face like solid granite. She does not bear a weapon. Will they make her fight unarmed? From the look in her eye, this won't be the first time.

A rush of pure fury bursts through my veins. I've had enough of this. I don't know if Castien is ready, but I will not wait and see Khas brutally hacked down by this Skull Crusher. Pushing the double doors wide, I step into the hall.

The effect of my entrance is immediate. Every eye in that room swivels to fix on me. All shouting and cheers abruptly cease. I can feel the questions erupting in the silence: Who is that strange little human with a book tucked under one arm? Nothing impressive, nothing worth the notice of these grand Lords and Ladies, and yet . . . all of Biroris Hall goes painfully silent. Because there's something in the atmosphere, something they can neither understand nor explain. Some deep magic, prickling on the edge of their fae awareness. I smile. Castien did warn me my entrance might cause a moment of shock. We counted on it.

Then Sis breaks the spell, leaping to her feet, the chains around her ankles rattling. *"Mar!"* she shouts. Her voice seems to awaken the assembly. The fae turn to each other, murmuring, whispering. Estrilde sits up straighter in her throne, both hands gripping little Sor as she stares across the hall at me.

"What are you doing with that child?" I demand, my voice ringing against the tall gold pillars.

Estrilde's lip curls. "Whatever I wish," she replies. "I do what I like with my belongings."

My long years spent as her Obligate validate every word. A chill ripples down my spine. "He does not belong to you. You will give him to his mother. Now."

Estrilde's face is a careful mask, but I see the fear simmering in the depths of her gaze. She cannot let her courtiers suspect how deeply my arrival has unnerved her. Lifting her head, she utters a derisive sniff. "The creature's mother requires motivation to perform. She is a favorite of Aurelis—she cannot disappoint my court."

The Lords and Ladies murmur their approval but cut off again abruptly when I take three bold steps into the hall. "You will release her," I say. "Her and all the trollfolk you hold captive in your house. And"—I lift my hand, pointing straight at her—"you will get out of that seat."

"Will I?" Estrilde settles back more comfortably and strokes Sor's head like a lapdog. "And by what right do you make such demands, human?"

"My right as queen."

"Queen?" Estrilde's laugh is like liquid gold, but she cannot disguise the telltale tremble. "And who made *you* queen of Aurelis, pray tell?"

"Her king."

His voice fills the whole hall, ringing to the highest reaches of the ceiling, powerful and brilliant like a sun-sharpened blade piercing storm clouds. Even as he speaks, the dark figure of the Skull Crusher steps forward and throws back his hood. Disguising glamour melts away—and there he stands. Castien Lodírith, son of Lodírhal and Dasyra, heir of Aurelis. He is clad in gold, and his long hair shines like a river of night. A gasp ripples through the court. Every eye in that room is transfixed by him, my own included. He completely steals the breath from my lungs.

Lifting high the battle ax, he gives it a shake. Immediately more glamours vanish, revealing its true form: a broad troll sword. He tosses it to Khas, who catches it easily in her shackled hands. Then, unarmed, he turns to face Estrilde. All around the room, weapons are trained upon him. Guards stand at attention, some hovering in midair, suspended on great golden wings, their lances poised and ready to be hurled. None of them dares make a move, however. They all recognize the power brimming inside him, the might of Aurelis's king come home to reclaim his kingdom.

Estrilde stands upright, still clutching little Sor in her hands. "Give the baby to his mother, Estrilde!" I command, my voice echoing in the stricken stillness. Her eyes still fastened on Castien, Estrilde plunks Sor into Sis's arms. Sis immediately leaps from the dais and races to Khas's side. Khas urges the girl to stand behind her and remains in battle stance, her sword upraised. But I can already see that this battle is over. It was over before it began.

Castien holds Estrilde's gaze. The air between them bristles with tension, with the aura of his majesty and the feebleness of her resistance. As I watch, her glamours melt away. First her horns vanish in little ribbons of vapor, then her great height shrinks, her tall, strong form becoming hunched and pathetic. All the golden light which shone from inside her fades, leaving her gray and shrunken. She simply cannot bear to exist in the presence of her king.

"Kneel," Castien says.

At his word every one of the Lords and Ladies in that hall drop to their knees. The guards toss aside their weapons and throw themselves down, heads bent, backs bowed, genuflecting before their master. Estrilde resists for a breath longer than the rest. Even now she seeks to hold onto that which she had believed to be in her grasp—the kingdom that was never meant to be hers.

Castien takes a single step forward. He doesn't say a word, but it's enough. Estrilde falls to her hands and knees, the last of her glamours dropping away entirely. "It's not my fault!" she cries, her voice hollow in that huge, captivated space. "It was Ivor, it was always Ivor. He enthralled me! He made promises I couldn't resist. It's the human blood in him, beguiling me with human lies—"

"Enough."

Estrilde's voice cuts off as though her vocal cords were snapped. She gapes up at her king from hollow eyes. She is utterly wretched and ugly, though her skeletal frame is still clad in that luxurious pink gown and dripping diamonds.

"My dear cousin," Castien continues, his voice and presence filling up every square inch of this mighty hall, "you are hereby banished from Aurelis from now to the end of your days. I strip of you all titles and privileges of a princess of the Dawn. If you are found anywhere within the bounds of my kingdom by day's end, your life is forfeit."

Estrilde lets out a wail, tearing at the ragged strands of her hair. "Where am I to go, Castien?" she cries. "Where in Eledria is there a place for me?"

He shrugs. "Go to Noxaur. Seek asylum with Lord Vokarum; I understand the two of you are quite chummy. I'm sure he'll find a place for you, perhaps in his Wild Hunt."

A wretched shriek rips from her lips. At a gesture from Castien, her own guards swoop in from all sides, take her by the arms, and drag her away, still weeping, still pleading, and, at the very last, cursing. All eyes in that room watch her go until the double doors shut behind her. Then they snap, huge and staring, to fix upon their king.

Castien faces them, turning slowly in place as though to meet each gaze in turn. "Your king has returned," he declares and holds out his arms. "Is there any here who wish to contest my rule?"

All the kneeling Lords and Ladies lift their heads. As though in one voice, they declare, "*Long live King Castien! Long live Lodírhal's heir!*" Their chant rises, a pulsing song that ripples up the walls and rolls out through the high windows, carried across all Aurelis City. Soon I hear more voices taking up the cry from beyond the hall, until it seems the entire kingdom echoes with the sound. *"The king has returned. Long live the king!"*

Castien's eyes meet mine at last. He holds out a hand to me. I go to him and stand by his side in the center of that hall. Fear weakens my knees, and I need the support of his hand at my waist to keep me upright. I'd never imagined myself as queen. I'm not right for this role, don't deserve this honor. After all my many failures, why should I find myself now in this place, beside such a man? Happily Ever Afters belong to heroines, not problematic characters like myself.

But when I look into Castien's eyes, I see nothing but love shining there. I may not deserve this, but what does that matter? The love he offers goes far beyond deserving. Besides, I can spend the rest of my life doing everything I can to become the kind of woman who merits such love. Maybe in the end, that's enough.

I return his smile. Then I reach out and take Sis's hand, pulling the girl to me in an embrace. As we stand there in the center of Biroris Hall, the chant of the crowd changes slightly and becomes: *"Long live King Castien. Long live his queen!"*

Khas steps forward suddenly and kneels before us. She offers up her sword to Castien, the blade resting across her flat palms. He takes it from her hands. "Rise, noble Khas," he tells her. "You are no longer my subject, daughter of Valthurg."

She obeys, getting slowly to her feet, her chains clattering.

When she lifts her eyes, it's my gaze she seeks. "Mixael?" she asks in a low growl.

"He's home, Khas," I answer at once. Tears cloud the edges of my vision. "Home in Vespre, waiting for you. You're to go to him at once."

Her face lights up in a smile brighter than all the golden light of dawn. And just for a moment every loss we've suffered, every terror we've faced, is made right in her unabashed joy.

EPILOGUE

TWO YEARS LATER

"OSCAR, LOOK! IT'S ABOUT TO BEGIN. WATCH THE PRETTY moths, sweetheart."

My son yawns enormously and squirms in my arms, twisting his whole body in such impressive contortions, I very nearly drop him onto the hard platform steps.

"Here now, young man, none of that!" Castien gracefully swoops to my rescue, taking our miraculously boneless child and popping him up onto his shoulders. Oscar peals with laughter and pulls his father's pointed ears, delighted at this new lofty view of goings on. I breathe a sigh of relief and straighten the front of my bodice, which chubby hands had pulled askew. I'm wearing a gown of soft seafoam green trimmed in delicate lavender flowers, wide at the neck, gathered just below my bust, with ample skirts to accommodate my swollen abdomen. Castien took one look at me when I put it on and told me it was quite unfair to the new queen of Valthurg for me to be seen out in public looking so ravishing. He's a fool of course. But he also means it. Even the size of a small whale, I captivate his full attention.

I thread my arm through my husband's elbow and lean against his shoulder, a smile on my lips. Truth be told, I'd be happy to squirm and fuss a little myself if it meant someone would take me home and tuck me into bed. The hour is late, and I've been working long days in preparation for my upcoming confinement.

But I couldn't miss *Hugag*—the night of the Great Flight. It's been many years now since the sacred moths crawled out from their subterranean cocoons and took wing for the starlit heavens above Vespre City. Throughout the seven years the island drifted on the Hinter, there was never a sign of them. Since King Anj's ascension to the throne, he has been working tirelessly to reestablish anchors and bind the island back into conjunction with the rest of Eledria. Gates have been reestablished and new ones built, leading to every one of the Eledrian realms. All signs would indicate the *hugagug* will return tonight, but we can only wait and watch and hope.

The crash and groan of *bugdurash* music fills the air. Castien and I stand on a platform above the sacred circle of crystals, observing the dance taking place below. We are in company with King Anj and his bride, along with other noble guests from across Eledria. There was some resistance at first among the kings and queens against acknowledging Valthurg as a sovereign nation. King Anj benefited tremendously by the support he received from Aurelis, and he has not forgotten what he owes my husband. Thus we stand in a place of particular honor on the king's right hand, in full view of all those gathered below.

I look around the *Gluronk*, searching out the faces of my people in the crowd. Dig stands as close to the dancing circle as he can get, proudly watching Umog Hith, his young wife, as she performs the stomping, rolling steps of the circle dance with her fellow priestesses. I still can't believe my boy is old enough to be married . . . and he won't be the only one for long. Both Har and Calx have sweethearts of their own. I spot Calx a little farther back in the crowd, taller now even than big Har. He catches my eye across the way and flashes me a diamond-tooth grin.

Someone tugs at my sleeve. I turn and smile into Sis's eyes, level with my own. She grins hugely at me and points to the *gubdagogs* decorating the outer edges of the *Gluronk* circle. "That one's mine, *Mar*," she says proudly.

"And it's the best one by far," I tell her, though I'm certainly not one to judge. *Gubdagogs* remain as baffling a mystery to me as they ever were. But everyone says Sis is the most talented *gubdagoglir* ever trained under Umog Grush. *Princess* Sis, I should say, for she and her brothers were all officially adopted by Anj when he married their *mar*. Who would have believed that a handful of *grakanak-balja*—orphans, without name or standing within their own community—would become such prominent members of troll society? It is certainly a new age for troll kind under King Anj and Queen Lir.

Sudden tension comes over the crowd. The music stops, and everyone stands with their eyes upraised to the moonlit sky. Waiting. Hoping. Will the moths emerge from their caves and fly once more? Is the city truly healed from all it endured? Between them, Anj and Castien have worked miracles to reestablish Valthurg's standing among the realms. I've worked my own share of miracles as well, of a different but no less valuable kind, confronting and ending the existence of innumerable Noswraiths over the last two turns of the cycle. Sometimes the enormity of the task threatens to break me in two. But a night like this, brimming with so much hope and expectation, leads me to feel that it's all so much more possible if only . . . if only . . .

The air erupts. All the trolls gathered round the *Gluronk* open their mouths and let out a single, simultaneous roar. Even though I've heard it once before, I cannot stifle a scream and clutch my husband's arm. Little Oscar, by contrast, opens his mouth and joins the shout, his joyous voice melding with the chorus.

The next instant wings fill the air. The *hugagug* moths, emerged from their cocoons, crawl out from the depths of the earth and soar to the heavens, dancing together in perfect synchronization. They surround us, silken wings brushing our cheeks in delicate kisses before funneling skyward. Their wings catch the moonlight, reflect it back in myriad colors, dazzling to the eye. They're thicker than ever, millions upon millions of them, blocking out the moon and the stars.

Then they're gone, dispersed across the sky, making their way to some distant habitat. They'll return at some point, of course, to lay their eggs. And the cycle will begin again. Renewed.

I breathe out a sigh, one hand pressed to my heart. The sensation of an intense gaze fixed upon me draws my attention. I look up to find my husband looking down at me, his eyes dancing. "Oh, Castien!" I sigh, blinking back tears. "Castien, wasn't it beautiful?"

"Not bad," he replies with a grin. "But I confess, I was rather distracted." He leans down, Oscar squealing and gripping the hair on top of his head. He draws his mouth close to my ear. "No wonder Eledria has to offer can rival the sheer beauty of your face lit up with delight."

Heat rises in my cheeks. Though he doesn't say it, I read the promise in his eyes of all the delights he intends to bring me when we are alone together once more. Suddenly I'm not as tired as I was a few moments ago.

Dancing in the *Gluronk* continues, the strange troll music filling the air once more. It's beautiful and strange, and I enjoy the sight, but am relieved when at last Queen Lir turns to her assembled guests on the platform and invites us all to return to the palace. She and Anj lead the way, and Castien and I fall into step behind them. Lir takes a moment to squeeze my hand and ask if I'm all right, her gaze dropping to my swollen abdomen. I smile to reassure her, but she takes care to set a sedate pace, for which I am grateful.

The palace is lit up for celebration tonight. It's so different from the last *Hugag* Night I witnessed. Then everything had blazed with golden light in honor of the Prince's Soliran guests. Now all is suffused in moonfire glow and the gentle pulse of troldish *lorst* stones, which cast everything in a magical glimmer. Vespre Palace has never been more beautiful.

"Dancing or feasting first, my love?" Castien asks as he leads me inside.

I place a hand across my stomach and give him a look. "Guess."

He chuckles and guides me to a comfortable seat, which I suspect Lir ordered placed specifically for me. Trolls don't care for cushions and footstools, but I am certainly grateful for both. Castien removes our son from his shoulders and plops him in my arms, promising to return with *mog* cakes in short order. He darts away, weaving between the dancers who already congregate on the dance floor. He's so light and graceful on his feet, and I watch him until he disappears into the crowd. Even in this company of Eledria's elite, he is still the most beautiful being I've ever seen.

Oscar rests against my shoulder, drifting away into drooling slumber. He's so sweet, so innocent like this, it's easy to forget how quickly he can rally into the living embodiment of trouble. I wrap my arms around him, rest my cheek against the top of his curly head, and enjoy the peace while it lasts. I watch the dancers whirl, memories creeping back in on the edges of my awareness. How vividly I recall watching Castien dance with Ilusine, the pair of them so golden and shining beneath the magicked lights. A dart of pain stabs my heart even now, so many years later. I don't often let myself think of Ilusine. We've not heard anything of her, and I wonder sometimes if she ever managed to make her way back to Eledria, in some distant timeline. Or is she still out there in the mortal world, searching for a way home?

Thoughts of Ilusine never fail to bring Danny to mind soon after. I close my eyes, and for a moment, the beauty of the palace ballroom vanishes, replaced by a different image: my childhood friend, collapsed on the floor of the witch's cottage. Cold. Heartless. Ilusine had promised to get him home safely, but what kind of man did she return to Kitty Gale's care? I can only hope he is still the same brother, doctor, and friend he always was.

As I always do when thoughts of Danny and Ilusine intrude, I whisper a short prayer to the gods. I send another one up for Kitty as well. That I never got to tell her goodbye is a regret I will carry to the end of my days. I love the two Gale siblings still, though the paths of our lives have irreversibly diverged. I hope they think of me now and then and remember the friendship we once shared. I hope in the long run they were better for loving me as I am for loving them.

I breathe out the prayer and in that breath I let them go. Again. It's funny how one must continue to practice the art of releasing, how it is an ongoing choice to relax my grip on the past and not try to snatch it close again. But I'm getting better with practice.

Mixael and Khas whirl by on the dance floor. Young Sor clings to his mother's back like a little monkey, laughing in wild glee, his curls bouncing. Khas is absolutely breathtaking of course. Mixael continues to wear age on his face, though the air of Eledria might have restored him to perfect youth if he so chose. He is still handsome, and his smile is like a flash of pure sunlight in this twilit realm. He is now the sole librarian of Vespre—a tremendous task. But he does not work alone. I spend most of my days traveling back and forth between the two libraries, assisting Mixael in bindings and sometimes carting prepared volumes back to Aurelis. Slowly but surely Vespre will be emptied of all its Noswraiths. It must be done with great care and precision, however, as we prepare vaults in Aurelis strong enough to receive the grimoires.

Despite the hugeness of the task, it is undeniably easier than it used to be. I've been honing my skills, finding ways to liberate and lay to rest more and more of the smaller wraiths. I've trained Castien and Mixael as well. Not long ago Mixael succeeded in laying the Thorn Maiden to final rest, liberating the tortured remains of his father's creative soul in the process. Now there was cause for celebration! It also sent the other Greater Noswraiths cowering into themselves once more. The grimoires lie quiet, afraid of drawing attention. I don't remember the last time we dealt with an outbreak.

The Doomed City is no more. Valthurg is a thriving place, brimming with hope and promise. There was a time I wouldn't have believed it possible. Yet here I am, and here we all are. Or at least . . . most of us . . .

Castien still hasn't returned with those promised cakes, but I suddenly find I'm not hungry anymore. A powerful compulsion comes over me. Biting my lip, I look down at Oscar's sweet face. He's nodded off, lulled by the dancing. His snores are soft in my ear.

I adjust my grip on his warm little body, wrap his chubby legs around my middle, and secure my arms under his bottom. Then, rising from my comfortable seat, I slip away from the party. I don't weave and glide through the dancers as gracefully as my husband did, but I make my way well enough and venture out into the quiet stone passages beyond the ballroom. A smile plays on my lips as I recall the last time I escaped a ball on *Hugag* Night. Castien pursued me and . . . well, that was a night to remember in more ways than one. A night of beauty and tension, a night of tentative hope followed by fear. So much fear. That was the night I faced the Eyeless Woman for the first time and recognized the horror I had brought to life in this world.

Yes, those memories are hard. But also good. I can look back on them now and see more than just my mistakes and failures. I can see the path I have walked, the growth I have endured. I am still growing to this day, and I will dwell on that fact and not dwell on horror.

My footsteps are heavy, but they carry me at last, panting and puffing up the library stairs. I can still hear music in the distance, bright and lovely. It follows me even when I push open the door and step into the quiet of the upper floor beneath the crystal dome.

For a moment I stand in the doorway, breathing in the smell of this place. The smell of ink and parchment and leather, the smell of dust and ancient, forbidden knowledge. The smell of latent magic, always just on the verge of waking. The Noswraiths are all dormant, sleeping. If any are aware of my presence, they recognize me and make themselves smaller, eager to escape my notice. But I will get to all of them eventually. And I will look each of them in the eye and speak their true names. I just need time.

But not tonight. Tonight is a night of remembering.

My heart, drawn with purpose, guides me across the library to my own little cubicle and desk. Oscar cradled in my arms, I take a seat before the pile of unfinished work. Yet another memory intrudes on my thoughts—memory of my first day working at this desk, the Dulmier Fen spell in front of me. How afraid I was! How completely in over my head in every respect. I could not then have believed that I would so soon feel at home here in Vespre. Here in this library, surrounded by nightmares beyond description. I found my purpose, found my calling. Found people with whom I could build a life full of meaning. And though I'd resisted with everything I had, in the end I'd ended up where I was meant to be.

I push aside a few stray papers, my hand searching for something. I find it tucked in one of the little cubbies and draw it out: an onion skin notebook, old and worn on the edges. There's no spell contained within its pages, no hidden nightmare or wraith. That isn't to say that the man who wrote the words contained herein wasn't powerful—indeed, he was a great mage, brimming with deadly potential.

But not everything he wrote was evil.

"Here's a story, Oscar," I whisper into my baby's ear. "I thought you might like it." I open to the first page and begin to read the opening lines:

"Once upon a time, there was a sister and her little brother, and he was very brave. As long as they could be together, they were both very brave, no matter what happened. One day, their mother said to them, 'You must venture into the Dark Forest, my children. For your father is sick, and it is up to you to find his cure. But you must be brave, strong, and always loyal to one another, or you cannot hope to survive the journey.'"

I read on, allowing the unfinished tale to spill out from my lips. In this story, in this version of reality, both brother and sister cling to one another through every trial and tribulation. In the end they return home triumphant, their father's cure in hand . . . only to find their father has already perished and their mother as well. They are orphans alone in this world.

My brother's handwriting trails off, the final lines blurred and difficult to read. But the story doesn't end there, not anymore. I have added to it, and I keep reading now, softly, my voice little more than a whisper.

"Only they weren't alone. They never would be alone again. Everything they endured in the Dark Forest had only strengthened their bond. And the sister turned to her brother and said, 'No matter what happens, I am here for you, and you are here for me. We have each other. Forever.'"

Tears stream down my cheeks as I reach the last few words. I dash my hand across my face, determined not to cause more damage to these already frail pages. Perhaps one day soon I will copy it down in a fresh volume so that my children may read it to each other. For now, however, I let our combined handwriting—mine and my brother's—carry the magic and truth of this tale. A truth my brother forgot for a little while perhaps. But I haven't. And I won't.

"Darling?"

I startle in my seat and turn to see my husband coming toward me, a plate of *mog* cakes in hand. His face, illuminated by starlight, is lined with concern. "What are you doing up here?" he asks.

I close the book gently, unwilling to share it and its contents just now. Instead I smile and tip my head to receive his kiss on my cheek. "Just remembering," I say.

"Remembering what?" He perches on the edge of my desk and sets aside the plate.

"Not what. *Who.*" I sigh and look from the cubicle about the open library. "They all feel so near tonight. Nelle Silveri and her wyvern. Andreas and Thaddeus Creakle. Vervain and Umog Grush. Ilusine and Danny and . . . and . . ."

"Oscar," my husband finishes for me. He takes my hand, his thumb running back and forth over my knuckles. "I know you miss him."

I sniff and nod. "I do and I . . . I don't. I miss my brother, the boy I knew. I miss what we once were to each other. I don't miss the man he became. But I don't love him any less." I stroke our child's sleeping head and release a small sigh. "I wish he could have known little Oscar. I wish he could know that the cycle is broken, that Edgar's hold on our lives is no more." I look up at

Castien, tears blurring the edges of my vision. "Sometimes I can't quite recall his face. When I think of him, it's our little boy I see instead. As though our Oscar has somehow taken over the space my brother once held in my heart. I don't know if that's good or bad. It simply is."

Castien nods his understanding. Strains of distant music sing lightly through the open door, silver and bright, as though written for the stars themselves. Hearing it, my heart lifts once more.

"Dance with me," my husband says suddenly, holding out his hand.

My lips quirk to one side. "Am I *obligated* to dance?"

He snorts. "When have I obligated you to do anything?"

"Oh, I can think of an occasion or two!" I reply but take his hand. He pulls me up from my chair, wraps his other hand around my waist, and draws me and our sleeping child close to him. Oscar's fat little rump and my own swollen belly prevent him from pressing me as close as he might like. But he looks into my eyes and smiles a smile that shoots warmth all the way to the deepest places of my soul. I blush and drop my gaze. Then blink in surprise. "Castien!"

"Yes?" he asks with perfect innocence.

"I know I did up every single one of those buttons before we set out this evening. How in the world have they all come undone?"

"Oh my." He looks down, blinking in mild consternation. "I wonder how that happened? Perhaps I'm cursed."

"Cursed to perpetual button-slips?"

"Yes. Someone must have gone and bargained something dire indeed to lay such a curse upon me. But what's to be done?" He catches my eye. "I suppose you'll just have to suffer it, Clara, my Darling. Do you think you can bear to?"

I roll my eyes. "I suppose I'll have to find a way."

He laughs then, his voice echoing up and down the many levels of the library, and whirls me away in the rhythm of that song. If any of the Noswraiths hear him and wake, they watch silently from between the covers of their grimoires and make no move to interfere. For there's no room for nightmares in this little sphere of existence that holds the three of us. Only dreams.

About the Author

Sylvia Mercedes makes her home in the idyllic North Carolina countryside with her handsome husband, numerous small children, and the feline duo affectionately known as the Fluffy Brothers. When she's not writing she's . . . okay, let's be honest. When she's not writing, she's running around after her kids, cleaning up glitter, trying to plan healthy-ish meals, and wondering where she left her phone. In between, she reads a steady diet of fantasy novels.

But mostly she's writing.

After a short career in Traditional Publishing (under a different name), Sylvia decided to take the plunge into the Indie Publishing World and is enjoying every minute of it. She's the author of the acclaimed Venatrix Chronicles, as well as The Scarred Mage of Roseward trilogy, and the romantic fantasy series, Of Candlelight and Shadows.

Printed in Great Britain
by Amazon